THE STUD BOOK

Also by Monica Drake

Clown Girl

a novel

THE STUD BOOK

MONICA DRAKE

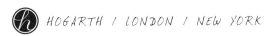 HOGARTH / LONDON / NEW YORK

Copyright © 2013 by Monica Drake
All rights reserved.

Published in the United States by Hogarth, an imprint of the Crown Publishing Group, a division of Random House, Inc., New York.

www.crownpublishing.com

HOGARTH is a trademark of the Random House Group Limited, and the H colophon is a trademark of Random House, Inc.

Library of Congress Cataloging-in-Publication Data
Drake, Monica.
The stud book: a novel/Monica Drake.
p. cm.
1. Friends—Fiction. 2. Families—Fiction. 3. Parenthood—Fiction. 4. Portland (Or.)—Fiction. I. Title.
PS3604.R354S78 2013
813'.6—dc23   2012032560

ISBN 978-0-307-95552-4
eISBN 978-0-307-95553-1

Printed in the United States of America

Book design by Elina D. Nudelman
Jacket design by Megan McLaughlin
Jacket photography: Howard Sokol/Getty Images

10 9 8 7 6 5 4 3 2 1

First Edition

For my family, in all directions.
Where would I be without you?
And especially for Monica Robertson,
with all love and gratitude.

THE STUD BOOK

Adaptive Behavior

Say you're a night crawler in warm ground. Your body is a tube within a tube, soft as foreskin. You're a hermaphroditic sex organ burrowing through dark earth, a reproductive decomposer.

Fully loaded with two sets of testicles, two testes sacs, ovaries, sperm, and eggs—seminal vesicles, seminal receptacles; the parts sound almost spiritual, nearly Catholic, really—and you have what it takes to build an army, a generation.

The heartbreak? You're not an asexually reproductive creature, like a lonely sea sponge or a budding hydra. You can't fertilize your-self.

You have needs.

Your job is to find another earthworm, a dew worm, an angler, to swap sperm, fertilize your eggs, and incubate them in a slime tube, a bellyband, a pale pink saddle you'll wear briefly around your waist until you slip it off over your head like a silky nightgown. Charm your way into a biological destiny.

Blind hermaphrodites find each other in the dark. It happens all the time.

Sarah stepped over one pale banded worm on the damp asphalt

walk of the Oregon Zoo. She saw the bellyband—the slime tube—and thought: *Babies! So dear, even in a lowly worm.* She carried a timer and a clipboard, pulled her coat closed against a fine rain, and leaned on the railing of the mandrill habitat.

Inside the enclosure the kingpin man-ape gave a flying leap. Leaves tumbled in his wake. He moved from his high perch to a low branch, and on the way flashed his penis, where his body was as red as a rash.

If that mandrill were Sarah's baby, she'd powder his rash. Not with talc—talc is pure cancer. She'd dust sweet cornstarch on the flaming red genital area between that mandrill's muscular, hairy thighs. Except his wasn't really a rash and she knew it. Baby fantasy over. She was a professional. Mandrill penises are red; their scrotums are lilac. He'd be a grotesque infant, big and buried in hair.

The sky was blanketed with gray clouds as bright as aluminum, hiding a winter sun. Visitors moved in tight packs in the rain over the tended zoo grounds. Kids lurched ahead of their parents, with room to roam and no streets to cross. A sullen flock of teens clustered at a cement picnic table around a paper basket of French fries. They had a fat pink baby in a fat pink fleece jacket in a stroller nearby. Who was the mother? They were all kids themselves.

Sarah was twice their age and watched their parenting, or lack of parenting, as though the teenagers were her assigned animal behavior study.

If her first baby had survived, the child would be three years old, with sticky ice cream–coated fingers pressing against the glass in front of all the animals.

Her timer beeped. In the mandrill enclosure—and you don't say "cage" in a modern zoo, but "enclosure"—a newborn named Lucy clung to the rich olive hair of her mother's chest. The two huddled on a shelf against a back wall. The mother ate nits from Lucy's coat. Sarah marked "Grooming" on her chart.

Sarah would eat bugs from her own baby's hair if that was what motherhood required.

That baby mandrill was Sarah's field study. The patriarch, though, with his strut and flash, was a steady distraction. The more color a mandrill shows in his red, white, and blue behind, the more testosterone is cruising through his system, and this one advertised his virility like a flag.

His ass was an ornament, in evolutionary terms.

On his branch, this head honcho tugged his golden beard. He clambered and waved his ornament like a second face there to say hello. On sunny days visitors snapped photos to post on the Internet. They took videos. What a crowd-pleaser! With an ornament like that, you'd think survival of the fittest was about drawing hits on YouTube.

The timer beeped again. Baby Lucy banged a stick in loose straw on the shelf where she perched. "Play behavior."

One of the lone females followed the patriarch, walking close behind, like his flash ass was the ice-cream truck and she had change in her pocketbook. This was mandrill flirting.

Toward the back of the cage, another female sat with her legs tucked against her body. She was pregnant, the previous customer to chase that ice cream. Mandrills generally don't show pregnancy the way humans do, but this wasn't her first round. Her body had thickened, the muscles grown slack from carrying earlier offspring, and this time her pregnancy was pronounced.

A woman with a stroller pushed past, her baby under a clear plastic rain liner like a little biosphere—didn't babies suffocate under plastic? It certainly wasn't teaching good habits. But at the same time the plastic dome made the baby seem precious and revered, like a diamond in a case, or a doll tightened down inside its plastic box.

If Sarah's second baby had survived, it'd be twenty-three months old by now, spitting out the names of animals from around the world.

Toward the zoo entrance, on the horizon, a white van edged its way over the top of a distant hill, KZTV NEWS written on the side.

The timer beeped. Lucy rested snug against her mother, mouth on a teat. The mother wrapped a protective hand around her child. Sarah marked "Nursing."

The news van stopped where the paths grew narrow. Its sliding door opened, and a crew tumbled out. First came the reporter, a correspondent out in the field, identifiable by her markings: a helmet of blond hair, a large head, a tweed skirt-suit. Why was there a news van on zoo grounds?

One of the teen girls stood up from the picnic table, stretched, and showed a lump under her coat like a beer gut, another baby on the way, or maybe both.

Another baby?

Sarah bit the end of her pencil. The news crew approached on foot. The reporter, in heels, skittered along the curving path like Dorothy on her way to see the wizard, flanked by her loose-legged cameraman and a bearded guy in a headset. The cameraman balanced a shoulder cam over his puffy winter coat. A woman so young she was practically a girl carried a clipboard and led the way, their own little Toto.

They traveled toward Sarah. Her guess? They were hunting for a feel-good story on baby Lucy. She saw it coming: They'd want her expertise. She'd have to hold back. She didn't work in PR, wasn't authorized to answer press questions. Zoo publicity was a tricky business of walking a line between PETA protesters and wealthy donors. Portland is a city of vocalized opinions and insta-activism. Sarah's job was strictly to compile data. The reporter would ask about the mandrills. She'd have to decline. She felt a conflict of interest creep closer with each step of the news crew on the rain-darkened asphalt trail.

She was proud to work for the zoo, in an amazing community of caring people. The air that greeted her daily inside the zoo walls was a particularly habitable atmosphere. Her role was small, but it was hers.

Breeding was a tightly planned eugenics exercise. Animal curators worked with the algorithms of the International Species Information System to determine who would breed and who, of the genetically redundant, was given birth control.

Every zoo manages a budget. They know how many animals they can support and have data to prove who brings in the income—Pandas! Elephants! Monkeys!—while the lazy sun bear and the Visayan warty pigs serve as chorus girls.

Each mandrill birth was recorded in an international studbook, an official intergenerational record of who has sex, who's born, who lives fast and dies young. The studbook is like Mormon genealogy listings, all those famous *begat*s in the Bible, or *People* magazine for caged animals singing the song of celebrity births. It'd be gossip if it weren't seriously about bolstering the genetic makeup of dwindling animal populations.

Sarah collected one thin current of data that fed into behavioral documentation, noting which captive infant animals thrived and which failed.

The young woman with the news crew traipsed in white Keds that miraculously stayed white even in the rain. She seemed to grow younger as she came closer, and smiled, baring friendly teeth. Sarah hated to turn her down, sensing a kindred spirit—they both had clipboards!—but it was zoo policy.

The girl, the woman, reached out a hand as though to shake, to touch skin in a behavioral display of goodwill, and Sarah put her hand out, too, only then, instead of shaking, the girl tucked her clipboard under her arm and rolled her hand, calling the reporter in like reeling in a fish. The correspondent stepped in close, then closer, bringing along a cloud of hair spray.

This is how elephant cows assert dominance: They sway closer and closer, until one cow gives up ground.

Sarah was that cow. She gave up ground. The reporter stepped a sharp heel on the mother-father hermaphrodite worm where it inched along the asphalt, right on the bellyband. Her foot skidded. Babies! She caught herself as if it'd never happened.

The reporter's hair blocked Sarah's view of the mandrills. When the timer beeped, Sarah said, "Excuse me—"

The teenagers at the table watched them like they were on TV already. The human primate in the stroller sucked its pacifier while the man-ape flashed his best feature. Sarah bobbed her head to one side of the reporter's hairdo then to the other, trying to do her job. It was important work! She was here for the zoo, for science, for the future of humanity! She'd definitely turn down their silly little media request, hoard her specialized information.

If her third baby had lived, it'd be six months old, in her arms. They wouldn't crowd her this way if she were flanked by her children. She'd be a different person, hold a different place in the world. She'd have what Georgie—the old Georgie, Sarah's child-free, academic drinking buddy, that denizen of the life of the mind—would have called, as though from a great intellectual distance, the "cultural legitimization conferred through motherhood."

Was that ever such a bad thing?

But Georgie had changed. She had a baby, the legitimizing child.

The only infant in Sarah's care was Lucy. She'd protect Lucy's privacy.

The girl with the clipboard said, "Ma'am? Sorry. We need you out of the frame."

The Road to Hell

*A*cross the river Georgie wore the blood-marked abdominal smile of a fresh C-section and navigated the short hallway of her two-bedroom bungalow. She had a round of prescription pain meds and a baby, like a warm bundle of fresh laundry, wrapped in a blanket in her arms.

It was lovely to carry her own perfect girl-child. Out of nowhere—or really, specifically, out of Georgie's body, out of her uterus, out of the slash cut in the middle of her gut—there was a baby! Right in their house. Once they'd let a stray cat in, and those were weird days. Suddenly she and her husband held cat energy in the house, an animal curling around their feet, asking for food and love. A baby was even more dreamy and surreal. She kept thinking about that cat now, how it had come and gone, leaving cat hair on an armchair, traces of itself. This baby was here to stay. Georgie reached for her drugs.

Oxycodone is a cute narcotic, delivered in small pills like toy medicine. You could feed those pills to a mouse, a rat, a teacup Chihuahua. She shook the pills in their plastic container and they put on a ragtime rattle of a show for her darling newborn daughter. With its fine rattle that bottle was practically a Waldorf learning tool, except instead of the requisite Waldorf wood it was made out of plastic and painkillers.

Georgie clambered across the broad expanse of their California king with the baby clutched tight to her chest and the pills in the other hand, her hand wrapped around the vial, her knuckles against the bed. C-section stitches tugged across her bikini line. "Oof!" She said it out loud, like a cartoon character, a plea for sympathy, even though she was alone.

She was alone except for her daughter, anyway. That was the whole thing about being a new mom—always alone and never alone. Always with the baby. Always with this new nonverbal companion.

Humble would come home soon.

The baby's fingers lay outside her pink blanket like a little row of roots, white and thin. Until she held her own child, Georgie hadn't known anything about mother-love. Now it crowded her body, clotted her heart, made her want to cry. Maybe it was the painkillers that made her want to cry. Either way, she was high and happy and sad and the whole thing closed like a hand around her throat.

She couldn't hold that baby tight enough.

She had a blue triangle tattooed on her bicep—the "rhetorical triangle," her favorite paradigm. She drew the triangle on the whiteboard each year, the first week of her freshman English classes, as an illustration of how all meaning is made.

The three points of the triangle? Author, audience, and text, as they say. An author puts a text in front of an audience, and meaning is conveyed. Change any one component—new audience, new author, new book—and the meaning changes, too. It could be a slight shift, or massive. In class it sounded clear. Across her other arm, in the rounded font of an old typewriter, a second tattoo asked ANY QUESTIONS?

The soft spot of her baby's fontanel pulsed with each breath, making tufts of the girl's dark hair dance up and down.

In the rhetoric of new life, Georgie was author and audience both. Bella was the text, that daughter she'd drawn into existence. The meaning of the world shifted from the life of the mind to the bloody, seeping, heartbeat center.

Parent/Baby/World: All meaning came from that juncture.

Any mind-body split was blasted out of the water once her own body was nurturing a new mind.

She had a third tattoo on the small of her back, a tribute to French feminist philosopher Simone de Beauvoir. It read THE SEC-OND SEX, after one of Beauvoir's seminal titles.

Seminal—could you use that word with a woman's writing?

Weird.

But yes, Georgie had a French feminist tramp stamp.

She'd dropped out of high school. Now she had a PhD, because every dropout has something to prove, and she proved she could handle school all the way through. She'd learned to speak the language of the academy. It spoke right back, too, which is to say *the legitimizing pedagogical institutions had granted investment in the (re)-formation and reification of her gendered body.*

Ha!

In other words, she was a woman, a mom, with a PhD.

Bella was three days old. Georgie's underwear was a day newer than that. One of the first adjustments to motherhood was that she'd bought a six-pack of granny panties—the kind that came all the way up—because every pair of her bikini-cut version hit exactly where a row of fish line–style thread was stitched through her skin.

Doctors called it a "bikini-line incision." Georgie never realized "bikini line" was a precise anatomical designation until she tried to put her own clothes on.

The el cheapo granny panties came in fuchsia, turquoise, and glaring white. Each color made her ass look larger than the pair before it, but they didn't rub against the stitches. They wrapped over her skin like a comforting hand. She settled into her nest of blankets, books, and magazines, and reached for the remote, turned the TV on, but kept the sound down. How much TV is bad for a newborn? That's what it means to be alone and never alone—to reconsider every urge.

What she really wanted was a full-bodied pinot noir, a gin and tonic, a pale pink raspberry martini. Doctors said alcohol would leach into her milk and dim her baby's growing brain. They used to prescribe stout to bring the milk in, but she didn't have those old-school doctors. So instead of a Guinness, Georgie had oxycodone and a big glass of water.

When she asked whether oxycodone in her bloodstream was okay for the baby, the nurse said, "You wouldn't want your baby to have a mom in pain, would you?"

She didn't want her baby to have a mama in granny panties, either, but there you go. Not everybody gets what they want.

She curled a hand over her daughter's head, cradled and covered that constant pulse of the fontanel. "We'll be okay." She pushed the baby blanket away from Bella's chin. The girl's tiny red mouth was open, her eyes closed, long lashes resting over her pale skin. Her mouth was a little heart, with all the love in the world collected there.

Bella slept like her father. He could pass out anywhere. It was a way of trusting the universe. Georgie didn't even trust herself.

She flipped channels until she saw the familiar curve of a pregnant belly. The warm enthusiasm of a trained woman newscaster came in as a voice-over. "The zoo will soon welcome a new resident!"

The flat color of local video scanned the pregnant monkey, hunched and fat. Georgie sat up straighter in bed to distinguish herself from that slope-shouldered simian. That was one difference between humans and other primates—we walk upright. Upright!

The vial of oxycodone was still in her hand. She moved her legs and the blankets shifted, books tipped and adjusted. The news camera cut to a baby mandrill, clinging to its mother.

The new infant would be born in December, born on the cusp of the schizophrenic season. Georgie had read all the books, the articles. She knew the threats: more schizophrenics were born in winter months, with numbers peaking in February, even bleeding into early March. Bella was born in November, just as that curve on the graph of probability started to climb. If she'd planned things better, Georgie would have given birth in August.

Could primates even be schizophrenic?

Any questions? Her tattoo was so cocky! With a new baby, she was all questions.

She reached both hands around her daughter to press and turn, to coax the childproof lid off the pill vial. The camera cut away from the mother and baby. For a moment there was Sarah, on TV. Huddled near a garbage can, near a pack of teenagers.

Sarah?

Sarah was pale. Her hair needed attention. It was soaked, and maybe that's just how hair looks when a person works at the Oregon Zoo in the rain. Except Sarah was wild-eyed, too, and that made it all worse. She looked a little nuts. Guilt tapped at Georgie's chest, a reminder: Sarah's phone calls, those kind offers to come hold the baby. Georgie wasn't ready to see anybody, to put on pants, or even a skirt.

Besides, Sarah could be kind of a downer.

The thing was, Georgie felt guilty for having a baby when Sarah had only miscarriages. She'd bought Sarah a satin bathrobe after the first one. She gave her a stack of novels and a bottle of pear brandy after the second. With the third, she'd stayed around for days, made dinners, washed Sarah and Ben's dishes. What else could she do? She didn't promise not to have her own.

She cupped a hand and shook the vial to tap a pill into her palm.

Sarah started backing out of the frame, then bent and picked a pale pink flower off the macadam of the zoo path. No, it wasn't a flower; it was a pacifier, clutched in Sarah's pale, reddened fingers. Georgie squinted and leaned closer. As she moved, the mess of meds fell forward like too much salt from a shaker. They fell into her hand, bounced over her fingers, and scattered on the bed, on the blankets. On the baby. White pills rained down on the small, sweet, open cavern of baby Bella's red heart-shaped mouth.

"Fuck!" Georgie moved fast but couldn't think. Were there pills in Bella's mouth? That trusting, trusting, open mouth. She wanted to shake the baby, shake pills out, but you can't shake a baby—people go to prison for that. Shaking a baby can cause brain damage and death. She held Bella closer and tried to see into the dark space between those little lips and toothless gums. "Jesus, Jesus, Jesus," she chanted.

The fontanel's pulse was an accusation.

Georgie lunged out of bed. Her foot caught in the sheet. Bella was in her arms. Stray pills bounced to the floor along with the flutter of magazines. Her stitches yanked against her gut as though to hold her back, like an invisible internal seat belt. She turned on the ceiling light and tipped the baby's head toward it, to see better inside her tiny mouth. There it was, there it was! There was a glimpse of white, a pill on her baby's tongue. She'd thrown a bull's-eye, made a half-court basket, sunk the eight ball, except this round she didn't want to hit the mark.

Georgie's finger had never seemed so thick as it did when she tried to fish inside Bella's mouth. She was afraid she'd force the pill down. Bella screwed up her face and pulled her hands out of the swaddling blanket. Georgie moved her finger into Bella's mouth again. Bella tried to suckle.

Ah! Don't! Georgie pulled her finger away and whispered the words, a prayer, "Don't suck anything down." She laid the baby on her side on the bed and tried again to press a finger over those sweet toothless gums. Bella screamed. Her face turned red. She was a good screamer. Her tongue was a bird's tongue, narrow and strong. And there was the pill, stuck to the side of her tongue. Georgie reached in, tapped, flicked, touched the pill until she managed to knock it off the side of Bella's tongue, out of Bella's mouth. The tablet was soggy and eroded, but otherwise whole.

Thank God.

Georgie picked up her whole reason for living and let the girl shriek in her ear while she collected pills from the sheets, the blankets, the floor. She counted as she found them. She reached for the phone. Then she dropped the phone and went back to counting, and she grabbed for the phone again because with her baby in her arms she didn't have enough hands and didn't know which to do first. She needed backup—somebody at home besides the baby. Alone and never alone: If she were really alone, there'd be no problem, no baby's mouth, and no pills.

But that wasn't what she wanted. Not at all.

She needed a team, a crew. Mostly, she needed her husband. Where was Hum? He'd taken five weeks off for paternity leave and still went out most of the day like he had somewhere to be. Georgie found two more pills on the floor. Bella yodeled in her ear. "Hush, hush, little peanut."

Georgie's milk let down, warmed her boobs, made them hard and high as implants until milk spilled out and soaked her nightshirt. Doctors said the leaking would stop when her body adjusted. She was a generous fountain.

She hoisted her shirt to let Bella latch on. Thin white milk ran in rivulets down Georgie's stomach.

She stood hunched over and sliced open in the middle and

stitched back up; her warm daughter nursed under the drenched and clinging nightshirt. Georgie dialed the pediatrician and scanned the floor for stray drugs. She stuck the phone between her ear and her shoulder.

There should be a book illustrating how to nurse, cradle a phone, panic, call 911, and count stray pills on a dusty floor.

She'd started with twelve pills. She'd taken three on Saturday and one at night, and then . . . after that? She had five left. Was that right? Five, and one was soggy. She put the soggy pill in her own mouth and drank water to wash it down. It stuck in her throat. Or something stuck in her throat. Maybe it was guilt.

How much of that soggy pill had seeped into Bella's system?

There'd be oxycodone in Georgie's milk. Could Bella overdose now through nursing?

She used a finger to pry the baby's mouth off her nipple. Bella screamed louder than ever. The ringing phone tumbled from Georgie's shoulder and knocked against Bella's head on the way down. Shit. A red welt raised against the girl's skin, near her hairline. Was that a problem? How protected was a baby's brain? If anything happened to Bella, Georgie would kill herself. She'd have to. There were so many ways to fail. All she had was good intentions; the road to hell was paved with babies.

Giving birth was the original blood oath.

She could still hear the phone ringing on the other end, now a tiny sound, like one an insect would make. "Just wait, wait," Georgie whispered, and bent to find the phone on the floor. She was on her knees. She could barely hear over Bella's howl. Three days old and the girl was a boob-aholic. A recording came on: "If this call is a medical emergency, please hang up and dial . . ."

Georgie found the phone under the bed and pulled it out, covered in dust bunnies.

Was her call an emergency? That was half the question. Bella's wail was strong. She hadn't passed out, anyway—always a good sign. Georgie pressed zero for pediatric advice. "Shh, shh, shh . . . darling, darling, darling," she crooned against the side of Bella's head, into the welt, now a lump, against her silky hair. "My sweet girl."

A receptionist came on. The woman asked the birth date of the patient, the patient's name, and the patient's doctor's name. Then she asked, "What is the nature of the problem?"

"I have this prescription," Georgie said. "The baby got into the prescription." She ran a hand over the sheets as she talked, checking for more pills.

"The baby got into the prescription?" the receptionist repeated. "Tell me the child's birth date again, please."

The baby, Bella, was three days old. She couldn't lift her own head. It was an accident if she found her mouth with her hand. "I mean, I spilled the pills, and the baby got ahold of them."

"Got ahold of them?"

That baby was a precocious drug addict.

Georgie said, "I dropped an oxycodone in my daughter's mouth. I got it out, I just don't know anything. I don't know what might've happened—"

"You've retrieved the medicine at this point?"

"It was pretty much whole." Georgie was glad to say she'd done one thing right.

"Keep the pill to show doctors in case they request it."

"Keep it?" Georgie said. "I took it."

There was a silence on the other end of the line. Then the receptionist said, "The advice nurse will call you back."

Georgie heard caution and a controlled urgency in the woman's voice. It dawned on her: They'd call child protective services. They might. Would they?

Shit.

The butter pecan walls went swimmy. She sat on the side of the bed and tried to breathe. "I'm new to this." They couldn't take her daughter away! It was her first child, her only darling. But really, they could. That was the thing.

The hospital had given her those pills. They'd sent her home with the baby. They'd set her up. She said, "This must happen all the time." She tried to talk over Bella's screams, and her voice came out high and thin and broken. Where did other people learn how to take drugs while holding a baby?

The woman said, "Do you need a referral for a counselor?"

"A counselor?" She was ready to cry but didn't need a counselor. The baby was the question, the concern. Little red-faced Bella spit up on Georgie's arm.

The woman said, "Some new mothers have difficulty adjusting—"

This woman would make her cry. Georgie hung up on the

receptionist. The advice nurse could call back. They had her contact information.

She carried her howling daughter to the kitchen, sang the alphabet softly, and used a dish towel to wipe the white patch of spit off her arm. Maybe that spit-up solved the drug question, like a self-induced gastric lavage?

In the kitchen, on the counter, in a six-pack of bottles, there were six servings of formula sent home as free samples from the hospital. For all she could tell those formula samples were made by McDonald's in a third world country using slave labor and antifreeze. They were the precursor to fast food and a slow waddle.

At least it wasn't organic. Organic baby formula sweetened with rice syrup was full of arsenic half the time. She'd read the reports.

Bella started to wail again; Georgie's milk was a drug deal that couldn't happen. What was the advice for this?

She and her daughter waited together, alone. They waited for the phone to ring, for Humble or a nurse to call. Georgie cracked the lid off a bottle, and it came off with a pop. She screwed the artificial nipple in place and tipped the bottle to Bella's blessed mouth.

Bella didn't want it. Georgie started to pull it away, and a reflex kicked in—the girl latched on to the fake boob. Oxycodone, that opiate, eased its way into Georgie's blood, and she started to feel lighter. The pain in her stitches backed off. She took a breath and relaxed against the counter.

The phone rang, and caller ID showed it was the hospital. It was either the advice nurse or the baby police calling to tell her she'd failed as a mom. The baby, her living dissertation, was perfect, yes, but Georgie wasn't.

The phone rang again, singing its song.

The hospital knew where they lived. They had her address, her employer, her health insurance ID numbers.

Georgie needed to lie down. Bella was still breathing. Even the red welt on her head had already quieted.

"We'll be okay," she whispered, giving voice to what she most wanted to hear. She'd be her own advice nurse. Her voice was good enough. She was in her house, in this room, on her own with her daughter, alone and in it together. One more ring and the phone would go to voice messaging. This was her job: to raise her daughter.

The doorbell rang.

The doorbell? Hum wouldn't ring, unless he'd lost his keys. It was a visitor, a stranger, maybe a pair of Jehovah's Witnesses.

It might be cops. Paramedics. Child protective services. Could they have gotten there so quickly? Of course they could. Georgie's soaked nightshirt clung to her boobs and postpartum stomach in a frump's rendition of a wet T-shirt contest.

Oxycodone slowed her brain's synapses, let the endorphins step in, and lifted her head in a clouded way. They offered the best advice in the room: Go back to bed. She moved away from the door and windows and carried Bella to the bedroom. The doorbell rang again. Georgie's heart knocked in response. She took a breath. She was okay, as long as she didn't open that door.

Then the phone started again, too.

The phone, the doorbell, the phone—Georgie slunk away from them both.

This is what separates humans from animals: free will.

She had TV. She had the comforting hand of granny panties and narcotics. Her daughter was fine—awake and nursing. Nobody looked high! Neither one was nodding off. Well, okay, Bella was nodding off, but that was normal for a newborn, right? Georgie tickled the girl's foot and saw her eyes widen, evidence she was alert. Together the two of them climbed into the privacy of sheets that smelled like sweat, like their bodies, like milk and blood and piss and love. She climbed back into her nest of blankets and books.

Safe.

Where was Humble? She needed him to come home.

A hand slapped against the bedroom window from outside. It was a hard crack, like a bird breaking its own neck against the glass. It was a bad omen, and Georgie jumped at the noise. She sat up, looked, and saw that it wasn't a bird. Worse: it was human. There was a palm, fingers, and a thumb, splayed, for a moment flattened against the pane.

Dead Girl Solitaire

"*E*ver play dead girl shots?" Humble Johnson slouched at the bar. The first wash of alcohol encouraged his brain to move gamely.

The bartender said, "Dead girl shot?" He leaned forward to better hear over the music. The bartender was young, with hair in his eyes and in a button-down shirt. He was relaxed behind the counter, like somebody's son hired to mix drinks for a family wedding.

Humble said, "Shots." He lifted his glass to illustrate. "Drinking game."

The bartender shook his head, tossed a damp rag into the air, caught it, and wiped the hardwood counter down. A disco rehash blasted a rattling sound track.

A couple sat beside Humble. The woman's back made a wall where she turned away to share a plate of assembly line–style calamari with her date. She twisted around to look at Humble, a greasy, fried circle held between her fingers like a wedding ring. She sized him up. She swiveled away again and used her other hand to flick a strand of her long dark hair.

Humble Johnson hadn't played dead girl shots in years, but he thought about it sometimes. Did anyone play anymore? He'd played in college at Oregon State, in the lounge, surrounded by the smell of pressed-board furniture and the sweat of his dorm-mates.

The bartender pulled a beer for somebody farther down the row.

Humble hunched over his bourbon, elbows on the glossy wood of the polished bar top, what had once been a slice of the body of a massive old-growth tree. A hundred years earlier when loggers ruled, when a tree in Oregon was bigger around than an SUV and SUVs didn't exist yet, somebody needed a place to set a drink and so felled timber big enough to knock out a neighborhood.

This place had been a logger's watering hole turned wino's haven. More recently a pair of midlife bankers had bought the building and hired a Vietnamese crew to peel molding plywood off the windows. They aired out aged smoke, put up red velvet and gold-flecked wallpaper, and lined the glass shelves with a higher grade of hooch. Humble Johnson, forty-two years old, born and raised in Portland, used to ride his tricycle on the sidewalks around there. He'd waited for the TriMet bus at a bench just down the block. He'd been drinking in that bar and elsewhere for more than twenty years, maybe as long as the bartender had been alive. His history was written in dive bars, laced with malt winds off the old Weinhard's brewery—the Swinehard's Factory, his friends called it. The Swig Hard, the Swill. Beer foam runoff filled the streets back then.

Nobody would put up with that shit now. Beer foam in the streets? The brewery shut down. The "Brewery Blocks" had been converted to a stretch of condos and art galleries. The old Industrial Northwest had been renamed the Alphabet District, like some kind of baby crackers or cheap soup.

When did people get so delicate?

It's a special crowd that settles in to the amber candlelit glow of booze and mirrors before mothers of the neighborhood call their children home to dinner, before a standard workday ends. Humble was part of that crowd. It warmed the cockles of his heart, whatever the hell cockles were. In this haunt, on a strip of northeast Portland, the new owners had added three flat-screen TVs. One, almost overhead, showed the news. Another, just past the pool table, *CSI* reruns. The third was a string of ads.

He watched TV, all three of them, and waited for a girl to die.

Bourbon coated his tongue and burned its way down his

throat. He watched the news. His guess? Dead local girl inside of fifteen minutes, almost to the weather report, halfway to sports. He would've laid that bet.

The way you played the game was, watch TV with drinks ready. When you see a dead woman, pour a shot and throw it back. When you see a girl pulled out of the river, fake-looking TV-land strangle marks on her pale neck, chug a pint. When you see a glamour girl splayed-legged and faceup, dusted blue, dressed just enough to please the FCC, shout "Skoal!" and clink glasses and bottoms up.

Humble missed those days. It'd been fun.

On the *CSI* rerun, a dead girl started the episode. Humble's internal meter told him there wouldn't be another body there for a while.

You could lay bets. With the TV off, you could bet how many minutes until the dead girl showed up, turn the TV on, and time it. Bet how many channels and flip through. You could bet how many channels until the dead girl, or how many channels, at any minute, were showing a dead girl.

So many ways to play the dead girl game. Drunk, it's better. When you play it right, you're wasted.

The bartender surfed. He landed on VBTV, Vampire-Based TV, all hot chicks, dead and undead at the same time. That channel wasn't even fair to bet on—it was too easy. Humble said, "Go," and the bartending kid did, and Humble felt himself command the space.

Another channel flashed the fat body of a monkey. Closed captioning read . . . EXPECTING A BUNDLE OF JOY . . . That knocked-up monkey looked right at Hum. It looked as though it knew him. Under the stern eyes of the monkey's gaze he thought he ought to get up and go home to his wife and their new baby, their daughter. Then the channel changed. Any urgency he'd felt faded into the warmth of bourbon.

Home?

Home to Georgie, with her stitches in her gut and her bad back, her postpartum gas and grievances. Bella, that elfin thing, was red faced and scowling. He loved them both. He did. He loved them in a way that made him half-sick, to see them waiting at the door, Georgie smiling hello, Bella still wrinkled and squinting, everyone eager to be a family. His daughter was a sleepy pink kidney bean. She was as fresh as a car from the factory, everything new, no miles; no scars, no flaws, no resentments. All the world would do was mess that up. When he looked at her, Hum was reduced to the role of a gnarled tree in an enchanted forest waving old limbs and warning, "Go back! Go back! Danger ahead."

He loved them in ways beyond his practiced levels. He'd never envisioned himself getting married, but then they did and it'd been his idea, really. That was okay. They'd been married for ten years. He never thought they'd have kids, and now they had one. It made him feel myopic, like he couldn't see past the next year, or maybe past what he'd already done. But the baby thing? It brought out, in Georgie, a new level of need. Their easy marriage had been a loose knot. Put a baby in the picture, and it pulled those bonds tight.

Humble was self-employed in computer maintenance. This was supposed to be paternity leave, but Georgie and Bella both slept so much he hadn't figured out why they needed him home. He itched to order another round, linger in this drinker's limbo. When the bartender didn't catch his eye, he almost got up to head home.

Instead he laid a bet against himself: If the next dead girl showed up within two minutes, on any one of the three TVs, he'd stay. He'd have another bourbon. If the girl didn't show, he'd pick up his keys and coat and close the tab. Two minutes. The answer to the question that was the rest of Humble Johnson's evening, or the rest of his life, he laid in the dead girl's stiff blue hands.

A real woman, alive, reflected in the mirror, stepped in behind him. She was tall and thin, her hair streaked red and blond like cedar. She shook rain off her dark coat and hung it on a brass hook on the side of a booth. The woman was young, in one T-shirt layered over another, with sweet curves and a high, inviting ass. She turned toward the bartender, caught Humble's glance in the mirror, and said, "Hey. I know you, don't I? You fixed my old PC." She twirled a barstool with one hand.

Over her shoulder, a crew of men stumbled upon a dead woman near a river. That dead woman's body gave Humble what he needed. It gave him a gambler's permission to stay.

Visitors

Nyla stood on the white cement of Georgie's driveway. Dulcet stomped her way out of the boxwood bushes that lined the house. She used one hand to balance a wobbling pink bakery box. With the other she brushed off dried leaves that clung to her skirt. They'd come to see the baby. They'd called, knocked, rang the doorbell, slapped the back window in case Georgie didn't hear them at the door, and still nobody answered. She'd said she'd be home.

A white curly-haired dog jumped against Dulcet's shin. The sleeve of her satin coat flapped against the claw of brambles. That coat was like something a boxer might wear, in beige satin the color of skin, with wide white cuffs at the sleeves. On the back, in a cursive script, it read:

More Established Than the Rules

It was a tour coat from a show she'd put together about sex before social norms—her own fantasy of prehistoric promiscuity—a sleeper show in three cities playing to an audience of six, or two, or a janitor, with Dulcet stripping down onstage in rooms the size of a bedroom. Edging up on forty, she, too, was more established than the rules and moved like she knew it.

Her T-shirt read I AM WOMB-MAN! HEAR ME ROAR, written in Sharpie. Now she said, "What the hell?" She was tall, made taller by her clogs, and scrawny-thin, all sinew and muscle, with big hands. She snapped her fingers at the dog. "Down, Bitch."

"Do you have to call her that?" Nyla said, and eyed the house's front door.

Georgie wouldn't answer the phone. She hadn't been out of the house much at all, or at least nobody had picked up the *FoodDay*, those free food newspaper inserts full of ads. They'd piled up on Georgie and Humble's front step, making it look like a house neglected.

"Sweet little Bitchy Bitch." Dulcet ran her free hand over the dog's curly head. "Little Bitchybitchybitchybitch."

"That is not a name." Nyla was soft in all the ways Dulcet was hard. Nyla was short and dressed in a sage-green windbreaker over worn yoga clothes. Her honey-brown hair was tucked back in a loose ponytail. Dulcet's bleached hair couldn't have been shaved any shorter without scraping her scalp. They'd known each other since sixth grade. Back then, almost thirty years earlier, they'd pooled their money and bought a tub of ready-made frosting at the 7-Eleven, chasing the same sugar high.

Dulcet said, "It was on her papers, at the pound."

"That's her gender, not her name."

"It might be her breed, too," Dulcet said. "A bichon bitch?"

"Bichon frise," Nyla said. It grew dark early in Portland in the winter. Some gray days it never got light out at all. The lights were off inside the house. Nyla said, "Georgie's probably asleep. Those first baby days are exhausting."

Dulcet said, "So we're stuck with a thirty-dollar cake?" She used one hand to point, as though cocking a gun at the cake box.

"After you've had a baby the whole world shifts." Nyla gave birth to her first child, Celeste, when she was barely twenty. The girl's full name was Celestial; that's how young Nyla had been when she'd had her. She'd named her daughter after her favorite tea, Celestial Seasonings. If it'd been a boy, she would've named him Stash. Now Celeste was off at Brown.

Nyla's second child, Arena, was in high school.

Dulcet handed over the cake box. Bitchy Bitch lunged in an effort to snag the cake midtransfer, but she was a short dog with no luck.

"Babies are parasites."

Nyla said, "We all start out as babies."

"All parasites." Dulcet pulled a lighter out of her bag. "I hope she doesn't make me hold it. If I wanted to hold a baby, I wouldn't have had that eighth-grade abortion."

"Or sophomore year," Nyla said.

"That one, too."

Nyla had been there for Dulcet through them both, more or less. With the first, she was still so young and clueless she honestly thought an abortion was dental work. Seriously. She'd had to look it up.

Dulcet said, "Thank God, or the Great Teutonic Dawn Goddess of Fertility, or whatever, that there's a total surplus of babies. My baby-making skills aren't needed."

They walked back to Nyla's old Jetta wagon. Nyla rested the cake box on the hood of her car, opened the top, and ate fresh fruit off the cake one glazed piece at a time.

"Avoid pain, seek pleasure," Dulcet said. "Babies are all about pain." If the goal of living is to balance the wonder of life against the fear of death, Dulcet needed help finding that wonder ever since she watched both her parents crawl out of the world early.

Her mother had turned a dark yellow before she died. Her father had been simultaneously both bloated and emaciated.

They left her with pills, by way of an inheritance.

She kicked a foot at a pair of high heels near the curb. "The cream of the crap. Pretty good, for hooker shoes."

If New York is the city that never sleeps, Portland is the city that never throws anything away. Streets are littered with paper signs screaming FREE! Free cardboard boxes, ironing boards, weathered chairs, stereo systems, and paperbacks. It's a materialist's cornucopia. Except for the rain. Then it becomes a multileveled mold collection.

She kicked off a clog and slid her foot into one of the free shoes. They were dark brown with a pale blue piping that matched perfectly the blue veins over her instep. She kicked it off again.

Dulcet rummaged in her oversized purse until her hand

emerged, pale fingers laced around a slim clay pipe. She slid it into her coat pocket and dug through her bag again. This time she pulled out an amber vial of Vicodin, a wad of Kleenex, and a bottle of K-Y, and piled them all on top of the car.

In sixth grade, when they met, they'd been twins in their indulgences. These days Nyla opted for the endorphin high of power yoga. She asked, "You're going to smoke?"

"I have a license."

Nyla said, "To smoke in the car?"

Dulcet pulled out a string of condoms, a fistful of pens, and a sleeve of Vicks cough drops. She turned the purse upside down and unloaded the rest of the contents on the car's roof. "You have a license to drive, I have a license to smoke. We're covered." She found what she sought and held it up, victorious: her baggie, clouded with use, and the dried herb inside.

Almost immediately a cop car turned the corner at the end of the block. With the low rumble of an engine meant to move at higher speeds, the cruiser made its way to the curb.

"Shit." Dulcet dropped her stash back in her purse. "Am I bugged, or is this whole city on camera now?" She wadded up the string of condoms. She swiped at the K-Y too fast and sent the bottle flying in a nice arc. She reached again, like a cat batting at a moth, and knocked it out of the air. It fell into the sprawling box of FREE! molding party clothes. Dulcet turned away fast, acted like it wasn't hers anymore, not at all. . . .

The cops parked nose to nose with Nyla's beater.

"Do they ticket if you're parked the wrong way?" Nyla murmured under her breath. She pushed the lid on the cake box closed. Two cops got out of the car, both tall and big, in their dark uniforms. Bitchy Bitch leapt up to say hello. Dulcet snapped her fingers, and thank God, the unleashed animal doubled back.

Twenty years earlier nobody'd even carded in Portland bars. You could live well in an abandoned warehouse—it wasn't against any law that was enforced. The tofu factory would give away the corners they made when they cut round burgers out of square pieces of tempeh. Alternative living was that easy. Now people were shot by cops for pissing in an alley and the only thing easy was to get on the wrong side of the law. So much for the Wild West! Still, the streets smelled sweet with herb, smokers smoking and taking the risk.

The first officer hitched up his pants. The second squinted toward the house like he needed glasses, then headed up Georgie's short driveway.

Through a front window, there was a flash of Georgie's pale face and what seemed to be the inadvertent wave of a white hand against the darkness as she reached to close a curtain.

Dulcet wrapped her fingers around Nyla's arm, holding her back. When Portland's finest were involved, Dulcet's inclination was to run.

But Nyla was a mother and carried that authority. She lifted the cake in its box like it was her turn to bring the school snacks, shook Dulcet off, and followed the cops to Georgie's door with one arm swinging, the other holding the box tight against her side. She asked, "What's going on?" to the backs of the officers—their short haircuts and thick waists where they spilled over heavy belts. "Is there a problem?"

Dulcet followed more slowly, with her bouncing dog circling at her feet.

The first officer knocked on Georgie's door. The door creaked open.

Georgie smoothed her hair back as she ducked around the door. Her skin was splotchy. She cradled her baby, blinked, and through a fleeting, shaky smile, offered one word. "Yes?"

The officer asked, "Everything okay here, ma'am?"

"All good." Georgie's eyes were blue and watery. Her face seemed superimposed on her neck, the way her head bobbled. She was barefoot, in worn flannel pants and a sweater. A soft blue night-shirt poked out in a ruffle below the sweater's edge.

The officer asked, "Mind if we come in?"

She let them in without resisting, without asking questions, as though out to prove her own innocence by a sheer willingness to comply. Did she know what this was about? She moved away from the door. The house was dark inside, the curtains closed. Dulcet, Nyla, and Bitchy Bitch followed on the heels of the cops.

Dulcet whispered, "Did you call them?"

Georgie shook her head, a swift, secret negation.

The officers walked from room to room, restless animals, and gave a cursory glance to the bedroom and bathroom. The two men were as tall as Dulcet and twice as wide. "You have one child?" the first officer asked. He held up a thick finger, a simple illustration: one.

"That's right." Georgie held Bella tightly to her chest. The baby was calm, sleeping.

Bitchy Bitch nosed a Diaper Genie near the front door.

The women clustered in the kitchen, leaned against the counters, and were mostly silent, as though they'd be arrested if they said the wrong thing; nobody knew what that wrong thing was. You have the right to remain silent. . . . That was the only right they could count on. They waited together the way they had years before when somebody had called the cops on their parties, or when they sat in cars, pulled over for speeding tickets. If you moved slowly, didn't argue but went along with it, there was a good chance the cops would go away.

One of the officers said, "We got a call from a concerned party. Thought there might be trouble." He ran his eyes over a chipped plate with a piece of toast on it, a half-full glass of orange juice, an open bottle of baby formula, and three white drips on the counter. A package of cloth diapers rested near the door.

Nyla slid the cake box onto the counter.

The second officer asked, "Are there any other children in the house?"

Georgie said, "No." She said it loud and clear, as though testifying.

"Anybody else at all?" he asked. Georgie shook her head. She might've raised her right hand, if the baby hadn't been in it, and sworn to tell the truth, the whole truth, nothing but the truth—*and nothing except exactly what you want to hear, officer!*

The cop looked at Dulcet, then he looked at Nyla, studying each of them in turn.

"We just got here," Nyla said.

They were big men with big shoes and heavy tools, trying to solve a problem they couldn't see.

One looked at Dulcet's shirt. "Womb-man, huh?" he said, and smiled.

She pulled her satin coat closed over her shirt.

After a moment, the second officer looked toward the first and said, "Okay?" That was their conference; they made a silent decision. The first put a card on the kitchen counter with his name and badge number on it. "Take care," he said, satisfied.

Once the police were gone the small house felt a little bigger, the air a little lighter. The women could move. Nyla asked, "What was that all about?"

"Jesus H. Christ," Georgie said. "God almighty." She held the baby in one arm and reached the other down her flannel pants. Her hand came back up with a vial of prescription pills. She slapped the vial on the counter. Dulcet and Bitchy perked up their ears.

"A mistake." She wrapped the baby blanket more tightly.

Nyla said, "Oh! She's got a little bonkie-bonk on her sweet li'l noggin." She leaned in to kiss the baby's head.

Georgie pulled Bella possessively close and ran a finger over the red patch on her girl's white forehead. "I hit her with the phone."

Nyla blanched.

"It was an accident. It fell on her." Georgie moved away, toward the bedroom. "You can have those pills. If the phone rings, don't answer."

Dulcet said, "But these drugs are yours. They're legit—"

Nyla added, "Georgie, that's enabling."

Georgie, in the next room, called back, "It's nurturing. Dulcet needs pain pills." They knew one another well.

Nyla called after her, "Do you need anything, while we're here?"

Georgie's only answer was the rustle of a comforter and pillows tossed on the bed. Dulcet studied the label on the vial like a fine bottle of wine. She cracked the lid and took out a tablet.

"We love you!" Nyla shouted.

Dulcet swallowed her pill with a handful of water from the kitchen faucet. She pulled out her pipe and her stash, and ran the pipe through her damp fingers. "Not much of a welcome."

In the back room, the TV spoke in a low murmur.

"New moms are a world of two. When you're nursing, your body fills up with chemicals, relaxing hormones—"

"Relactating," Dulcet offered.

"—that make you happy to lie around."

"They have synthetic drugs for that now," Dulcet said, and wiped a drip of water from her chin. She rested her baggie on the counter then packed the pipe. She said, "Who wants to stick around to be your own kid's best cautionary tale? It's a setup." She let her lips find the narrow stem of her pipe and took a swift hit.

Nyla opened the cake box and touched a finger to what was left of the glazed fruit on top.

Dulcet's exhale filled the kitchen with smoke. She tipped her head back to blow the smoke up. Her thin neck was marked with tendons. Her eyes softened.

Nyla hissed, "Sweetie, there's a baby in the house!" She turned on the fan over the stove, opened a kitchen window, and flapped her arms to drive the smoke out.

Dulcet said, "Doing what I can for the planet, supporting hemp farms, right? Hemp fields pull carbon dioxide right out of the air."

Obligingly, she blew into the fan's updraft.

Nyla flapped both hands at the smoke as though trying to fly, to urge the toxic air out. She said, "Arena wasn't a cuddly baby. She wouldn't look at me. For a long time, I thought she was autistic."

Through yellowed teeth, and as Nyla did her flapping dance, Dulcet said calmly, "Arena turned out perfectly fabulous."

The Future Is Unwritten

Arena had slipped from her high school halls to sit on the edge of a turnaround pit on the side of the road across the street from school, just far enough away to escape the rules. She gave a gentle pat to the dead ferret wrapped around another girl's neck. A yellow sign over their shoulders read SLOW CHILDREN. Someone had spray-painted an arrow pointing down from the sign to the spot where Arena sat, where smokers and stoners regularly perched along the decidedly uncomfortable corrugated aluminum railing meant to keep cars from sliding into the parking lot of the veterinarian next door.

She was a lanky colt in a tiny T-shirt that said I ❤ POPCORN and skorts, that skirt-short combination, short enough to fit the child she'd been five years earlier. Her dark hair hung like satin.

The girl in the ferret pelt, with a jumble of black dreads, watch-gear earrings, and lace-up boots, rested beside her with her eyes closed.

A guy sat cross-legged in the gravel, wearing the outfit of dis-enfranchised white boys since the breakout of the Clash thirty-some years earlier: a T-shirt, black jeans, and Converse. Arena knew the Clash from listening to her father's records. She listened to vinyl in her room most nights, imagining her father's voice channeled through scratches and guitar riffs—the Melvins, the Clash, the Wipers. Romeo Void. Even the Slits and Wendy O. Williams channeled her dad, because otherwise? She could barely remember having a dad—only knew what it felt like to want him.

The girl in the ferret neckerchief opened her eyes to offer Arena a smoke. Her eyes were dark, and her smudged makeup was even darker. For Arena, looking directly into anyone's eyes was like looking at aluminum reflecting the sun, or a swimming pool on a bright day.

She was bad at it.

She shook her head no at the cigarette. "Why start something I'd have to keep doing? It's enough to brush my teeth and change clothes." She kicked her vegan-friendly Toms red wrap boots into the gravel. Her mom had bought her those boots. Her mom, a yoga instructor now trying to get a store up and running, was always broke but up on the good causes, and with every pair of Toms sold a poor kid somewhere got new shoes, too.

Arena pretty much was that poor kid.

"Who changes clothes?" This girl, total steampunk, had worked hard to look like she'd been in the same black rags since, what, maybe 1889? "Social pressure to change clothes is just a way capitalism keeps us on the rat wheel."

The Clash kid, in his own uniform, said, "Weren't you, like, Goth last year?"

She said, "Visigoth. It was a specialization, but I've evolved."

Arena said, "Smoking is the biggest corporate scam ever."

"Not if you buy the Indian kind." The girl scratched her head through her mass of hair. She had rings on every finger, spiders, cogs, and crystal.

The Clash guy said, "You sound depressed."

Arena asked, "Because I don't smoke?"

He ground the cherry of his cigarette out in the gravel. A button on his messenger bag read ALPHA NERD. He said, "Where's your zest for livin'?"

The Visigoth-turned-steampunk waved her cigarette. "Your spirit of adventure!"

"American Spirits of adventure. Blue pack." Alpha Nerd tapped his pack on the ground twice. "What'd you come out here for, then?"

"Reading break."

"Right on." When the girl nodded, her black dreads shifted in a thick mass. "They don't let you do that in there?"

"Not enough." Arena found a book in her pack, *Red Azalea* by Anchee Min. Inside, the school's hot halls smelled like crushed ants and gym shoes. If she sat in the grass of the school lawn by herself, that'd be weird. But when she sat with the smokers it was, like, sociably antisocial.

She opened the book to a dog-eared page. *Red Azalea* was a memoir about life in Mao's China, written by a girl assigned the role of a peasant. The author lived in barracks and slept in a room with eight other girls, each inside her own mosquito net.

Anchee Min wrote, "I spent the night of my eighteenth birthday under the mosquito net. . . . The air felt creamy. It was the ripeness of the body. It began to spoil. The body screamed inside trying to break the bondage."

Arena knew that scream.

"My body was in hunger. I could not make it collaborate with me. . . . I tossed all night, loneliness wrapped me. . . . The mosquito net was a grave with a little spoiled air."

In the school halls football players sent one another porn shots and videos of cheerleaders sucking them off, or whatever they could lift off the Internet and make look like it was their life. Lockers were decked out with raw beavers, boobs, and cocks, and slammed shut fast when a teacher walked by. Sex was everywhere—in mute shots of naked bodies, grunting videos, and jokes—but to read about sex without pictures was a totally new kind of thing.

She was maybe the very last virgin in the whole school.

Reading about sex was intimate. Reading about anything was like this really cool secret code from one brain to another, like ESP. Arena looked at the letters. How was it that letters turned into sounds? And sounds formed words and the words could mean absolutely anything and everything, even body fluids—and what exactly let her brain know how to decipher meaning from marks on a page?

Weird.

Writing was the most abstract art ever. She wrote in the back of her book, rough lines, making the letters as awkward and cryptic as possible. She wrote, "gOd." Then she turned the page to Alpha Nerd. "What do you see?"

He said, "God?"

She nodded. There it was, the collective delusion. She'd made him see God in a few lines.

Alpha Nerd, Son-of-Joe-Strummer, who probably didn't even know who Joe Strummer was, said, "Want a pick-me-up?"

She put a hand to her shirt, over the muscle that ran from her chest to her shoulder. A pink and white scar ripped through her skin there. She held her eyes open and steady. To let Alpha Nerd's eyes meet hers was an exercise in connecting, like hands over her body. He said, "First one's free."

She said, "You're that kid we learned about in seventh grade. In that peer pressure video?"

He grinned. "Everybody does it." It was a line from the film.

She reached out a hand. He put a packet in it. She tried not to blink. His damp hand brushed her skin. She could smell the earth below where they sat, the dirt and dust. She could smell oil on the ground, as though a leaking car had idled there. She closed her fingers around the package. This was new terrain. She'd stepped into the video of their seventh-grade cautionary tale. The paper of the packet was solid, like a promise, crisp as the page of a magazine.

Mate Choice Availability

Sarah's cell phone sang in her pocket. Her hands were numb with cold. When she answered, Nyla said, her voice a susurrant whisper, "I don't think Georgie's doing too well."

The zoo's air was filled with the scent of cinnamon and grease—the "elephant ears" cart workers had started making their daily sweet fry bread—and Sarah felt that disconnect of being close and far away at the same time, a friend's voice in her ear, the news crew blocking her view. She had the pacifier laced around her index finger. Absentmindedly, she tapped its rubber nipple against her cheek.

"You saw Georgie? I can't get her to call me back." Yes, it was a selfish hand that tightened down against her heart, but she, Sarah, was meant to be first in line to see the baby. She would know how Georgie was adjusting—her oldest friend, her friend from Lincoln High! Her friend who'd never moved away.

Portland had, for a while twenty years earlier, been low on young people. Portland, Oregon, you had to say, because somehow even the tiny spot of Portland, Maine, loomed larger.

When they were right out of high school there was a small crew of downtown club kids, so small it was easy to think you knew them all. It was a tiny scene with a big, weird social pressure to say, *Yeah, I'm heading to LA soon.* Or you could say SF, or maybe San Fran. You might say, *A friend invited me down.* Maybe you'd really go. Sarah and Georgie didn't even pretend.

Georgie's own mom had left back then, moved out of town like some kind of runaway—a runaway mother nobody went looking for.

Those years mattered! Sarah and Georgie rode clunker Goodwill bikes on streets that emptied out after dark and drank in dive bars where nobody asked their age. They colonized the old-man bars, laid the foundation for generations of hipsters who'd come along since. They drank at Satyricon, and saw Poison Idea and even Nirvana before Cobain really made it.

Portland's last bastion of the permissive West died when they closed Satyricon's punk rock doors. The club reopened for a while, under the same name, but it was thin and watered-down. It was in the original version where Sarah and Georgie saw Courtney Love in the bathroom, where they dodged a flying bottle when someone—Courtney?—flung it. It was definitely Courtney's hand in the mythology of their shared memory. Even when they went to college, they only went to Portland State University, a commuter school downtown.

Now the dollar theaters were six dollars and all parking was metered.

Nyla and Dulcet were native Portlanders, too, though from the east side of the river. Grant High School. Sarah had known them almost twenty years—a long time, yes, but still she knew Georgie first.

She pressed the phone to her ear. "In what way isn't she adjusting?" Her words came out through a tight jaw.

Nyla whispered, "She's in the bedroom."

"Georgie invited you over?" Sarah's voice caught as she said it. She spun the pacifier on her hand, as a way to keep from shaking. The TV crew started rolling up their cables.

Nyla said, "We dropped in."

We?

"You and who else?" Her voice cracked and her throat was raw, as though an alchemy of grief, jealousy, and guilt flourished in the onset of a sudden virus.

"Dulcet," Nyla said.

Of course.

"She gave Dulcet all her painkillers."

Dulcet would love that, Sarah thought. It wasn't that Sarah wanted painkillers. She just wanted to be first in line for the offer, for any offer, from her friend.

She kept in check an urge to slide the pacifier into her own mouth.

Across the grounds Dale, the zoo vet, made a lazy S curve down the asphalt paths on his mountain bike. His jacket said zoo vet in white letters big enough to read across a stadium. He wore shorts all winter. He had an Oregon tan, which is to say no tan at all but the pink flush of bare skin working hard in a cold rain. His muscles shifted with the effort of an incline. He was a specialist in cardiovascular fitness and circulatory systems, and believed in constant motion. Sarah said, "Is she adorable?"

Nyla asked. "Georgie? She's worn out."

"I mean the baby. Of course the baby's cute." Cuteness in infant mammals is a survival skill. Sarah imagined a cross between Georgie, Humble, and little Lucy, the newborn man-ape.

Sarah had met Humble before Georgie did, years ago. They'd gone on what might be called one date. Back then, Humble drove a worn old Mercedes, and he coddled it. Sarah had her dog with her, Shadow, a cuddly new puppy that smelled like summer sun. They'd met up for a beer in the park. Late at night, after dark, he offered her a ride home, but it had pained him to allow her pup in his car. He couldn't hide it.

That was the dividing line: How could she date a guy who begrudged her dear dog-baby?

Ben moved in with Sarah. He loved Shadow from the start! Now the dog was their aged and pampered thing, almost fifteen years later.

Georgie met Humble at a party in Sarah's one-room apartment. Georgie didn't have a dog. That baby? If things had gone differently, it could've been Sarah's.

Then it would've been supercute. Ha!

Almost as cute as the baby she'd have with Ben, anyway.

All babies are adorable. They're built that way, with big eyes, big heads, and button noses. Then that strategic, stumbling, and vulnerable walk kicks in.

The Cuteness Factor.

Grown mammals nurture and protect baby-faced creatures. Reptiles lay eggs and crawl away, and that's a good survival strategy because otherwise they'd eat their own offspring. A lucky anaconda turns out a litter of maybe sixty at once, some alive, some dead, others as unfertilized eggs. It's the original combo meal, a built-in food reward for procreating.

The offspring who survive are the ones who slither off fast. Let that be a metaphor to get your ass out of your parents' house, right?

Nyla said, "It was weird. Georgie let the police in to look around. They left. Now she's sleeping."

Sarah asked, "Police? Why the police?" So even the Portland police had seen the baby before Sarah? She was totally last in line!

"I don't know. Apparently they'd gotten a call?" Nyla said.

Dale charged his bike through a murder of crows; glossy black bird wings filled the air. Sarah's timer beeped. Baby Lucy was in motion, motoring.

The news crew marched toward their van. Dale's nylon shorts flashed in the gray light as he pedaled from one animal enclosure to the next.

"I should be there." She tapped the pacifier against her thigh.

Nyla said, "It's all right. We're on our way out. But, hey, I hear you're due for a new baby, too." Her voice was a happy singsong.

Sarah's heart stopped; her face flushed. Nyla'd heard? They'd been trying, she and Ben. Maybe she was pregnant. She hadn't taken the test yet. It was too soon—too soon to let herself down if the answer came up negative.

"At the zoo," Nyla said. "The monkey. It was in the paper this morning."

Ah! That pregnancy. Apparently this round—like an early labor, an early birth—PR had issued a premature birth announcement. Admin was either confident or strapped for funds, desperate to bring in visitors and sway voters to approve the next levy. Not all pregnancies made it to delivery. Sarah knew that truth in the memory of her body.

"It's exciting?" Nyla asked.

"Sure." The mandrill family kept up their Brady Bunch routine in the zoo equivalent of a split-level, ranch-style house: a split-level, semiterrestrial enclosure. Baby Lucy looked out through a wrinkled old man's face. Her ears were huge and pink, cute by design.

The thing was, that mother-to-be mandrill had already been declared genetically redundant and was given a birth control implant. She'd conceived against the odds.

"Can you put Georgie on the phone?" Sarah felt far away from her old friend. She heard the phone rattle. Nyla's voice moved to the background, calling Georgie's name. There was shuffling, and a wait.

Nyla came back on the line. "She's sleeping."

You can't wake a new mother from that famously hard-won maternal sleep. Those sacred baby naps! Conversation over.

Dale, that biological illustration of muscle and circulation, dismounted his bike on a forested hill. Sarah watched him with the scientifically engaged eye of an ethologist.

Dale had all the markers of a virile male animal in his prime: from his hair to his coloration, his flat abs, and the ready way he entered a room. He wasn't exactly good-looking, but so very healthy.

Sarah had her own fertility markers: full breasts, strong hips, good skin. Ben, her husband, was tall, which was a genetic plus in the brute world of animals, but he was a paper pusher. He spent his days at a desk in an office, making decisions on home loans. His slack shoulders had started to show the strain of sedentary work. He still had all his hair, though, that bloom of youth.

Thoughtful and kind, Ben was Mr. Steady, the most patient man she'd ever met. Being slow and gentle was one of his strengths.

Until it turned into a weakness.

He'd grown up in eastern Oregon, near the Washington border, near the Umatilla Chemical Depot, a chemical munitions storage facility. It was possible he had what the doctor called slow-moving sperm, or "low motility."

Patient sperm?

And he was slow to get his sperm checked. His logic was that heavy pot smokers have slow swimmers, and they make babies all the time, so it'd happen!

Sarah made him drink three shots of espresso an hour before sex. Caffeine sends the soldiers flying.

She'd meet him after work, with a steaming cup of coffee.

By now it was conditioning: Coffee was foreplay, and a hard-on was hope.

When she went home she'd pee on a stick then watch to see: baby or no baby?

The teenagers had disappeared and left her holding their DNA-laden, baby-spit-coated made-in-China pacifier. The zoo paths were dotted with families led by men in sagging jeans.

So why does a patriarch mandrill have that beckoning ass? Why does testosterone manifest as ornamentation? It's about mate choice availability: His ass draws the ladies and holds the family together. One theory is that a bright butt helps a male lead his colony through the dense plants of the rain forest.

In the distance, Dale, in deep purple shorts, straddled his mountain bike and pumped up the side of a hill into the thick green manicured shrubbery of the Oregon rain forest where it had been groomed to make way for Employees Only paths.

God's Angel

Late that night, when Humble still hadn't come home, Georgie called him, but there was no answer. She'd seen the conflicted way he moved around their house since Bella was born. He'd pick their daughter up, hold her close, one big hand spread across her tiny back, a perfect father. They had the same soft waves to their hair. His eyes might be narrow with sleep, and hers, too. Then half the time he'd put her down again, grab his coat, and head out without looking back. He'd say, "I have to work."

Maybe he really did.

A permanent clutch of love and panic had moved into their home—they'd brought a baby into the world! They had the most perfect child! They'd screw up.

Paternity leave is built on vague terms for the self-employed. A lot of people had Humble's phone number. When computers crashed, with small businesses on the line, they'd call him and he'd go and make things right. He worked whatever hours it took.

Maybe he was working now. That was possible.

And if he'd stopped somewhere for a drink? It wasn't a crime. If it kept him from feeling like he'd lost all autonomy, Georgie could hold down the home front.

This was the truth about having a baby and a PhD: She knew the prescribed cultural mother roles, from domineering Queen Eleanor of Aquitaine to domineering Peggy on *Married with Children*.

She'd read psychologist Erik Erikson's theories of "momism"— every frustrated, repressed, suicidal, alcoholic, promiscuous, flatulent, or dandruff-ridden man was driven to his weaknesses by a controlling mom or an infantilizing wife. Erickson postulated that mothers ran the family the way a boss runs a business, only with more castration.

Momism.

If men stood for individualism, women were enforced conformity. Men were active and women beyond passive, a symbol of the sedentary. Christ almighty.

She'd read *One Flew Over the Cuckoo's Nest* and all those academic essays about Nurse Ratched: The woman's role is to run a tight ward, robbing weak men of their masculinity. Wah!

She wouldn't let motherhood put her in that emasculating spot of perpetrator and victim in one ovary-packing, mammary gland–wielding package, chasing her man home from bars, setting a curfew like he was a derelict teen.

No. If Humble missed dinner, that was his problem.

Georgie wrapped herself in a wool sweater, pajamas underneath. She held Bella in one arm and ventured out to drag their garbage can back from the curb. A cop car passed at the end of the block. Were those the same officers who had come to see about the baby? She stayed on her porch until they eased on by.

A haggard neighborhood regular stumbled out of the bushes in their wake and lurched down the middle of the road. The woman had gray hair, a limp, and a bottle of Olde English 800 sticking out of a black plastic bag. Her voice was a croak. "So you had the kid! Let me see the baby." She hobbled over. She held her bottle by the neck, the bag sliding off like a badly fastened diaper.

Georgie pulled back the soft, clean satin blanket. Bella's eyelashes were delicate lines. Her nose was a perfect button.

"Oh, a lovely one." The woman's breath was diseased. Her teeth pointed in every direction. She said, "That's God's little angel you got there."

Who doesn't love a baby compliment, even if it drifts in a cloud of gingivitis?

The woman pointed an arthritic finger. "She'll turn on you, one of these days, you know."

It was a curse.

The woman's laugh was raspy with phlegm. She said it again: "Goin' to turn on you."

Were those flecks of spit raining down on Bella's newborn's skin? The baby's closed eyes fluttered, showing the tiniest vein decorating one eyelid.

"She will not." Georgie tried to keep her voice light.

"I got five li'l angels out there. Hell knows where they are now." The woman twisted the cap off her bottle. When she drank, she tipped her whole body back and flung an arm out for balance.

A pale blue polyester nightgown peeked out from under the woman's coat.

Shit. That nightgown! It was a flash of a nightmare. It was as good as Georgie's own, or close enough to it. This woman was a mother who didn't bother to get dressed, one possible future looming.

It was the wrong way to author a family.

It was a creepy reminder of the Gothic, within the family text.

Georgie lifted the edge of her garbage can by the plastic lip. With Bella in the other hand, she stooped to accommodate the can's height and dragged it from the street to the sidewalk. The bedraggled drunk laughed. The can hit the back of Georgie's foot at each step; like that laugh, it chased her home. Garbage chased her.

"I won't let you down," she whispered. She wouldn't even put the baby down, actually, didn't let her out of her arms.

The woman cackled and called out, "You read them baby books?"

Georgie didn't turn, didn't answer.

The woman said, "Here's my advice—don't worry! It takes a lot to kill a baby!" and she laughed again until she started to cough. Georgie heard a soft crash behind her as she scurried, as though the woman had fallen, but the laugh didn't stop.

Kill a baby?

"Can't go too wrong!"

Georgie was Quasimodo, staggering under her burdens. She'd surround her daughter with beauty, but there would always be garbage. She let go of the can when they reached the side yard and bent over her bundle, her baby. A car turned down the street.

Humble?

She peered toward it in the dusk and felt in her own hopeful gaze the wistfulness of a dog left home alone too long. The car slowed, then it lurched and veered around the drunk mama with the Olde English 800, who rose slowly to her feet to make her way, stumbling, down the center of the road.

Dulcet's Anatomy

Dulcet Marvel was a tall, cool waterfall of a woman raised on Rit-alin and Benadryl, built to last, entirely anti-baby. Why haul an-other little uterine hostage into the world to suffer through a rigged game? Why line up for public schools and cubicle jobs to work your ass off while the rich get richer and everybody else drops dead early?

She had her mother's hips and her father's hands. She had their silver serving tray and used it to hold jewelry, spare change, and pipes.

If she made it as long as her mom, she had twelve years left to live. If she lived as long as her dad, that might be closer to fourteen.

She didn't hate babies, though maybe hated the world. That was possible, although she liked some things about living. She liked a vodka martini and the dusty, bitter taste of a Percodan on her tongue. She liked damp sex, hot strangers, and late mornings. She liked that first sip of the first cup of coffee each day—you couldn't repeat the moment in the second sip, it wasn't possible—and she loved her little dog.

Her job was to teach teenagers how not to multiply. On an after-noon when the air in the school gymnasium that doubled as a school cafeteria still held the sweet scent of canned corn and cheap meat, while the city waited for their new mandrill to be born, while other women had babies in production lines at hospitals all over town or turned them out in home births, and in water tanks, and on the seats of public transportation, Dulcet was back in high school. She stood tall, nearly naked, alone in the middle of the gym under a ticking clock, in front of a crowd of teenagers who lined the bleachers.

She wore latex, her living anatomy lesson in a handcrafted, tailor-made transparent three-piece suit: a leotard-like one-piece latex swimsuit, a long-sleeved latex shirt over that, and a latex vest. The vest, marked with the wither of black lungs, was already on the floor. Her shirt showed white ribs and healthy lungs—the lungs of a country child! A nonsmoker! The shirt was as tight as a wet suit, with a zipper down the back. It ended at Dulcet's narrow waist. The suit below it was laced with internal organs. A flower of ovaries bloomed just inside the cage of Dulcet's hips. There was the curve of fallopian tubes, little question marks. She wore black boots, knee-high and high heeled. Her thighs were bare.

She was an anatomical superhero.

There were companies that specialized in latex women's body-suits for men, with hip padding and breast inserts. These suits let transsexuals walk the world in the ultimate female form. They came complete with catheters to let urine trickle from a man's natural penis, which would be hidden, down through the folds of a latex vagina.

What Dulcet wore was harder to come by: an anatomically correct illustration of a woman's internal organs made to cover a woman's body, with the vulnerability of the inside lacing the outside. In her anatomy suit she was beyond naked: peeled of skin.

With a laptop and a portable projector balanced on a chair, she'd already been through her PowerPoint demo on genital warts. Everybody loved photos of genital warts! Flash those on a wall, and the place went silent.

When she spoke into her headset microphone, Dulcet's voice boomed. She'd moved on to the particulars of hygiene. She said, "This is why, for the ladies in the group, you can't actually lose a tampon. Quell that fear! Listen up, males, men and boys. You're part of this too."

She was here to tell the story of the body.

She pointed to her lower abs.

"The vagina is a short cave. It's a major draw, but it's not the Grand Canyon. Don't let anyone tell you otherwise. It's not a black hole. The cervix is a barrier. If you lose the string or have sex without taking your tampon out—not that I'm advocating sex at your age, we already covered that—still, if it happens, save yourself an ER bill.

"Take a deep breath, relax, and bear down on those Kegels.

"You know your Kegels, right? Imagine a bowel movement. Then use your fingers. It's your body, you can touch yourself. I can give permission for that, right?"

Girls giggled. There was a flash—somebody stole a photo. The room was full of camera phones.

Dulcet glanced at the PE teacher, who leaned against the cinder block wall. She was about Dulcet's age, short with curly hair, dressed in the snug contours of a blue all-purpose tracksuit-turned-yoga-wear. The teacher nodded. Or maybe she flinched?

Everything in a public high school is politically on thin ice: All paranoia, all the time! Behind the teacher stood the vice principal, and behind her was the principal, a mini–Mount Rushmore arrangement staring out from the crowd.

Students fondled iPhones, BlackBerrys, cell phones, and games, the world in their palms. A few palpated the fake boobs Dulcet had passed around, looking for cancer lumps. Somebody flung one of the boobs toward the basketball hoop. It fell short. The PE teacher jogged over and picked it up. She gave a delicate scowl in the general direction of the audience but didn't blow the silver whistle that hung from a cord around her neck.

Dulcet said, "Nice shot. Now, fellas, listen up. You can help with tampon retrieval. Cut your fingernails first. If it's been in there a while, the retrieved tampon will stink. It will. It'll stink to holy Heaven. And if it's been in for a month, ladies, you might want to tell your doctor, but as long as you feel fine you'll probably be okay. What you want to look out for are symptoms of toxic shock, like fever, vomiting."

There were more flashes, more photos. Dulcet gave not one fuck about showing up on the Internet; her body was an extension of her public service work. If she started conversations in the blogosphere, that was good.

Besides, she didn't take a bad photo. She was chiseled. She was a professional photographer herself. She could pull it off.

The latex suit was sheer between the bright blooms of organs. An observant student might see the dimple of a belly button and dark spots of pubic hair behind the translucent drawing of a vagina and uterus.

She was drenched in sweat under the suit. Worse, she'd had to cover herself in lube first, in order to pull the latex over her own muscles, angles, and curves. Now lube and sweat mingled until the outfit was torture, like a bad weight-loss program.

She drank from a bottle of water that rested on a wooden stool at her side. She had a duffel bag at her feet, mostly for the fake boobs. Her job was to get the kids' attention.

She'd been over the gender-neutral parts: shown the pancreas and the appendix, traced the bronchial system, ribs, and heart. To some of these kids a heart was a cliché in a pop song, not a vital organ that could burst with too many of the wrong drugs. They needed to know what she had to offer.

A heart can skip and murmur even over basic things like a lack of adequate water or too little potassium. A brain is a fragile, adaptive organ. She had a dream of making a brain hat to show how drugs and frontal lobotomies worked.

She said, "Any questions?"

The room went silent, except for the ticking wall clock.

Dulcet said, "I don't do this because I'm court ordered to as community service, or because I get rich from it. I do it because I want you to be in charge of your own body. You're the ruler, and you can exist in your own benevolent anarchy as long as you know the rules."

She walked a few steps in one direction, eyes on the crowd, then turned and walked back the other way. In the audience, one hand crept up slowly.

"Yes!" Dulcet pointed to the girl fast, as though she were fingering a fleeing suspect. The girl slouched in the middle of the crowd. Dulcet said, "Kudos to you, first one to break the ice. Let me give you a prize."

When she crouched, the rubber suit folded and bunched at her waist. She dug in her duffel bag until she found what she was looking for, then stood and tossed a paperback toward the girl in the crowd. It was a copy of *Your Body: Right or Wrong?* Physical trivia. "Now, what's your question?"

The girl said, "How do you pee in that?"

Dulcet said, "I have a slit, in the latex. Who else?"

Another girl raised her hand. This one asked, "Are you, like, post-op sex change, or what?"

Dulcet wasn't sure she'd heard the question right. You had to get it exactly right on these school visits—conversation about transgender stuff had to be student initiated, or funding could be shut down fast. She put a hand behind her ear. "One more time?" she said.

The girl cleared her throat. She sat up a little straighter. She was heavyset. She said, "Like, were you born a girl, or a guy?"

I have a slit, Dulcet thought.

Her job was to answer with authority and respect. The other part of her job—the part that didn't show up on her résumé—was to physically remind kids steeped in media images that there's more than one way to be female. She was tall, strong, short-haired, big-handed, and elegant. And she was direct. She said, "I am a woman. But people can be born in a range of ways. Gender identity is a continuum rather than a dichotomy, right?"

She aimed for the all-inclusive answers.

A boy raised his hand, or at least the person looked like a boy. Dulcet tried to avoid assumptions. She pointed and said, "Yes?"

"If you're a girl, how'd you get so tall?"

She said, "I grew up, this is me. Now, any questions about your bodies?" She smiled in a way she hoped was kind, though Dulcet wasn't a big smiler; it made her face hurt.

Without raising his hand, a boy called out, "Are we going to get a naked man suit in here?"

Another kid cupped his hands and yelled at the first one, "Homo!"

Somebody else said, "Show dill weed how his cock works."

The kids laughed and one pushed another and then the bleachers were roiling with bodies. All the discomfort of not talking, not asking their questions, turned to the physical. Someone threw another fake boob. A kid caught it and flung it back. One boy collected three and juggled them. An A-cup skidded across the polished wood floor. The PE teacher picked it up, tucked it in her sweat suit pocket, and just like that she had a third mammary down low on her torso. A jellyfish of a double-D fell as though from the sky, right behind the first, and took a dive past the teacher's ear. The woman ducked, in a fine show of peripheral vision and fast reflexes. She said, "Let's say good-bye to our guest. Thank you, Dulcet Marvel! Make sure to return all the props in good condition." She led the kids in clapping, and they took that as a cue it was okay to leave. They clapped as they walked, a clapping stampede, like they couldn't get free fast enough.

Dulcet collected her rubber vest with the picture of smoker's lungs, and her bottle of water. The PE teacher picked up stray boobs that had scattered like hacky sacks. The laptop and projector belonged to the school. Dulcet pulled out her flash drive and looped the lanyard around her neck.

A lanky high school girl cut free of the pack and headed toward her. Dulcet knew these girls, the ones who snuck up quietly afterward. Hers would be a personal question: Pregnant? Overly familiar with genital warts? One boob bigger than the other?

As the girl separated herself from the crowd, Dulcet saw it was Arena, Nyla's daughter. She'd forgotten—Arena went to school there.

"You were great." Arena's voice was soft, lost under the high ceiling of the gym. "Here's your thing back?" She handed over a gelatinous fake boob. It was warm, palpated by the masses.

Dulcet said, "Thank you, sweetheart. Cancer, or no?"

Arena said, "I think that one's got it."

Dulcet found the lump between two fingers. Arena was right. "Perfect. That could save your life." They walked together toward the door. "So, you like this place?"

Arena looked away. "It's life as I know it."

They came to a closet in one corner of the gym. Dulcet said, "Well, this is my backstage." The PE teacher came up behind them, carrying more silicone boobs.

Arena said, "They didn't give you the faculty restroom?"

Dulcet said, "I don't want to waddle down the hall in the outfit, my parts showing."

"You wouldn't be the first," Arena said. She slouched, a sweet, shy girl, with her chest tucked in and her shoulders forward.

Arena's father had died in a car accident in the same year, around the same time, that Dulcet's father succumbed to cancer. Dulcet's parents had four kinds of cancer between the two of them—breast, liver, prostate, lung. It was a whole season, an era, of dying.

So when Arena was little and Nyla was newly widowed, Dulcet had gone to Nyla's house every day after she left the hospice. She'd brought Nyla wine, and brought the girls blueberries, strawberries, and overpriced gummy vitamins. She'd brought them Goodwill dresses and pens from the credit union, anything she could find. It was a way of grieving, to feed the girls vitamins and keep them dressed.

She and Nyla would sit together, ice packs on their puffy eyes, and they'd cry. They'd wash down Dulcet's dad's pain pills with Chardonnay, after he didn't live long enough to need them all.

Dulcet was still washing down pain pills ten years later.

She tried to be an aunt figure, somebody Celeste and Arena could count on, but she forgot birthdays and showed up late for school events and slept through their fund-raisers. She got too drunk at birthday parties, especially when she tried to be domestic, and she never brought the same date twice.

Did Arena remember the strange light of those winter afternoons, after her father's death? As the girl loped away now, she seemed relatively unscathed other than being so very much alone. Teenage girls were supposed to move in packs.

Dulcet ducked into the closet, a dark space, where one hanging fluorescent light warbled from the middle of the ceiling. The room was full of balls and orange cones, full of the smell of rubber.

The PE teacher had finished collecting latex breasts, and followed Dulcet. "We've got hand sanitizer for the props. Don't want to take home swine flu. Need any help?" The woman let Dulcet's fake boob collection tumble from her hands into to a tidy pile on the floor.

Dulcet said, "Actually, my zipper." She pointed at her back. It was hard to lift her elbows all the way up, to reach her back, in that slingshot of a suit. The teacher hesitated. Dulcet said, "It's under the vertebrae." The zipper was camouflaged by a thin drawing of bone.

Dulcet felt cool air. The zipper went down. The teacher's breath moved over her neck. "That was a terrific presentation."

"Thanks." Dulcet shook her way out of the tight shirt and tossed it onto a mesh bag full of volleyballs. She'd rinse it at home.

Now she was in the latex bodysuit with the heart and arteries on it. A green scrawl drew the lymphatic system; the endocrine system was in blue. Dulcet knew well where the cancers lived that caused her parents' deaths.

"You do a lot of these?" the teacher asked.

"Pretty regularly, in the fall." Dulcet dug in her canvas bag.

"It's full-time?"

Dulcet pulled out her Volcano vaporizer, a metal, cone-shaped smokeless smoking system, a way to get high without wrecking her lungs, setting off fire alarms, or getting busted by the smell. "Mostly," she said, "I'm a commercial photographer. Nude portraits." She moved a crate of basketballs to get to an outlet. "I patch together a living."

Dulcet plugged in her Volcano. She could wait to get high until the teacher had gone, that was an option, but the PE teacher didn't seem to be going anywhere too soon. Dulcet had already waited through her own presentation. She knew how to be patient. She also knew that patience came easier when she was high, and the Volcano would take a while to heat up. "I've got a chronic pain problem. This is totally legal." She loaded the chamber with weed.

The PE teacher asked, "What kind of pain?"

Dulcet pulled the straps of the latex leotard-like swimsuit down over her shoulders. The suit clung. "Skin, bones, joints. Fibromyalgia, restless legs syndrome, TMJ. You name it." She rubbed her jaw. She took both hands and twisted her head sideways until her neck cracked. Ghost cancer, a perma-hangover, love wedged in with bone-deep loss—who knew where the pain came from? It was always with her. She said, "Doing the body show makes my bones hurt."

She peeled the suit lower. Her breasts sprung out, small and high.

Her goal? To feel and not feel, at the same time.

The Volcano whispered a promise only Dulcet could hear. Her mouth practically watered. Only pot and meds lifted the pain. The latex suit bunched around her waist. She left it there, let her damp boobs breathe in cool air. She bent and attached a valve and a balloon chamber to the Volcano, to collect the pot vapor. Dulcet had never been shy. She'd made a decision a long time ago to skip the shy routine.

The PE teacher said, "I'm a registered massage therapist."

She touched Dulcet's neck with a mix of professionalism and an invitation. Dulcet knew how this worked: When she wore her organs on the outside, showed that cartoon version of every heart and liver, it sent out a signal of easy familiarity. When she pulled the suit down, let herself be naked, strangers were willing to take risks.

She was a body, intimate and public at the same time.

The teacher smelled like roses and rain. She rubbed her thumb in small circles along Dulcet's upper vertebrae and said, "Sit down." Dulcet sat on a step stool. It was a low place for a tall woman, almost like sitting on a curb. She relaxed under the teacher's hands.

"I work on micro-muscles. Most people only tune in to the larger muscle groups. They don't realize how many muscles a body has."

Dulcet said, "I do."

The balloon on the vaporizer moved as though ready to inflate.

The PE teacher reached forward, a hand on both sides of Dulcet's clavicle. She said, "Come see me, at my practice. I'll give you a card. You don't have to be in pain."

One hand inched down Dulcet's bare skin as though counting ribs. In that gesture was a question: Where were the limits of this particular intimacy? It was a conversation between two warm bodies alone in a badly lit room.

This was another moment in Dulcet's sweet skin-story, nobody's business but her own, an exchange between humans. No condemning bearded God paused to look down from his elitist Heaven and dangle that carrot in the shape of a cross, that bribe—a trick to pass up life's libertine liberties.

Dulcet said, "If you'd want your picture taken, we could trade. I do nudes."

The teacher's breath brushed Dulcet's ear, with the scent of mint.

The door cracked open and light cut in. There was a curvy silhouette, a woman in high heels whose hair glowed like new snow on a winter night against the dark of the poorly lit room, and as Dulcet's eyes adjusted she saw the principal, Mrs. Cherryholmes, under that halo of weak fluorescents.

The teacher straightened up and scrambled backward.

Mrs. Cherryholmes jumped back and almost closed the door again before she got herself together to step forward. "Ms. Marvel, your check." She waved a white envelope. There was a tightness in her voice that implied that their conversation wasn't over.

Dulcet's whole job could be over.

Her green lymphatic system and blue endocrine system, those pretty graphic designs, were bunched up in the latex at her waist. Without getting up, she said, "Thank you."

Mrs. Cherryholmes put the check on one of the industrial shelves. The teacher made herself busy organizing soccer balls. As the principal started to turn away, something else caught her eye. She said, "What is that?"

The Volcano.

"Mine. It's medical equipment." Dulcet's voice came out low, gravelly and relaxed.

The principal studied the Volcano, her eyes steady, taking it in. "Nice to work with you, Ms. Marvel. Ms. Tompkins, please see me in my office when you have a moment." She closed the door.

The room went dim again. It smelled like rubber and sweat. Dulcet said, "So you're Ms. Tompkins?"

Ms. Tompkins said, "I have to go." But instead of leaving, she moved further back into the storage closet, to a rack of industrial shelving, and found a small box. She took out a card and handed it to Dulcet. "My massage therapy business," she said. "Call me."

Fifty Things You May Not Need to Worry About

*T*here are three rules for writing a novel. Unfortunately, no one knows what they are.

Ba-da-boom!

W. Somerset Maugham famously said that, and he said it again now in Georgie's ear, and he threw his head back and laughed.

His words were scrawled on a piece of paper tacked to her wall. She was at her computer, a desktop set up in the dining room. With a one-term leave from an adjunct teaching job at Portland Community College followed by Christmas break, this was the moment to dust off her dreams. It would be the longest consecutive stretch of time she'd had off from work since she was thirteen, since her mom transferred with Nike to Malaysia and her dad forgot how to buy groceries, since she got her first period and had to take the city bus to buy her own tampons. At thirteen she washed cars. She made blackberry pies from berries that grew in an alley and sold them by subscription to residents in a retirement home.

Twenty-five years later, this was her big break. Her plans for maternity leave? She'd write a book. *Author* a book, even. She'd been patching one together for ten years already, in bits and pieces—it was her PhD dissertation: *Implied Narrative and Suppressed Symbol in the Paintings of Élisabeth Vigée-Lebrun.*

She could smell the best-seller possibilities!

With a shift in tone and scope she'd turn her dissertation into a commercial manuscript—play up the romance, the tragedy. Manufacture a lot of deeply felt emotion.

Pssst! They don't tell you this in grad school, but here's a tip: People go nuts for deeply felt emotion.

Vigée-Lebrun was a beautiful raven-haired portrait artist who flattered her patrons and worked her way into Marie-Antoinette's life as a court painter. She lived at the Palace of Versailles with her infant daughter. When the French Revolution hit, when Marie-Antoinette lost her head, Vigée-Lebrun and her child escaped overnight, in a seriously competent mother moment.

This woman's life was destined for the big screen! Georgie opened the file. Bella slept in her bassinet. The house was quiet. First thing Georgie did was revise the title of her work: *The Secret Narratives of Vigée-Lebrun.*

Readers love secrets.

Success inched closer. Somerset Maugham could have his laugh, but she'd win out and find her own rules. Her writing project had a nerve-racking sense of suppressed urgency.

Back when Georgie's mom left town, Georgie dropped out of school. Social workers tracked her down. Her dad must've given them Sarah's address. She was with Sarah's family, eating their Pop-Tarts, bread, and tuna. She had Pop-Tarts hidden in her pockets. Heat pumped out of the vents in Sarah's house, a minor miracle. She slept in Sarah's extra bunk bed, on an extended sleepover, ready to leech love from a family that wasn't hers.

She was a stray.

Now the bruised feeling around her C-section incision had started to lessen. Bella, mid–baby dream, scrunched up her face like Margaret Thatcher on a bad day—like Marie-Antoinette, when politics took a wrong turn—but still she slept.

What could go on in those new dreams? Freud suggested dreams were about working through repressed urges. What would be repressed in a newborn baby? Maybe Freud didn't take care of enough babies.

Georgie readied her hands over the keyboard.

To spell and *to cast a spell* came from the same Middle English, the same source and sorcery, the same impulse and high hopes: to charm an audience.

The goal was to get the right letters in the right place, the right words in the right order, and seduce. She started to type, launching in earnest into her project, and at that very second, as though tied to the touch of Georgie's fingers against the keyboard, Bella woke up and began to cry.

That angel. The girl's face got so red! Was that natural? Did babies ever have aneurysms with all their screaming? And what were those blotches on her cheeks?

Georgie picked Bella up to croon in her ear. Then she saw marks, little crescents, etched in her daughter's forehead. Claw tracks?

They weren't deep. It was like a rat had prodded the child.

A rat?

If Georgie were to call the advice nurse again, what would she say? Hey, remember me, the one who gave my daughter drugs? I have one little question. . . .

No. Instead, she turned to the computer, held Bella in her arms, and typed, "baby + blotchy + cuts on forehead." Thousands of answers and nonanswers came up, a world of parents trying to sort things out from home.

One search result read: cancer.

Georgie's heart, her blood, her brain—everything stopped, instantly sick. She held her daughter closer. Cancer?

Oh my God! They'd spend every minute together. Life was short.

She tipped the baby back and looked at Bella's face again. The splotches had subsided but the slim nicks in her forehead were still there. She pulled the sweet bundle closer, talking herself back off that ledge: not cancer, not cancer. Not everything is cancer.

There were other answers to choose, all more reasonable, more manageable. That was the beauty of Internet medical advice: options.

Georgie had Googled health and baby answers every day of her daughter's life so far. And as this thought crossed her mind, she reenvisioned her whole book proposal: new idea, new project. It was so clear! It wouldn't be the book she had set out to write ten years earlier, but it was the book that mattered now, the one that'd save her sanity. She opened a blank document and typed:

Fifty Things You May Not Need to Worry About in Baby's First Year (But Can If You Want To): A Hypochondriac's Guide to Child Care

She started a list:
1. *Crazy newborn waking-up faces*
2. *Crossed eyes*
3. *Acts deaf*
4. *Funky breathing*
5. *Poop styles*
6. *Crying jags*
7. *Staring*
8. *Red face*
9. *Bruises*

She wasn't a doctor. She was a mom who knew how to self-soothe, as they said in babyland.

She wrote:
10. *Baby:*
    a. *Sleeps all the time*
    b. *Sleeps when held*
    c. *Sleeps when swaddled*
    d. *Never sleeps*
    e. *Looks half-asleep when its awake*

Her daughter wasn't even a week old, and there she had it—ten ways to go insane. Another day or two, this book would write itself.

She'd never leave the house again. She'd stay home, write books—cast those written spells—and coo at her baby until the baby grew into a girl who could talk. The two of them would talk together. Everything that mattered was already there in those dark rooms.

She was still on the computer, rocking Bella on her lap and darting from one link to the next, when she came across a notice: "Lit Expedition: Ecotours of the mind."

It was an upcoming conference, scheduled for Portland. It was a world of major literature in her own backyard, less than two months away. It was listed as "The First Annual . . ."

It couldn't be annual if it hadn't even happened once yet. She had an urge to grade that line like a freshman placement exam. But no, she'd let it go—that wasn't the relationship she had with the material.

This time, she wanted in.

Johnny Depp was listed as keynote speaker. Johnny Depp?! Gilbert Grape. Captain Jack Sparrow. Edward Scissorhands. Donnie Brasco. The Johnny Depp who channeled Hunter S. Thompson, with his thin mustache and shaggy hair, the man whom she'd known since *21 Jump Street*, who was entirely familiar yet unreachable and surreal. That man was coming to the Oregon Convention Center to wave at a crowd and talk about environmental literature?

Okay. So she'd leave the house after all.

Even Vigée-Lebrun, that rococo painter, knew when to exit the castle.

This—*this!*—was the balance Georgie sought as her book project swerved from the academic to the popular then into a list of neuroses and baby poop. The life of the mind. Bring it on. She e-mailed her name to the organizers. She typed, "Hello, I'd love to volunteer to introduce speakers for your upcoming conference." Calm and polite.

She hit "send."

And before that message disappeared, she saw her mistake: "Hell, I'd love to volunteer . . ."

Ah! One dropped letter and she'd turned her voice on the page from an English major with a PhD into an enthusiastic cowboy.

Hell yes. She'd love to volunteer!

She put on classical music. The music was for the baby but also for her. It was Brahms's Academic Festival Overture, conducted by Leonard Bernstein. The music was thrilling! It was the dance of Georgie's high hopes set to a score. The conference would be her way of stepping back into the stream of the academic conversation. She needed it.

Please, please, please.

The organizers got back to her mid-overture. They said they'd love her help—they were desperate for volunteers!—but also that they wouldn't have exact assignments until the day of the conference.

Georgie wrote back, pecking at keys on the keyboard one letter at a time, one-handed, while she held Bella against her chest. She typed, "Thank you!" She couldn't say it enough. Then she added, respectfully, "One detail. If I don't know my assignment in advance, how will I have time to research and write the introductions? I'd love time to think about it." She wanted to put her writing skills to use. Her mind hadn't gone with motherhood; she was still part of the discourse, the academic dream. The blaring classical music, that Academic Overture, was the sound track to Georgie's life.

And as soon as she hit "send" again, she saw her mistake: "I'd love time to think about tit."

Tit.

Crap! This was the problem with typing with a baby in her arms, a nursing baby, a baby high on tit.

An e-mail came back: "Well write it. You get a copy the day of."

That was confusing. Well write it? She was missing a crucial piece.

Georgie e-mailed, "Sounds good. I'll write it, once I know who I'm introducing. Okay?" She tried to put a smile in her words without sinking to emoticons.

For a while, her in-box stayed quiet. There was an ad from Sears, and another from Doctor Sears. Much later another conference e-mail came back. "We'll write it," this one said, more clearly. "All you have to do is show up and read it onstage." Signed with a smiley face.

Less exciting, but fine, and still a way to keep her hand in.

She wondered who she'd be assigned: a writer, an editor, a theorist, a filmmaker? Somebody smart. Johnny Depp?

Ha. She pictured introducing him in his Willy Wonka glasses, or his Jack Sparrow makeup. More likely he'd be in a good suit. Somebody at the top would snag that assignment. Al Gore was a keynote speaker, too. Michael Pollan would be there, and all the superstars would be far out of reach. Georgie would likely be assigned an obscure academic on a back stage.

One of her exes, a professor named Brian Watson, hit up all the lit conferences. He usually sat on a few panels, ran a seminar or two, and chaired a hiring committee. She'd seen him at more than one hotel lobby cocktail party. Brian Watson had been a tenured full-time professor since he finished grad school two decades back.

When Georgie went back to teaching in the spring her goal was to become full-time faculty. Her department chair, Dan, was on every committee. His vote would be key. Maybe she'd introduce him at the conference. That'd be okay. Not thrilling, but still an opportunity. Georgie hitched up her shirt and let her baby nurse again, turning over her body while she herself lived in her mind, the idea-driven world of plans.

.⸱ ⸰.

That evening when Humble came home, Georgie and Bella rested in the indentation of their collapsing couch. Georgie said, "Guess what?"

Humble jumped. He said, "Jesus, it's dark in here. Thought you'd gone to bed."

The sun set early in the winter. Georgie, in her cave with her thoughts, hadn't bothered to turn a light on. She and Bella were fine moving around in the soft glow of the computer.

Humble poured a drink from a bottle of bourbon they kept on a low shelf in the dining room. He dropped down onto the couch beside her and put his bourbon on a side table. His body was warm. He was a big man, with solid shoulders. He pulled the blanket down, away from the baby's face. "How's our girl?"

He smelled like a bar.

They used to go out for drinks together, sit in a bar midafternoon sometimes. Back then it felt like vacation. When she got pregnant, at first she'd still go along—have a soda and bitters and chew on a maraschino cherry to calm her stomach.

He put his finger in the girl's palm. Bella closed her hand. He said, "You fill out the life insurance papers?" His words knocked into one another.

"Oh, jeez," she said. He'd been asking Georgie to fill those out. *If you died today.* . . . It was a threat, there on the front of the glossy brochure. The threat that came with bringing a child into the world: abandonment. She said, "Did you drive home like that?"

"Like what?" he asked.

"Drunk," she said.

The phone rang. Neither of them moved.

When the phone rang again, Humble made an obvious effort to not slur. "You wan'to answer?"

No, she didn't want to answer. Sarah had already left a dozen messages about coming over. The house was a wreck and steeped in Georgie's own unshowered, sliced-open, stitched-closed, nursing body odors. She turned to the window behind the couch and pulled back the curtain to look out.

"You could throw a little party."

A party for the baby. Who was he kidding? She'd have to get dressed, for starters. Sarah would leave in tears. Dulcet would show up high. Nyla would fixate on "spiritual midwifery" and the home births of her own two children. Ugh.

Portland was packed with happy mamas who birthed babies at home. Each one chalked it up to her personal, unique, deep-seated womanly wisdom. They preached natural birth as the only valid birth experience.

Georgie had bought into that narrative, too, until Bella.

Georgie had cracked a tooth, gritting against the pain of labor, when Bella was ready to be born. In the hospital, the epidural was a soothing cocktail. Then everything had gone into emergency mode. There was an oxygen problem, the obstetrician said, reading a monitor. They'd wheeled Georgie into the operating room without time to talk and jacked up the drugs, so many painkillers through her spine she couldn't lift her arms.

They hung a blue paper curtain between Georgie's head and her body because what they were about to do was brutal. They cut a fast line, let the blood seep, lifted her baby girl out. Bella's long legs unfolded like a little foal's. Georgie felt like a floating head. The rest of her body wasn't her own—it was numb, bloody, being stitched closed by strangers—but she saw her daughter, and they handed the baby to Humble, and she was beautiful. It wasn't a natural birth. Whatever. It was the happiest, bloodiest day of Georgie's life.

Bella was born alive and sans brain damage. So what if it wasn't in a candlelit bath of balanced sea salts set in the middle of feng shui-ed master suite, right? So what if it wasn't in the chicken coop of an urban homesteading commune.

Humble turned on a light that cast him in a warm yellow glow. He could star in an old French painting, flattered by Vigée-Lebrun, dressed in the rococo ruffles of royalty.

He poured himself another shot. Georgie saw him sway. "How many drinks have you had?"

"Enough to quit counting. You want a Breathalyzer?" He leaned over to give her a bourbon-soaked smooch.

"Don't put me in the cop role." That was the road to momism. Georgie felt herself walking a thin, nervous line: She had a family now, the very thing she'd lost as a kid. Her own mom would've been planning an escape.

He stumbled, and she thought for a moment he'd crush her and Bella both. She held a hand up, to protect Bella, but Humble found his way.

She said, "Listen. I volunteered to work on a conference, with Johnny Depp."

The Gift

Days later, Sarah folded herself into her husband's car, into that cloud of leather polish and spent gasoline, with a wrapped present on her lap. A week had passed since the baby was born. Sarah was like an aunt to that child! She would be, anyway, given a chance. She was out to practice her "aunting behavior," as the ethologists called it. She'd treat that child like family.

Ben got in on the driver's side.

In the tight box of a car, Sarah bent over her knees, over the gift, and gagged. She wiped a hand to her mouth then hacked again, a cough mixed with throat clearing. The present crinkled under the pressure of her chest against it. "Oh, God, I spit up a little on the cute bows." She picked at the curling ribbon.

Ben asked, "You okay?"

"Sure, I'm great. It's a good sign, right?" She looked for anything made of wood to rap her knuckles on. The dash was plastic, the seats leather, the floors covered in carpet. Paper was like wood, or had been when it was still alive, before it was made festive, girlish, and metallic. She tapped her hands to the silver and pink wrapping paper, then she tapped her head. She tapped her breastbone, not for luck so much as to urge back the sense of vomit rising.

The pregnancy test was positive. They had a baby on the way! It's good to be queasy in the early weeks of pregnancy—it shows a body tilting into new hormones, adapting as a host, though maybe what she felt was only prenatal vitamins resting heavy in her stomach, a minor flu, bad food.

"I shouldn't have had that Saint André." Bacteria in soft cheeses, that's not good for unborn babies.

Ben said, "Brie won't kill you."

Saint André wasn't exactly brie. It was a triple crème, richer and fattier and harder to resist. She said, "I'm not worried about me."

If her pregnancies had worked out, their backseat would be crowded now. The floor of the car would be flecked with cheddar goldfish crackers and Pirate's Booty.

He put his hand on hers, on top of the present. "We could see this kid another time."

"Now is good."

"Are you going to hold the baby?"

Sarah said, "Of course I'll hold her."

Ben shifted the car into reverse and backed down the driveway. "Are you going to cry?"

She'd fallen apart at the baby shower when a friend of Georgie's from work brought a cake shaped like a woman's body with a plastic baby floating in an amniotic fluid made out of pale Jell-O. It was awful. She'd played the toilet paper game, guessing Georgie's size at eight months by tearing off a length of toilet paper, but she had to dry her eyes on her game piece. It kept getting shorter.

When she turned in her estimate, what she had left of that strip of toilet paper was damp, blackened with mascara, and tiny. She had to guess that Georgie was toddler-sized, maybe even what they called eighteen months in the infant section, and then she bawled again!

She sobbed over the itty-bitty booties that served as table decorations. She'd totally made Georgie's baby shower about herself, her own big void, her drama. Jeez Louise.

She couldn't help it—babies made her cry.

This time, it wasn't a party, thank fucking God. It was a visit. And this round she was pregnant. Again. That was her secret strength. She said, "I feel really good. I'll be fine."

Georgie opened the door holding Bella bundled in a blanket. Sarah and Ben, on the porch, made all the right sounds—they exclaimed: They were glad to see her! The baby was beautiful! Georgie looked great!

Sarah couldn't hear whatever Georgie said over the baby's scream mixed with the grind and shudder of a jackhammer down the street, that familiar, loud language of a neighborhood intent on gentrification.

Georgie still looked half-pregnant, and, of course, nobody had expected her to put on makeup for their drop-in anyway. Maybe it was a leave-in hot-oil treatment that separated strands of her hair, showing a little scalp here and there? She had on some kind of Western-style shirt with pockets and big pearl buttons on the front like overstated nipples. The paisley swirl of the fabric was marked with dried milk patches.

"Come in," Georgie said, or something close enough, and moved out of their way.

The house smelled sweet, tinged with sour milk. Right away Sarah heard Nyla, midsentence, saying, "You can still have a vaginal birth after a C-section. Women do it all the time!"

Dulcet and Nyla were in the living room eating small sandwiches. Sarah hadn't known they were coming. Yet again, they'd gotten there first. Neither of them had a regular job. They could show up on short notice, a total advantage.

Arena slunk in from the kitchen, tall and sullen and gorgeous, with a handful of olives. That was pretty much everybody. Sarah was last.

"Come meet the latest enfant terrible to join our tribe," Dulcet called out.

Sarah wanted a visit alone. Georgie owed her that much.

Ben hung up his old jacket and surveyed the room in an open, neutral way, offering a smile for whoever stepped in front of him.

She'd worked hard to get that visit. She'd called and called back and didn't give up. Now she concentrated on keeping her smile easy—everything was fine!—and didn't look down when she reached to hang her coat on the hook near the door, where she caught her foot in a trap and almost fell. A bouncy chair bit her ankle like a bad dog.

The bouncy chair was little, pink, and lined with dangling toys. It burst into a slow, sad, and creepy version of "Twinkle, Twinkle, Little Star." Raggedy Bitchy Bitch leapt off the couch and came bounding to bark at the chair. Sarah still had the present in one hand and her coat in the other. She tried to kick the contraption off her foot but it held on, plinking out its little song.

Dulcet grabbed Bitchy by the collar, swinging and spilling what looked like a mimosa from a martini glass in her other hand. Champagne and orange juice doused the baby's chair.

Dulcet said, "Settle, Bitch. Jesus. Do you have a towel? Sorry about that." She didn't sound sorry so much as vaguely entertained.

Georgie joined the chorus of apologies. She clutched the baby, bent, and jiggled the chair off Sarah's foot.

"Good thing there's not a kid in there," Dulcet said, and swigged what was left of her sloshing drink. Sarah finally got her coat on the hook. A bassinet crowded the living room.

"I saw you on TV," Georgie said. "With the pregnant mandrill. That's fantastic. Is everyone at work thrilled?"

"They're hoping it'll help the levy pass," Sarah said, in a controlled voice that came out a little flat, verging on hostile. That wasn't how she meant it, not at all, but it was true—babies born to a zoo are about gaining funding, cultivating recognition, and maintaining a diverse population. Sentimental enthusiasm was for the press.

Nyla said, "I heard they're throwing a baby shower."

"Really?" Sarah choked. A pregnant mandrill cake? She pictured the amniotic fluid in Jell-O, a mandrill figurine inside. PR handled public celebrations. She was in the research wing, an entirely separate field. The Oregon Zoo was a research institution, and one of the best, dedicated to preserving endangered species. She was proud to be affiliated. "They wouldn't. It'd be anthropomorphizing." Sarah couldn't handle another baby shower.

The next baby shower she went to would be her own.

"They throw a party for Ellie every year," Dulcet said, and shrugged. "That's anthropomorphizing."

Ellie was the zoo's firstborn baby elephant, now a fifty-year-old matriarch. She'd given birth to six babies. Four of them had died, though nobody tried to think about that. At her birthday everybody wore giant paper elephant ears. They sang "Happy Birthday" while she demolished a three-layer wheat cake with bananas planted on top.

"She's alive. It's a PR risk to let the public invest emotions in an unborn animal," Sarah said, and her voice warbled.

"It's a risk to invest love in a living animal," Dulcet said.

Sarah ran a nervous hand over the terry cloth sides of the new bassinet. There was a gift certificate on the table: Good for one "gyno-steam treatment" at the Opening to Life Spa.

"I'm going to steam my opening to life," Georgie said, and gave a sort of awkward plié, the baby still in her arms.

"We went in on it," Nyla said. She and Dulcet were good at hanging out together because they could both make a dollar go a long way. "It's an herbal postpartum vaginal steam bath. Drink?" Nyla tipped a green bottle over an empty glass.

Ben said, "I'd love one."

Sarah knew that about Ben—he really did love a good mimosa. He loved mixed drinks and fizzy drinks and things with umbrellas.

He wasn't afraid to ask a stranger for directions, either, going against gender statistics. Sometimes he even sat down to pee, which was fine!

Sarah said, "Virgin screwdriver for me."

Nyla poured while she narrated, "Regional, organic sparkling wine, raised on an eco-vineyard in Yamhill, with no sulfites added." Yamhill was a sleepy town in the low, folding hills of Willamette Valley.

Nyla was in the process of starting up a tiny eco-friendly store called LifeCycles, devoted to simple and transitory pleasures. When she found extra money she spent it on food and wine, the Portland way: Even when the economy tanked, when nobody bought what the news referred to as "durable goods" and the regional Goodwill stores had the highest sales rate in the nation, when renters made up the biggest demographic and everybody rode bikes because their old cars broke down, even then Portlanders blew through cash on microbrews. They'd pay for wine, grass-fed cattle, and Pacific coast sushi. They spent big on tattoos—that most durable of durable goods.

The baby screamed.

This is where Ben, if it were still the 1950s, would've said, "Great set of lungs on that kid!" clapped the new father on the back, and shared a cigar. Instead he sipped his mimosa. He asked, "Where's Humble?"

Georgie fluttered a hand in a half circle then above her head. "Organizing the attic." The baby kept up its wail.

"One way to use paternity leave," Dulcet said, and picked at the tray of tiny deli sandwiches. They were baby-sized sandwiches, scaled in a cute size to honor the infant.

As though newborns even noticed lunch meat.

And as though those small pink slices of soft meat inside the bread weren't eerily akin to the soft vulnerability of baby flesh. Sarah, nervous and half-queasy, saw the sandwiches as foreign, a strange behavioral ritual of a deli-worshipping tribe.

But they also looked kind of good.

Arena sat on a window seat and pulled her knees to her chest, shrinking away from the baby's screams.

Nyla said, "The beauty of bringing a baby into the world these days is, in part, that it automatically turns the new parents into environmentalists. You can't have a baby and not care about the planet, right? It's that awareness of future generations."

Dulcet ate maraschino cherries out of an open jar on the table. She flicked juice off her long fingers. "Then who shops at Walmart?"

Nyla ignored her. "Giving birth to a child gives birth to the parents. They're new people. It's like crossing an invisible border."

Sarah's stomach hurt, she wanted so badly across that border. She was an illegal immigrant peering into the land of maternity, deported three times already.

Dulcet said, "And the rest of us?"

Nyla said, "You don't appreciate everything your mom does until you have a child of your own. Then you know."

"What if she didn't do much?" Georgie asked. "Just checked out early."

Nyla reached to adjust one of Georgie's tiny flower earrings, turning it right-side up. She said, "I could lend you my postpartum kickboxing cardio DVD if you want, *Blast the Flab*. I use it all the time."

Georgie winced.

Sarah spoke up. "That's postpartum. It's normal."

"Normal fat," Georgie said, and patted her stomach. The baby in her arms was making a quieter howl now, more like a song off-key.

Sarah moved in close and reached her arms out. She said, "You look fantas—"

Georgie unsnapped one of the pearl buttons on her Western shirt. There was a flash of brown nipple. It was a nursing shirt. The pocket was a trapdoor.

Sarah's words broke at a splash across her cheek.

Georgie said, "Oh, jeez."

Dulcet gave a wheeze that passed for a laugh, palmed one of her own flat breasts, and said, "Fucking God. It'd be almost worth being preggers just for the boob juice act."

Over Bella's wail, Georgie half-shouted, "I don't have any diseases. They tested for all that." Breast milk is a blood product. Georgie hoisted her now-exposed boob.

Arena's pale cheeks turned red, a blush climbing. Yes, it was breast milk that hit Sarah's face, shot from Georgie's boob like a water pistol. The baby latched on, and the room was newly quiet, the screaming replaced by only a sucking sound. Even the jackhammer was a distant rattle. There was a scrape against the floor upstairs. Humble moving furniture.

Georgie came at Sarah with a napkin and dabbed at Sarah's face, with her boob still out and the baby in her arms, all those suckling sounds and the cloud of milk smell. It was too much, too close—the smell clotted Sarah's throat and tugged at the side of her mouth, forcing a grimace.

It was worse than the baby booty table decorations, worse than the amnio cake.

Georgie said, "Have some food." This is what mothers do: nurse babies, feed a crowd.

Sarah would, in a little over eight months, magically transform into that competent mother hostess queen. She swore she would. For now she turned away and adjusted pillows on the couch.

Georgie cradled the baby's head in her palm and whispered, "Sleep, sleep, sleep."

Sarah watched uneasily, with a mix of greed and nerves. She watched like it was porn.

She watched like she was a failure.

Her hands trembled. Small-brained animals, hamsters and rats, sometimes eat their offspring in a kind of twisted overprotection. Polar bears do it, too. Sarah understood the impulse: insatiability.

Nyla and Dulcet seemed immune to the urge, as they picked through tiny foods and refilled their glasses. Ben was calm, looking at art on the walls.

When baby Bella drifted off to sleep Georgie eased her off her breast, snapped her shirt again, and rested the sleeping bundle against her own shoulder.

"She's a delicate little bonbon," Sarah whispered. The baby was a secret that'd take a lifetime to unfold. She had a distinct blue vein that ran along the side of her face, like a river drawn on a map. It was life.

"Want to hold her?" Georgie asked.

There it was: the question that came with only one answer.

"Sure!" Sarah squeaked, in a single note so high and quick that perhaps only Bitchy Bitch's ears could pick it up. She held out her arms and tried to stay steady. They swapped Bella from one shoulder to the next, one patting hand to another, and Sarah thought, *Okay, I'm doing it.* She looked to Ben to show him what she could do: hold a baby and not cry.

She concentrated on the baby against her chest, the tiny weight, radiating heat. Her lower lip trembled. The baby seemed to grow more fragile in her arms. She could squeeze that child, right up against—right into—her own body. She was a stand-in for the infant's whole soft world. Nothing about Sarah's hold on the baby felt natural; she worked to make it look simple.

Advanced maternal age. A doctor wrote that on a chart at the hospital under Sarah's name. "Aged primipara," they wrote, which was nothing like an aged prima donna. Later, they changed "aged" to straight-up "elderly."

It was like being diagnosed as an old hag. Waiting for death.

And here she was, that old hag, with a baby in her arms! Despite what they said, she was happily, victoriously, secretly pregnant. She turned in a slow waltz while Georgie pulled the ribbons from the present they'd brought, then let the paper fall open. *"Goodnight Moon,"* she said. "How sweet! We love it."

Sarah stopped mid–box step. "Do you already have a copy?"

Georgie gave Sarah a reassuring smooch on the forehead, and again brought her into the maternal nimbus of sweat and milk. Sarah felt a rush of heat behind her eyes. She held back her nausea.

Nyla picked up the wrapping paper and ran a finger over the metallic polka dots. "Is this recyclable?"

Arena, that lanky child, bit a nail, looked at her mom, and cringed. Humble came through a swinging galley door. His thick hair had a cobweb in it. He gave everyone a nod, a handshake, a hello, and checked the bottles on the table. He said, "Let's get these guys some good stuff."

"That is good," Georgie said.

Nyla chirped, "One percent of each sale supports urban gardens for terminally ill homeless refugee children."

Humble was already in the kitchen. He came out with two beers, one for himself and one for Ben. "Enough with the girls' drinks."

Ben traded his nearly depleted cocktail for the brewski. But he really did love a mimosa. Sarah thought, Who was he to pretend?

Humble brought his bottle forward fast and clinked it against Ben's bottle. Beer sloshed.

With that clink, Bella woke and squirmed in Sarah's arms.

An awake newborn was more complicated than a slumbering one. Sarah felt Bella writhe and brought her forward. The baby was making such cute faces! "Is that a smile?"

They leaned in close. Georgie said, "Her first smile."

Nyla said, "She likes you."

"You smell like mama's milk," Dulcet said. Sarah had milk in her hair. Dulcet smelled like yesterday's booze.

The baby huffed, red in the cheeks.

Nyla said, "It might be gas."

Arena, living, breathing evidence of Nyla's expertise in raising babies, stretched one long arm, yawned, and turned away, exuding a teenager's discomfort in her own skin.

Sarah said, "She's warm."

"Go ahead, take the blanket off," Georgie offered. And they un-wrapped the baby, that prettiest of presents. The women cooed and laughed and touched Bella's soft legs. The men nursed their beers. Sarah relaxed. Babies liked her! This one did.

She reached for a sandwich.

She could hold a baby and eat a sandwich, and that had to count as maternal competence.

Humble said, "That's an honor, you know. Georgie never puts her down."

Georgie waved the comment off, but said, "I don't want to put her down, actually." She started to reach for the baby back, then she checked herself. "An abandoning mother is not a mother," she said. It came out with the rhythm of a jump rope jingle, as practiced as the voice in her head.

"It's not abandoning to put her down," Humble added. His voice was kind.

Georgie looked, as though from a great distance, to where Bella rested in Sarah's arms. She said, "I heard about a literary festival coming up and volunteered to introduce a few speakers."

Behind her, Humble said, "You're really going through with that?"

Georgie said, "Bella can stay with you. It's one afternoon."

"What if she needs—" Humble held a hand to his own chest, cupping a porn-sized ghost boob.

"I'll pump. It's an international event. Johnny Depp'll be there. It's called Lit Expedition. Ecotours of the mind," and she laughed at the tagline.

Dulcet asked, "Johnny Depp writes?"

Nyla said, "Maybe he'll talk about what it's like to have a private island in the Bahamas. With global warming, that estate will be under water."

Humble turned to Arena, his voice booming, "You good with babies? Want to babysit?"

It was sudden, the way he shifted his energy. Arena flinched. "I think so." She looked at the floorboards.

"Think so?" He bumped his hip into Arena's shoulder. She gazed out the window, in a clear effort to ignore him.

"Of course she is." Nyla nudged her daughter, too, more gently, and the girl was jostled between them.

Sarah rocked the happy baby, moved her from one arm to the other, and took a bite of the sandwich.

Humble said, "Or we could call Aunt Sarah when we need a night out."

Aunt Sarah. He'd read her mind! Her dream was to be that child's aunt, though with a baby of her own. Aunting behavior was the helpful but strained, desperate social role of the old maid animal. It was a subordinate, childless female making herself valuable.

Sarah would have her own child in eight months. Then her aunting behavior would transform into cooperative parenting. She said, "Anytime."

She felt a drip on her arm, near her wrist. She looked. It was the dark yellow of deli mustard leaked from her sandwich. This was the kind of thing mothers put up with: compromises. She shifted Bella and licked the mustard off her skin. Her skin was warm. The mustard was warm, too. It was grainy with a taste like sour milk and compost. It didn't taste like mustard.

Dijonnaise, perhaps?

It didn't taste like mustard at all.

Georgie froze, her face still, eyes wide, then she poured a fast glass of wine. "Swish," she said.

Sarah wasn't drinking. "No, thanks."

Nyla said, "There's not much in baby poop in the first weeks anyway. Just breast milk, right?"

Baby poop?

Humble said, "Get that kid changed."

Bella's cotton diaper rested loose around her pink baby thighs. There was no mustard on those little sandwiches.

No Dijonnaise.

And Sarah thought again, *Poop*, the word an echo of the bitter taste, and she nodded yes, she would take the wine. She lifted the glass, swished, and spit back into the glass.

Poop coated Sarah's tongue like oil. Grit caught in her teeth. Her eyes were hot, and she couldn't quite see. She'd already been queasy, and now she gagged, nearly vomited. She made a yakking squawk, the sound of a dying bird. Bella started to wail.

Sarah couldn't pass her over fast enough.

Humble took the baby so gently; he was a handsome, sensitive, fatherly man. It was about as much as Sarah could stand.

If soft cheeses bred deadly bacteria, what more did she have to worry about with poop in her teeth? That could kill a fetus, for all she knew. Her baby would never be any safer than it was right now, hidden deep inside her body, and that wasn't safe at all.

Her vision clouded as she tried not to cry. She tripped again on the bouncy chair, stumbled, made her way to the bathroom with the thing chiming "Twinkle, Twinkle" still half on her foot, kicked it off, and closed the bathroom door behind her.

She spit in the sink, rinsed her mouth. She looked through the cabinet for Listerine. There was nail polish. Comet. Clinique Take the Day Off makeup remover. She hung her head, willed her throat to relax, and tried not to cry. Mascara had migrated into the creases below her eyes. Who had sold her that clumped and flaking paint? Sarah looked like an aging Ace Frehley.

Advanced maternal age. The diagnosis was drawn on her skin.

Next to the tub she saw not one but two more copies of *Goodnight Moon*. Two copies! What did she, Sarah, know about babies? Only the most obvious things. What everybody knew. She should've bought a damn gyno-steam treatment, an "opening to life" herbal refresher.

Old hag.

Her throat choked up and she gagged, hacked, and then spit again.

Through the hollow door and down the hall, she heard Nyla ask, "How far along is she?"

Sarah froze. They were talking about her. They knew.

She thought of the zoo, her body a cage: *It isn't good to let the public emotionally invest in an unborn animal.*

Then the conversation was a radio off the station, a static of voices. Sarah wiped mascara from her face and drank tap water from the palm of her hand. She wiped her hands on her skirt and over her hips, adjusting her clothes, her body, herself.

As she walked back into the living room she looked steadily from Ben to Georgie, to Nyla and Dulcet. Arena sat curled up on the window seat and tapped on her iPhone. Maybe she was texting somebody: *Just saw Mom's friend eat baby poop! LOL.*

Whatever. Sarah smiled and tried to act like she meant it.

At first, nobody said anything. Georgie raised a glass of soda water. She burst out, "Congratulations!"

They were all so happy! They drank and beamed her way. Humble, with the baby in one manly arm, gave Ben the uneasy glance of a guy ducking from his own unstable emotions of raw papa love.

Sarah said, "You told them?"

"They guessed." Ben shrugged. Of course they did; it wasn't hard to guess. They'd seen her through three miscarriages and knew they'd been trying. Ben was happy, too. Dulcet refilled her own glass, because booze and a toast was what passed for emotion in Dulcet's world. Bitchy scrambled to find a crumb on the floor. Georgie said, "Let me get you something."

She disappeared upstairs and came back wrestling a pillow twice as big as she was and as wide as Humble's shoulders, only with a hole in the center. "It's a pregnancy pillow. You can wrap your legs around it, or use it to take the weight off your stomach. The fabric wicks water away from your body when you sweat."

So it was a pillow full of Georgie's dried pregnancy sweat? A pillow she'd tucked between her legs, under her own sweating, baby-filled stomach. She pressed it on Sarah. When Sarah took it, it was like carrying a giant doll. "Sure you're done with it?"

Georgie was certain. "I don't need it anymore. Now I snuggle my baby."

Right. Sarah leaned the pillow against the wall by the door. Her voice was soft and disappeared into the noise of the party as she said to Ben, "I wasn't ready to tell anyone."

Humble tapped Ben on the arm and said, "Let's have a drink, buddy. Later this week?"

Ben hesitated, then said, "Yeah, sure."

That night, Sarah and Ben lay in their bed in the dark. The house was warm. Their old beagle-terrier mix, Shadow, wheezed where he slept nearby. He'd started snoring in his old age. He was slowing down these days.

Georgie's pregnancy pillow sprawled over an armchair, emanating the scent of Georgie's world. The moon cast a thin line of light in between their curtains. Goodnight, moon. Their lives weren't hard. Sarah loved her work. Ben did well as a mortgage underwriter, even through the housing collapse. They could coast to retirement.

They could be as good as dead already.

Ben whispered, "Do we really want all that?"

Sarah turned toward him. "We do. Of course we do."

Conception was a harsh business. Slam two gametes together hard enough, you get a zygote. You could potentially get other things too—chlamydia, AIDS, the rage of human entanglements, the big-time energy suck of courtship and nesting, the credit card charge of IKEA baby furniture making everybody a slave to work.

That was the cost of copulation.

Ben put his arms around Sarah, one hand over her stomach. Under his hand, under her skin, their child was made up of cells dividing and multiplying, creating enough of all the right pieces to build a human. The reproductive act is an unacknowledged death in the face of life: an egg and a sperm had committed their tiny double suicide to create the zygote of the next generation. Sarah and Ben would give up their old lives to make a new one.

This destruction of the self in the name of creation is a dead-serious bonding.

"I love you so much," she said, and reached for a stainless steel bowl on her nightstand. Her words were cut short as she spit into the bowl, put the bowl on the floor, and hung her head over the edge, waiting to see if she'd hurl. Morning sickness sometimes ran into the night.

She stretched her arm to touch Shadow's fur, where the dog slept on his dog bed. Ben rubbed her back. He whispered, "I love you." His hand found its way to her shoulder blades, beneath the thin, worn spaghetti straps of her cotton nightgown.

She said, "We want this more than anything. It'll be wonderful. Besides, we're already on our way."

The Telltale Heart

*H*umble let himself into the dark house, peeled off his coat, and draped it over a chair that sat near the front door. The floorboards creaked under his feet. The only other sound in the house, a mechanical heartbeat, pounded through the ceiling from upstairs. Georgie played a white noise machine to help Bella sleep. The heartbeat, complete with the ragged murmur of blood flowing in and out of ventricles, was meant to reproduce the sounds of the womb.

Thump-thump. Thump-thump.

She turned it up so damn loud, it sounded like they lived in a womb.

That heartbeat was the sound track for a murder scene. Humble felt guilty entering his own house—creeping; that heartbeat's thump was an accusation, and turned his careful tiptoe into creeping.

Thump-thump. Thump-thump.

He saw the glow of a night-light down the hall, in the kitchen, and walked toward it—crept toward it, quietly. *Thump-thump.* Then he saw Georgie, naked from her head to her painted toenails, standing next to a cold chicken on a plate on the counter. She held a glass of red wine. Her pubic hair was a dark patch just below food level.

Her C-section scar was angry, though healing, at cutting-board level. She peeled white meat off the carcass and put it to her lips. Her eyes flickered toward Humble.

Her skin was powder white, white as cocaine where the night-light hit her curves, paler than roast chicken. She said, "Look, I put the baby down, right? She's asleep upstairs. Proud of me?"

Thump-thump.

He moved around her and pulled himself against her from behind, up against her tattoo, where it read, just above the curve of her ass, THE SECOND SEX. The French feminist philosopher was honored in that sweet spot, which was so wrong and exactly right.

"What can I say? I have abandonment issues. I don't want to leave her alone."

He said, "You're a goddess," and moved in closer, his clothed body warm against her naked skin.

She wiped the back of her hand against her mouth. He'd called her a goddess back before they were married, when they first met, at a smoky party in Sarah's apartment. Goddess of Jägermeister.

When they met she had a pint of Jäger tucked into her cleavage, a cold bottle growing warm, a dark green dress cut low. She pulled out the bottle and made him beg. He was willing. She poured it into his mouth, a big joke, and sticky liquor spilled onto his Social Distortion T-shirt. MOMMY'S LITTLE MONSTER, the shirt said. Where'd that shirt go, anyway?

Now she picked up a drumstick, took a bite, and then held it over her shoulder. He bit the meat she offered. Her pale ass rubbed against his worn jeans.

He ran a hand over one of her breasts, and felt her heartbeat below, under the cage of her ribs. Her heart was faster than the electronic beat, a quick dance step. Her breasts were huge, milk-filled, white, and marked with the darkened nipples of pregnancy, the thin lines of blue veins. He loved her body, extra pounds and all. His cock rose to the occasion, a show of appreciation.

And the electronic heartbeat thumped through the floor, muffled. He whispered, "Do we need the horror flick sound track?" He rubbed his hard cock, trapped under his clothes, against her naked skin.

She said, "It helps." She turned in Humble's arms, soft and

warm and naked, and moved against him with a comfortable frankness, more woman than girl.

Humble said, "She's already sleeping, right?"

She dropped the chicken leg back on the platter. Humble took her hand. Her fingers were greasy. He said, "I miss you." He missed seeing her alone, without Bella in her arms. He pulled her toward the living room, toward the couch. "What happened to that green dress?"

She said, "Green dress?"

"Goddess of Jägermeister?" he said.

"Ah. Goodwill, I think. Or Freecycle. Maybe I put it out at the curb." She moved into his arms.

He unbuckled his pants. His belt dropped to the floor, and they flinched at the clatter. That'd wake their light-sleeping angel. He said, "Shit."

"Shush. She'll be fine." Babies were supposed to sleep like babies, right? Theirs, though, slept on the alert.

Georgie and Humble moved down together, onto the couch. One of them knocked a book off a coffee table. It hit the ground with a loud smack. They froze, Georgie on her back, Humble still in his shirt, otherwise naked, leaning over her.

The house was quiet except for the heartbeat. *Thump-thump.* "It's okay," Georgie said. She reached for Hum's shoulder.

Then Bella's siren wail cut through the sound of the muffled, pounding heart. It was the howl of a baby crying as though newly arrived, already late to the party.

Mr. Slips

Ben worked in a cube farm on the fourth floor of the old Standard Premiums Life Assurance building. Life assurance was along the lines of life insurance, only with a British parent company, and they offered investment advice as well as insurance. He loved that set of words, "Life Assurance"—like they sold a solid pat on the back. These days the building was divided. The mortgage company where he worked occupied a floor and a half. When Ben needed to camp out in *el baño* he'd take the back stairs to somebody else's floor, to a place where his big shoes wouldn't immediately be recognized under a stall door. He'd find one of the few bathrooms located in a hallway, not embedded in the offices of a bank, a real estate broker, or a skin rejuvenation clinic.

If he used the toilet on his own floor it was a parade of feet outside the stall, a waterfall of piss and shoptalk, a chorus of *Hey, how's it going?* He didn't want to mix his stink with the guy who, for the rest of the day, sat on the other side of his cubicle, shared his lunch break, and swapped turns at the microwave.

He carried his newspaper folded in quarters and tucked inside a mortgage file, alongside somebody's credit history, a borrower's lifeline drawn in financial choices. Then he marched down the hall, nodded at coworkers, and checked his watch like he had a meeting.

A meeting with his bowels and his newspaper.

Ben didn't take smoke breaks. He cruised through a week's worth of files before Wednesday. He helped other underwriters with the mess they made out of VA loans. He deserved time away from his cube.

He found a bathroom with two urinals, one stall, and nobody in it.

He settled in, pants around his ankles and a cup of coffee on the flat square space afforded by the metal box of a toilet paper holder, then dropped the ruse mortgage file to the floor. Overhead an automated room deodorizer gave off a hiss and released the scent of sweet oranges. Ben unfolded his paper to the front page. He turned to the page behind that—world news and politics—and there she was: his college girlfriend. Hannah. His stomach lurched and gurgled, instantly sour. He recognized her smile even before he saw the headline—before he saw that she'd just been elected senator.

Well, state senator.

He'd known she was in the running. He'd seen a glimpse of her on TV at night. Mostly, he hadn't let himself think about it. In the black-and-white AP photo, Hannah stood at the top of a short flight of metal stairs. A photographer had snapped the picture as she twisted back to wave, her head slightly ducked to accommodate the short airplane doorway. Who was she waving to? Maybe she waved to her not-so-new-anymore husband, her fans, the world. Somebody outside the picture. She wasn't waving to Ben, where he warmed his throne. Ben was out of that picture for good.

He leaned forward in a slouch and the automatic sensor on the toilet sent a silent message; the toilet flushed, swirled, and sprayed atomized toilet water on Ben's cold flanks.

He folded his paper back, keeping Hannah's photo on top. He pulled the paper closer. If she'd aged, the details were lost in cheap ink. She was a natural beauty, unfettered and makeup free. Ben ran a hand over his own forehead then through his thinning-but-still-thick (as the fifteen-year-old at Kuts-R-Us assured him) head of hair.

Hannah had one of those lady politician cuts now—between short and long, girlish and womanly, conservative and liberal—but it didn't look bad, and it wasn't molded into a helmet of hair spray. Her skirt was square and plain. Her jacket matched. She was pretending to be a Kennedy. But her calf, above a dull shoe, raised up in a sculpted muscle, and in the line of that muscle, Ben saw she was still there, the girl he'd once screwed, hidden under the costume. She was radiant.

As far as he could surmise, she'd never had children.

He ran a finger over a shadow that hinted at the curve of her ass.

In the old days she'd cut her hair herself. She'd sit cross-legged on her bed in her dorm room and cut her pubic hair, too, with these big, cheap black-handled schoolteacher scissors. She'd cut, make a face, and say, "Yikes!" Then she'd laugh and throw a clump of pubes in the general direction of the wastebasket.

Her roommate hated her.

Ben knew a few things about Hannah. If there was one person who could stir up a sex scandal as she climbed her way into office, it was him. Maybe. It was a powerful feeling, to be in on a shared secret past.

The thought lasted one second. What did he have? He had old news about straight, white, single college kids getting it on, and one of the kids was him, back when he was skinny and sustained by the world of big ideas. He didn't party in college. He studied, and then he fell in love.

That was all before he met Sarah, before his life found its shape.

What was the worst thing they'd done, he and Hannah, and the best—the hottest, sketchiest sex they had? She had these sheets, these stupid Holly Hobby sheets from St. Vincent de Paul, a church thrift store, and he remembered the way she'd wake up warm and naked next to him on a bed of pink and blue, and right away he hated himself for being such a sap. *Hot sex, hot sex, hot sex,* he drilled the words in his head and tried to remember.

Outside the stall door a faucet turned on. Ben listened, scanned the floor. There were no feet. Nobody had come in. It was automated, triggered by a ghost, a fly, a blip in the mechanism.

In college, if his life was set to run like a machine, he hadn't noticed it yet.

Hannah, a star on the swim team, had the X of a Speedo permanently tanned into her back. Her ass was pale and plump. She wore earrings only when she wanted to impress somebody. Ben pulled the paper closer. She had earrings on.

His cock lifted between his legs. He shifted the paper to his left hand, to reach down with his right and tug his balls. He listened for the door. He'd stop if he heard footsteps. He could stop. Yes, he was a freak, getting hard while he sat on the shitter like a woman, but it felt good, that heat and rise. His scrotum contracted under his fingers.

He didn't want to stop.

There was a time when he'd been walking with Hannah, and it was night. They'd gone off campus to see a band—some kind of thrash metal theatrics, all fake blood and pus. It was a band with guys named things like Flattus Maximus and Beefcake the Mighty. Jesus. Those days, he'd followed Hannah everywhere. The show had been in a warehouse district. They had to walk a ways that seemed farther after the show than on the way in, down empty side streets.

Hannah had worn these white high heels.

He ran a hand over his cock. He hated himself for pulling his pud in a public toilet. It wasn't right, but also—big deal! His inner Puritan could buzz off. There was nobody else there. He was alone in the bathroom. He was alone almost everywhere he went, really. Why stop? He gave another tug. He paid his mortgage, he had a strong credit history. If he applied for a new loan, he'd be the easiest credit file in town. He spit on his hand, cupped it, and rubbed his damp palm over the head of his cock.

His wife was great. He loved his wife.

There wasn't enough time in a lifetime to show Sarah all the love he had for her. There wasn't enough safety, enough security, in an uncertain future to keep her as safe as he wanted to. Everything he did was for Sarah, and he respected her! Respect was crucial. She was gorgeous, smart, and patient. She was his twin, his body; when he looked at her, he somehow saw not some other person, but a part of himself. They were on the same page, all the time—he could trust her.

Now she marked the dates they had sex on the calendar, which was okay, until friends came over, and then it seemed a little weird. She highlighted her fertile days in yellow. She'd started using a computer program to keep track. She walked into his mind, his fantasy, and he had to push her away. This wasn't about Sarah.

Coming back from the show, twenty years earlier, Hannah's shoes had cut into her feet. She complained. She was drunk. She leaned on his shoulder. He was stumbling, too drunk to drive, but not so wasted to think he could drive.

He pushed her up against a loading dock. No, wait, she pulled him closer. It was her move first. When they made out, their mouths were sweet with beer and mashed together, and they fell or folded themselves down onto the cement stairs.

Her legs were so long in those white shoes she was taller than he was. He'd climbed on top of her and hitched up her skirt. No—that's not it. She'd pushed her way on top of him. She'd been the one jerking on his fly. His black jeans. His effort to be some downtown kinda cool. His head was against a cement piling, something to keep trucks from running into that part of the loading dock. It cut into his neck. He said, "Somebody might see—" his voice broke, and Hannah laughed.

She pulled open her button-down shirt and showed him her bra, then her tits underneath. Her bra opened in front that easily, with one twist of her fingers like she was turning a key in a lock. He didn't want to do it. He was scared. She said, "Come on, there's nobody here. It's dark."

It was downtown. Public. He said, "Let's get back." To the dorms, he meant, that warm, safe place.

She grabbed him through his jeans and gave a squeeze that made him yip.

But that was years ago. He'd been drunk. Maybe he had it wrong. Memory is as faulty as anything. Could be he'd climbed on her. Maybe he'd undone his pants and lifted her skirt. It was his memory now. He could tell the story the way he wanted to remember it, full of the weight and curve of her boobs and the taste of her skin. Could be she was the one who said "No," who said "Wait," and maybe she didn't mean it. He ran his damp hand faster over his tight rod, and then again, and he didn't want to stop but he knew he should but why should he? He remembered how soft she'd been, and how sure of herself, and when he saw her now, in the paper, it was like she was there for him, like she hadn't left him so long ago, like she hadn't given the It's-not-you-it's-me speech, and he remembered instead an earlier evening when they first met, the way she whispered, "Come to my room," and he closed his eyes and heard it again in his head and he couldn't help it he shot his wad and pressed his cock down, felt the kiss of water, sent spew to lace its way through the toilet bowl and he hated himself even as he groaned, as he breathed, as he crunched the newspaper in one hand.

When he opened his eyes, he'd gone blind—all those warnings he heard as a kid, and now here it was, he was blind! The bathroom was uniformly black. He couldn't see the stall door in front of him. He couldn't see his own massive shoes.

No. That wasn't it. He'd been in one place for too long. The motion sensor.

He waved the folded newspaper over his head, a gesture that fell between a command and an SOS. The lights stayed off. The toilet, that overeager red-eyed bastard, saw the wave of the paper in the dark and flushed again beneath him. He waved the paper once more. No luck. He fumbled and reached a hand out into the complete darkness, until he jammed his fingers against the stall door. He found the lock—he could reach it from where he sat—unlatched it, and pushed the door open. But the door didn't trigger the motion sensor. either. Who'd designed this space? He sat in the dark for minutes, or maybe seconds. Either way, too long. What if the whole building had gone out? Or the whole city? Maybe it was a power shortage, or a terrorist attack, and he was on the toilet with his pants down.

It was a darkness so thick, so entirely absent of light, that Ben started to see shapes in it. He saw something yellow flickering always just to the side of his vision. He lost sense of the space, thought the walls were closer than they were, then farther away, and when he reached, he never had it right. The pitch-black room started to seem full of motion, full of space without the confines of visible walls. He could practically see molecules floating in the air. He knocked his coffee over, heard the clatter, and felt the cup hit his bare leg. Lukewarm liquid seeped into his sock. And there was that little hiss overhead again, as the air freshener gave a wheeze and crowded the dark with its scent of oranges.

That air freshener acted as a timer, triggering Ben's guilt: Nobody should stay in the john long enough to hear a timed air freshener twice.

One shoe was soggy with coffee. He had to risk everything,

to get out. He stood up and shuffled forward in the dark. He shuffled and he waved the paper. He swung the stall door open, hoping the radius of that motion would be enough to turn the lights on. The door swung open, then closed, then open again, in the dark. He stood and waved the folded-up newspaper just past the border of that stall doorway. He shuffled a tentative step forward in the pitch black, then another, and still nothing happened. His pants were around his ankles. Clearly this was going to take more commitment. He bent to grab his trousers and pull them up, and when he did, smack—fuck!—there it was, the crack of his face against porcelain, the sink. That sink was closer than he thought. Who moved the goddamn sink?

The automated faucet turned on, triggered by the swing of Ben's head as he fell to his knees. That sink mocked him—the whole bathroom could go on with or without Ben. He was nothing. The door opened. Finally the lights came on. Some big moose stood in the doorway. Blood ran rich from Ben's nose, and he moved his nose with his hand. It clicked sideways, bone against bone, and he was instantly sick and light-headed. There was a taste of metal in the back of his throat and his eyes swelled shut even as he tried to see straight, tried to sort out two sinks or one sink, two or one, every line doubled and blurry. He blinked and squinted, and felt his head swim.

The guy who'd tripped the light just held the door open for fuck's sake. He didn't back out or come in, like he was waiting for a prom date that would never show. Ben clutched the folded newspaper in one hand, and there she was, the love of his life, smiling—two of her. No, one. Then two again, the lines wobbling—about to fly off in a private plane. She'd been voted into office! People loved her! He loved her. Ben loved her. He'd voted for her, too. He filled in the little red circle with such sweet, sweet care. His cock was out, limp and exposed. Humiliation, pain, love, and Hannah—it was all familiar. Before he passed out, before he fell against the tile floor and before the paramedics came, for a moment he felt so young again that it was almost all right. The taste of blood in his mouth was salty as sex. It was like he was in college, and in love, half-drunk, out on the town, heading back to the dorms with Hannah.

Neither Created nor Destroyed

*A*rena was trapped in the Temple Everlasting of Life on Earth. She could see the world out the storefront window but was too shy to duck around the skinny guy who'd lured her in. "Are you happy with the shape of your life?" he asked. Arena nodded. She'd be happier if she could get out of there, politely.

Behind him a wall was covered with photos of the cosmos torn from magazines: black holes and the Milky Way. One read URANUS IN INFRARED. Those words made her queasy in ways she couldn't articulate even to herself.

The guy was maybe twenty, in a necktie and a white shirt, dressed as though for some kind of office job. Was this place his job? It wasn't an office. It smelled like mildew and was cluttered with half-unpacked boxes. He said, "Let me tell you about morphic resonance." His fingers were long, and they tickled the air as though he was flipping through an invisible Rolodex.

She held a smudged address on a slip of paper—her mom's store, LifeCycles. She'd gotten off the bus, walked down NE Williams, and met this man on the street, where he stood on an oil-stained square of sidewalk. He'd invited her in with the words "Hey, beauty, when's the last time you found a genuine bargain?"

She and her mom bought her back-to-school clothes in dustier retail corners, and called them legit. She wouldn't have gone inside except she believed his place was some kind of store. She thought the word "temple" on the front was ironic. She thought the word "bargain" was sincere.

Was there somebody else, in back in the dark? Somebody very quiet?

He said, "If you control your energy, you control the future. It's a resource."

She tried looking into the guy's brown eyes, past the fringe of inky lashes, to read if he was a rapist, a psycho, sincere, or just lonely. How would she know? She couldn't even look at him for long. The eye contact thing unnerved her. She ran the slip of paper through her fingers.

The temple was narrow and dark, lit by the glow of altars. White pedestals marked the floor like in an art gallery, basically, only a crowded gallery and with the lights turned off. It was like a gallery that couldn't pay its bills. He said, "What you do now will impact the lives of your children and grandchildren, the future of humankind."

Was that a threat?

He said, "We've seen it with littering, clear-cutting, and then reforestation. But it's bigger than that. If you've got ten minutes I'll show you tricks to expedite human enlightenment."

Her eyes had started to adjust to the dark. There *was* somebody in the back—a face. A man. It was Albert Einstein, in plaster, on a pedestal. He looked out from a dim halo of orange light, his usual cloud of hair a solid thing now. These were altars to science.

When Einstein looked at her, Arena had no trouble looking back. Maybe the temple was like going to OMSI, Portland's science museum. That'd be *edifying*, as they told the kids on every school field trip.

She let the temple sales-guy guide her through his showroom. His words held the bite of mints, his skin breathed soap.

He said, "Take the Egyptians."

"Okay," she said, as though he were actually offering them to her.

He led her to a mural on a northern wall. There was a honey-colored image of pyramids and an anorexic dog-headed god, like something copied from a middle school textbook, painted right onto the cinder block. He said, "The Egyptians were in touch with the divine."

Letters stenciled on the lumpy concrete wall read WHAT RE-MAINS AFTER CORPOREAL DEATH?

He shepherded her to a second display, where another sign, stenciled on the same wall, read GREEK PHILOSOPHERS ASKED DO WE HAVE AN EVOLVING INTERGENERATIONAL CONSCIOUSNESS?!?!

There was a life-size picture painted on a square of freestanding glass of a man, presumably a Greek, with a broken nose and a laurel wreath.

The man at her side, also maybe a Greek, said, "All cultures dabble in understanding the great mystery. African holy men and Indian gurus." She took another look at him. He was pretty hot, actually, in his underweight kind of way. If he wasn't a rapist, she was free to check him out.

On the wall it said HOW REALISTIC IS METEMPSYCHOSIS?

He asked, "Do you ever shed your clothes?"

"No." That was unnerving. She took a step back, then stumbled against a box on the floor in the dim light.

He caught her hand to keep her from falling. He said, "Of course you do. Everyone does."

She tugged her hand away from him. He let go easily. She read that as evidence he was okay, proof he wasn't a predator—proof of what she wanted to believe.

They were near the back of his narrow temple. Here he seemed older than she'd thought. Maybe pushing twenty-five?

Not all businesses are actually businesses. There might be reasons to shop only at the mall, at Lloyd Center, that place of predictable chain stores. Some kids grew up without ever seeing places like this; they only read about mysterious dusty shops in *Harry Potter*, as though every unregulated and irregular indie business tapped into the supernatural.

The guy gestured for her to walk around a partition. Anything could be back there. But he led and she followed and on the other side of it they came to a collection of musty old clothes, rags hanging from hooks. Words on this wall, smoother now, read THE BHAGAVAD GITA TEACHES US THAT WORN-OUT GARMENTS ARE SHED BY THE BODY; WORN-OUT BODIES ARE SHED BY THE SOUL.

A fat white canvas bag rested on the floor. The guy riffled through and pulled out a dirty sock and a wrinkled yellowing T-shirt. "Would you wear these?" he asked.

Arena said, "Is that your laundry?"

"Would you put this on?"

"No." She got around him, one step closer to the door. He was kind of crazy, he was so earnest. His laundry smelled like it came from a house with too many cats. They were in a maze of half walls. When she noticed the receding hairline at his temples—that other kind of temple—he seemed even older. Could he be thirty? She'd lost all sense of his age. He was a freak. He was confusing. She sort of wanted to like him.

Arena felt the weight of the room's darkness against her skin.

She had her cell phone in her backpack somewhere, and her mother's new work number on the slip of paper. She rubbed the paper between her fingers again, as though she could call her mom that way, like a cricket. Would it look paranoid if she got her phone out? She tried to stay cool.

"And what about this?" With a flourish and a fling of his arm, he slid back a dark blue curtain. Metal loops clanked up above where they jangled over a suspended curtain rod. Behind the curtain a suit and a halter-style dress hung side by side, dangling from pipes near the ceiling. The clothes were lit from the floor with mini-spotlights the size of flashlights. Maybe they were flashlights?

Arena said, "I saw that dress at Ross, last week."

"Really?" His face lit up. "I got it in a free box, out at the curb."

"Score." She nodded. "You got all this on the street, didn't you?" His whole temple was full of the kind of stuff you'd see out there.

He said, "My point is, you'd choose new clothes over worn clothes, right?"

"Especially if they're not my clothes." Really, she wouldn't wear the free dress, either. It was floor length and decorated with a fake gold chain belt and weird plastic stones, ready-made for a Carnival Cruise.

"What's your name?"

She almost didn't answer, then she did, because what difference did it make if he knew her name? "Arena."

"Perfect." He pressed a button on a wooden box, and a voice

came on: "Along with dead skin cells, we shed ourselves. Where do dead cells go? As they fall, are they energy or matter?"

She said, "Is that your voice?"

He nodded, and held up a finger to show he was listening. This was quiet time. His recorded voice continued: "Einstein solved that problem. They're both. Just as light can be both wave and particle . . ."

He said, "Embracing duality," raising his eyebrows and nodding. "That's the hallmark of genius." He was in conversation with himself.

They reached the Einstein light boards: "Mass and energy are but different manifestations. . . . Matter can be turned into energy, and energy into matter."

He said, "Hydrogen is two parts of each water molecule. Water is the key to life. With the hydrogen bomb, we've turned it into death."

$E = MC2$ was painted on a panel, balanced alone on a pedestal.

He pressed another button on a box, calling his own recorded voice to speak: "Energy cannot be created nor destroyed. Energy in an isolated system can only change form."

He said, "That's the key to reincarnation."

She said, "Einstein wasn't talking about reincarnation."

"If energy is always transferred, there's no death, right? It's impossible," he said.

"Are we even an 'isolated system'?"

He said, "Tell me. Do you *feel* isolated?"

She nodded slowly, and in that nod confessed: She'd been lonely her whole life. She didn't know how to talk to people or even how to look at them. She had her best conversations with her father's old records.

He took Arena's arm. She felt his energy and her own. He said, "Don't be nervous."

He turned to an old TV on a white pedestal. The TV showed footage of guppies swimming over the gravel of a creek bed. "Guppies can evolve in their thinking in less than ten years."

Arena said softly, "I didn't know guppies had thoughts."

The fish stayed in place as they swam against a current.

"Guppies are breeders. They're fish factories. But guppies

housed upstream, away from predators, breed less often than those in deeper water. That's interesting, right?" He tapped the screen. "This is morphic resonance. They're passing down knowledge generationally. They breed out of fear of death."

Was that what breeding was about?

She said, "Pet store guppies breed."

"Exactly! Because they see you—us, outside the glass—as predators." He said, "And we're not guppies! For them, ten years is generations. But if we, humans, give up our fear—live emotionally upstream from the threat of violence—we can evolve, too. We'll change from generation to generation, moving closer to an earthly awareness. Let me take your picture."

Uranus in Infrared, she thought. She could still see the photo tacked on the wall toward the front of the temple. "No. Thanks." She stepped away, not at all emotionally upstream from fear.

He said, "I want to show you something, about yourself."

"I know myself." She looked to the door. He'd be back to shedding clothes again next.

He put his hand around her wrist. "A photo of your palm."

"My mom's waiting for me." Her mom was waiting somewhere, anyway.

"It won't take long." He started to take the slip of paper, her mom's address, out of Arena's fingers. She closed her fingers tightly. He let go of her wrist and draped an arm over her shoulders instead.

She said, "Photos show up on the Internet—"

He said, "Your energy is already out in the world. We're all one on an energetic level. Look." He nodded toward photos tacked to a felt-covered board, each one of a tiny glowing sun against a black sky.

The pictures were pretty and mysterious. They weren't people, just shapes. Some of them were clearly ginkgo leaves, with the whole shape visible.

He said, "It's a visual representation of your bio energetic state."

Would it matter if her bio energetic state showed up on the Internet? She was intrigued. "How much does it cost?"

"I don't charge for enlightenment."

He waved a hand over a strange setup, a black bag on a table attached to a few wires. She slid her hand into the bag. It wasn't like any kind of camera. It wasn't a computer. What ran without a computer anymore? He tightened a drawstring around her wrist like a single handcuff, then pressed a button. A light went off inside the bag. They stood together, silent and close, until he reached underneath the strange flat machine, under the bag, like reaching under a skirt, and his hand came out with a photo.

He said, "You have a very orange aura. That's your dominant field. You're an adventurer, aren't you?"

Arena shrugged, unsure.

"I'll bet you enjoy a physical challenge." He looked her in the eyes. This time she really couldn't look back, and looked toward Einstein instead. He passed her the photo. Like the images tacked to the wall, it was a glowing sun, a comet against a dark sky.

She said, "I should go."

"Sure. Can't keep an Orange waiting." He smiled, showing his white teeth. "You chart your own path."

He ran a finger down her arm. She felt his energy tug against her own like a magnet. Instead of meeting his gaze, she looked at the photos on the wall. "They all look pretty orange. Everybody's an adventurer?"

"It's a self-selecting population. Only the adventurous give it a try."

She was in with a select crew. Like joining the marines.

On the wall in crayon, he'd scrawled LEAVES ON A TREE! DROPS IN AN OCEAN!

"Let me show you something else." He slid her backpack down her arms. Her back felt sweaty and naked with the pack off, like she'd lost her shell.

Another space on the wall said STEP ON ANTS! SLAP MOSQUITOES. IT'S ONLY ENERGY TRANSFERRED. THERE IS NO DEATH!

He said, "Put your hand in the bag again."

She put a hand forward, letting him guide it. He slid her hand into the bag and tightened the string. He stood behind her, wrapped his hand around her waist, breathed his minted breath, and said, "We live in a quantum universe built of tiny, discrete chunks of energy and matter."

His body pressed against hers. His discrete energy and matter pressed against her. Arena had never felt a guy so close. She was afraid to move. It made her sweat. He said, "We think we're individuals, each living our own story, but our lives are only subplots in one meta-narrative, as energy rearranges itself through the universe."

He snapped another picture.

Then he let go.

When he showed it to her, it was a picture of two setting suns, two burning orange fingerprints. "That's you," he said, pointing at the bigger mark. "The other is me. My hand wasn't there, but my energy was with you." He found a pen on the counter and wrote his name and phone number on the margin outside the image. "We're perfectly matched energetically."

He smiled his white smile in the nearly dark room and held the photo out, keeping it just out of her reach, inviting her to step closer, step away from the door, to follow him, as though that photo were bait.

Bargain Hunting

*D*ulcet was the living, breathing, boozing, and sometimes doped question in their group: What was the point of life after thirty-five sans kids? Sarah actually asked her that once out loud after too many Manhattans. It was the booze talking, coupled with Sarah's own freaked-out drive to reproduce, and Dulcet let it go by.

She was surrounded by baby addicts. There should be a support group for them all, Baby Addicts Anonymous. BAA, like the sound of an ever-expanding flock of reproducing sheep.

Having babies only palmed off the existential angst on the next generation. It was a way to cheat, not a solution to meaninglessness.

She'd been called decadent for her resistance to reproducing, but it wasn't decadent—it was restrained.

She'd been called childish, indulgent, shortsighted, by drinkers with big opinions, and she let it wash on by. Shortsighted? That was a laugh. She took the long view. Every story ended in death, right? It was childish to imagine otherwise.

And if people thought that having babies would somehow subvert mortality, by creating a genetic lineage? The short lives and single spawn of her own dead parents illustrated otherwise. Dulcet carried forward none of their values.

They were of the slave-save-and-die set. They saved exactly enough to afford their own funerals.

Yay! No, not really. It didn't play out as any sort of victory to their surviving child.

Dulcet made friends fast. She had no fear of going out at night alone. She'd worked in enough of Portland's bars that she could move from one to another with the familiarity of home. This morning her head had the dull, thick ache of one too many absinthe-tinis, and her body carried the spent sense of having used all her muscles—dancing high, good sex with a guy she'd known for a while, a long walk teetering home alone, and a hard sleep in her own bed.

That was the meaning of life.

It was totally cleansing, the fresh start of a new day.

She had bruises on one shin, blood blooming under the surface of her pale skin. Those bruises offered a weird portrait of life and death—was that the Virgin Mary's face?—and where had they come from, anyway? Some moment in last night's party. Now a barista waited while Dulcet clicked through the stack of maxed-out plastic in her wallet trying to pay for a triple Americano.

One thing about not having kids: There was nobody to inherit her bills. Total selling point! She was a single, adult orphan, an only child, uninsured, self-employed, a renter. Bitchy Bitch was all she had.

Her body would be cremated at the county's expense. She signed for the Americano and moved on.

At the cream and sugar station she tucked Sweet'N Low in her bra. It was an instant boob job—on one side, anyway. She'd been broke for so long, she made a habit of taking extra. A man came up with his eyes on her, ogling the Sweet'N Low lift.

His glance and her reciprocation: It was a transaction.

Life is one transaction after another, until somebody loses it—can't take the constant social exchange.

He said, "I've seen you before."

"Imagine that." Portland was small. She lifted a fistful of Sugar in the Raw packets.

His words? Another transaction.

He said, "In latex." His breathing was short and shallow. He put his coffee down and tapped a wooden stir stick nervously against his palm, a tiny self-flagellation.

She ran a hand along the neckline of her shirt, then did a stealth drop: Mission accomplished. Sugar in the Raw in the other side of her boulder holder. She carried a wallet, no purse, and preferred the freedom of empty hands. She adjusted the packets against her boobs.

The man said, "Latex with organs."

She stirred her drink, watching cream draw through the whirlpool. She only did the body show at high schools, and sometimes women's shelters, where no men were allowed. So this man was a principal, teacher, or janitor, harboring memories. He'd seen her as a woman with her organs on the outside. Clearly, he'd liked it.

"What about it?" She'd never discerned between dating and intimidating. She liked a forward guy.

He was a tall man, gone gray, but the gray was all right; it spoke of years. He had hazel eyes and a face that wrote his memoir in meat and cocktails.

Definitely more school superintendent than janitor.

He said, "I'd like to see that show again."

A skate punk edged around them for the pitcher of soy milk. A mom with a jogging stroller pushed her way to the sweeteners, jogging in place as she loaded up. Dulcet moved toward the bin of used newspapers. He followed.

She said, "Invite me back to the school." A clarifying test.

"I'd like to see it privately."

Okay. That was a crucial distinction. She said, "I don't put on the latex suit for free." She brought her hot coffee to her lips, as though to wash away her own words if they were to find the wrong ears.

"What's the price of admission?"

She held steady, turned, and pushed the glass door open, stepping into the sun, where Bitchy Bitch waited. He followed her to the sidewalk. It wasn't the first time she'd been approached. Her luck brought these guys around when the cards were maxed and the rent was due—which was to say, pretty much always.

A second selling point to being alone in the world, unattached, biologically singular, the end of the family line and lineage? The freedom to gamble. She was a free agent. Her body was the currency of her personal country; the trick was to finesse negotiations—establish an exchange.

She said, "You look like a man who understands the concept of billable hours." This was the meaning of life: bringing together bodies with needs. Some people are painfully lonely. She could help with that. She sized up his suit to estimate what the market would bear. It was contract labor.

Some might say whoring.

It's not like she was working a corner. They met buying coffee. That was perfectly innocent! Maybe she'd put her own body on the line, but nobody else's. There could be good money in it. If she screwed up, there'd be jail.

Studbook: Check

Sarah paced in a cinder block room overlooking the snow leopard enclosure. Her room was a cage, separated from the animals below by bars and a screen but no glass. In the wild, snow leopards use a personalized anal secretion to mark terrain. It means keep out, written in animal scent. At the zoo, that musky animal smell crowded the air, acrid and persistent. It clung to Sarah's clothes like smoke on a smoker, seeped into her skin and hair, and followed her home. In the evenings Ben put his nose to her hair and whispered, "Here kitty, kitty."

He hadn't put his nose to her hair lately, though, not since he'd smashed his face.

Her timer sounded a peep, like a baby bird, and Sarah wrote "Motoring" on a chart for Malthus, the male. Dame Anne sprawled on a fake sculpted ledge, her eyes narrow.

Sarah waited for a caterwaul. Malthus could mount. Why not? He'd sink his teeth so gently into Dame Anne's neck, force his barbed cock in, make her eyes open, her thighs quiver.

Kapow.

Uncia uncia. Once once. The Latin name for the snow leopard couldn't be more lonely or singular. Snow leopards are so instinctively antisocial, there's no official term for a group of them. It probably pained these two to share a cage, trapped in a cheap motel.

Sarah's job was to be a voyeur.

When the snow leopards screw, the world is on the mend. That was the thinking in trying to heal one tiny corner of the universe. Yes, it was reductive. Maybe it was alarmist. But snow leopards, almost extinct, wouldn't voluntarily breed in captivity.

In the wild they had bigger problems. Afghanistan was a war zone. That was one problem. And on the black market a snow leopard penis could bring in serious cash. It's hard to mate when you're being hunted for your mating tool.

Unlike humans, a snow leopard has a penis bone, a baculum. In Chinese medicine a ground-down leopard cock is all about virility: Bones bring on boners is the concept. Desperate, flaccid, impotent human mammals sought out powdered concoctions of flayed and crushed cat dicks. Some were duped by pig cocks labeled as leopard, and who could they cry to then?

Those same customers bought pills filled with powdered human babies. No joke. They bought anything that could screw or be youthful.

That was one side benefit of Viagra sales: A snow leopard out there might be able to keep his baculum; a dead fetus could have a burial. Pfizer could market the drug as an ethical, compassionate eco-hard-on.

Ha! Sarah thought of Nyla, with her constant environmentalism and intermittent OkCupid Internet booty calls.

The timer peeped. The cats held steady in their separate corners.

One theory was that snow leopards in the wild reproduced only when they had a habitat with enough prey to sustain the population. They were attuned to their habitat's carrying capacity. As an indicator, now these two said over and over again, with each flick of the tail, "Why bring babies into a worn-out world?"

Humans get it on even if it means they'll live as a family in a flat-tired Datsun on a dead-end road. She'd seen that happen.

Artificial insemination of big cats involves anesthesia, surgery, and sometimes flat-out death. The snow leopard studbook ran slim.

Sarah rubbed her belly, where a tadpole of an embryo was busy evolving. A dull ache had set in low down like somebody had ground out a cigarette on her gut, the rubble of broken glass. It could be a good sign, the embryo attaching. Or maybe it was the bitter burn of cheap coffee from the zoo's administrative offices. She allowed herself one cup of coffee a day, in line with the latest studies: one cup, and there was no risk of miscarriage, they said.

Her senses were heightened in pregnancy. She could smell the branches that decorated the cage below, the hay on the concrete floor, and the rabbit blood zookeepers washed away each morning.

Pregnancy is a battle between a host and new life, an opera built on chance and generations. This time, it was her opera.

She pulled a folding chair closer to the window, near the space heater. Her timer sounded. She peered over the edge. "Resting," she wrote again, for Dame Anne. Malthus paced along the glass in a flattened figure eight and looked off into the concrete bunker hallways of Cat Cavern.

Visitors against the window down below never looked high enough or carefully enough to see Sarah hidden in the trees, behind bars and mesh. Families would come and go, their faces blurry but their hands clear where they pressed against the glass. Now Sarah saw Dale press his white face to that same streaked pane. One marshmallow-pale cheek flattened between his creased palms and outstretched fingers. His mouth was a smear. It was like being mooned by an anonymous butt in a passing car on the highway.

She smiled out of habit, one social animal to the next, a flash of teeth to show goodwill. Dale stepped back and gestured that he was coming up.

"Hey," he said seconds later, too loudly for the silence-only space. He barged through a narrow metal door. "Soup's on. Rabbit delivery." He slid a cage across the floor. There was a scuffle of feet and claws from inside as the plastic kennel shifted.

The zoo fed the snow leopards live rabbits after hours. It was an experiment. Somebody thought it might help the odds—send the right message. The message was "Rabbits! Lots of rabbits." The illusion of a plentiful world.

The rabbits would wait. When the zoo closed, they would die.

"Maybe we should sacrifice a Nubian ibex," Sarah whispered. "That'd be bounty."

Dale locked his fingers, then bent and flexed his arms, a living diagram of blood pumping. "How goes the war?"

"Shhhh." She put a finger to her lips.

He pawed a second folding chair, knocked it from where it rested near the wall, and shook it open to sit beside Sarah. He traveled in a cloud of industrial-strength tick dip, the chemical scent strong enough to cut through the animal odor of the room. His strawberry blond hair lay damp, flat against his head, combed and parted. He said, "I'm knocking out a sun bear in about an hour. You should come watch. It's pretty cool. Dental stuff."

A knocked-out sun bear's yellow teeth? Sarah smiled. "Why would I want to see that?"

"I'll let you touch its fur." The vein in Dale's neck flickered to the surface. Those veins! They were intimate and public at the same time, like a lap dance. He said, "It's like a big teddy bear, but with massive claws." He clawed at her thigh and she pulled her leg away but he had her knee in one big hand and he squeezed and she laughed and he didn't let go. He handled her the way he wrestled doped seals.

A notebook fell from behind the official chart on Sarah's lap. Dale let go of her knee to lean down and pick it up. A sketchbook.

Between the thirty-second peeps of her timer, she'd used the side of a soft pencil to draw the contour of a snow leopard's leg, the sway of each cat's back, and the stretch of tendons. She could tell the two cats apart by the set of their bones, the angle of their jaws, and the width of their hips.

"Not bad," Dale said.

"My first major, way back when. Illustration." She'd made the cats look sexy. In her drawing they were close together, but only to save space on the page, not to save the species.

"Is that a major?" he asked.

She said, "It was where I went to school."

He lifted a page, then stopped, ready to tear it out. "Can I have it?"

She nodded. He ripped the page along the spine. He handed back the notebook but held the single sheet carefully between thick fingers. He held Sarah's drawing like it mattered. "I'll have it framed for the office."

It was a quick sketch. He was making too big a deal about it. He flattered her!

Her timer sounded. She checked the boxes: "Motoring," "Grooming." *Flirting*, she thought. Dale. Was he?

A kid slapped the glass down below and let out a howl. Rabbits kicked in their kennel. Everybody seemed happy enough. Some people despise zoos, and, of course, they're not ideal, but what is? In a way, it was paradise: mates and playmates batched into private enclosures, safe from predation.

All the snow leopards had to do was eat, screw, and look cool.

Dale rolled up the picture. He tapped the rolled paper on his leg. He said, "You could make the rounds with me, if you want. Catch a drink after?"

Sarah kept her eye on the cats, ignoring Dale's thigh where it grazed her pant leg. She ignored his hand as it stroked that white roll of paper, her picture, like an origami cock, his own fertility talisman.

He wasn't the kind of guy who'd need to eat a ground leopard baculum.

The timer rang. Malthus skulked. Dame Anne dropped her head as though to sleep. Sarah waited for the cats to take action.

Dale waited for an answer.

"I have to get home after this shift. My husband's under the weather." She made it sound like he had the flu. She made it clear that she had a husband.

She did have a husband. That was important! And she had his child—their child!—growing in her body. She swung her leg away from Dale's bouncing thigh.

He said, "It's been going around."

She said, "Actually, he broke his nose?" Her voice climbed, but she nodded as she said it, asking a question and answering at the same time. She said, "Smashed his face. Two black eyes."

Dale brought his eyebrows together, leaned in closer, and said, "No way!" like a grown frat boy crossed with Sarah's grandmother. He knew how to make her feel at ease.

She said, "Yep. Slipped, at work. I don't quite get it."

"At work?" Dale said. "He could sue somebody for that. What does he do?"

She said, "Underwriting." When Dale's face registered nothing, she offered, "Paperwork. Mortgage loans." That ache still bit at her gut, the grind of glass. Her timer sounded: "Motoring," "Sleeping," "Gossiping." Was it gossip to talk about her own husband?

Dale sat back and said, "Fistfight with an unhappy borrower." He nodded like he'd seen it before.

She said, "They don't even meet the borrowers."

Dale threw one hot arm over the back of Sarah's chair. Then she was between the space heater and Dale. His chest was so close she could've rolled into it. She got up, stretched her legs, and moved away from Dale's furnace: Let me not stand next to your fire.

There was a red spot on the chair she'd left, like paint. Sarah swiped a hand across the back of her cotton pants. Had she sat in something? Then she felt it, and it was on her hand. Blood. There was blood on her chair and on her clothes. It was her blood, and her baby's. It was the ache in her gut. How many miscarriages can a body have?

Dale's neck bloomed in splotches as he got up, too. Was he blushing?

She turned her head away. Quietly, through her teeth, she said, "Not again." Her eyes felt hot.

He said. "I'm a doctor. I'm trained in taking care of the body."

"You're a veterinarian." She felt her lip tremble, making it hard to talk.

He said, "I grew up with a big sister. It's okay."

Like his sister had a bloody miscarriage? Not okay. Not okay, not okay.

Dale said, "Miscarriage is sad, but it's natural. I see it in animals more than you'd think. It happens."

Nobody wrote those losses up in the cheerful zoo newsletters. Sarah choked on her own spit, on her tears. "It happens to me," she said, "four times now." It came out in a wail more plaintive than she meant it to be. She actually had a fleeting fantasy her words might sound brash.

"I can do this, if you want to go home." He reached for the clipboard with the chart. She let it go into Dale's hands. He put it aside and pulled his sweatshirt over his head. The white expanse of his abs flashed in the sickly fluorescents. Sarah blinked eyelashes thick with tears. She kept her gaze on those abs as though they were meditative, a still point in a shaky world.

She'd have to tell Ben about the baby. Round four. She'd been so sure, this time! She wiped her cheek with the back of one hand. The timer sounded. The cats? Motoring. Fucking around. Nothing. Those stupid, selfish cats. They could mate if they chose to.

Sarah wanted to mate. Immediately, even. This had nothing to do with reason and everything to do with loss.

She saw the smile on Dame Anne's face: Smirking. Mocking. Smug, and no box to check for it. Those withholding, passive-aggressive, aggressive animals with their pseudo-Darwinian line about not breeding, they wouldn't save the world from anything at all.

What kind of animal doesn't mate?

Georgie made it look easy! Nyla did this when she was practically a kid. Dulcet taught kids how to fight off pregnancy like it was a raging epidemic.

The whole study of eugenics was founded by Darwin's cousin Francis Galton. What kind of private things happened in that family to make those boys obsessed with baby making and survival?

The rabbits were getting it on in their kennel. She could hear the shuffling. Every rabbit was a premade pregnancy test.

Dale reached behind her and so brought her into his cloud of sweat and chemicals, the tick dip. He wrapped his sweatshirt around her waist. She was shaky. He took the arms of the sweatshirt and laced one through the other, and when he did, his hand grazed her stomach. He gave a tug. That sweatshirt was a bandage. Dale'd fix her up the way he fixed up every other hurt animal.

Down below, kids on a field trip laughed then screamed, ecstatic with the echo of their voices, laughing to spite her: obnoxious kids, the children she'd never have! She wanted to bite somebody, that's how it felt.

Dale said, "Do you need a ride?"

She didn't want to be anywhere, not even in her own body.

There were 250,000 people born every day, in the time it took McDonald's to sell four million burgers, both a disgusting production line.

Dulcet was right: Humanity was a disease, maybe a mental illness with physical manifestations, but still Sarah was ready to bring it on. A bleakness ran through her bleeding organs. She was a snow leopard, trapped in that space. Was this Ben's fault, or the chemicals of eastern Oregon?

Dale waited for her answer.

She shook her head. "Go floss that bear's teeth."

"I can take your notes to the office." When he reached for the door to the stairs, his forearm was a diagram of shifting planes.

He smelled like health.

"Where did you grow up?" she asked.

"Right here," he said, and guided her out.

Those veins along his legs, working the system in concert with his arteries and capillaries, would circulate blood to his penis and his heart. His vascular health could win an award. This man's sperm would make, for some woman—some other woman, some other *family*—all the difference in the world.

Denning Up

Vicodin, OxyContin, Tylenol 3. Diazepam and Ambien. Ben let the words tick through his mind in a chain of jagged syllables.

Prescription meds come with three- and four-syllable names; illegal drugs have one: pot, crank, crack, hash, blow, speed, smack, rock, dope, weed, junk.

His own name was one syllable. Ben.

Maybe he was illegal. Contraband. A bad boy. Except he heard his name, in his head, always in his mother's voice calling him in to dinner. She had a way of dragging his name out until it broke into two pieces—Be-en!—or else she'd use his whole name and make it three. He could still hear her voice, the way it sailed out into the blue sky, the yellow field grass. She was almost forty when he was born. He was almost forty now. She was gone. But for all those years, when she called out over the farmland, he went home to grilled tuna sandwiches, baked fish on Fridays, roast beef on Sunday.

Ben was a good kid, and soft as they came.

He and Sarah had their vials of meds lined up on the coffee table like appetizers. After four miscarriages and a broken nose, they'd amassed a decent collection.

Sarah took Tylenol 3, Ben took oxycodone. They poured whiskey in their coffee and let dishes pile up, making towers of bowls and plates. Georgie's maternity pillow claimed a corner chair. At night it made a fat shadow, like an intruder. Their good dog sat by their side.

Sometimes a miscarriage is fast. Other times, it takes days. By the third day Sarah said, "One of us needs to hunt and gather." Grocery-wise, they were depleted.

Ben ran a hand over the bridge of his nose. A hard kernel, like bone, rested under his skin and moved beneath his fingers. He could make it click, there in the radiating pain of a bruise.

He pressed it and it hurt in a way that made his dick shrivel, his spine tighten, his toes clamp down against his shoes. When he caught his reflection he was still surprised to see the deep, plum shadows and a jagged red line that worked its way up toward his forehead. The skin under his eyes had turned from purple to the first sallow lines of healing, a futuristic sunset. His nose, though, man. It was still a mess, with the crack of a bruise across the bridge and a new, flattened, sideways look to the rest of it.

Sarah squinted and her eyes traced a line from his nose to his forehead, then his hairline. He ruffled a hand through his hair and checked for stray hair in his fingers, always monitoring for hair loss.

It'd been a week since he'd "slipped on a wet paper towel" in a public restroom. That's the story he told: He slipped, fell, and hit a sink. Every time he said it he saw Sarah look him over carefully—with something like love, or concern, but then he'd see, in her squint, something more like flat-out suspicion.

"Dale, at work, thinks you could sue somebody," she said. "Seriously. A wet paper towel—that's dangerous."

Was she testing him?

Like he'd explain on legal documents why he'd been in a bathroom long enough for the automatic lights to turn off. He smiled painfully. "I'll go to the store." One of them had to do it.

He found his sunglasses on the mantel. In the winter, even the days were dark in Portland. Now it was evening. He put the glasses on anyway, gave a cavalier tap to the frames, and lurched toward the front door. When he picked up his keys, Shadow rallied, ears up: *Walk?* Ben ignored the animal and slid his cell phone into his front pants pocket.

"Ben? Don't. Sperm? Please." The phone.

Sweet Sarah. She believed radiation could be avoided. There was more radiation in that arid land where Ben grew up, where the sun beat down over rippling fields, than there was in that cell phone. His hometown was downwind from the Hanford nuclear site, east of Boardman, a coal-fired plant, complete with toxic spew. It was a golden landscape of big sky, sun, and cancer.

Everyone on the planet was bombarded by cosmic radiation, solar radiation, and radon that seeped up from the ground. Granite countertops off-gassed in rehabbed houses. That cell phone in his pocket? On the scale of things, it wasn't much of a problem.

But for Sarah, he took the phone out of his pocket again.

.᠊ ᠆᠊.

He moved through the warbled lights of the grocery like water. His head felt weird. Could a cracked nose cause a clot to form in the brain? Or else it was oxycodone talking to the whiskey in his blood, with an electric current of caffeine laced in. He picked up a carton of powdered sugar doughnuts, the taste of a road trip. Almost ten years earlier, when they were first together, he and Sarah had driven from Oregon to Las Vegas then down through the Southwest, to Tucson and up to Albuquerque. They'd lived on powdered doughnuts. Now when he lifted a pack of the same cheap doughnuts he remembered the way a pale sun rose over a Nevada campground, the air shifting from cool night to early heat, and Sarah's skin beside him in their joined sleeping bags. Maybe she'd remember, too. In the candy section he stacked three dark chocolate bars in his palm.

He found a fat pack of maxi-pads in the feminine protection aisle. That package was as big as a baby. A woman, teetering in high heels, looked his way. She looked again. Maybe it was the sunglasses, or the purple sunset of a bruise that seeped around the edges, or the way he swayed when he tried to stand, like he was on a boat. Was she taking an interest or appalled?

Ben pushed past her, rolling his narrow, high, modern shopping cart. The cart was so tall it forced his elbows to stick out in a way that seemed girlish. The pack of maxi-pads in his basket caught on the claw of a toothbrush display rack, and the whole thing crashed to the ground. He lifted the cardboard cutout—it was shaped like a giant toothbrush—but the maxi-pads were tangled in the metal hooks and toothbrushes swung and slapped like muffled wind chimes.

His maxi-pads were torn open. He felt the woman's eyes on his back.

Then his phone vibrated in his coat pocket. His first thought, his only thought, was: *Sarah!* With one hand still wrestling the cardboard toothbrush and its wind chimes of brushes, he used his other hand to slide the phone from his pocket. It wasn't Sarah; it was Humble. A text said, "C U @ Clive's."

God. Did Humble really use that text-speak? Even on his phone, Ben always wrote in complete sentences. Clive's was a bar. Clive's Dive. He'd forgotten their plan to have a drink. Humble had made the plan. Ben had only nodded. That seemed so long ago, before the miscarriage. He turned his head and knocked into the top of the cardboard toothbrush display rack—how was it supposed to stand on its own? The woman, in her heels, reached to help him. She stood the cutout up like it was a giant paper doll, moving with a calm competence.

When he got back with the groceries he told Sarah about his plans with Humble. He said, "I can cancel."

"You should go! You've had a lousy week," she insisted. Her bathrobe was open. She was naked underneath. She held a bloody dishrag between her legs like she was trying to stop a leak, to staunch bleeding, but really she was just catching blood as it ran out. There was blood on the white linoleum of their kitchen floor.

Ben pushed aside a pizza box on the counter, then moved a saucepan crusted with old rice. "It's not like we're really friends."

She said, "Of course you're friends."

They were, and they weren't. He knew Humble Johnson as one of Sarah's friends. Ben made what he considered his real friends in middle school, when they played Dungeons and Dragons and shared marching band practice. It seemed a leap to count Humble in the same category as friends he found when they were all kids turning into men, in a small town under the big sky.

Those old friends? One at a time they, or he, had moved farther away and quit going home. He'd moved to Eugene for school, then to Portland, looking for a bigger city.

He piled up moldy plates and stacked glasses to make room for the groceries. He sat an empty wine glass on top of the plates, then slid the economy-size pack of maxi-pads alongside the groceries in a little corridor of cleared space. "We'll set it up another time."

When Ben heard from the men he called friends, it was during holidays, in mass-produced letters written by wives. His old friends did family things. Ben had a wife, but not what they called a "family"—no kids, just that blood on the floor.

He said, "I couldn't leave you home alone."

Sarah kissed him. Their lips met in a quick hello. "I'll be fine. I'm schooled in all this by now." She tried to smile, but her smile twitched.

He slid another bag of groceries onto the counter, then took off his sunglasses.

She said, "Your eyes look better." She pulled the top of her robe closed but kept her other hand down between the folds of it, holding the rag.

The first miscarriage she'd been sentimental about. The second? Her jaw had tightened, and the way she spoke grew more clipped. It was a little chin lift brought on by disappointment, like a young Katharine Hepburn. During the third pregnancy her words, and her jaw, had softened again, but now here they were, round four, back to another pack of pads and blood everywhere.

She lifted the edge of her robe far enough to pull out her hand without getting blood marks on it. She threw the cloth in the sink. It slopped against the stainless steel. She rinsed her hands, ran cold water over the rag, and dried her hands by wiping them down the sides of her robe.

These miscarriages gave her license to be a slob. She slouched now. She'd put on a few pounds with each round of pregnancy, and those slight gains were adding up. She reached for the maxi-pads. The package was split, and pads sprang out like so much extra body fat in too-tight panties. "They're open?"

"I did that. An accident." The way the pads burst from their package reminded him of Sarah's body. He could pinch the new fat on her hips. He could kiss it and rub his hands on it for heat and good luck. She had a line of tiger's stripes in stretch marks over her backside—he saw them every morning, and he was the only one who did, and he loved it; he loved her stripes.

When they first got married, she wouldn't even change a tampon with the bathroom door open.

"Got the rest of my miscarriage kit?" She stood on tiptoe to look over the edge of the grocery bag. There it was: canned chicken noodle—the old kind of soup, the simplest, and cheap. It was what she'd asked for. She'd stir in lemon juice and one whipped egg, for an abbreviated version of a Greek avgolemono, a shortcut back to childhood comforts. When she was a kid, most of downtown Portland was owned by Greeks, all mom-and-pop stores. Greek food was Portland food, 1980s-style.

Ben had bought Tums, Tylenol, and red wine; three oversized dark chocolate candy bars from a company devoted to saving monkeys; two magazines, *Real Simple*—like anything was so simple—and *More*, the magazine for women teetering uncomfortably close to menopause.

She palmed the candy bar and said, "I'll be fine. Have fun. I've got to find underwear." She walked without lifting her feet, the chocolate in one hand, the other holding the maxi-pad in place.

He found space on their shelves for canned tuna and black beans. It had been a hard week. Other men could wear a broken nose and two black eyes like a badge, but he wanted to stay home forever.

Sarah was in sweats when she came back out, a matched set in snug cherry velour that showed off her curves. Ben took it as a good sign. She was trying. He put an arm over her shoulder and pulled her close. "Keep up on your pain meds, okay?"

Sarah was resistant to taking pills. Aspirin gave her hives. Zoloft, prescribed after the second miscarriage, did the same.

"It's not really that kind of pain, anymore." He saw her forehead, lined from wincing. She pressed into Ben's chest enough to move him away, then reached for the magazines and bumped the edge of the stack of dirty plates. The wine glass on top tottered. They both grabbed for it. Her hand touched it and his did, too, but too late—the glass fell and smashed against their blood-spotted floor.

She rolled her head back, closed her eyes. "My God. We're in squalor."

He went for the broom.

"That's all right. Go." She took the broom from him. "Just come back early. Don't stay too long."

"Don't worry about cleaning," he said.

"I haven't been." She nodded toward the piles of dishes.

"I'll do those when I get back." He wrapped his arms around her. She leaned into his chest. "Call if you need me. I'll have my phone."

"But not in your front pocket," she said.

"No, not in my front pocket." He loved her for her faith in problem solving, as though where he kept his phone could change their future. He kissed his wife good-bye.

Ben's Night Out

*H*umble was at the bar on a stool, watching his curly-headed reflection in the mirror between bottles of overpriced bourbon. It was a narrow bar, dark and crowded, with a giant TV hung up high in a corner. Ben made his way through the crowd. Everybody there— they were kids! Who was even twenty-one? He wanted to card the bartenders, the bar backs, the waitresses.

He'd been carded at the door, forced to pull out his cracked driver's license. The license showed he was forty years old. Some teenage girl hired to man the door scowled, furrowing her soft forehead in a way that made Ben want to give a soft pat to the top of her head on her dyed-black hair. She held up Ben's license, looked Ben in the eye, and moved her gaze back and forth between the two like she was trying to compare. Was she mocking the broken nose?

Whatever.

She handed the card back, and Ben went in.

The thrum and rattle of bar music was loud and seeped into his chest. People were laughing, already drunk. He was glad to be in. He needed this.

At home, Sarah felt a dull ache like a hand pressing too hard low down against her pelvis. It never let up. She called the hospital's advice nurse. "It's the third day," she said.

The advice nurse asked, "Are you soaking more than a pad an hour?"

"Maybe about that?" Sarah guessed.

Store-bought maxi-pads are high tech. They're more efficient than hospital pads. Hospital pads are about as absorbent as a wad of plastic bags. They're like something left over from a Communist work camp. If she'd been using hospital pads, the answer would've been yes, definitely yes. She'd learn that later, in the hospital.

The nurse said, "If you want to come in, we can do an ultrasound to see if you've passed the products of conception."

"I don't think I have."

"Well, it's up to you." That was the advice nurse's official advice: It's up to you.

She tried to call Ben. A phone threw out a few bars of funk like a tiny dance club in the next room. She followed the sound. Ben's phone rang and vibrated and danced to its own music on the slick white surface on top of the microwave.

Ben's voice came on through the phone at her ear, warm and efficient, probably coming all the way from some cheap digital real estate halfway across the globe, part of a computerized international answering service. "I'm not here, but leave a message!"

She started to call Georgie, then hesitated. She hadn't heard from Georgie in days. Now she'd call and talk about another failed pregnancy? While Georgie rocked her own baby to sleep? Pathetic.

Sarah's big plan was to get pregnant again as soon as possible, get back on the horse that threw her, do this to her body as many times as it took. She'd get back in the pregnancy cycle the way cutters sliced their skin, the way drunks reached for booze: compulsively, relentlessly.

Once she'd asked her doctor about movie stars—all those aging movie star ladies giving birth. Her doctor, an aging woman herself, lost all bedside manner. She snarled, "Surrogates," and waved a hand through the air, swatting off an invisible fly.

Sarah did not want a surrogate.

If they had to, she and Ben would take on fertility treatments. They'd get a loan, spend their savings, inject hormones, schedule intrauterine insemination or in vitro. It was a biological imperative.

"Goddamn, Shadow," she swore at her dear dog. Jesus. The animal was nosing at a bloody maxi-pad Sarah hadn't yet gotten all the way to the garbage. He looked up at her with that special anxious dog-love in his eyes: He wanted that pad. But he'd grown feeble in his old age. She kicked it away, held a hand to her gut, and limped to the back door, snapping her fingers and sending the dog out to the fenced yard.

Some day in the future she'd hold her own newborn son or daughter and, like so many other mothers, act like giving birth was natural and easy.

For now, she fell to the couch.

She called Nyla. Nyla was the most comforting of her friends, when she wasn't busy being an alarmist about global environmental collapse. And she'd had a miscarriage, too, a long time ago.

Voice mail picked up. Sarah said, "Where are you? I'm at home, having another miscarriage, goddammit." She blurted it out. Then she tapped her knuckles on the doorjamb for luck, the closest wood in reach. Maybe there was luck in wood, and if there wasn't any luck, it still didn't cost her anything. That's how she'd become in the months of miscarriages—desperate, superstitious, hedging all bets.

Losing so much blood over days made her nervous. Knocking on wood was what she had by way of an agnostic's prayer.

But with all that compulsive knocking, Sarah's message would sound like she was doing construction, checking beams for dry rot. She said, "I'm bleeding like crazy. When you had one, was it days and days, or a weekend thing? Anyway . . . I need a little distraction. My gut! It's sickening. It's worse than menstrual stuff. It's between the flu and a period. I don't know. Call if you want."

Sarah gave in and tried Georgie, though Georgie would probably be asleep, nursing, or bonding with her baby. *Play behavior. Grooming. Locomotion.* Sarah envisioned the tally, the check boxes of mother-offspring behavior. She couldn't reach Georgie, either, and again left a message. "I'm having another miscarriage. . . ." Her voice cracked. She soldiered on. "Could you call Humble and ask him to ask Ben to call me?"

Her voice, so weak!

As she hung up, she was more alone than in the moment she'd spoken to a distant machine. She tried Dulcet, her third and last resort.

᠂ ᠊ ᠊

In the dim orange glow of a cedar-lined room, lit only with salt candles, Georgie breathed a deep hit of gyno-steam. Steam seeped up between her legs. Her vaginal folds were hot and damp. It was like resting on a geyser.

Her C-section incision was on its way to becoming a scar. Everything smelled rich with herbs and pussy. The baby was on blankets and pillows on the floor. The spa was baby friendly, but when Bella started to cry Georgie eased off her throne, picked up the girl, and found her way back to her perch. She dropped open her white spa robe to let Bella nurse. The phone rang.

A sign on the wall urged THIS IS YOUR TIME.

Her opening to life was sweaty. The phone cried out again, its ringtone a classical riff, singing need. Georgie eyed the sign—YOUR TIME—and let the phone go.

᠂ ᠊ ᠊

At the bar the music was loud. Humble leaned toward the bartender, made a quick gesture, and there it was, another pint set on the dark red wood countertop. Ben hoisted the glass and let the foamy head roll. That first swallow of beer tasted like a party that shouldn't end. He wanted to order a second pint as soon as he touched his first.

He scanned the room. Knob Creek, Maker's Mark, Jameson, Crown Royal. Tanqueray, Luxardo, Chartreuse, Cynar, and Galliano: Bottles along the wall were as curved as bodies, the names like those of women Ben had only heard about—foreign exchange students, strippers, hookers, and cheap hotels.

Humble said, "You look like a fighter. Georgie told me you were a mess."

Ben could barely hear him over the noise. He said, "Georgie?" He hadn't seen Georgie. They had a deal—Sarah said she wouldn't mention it.

Sarah sat on the couch with her magazines, the phone, and the pack of maxi-pads within reach. She was too tired to get up but afraid to fall asleep, alone and bleeding. Ben would be home before it grew late. Soon enough she'd pass that little blue sac, the collection of misguided cells. Once that was gone—this collection of cells that refused to form a child—her whole body could calm down.

It was a natural process.

Animals had miscarriages. Prairie voles were known to have spontaneous abortions after hanging out too long with a male other than the father, in lab tests.

There was a stab in her gut, and Sarah thought, *Did this happen because of Dale?* He always sat so close, in small rooms alongside the cages at the zoo. Spontaneous abortion induced by impure thoughts? Jeez, she was getting more Catholic by the second.

The phone rang. She grabbed it. "Hello?"

The first sound she heard on the line was a baby's wail. It was a baby, crying! A baby had called her? She wanted to throw up. There was a rattling sound, not a baby's rattle but the sound of papers, somebody fumbling for the phone. Georgie's voice came on over the wail of the baby. She said, "Where's Ben? Does he know?" So she'd gotten the message.

Ugh. Sarah had to quit shaking. She said, "He's out with Humble, right?"

Georgie made a sound, a fast exhale, a breath of contempt. "They still met up?"

The baby's cry was quieter now, but still there, haunting and creepy in the background. Didn't Georgie know where her own husband was? Sarah said, "Ben needed a night out."

"You need him home," Georgie said. "What's going on?"

Then the line clicked. Sarah couldn't get away from the sounds of the baby crying fast enough. She said, "Dulcet's calling."

Sarah flashed over. She heard the sound of a party, a woman laughing, voices mixed together. Dulcet said, "How are you feeling?" Her voice was slurry, a few drinks in.

"Like hell," Sarah said, "but I'll be okay. Where are you? Georgie's on the other line. . . ." The phone clicked again. Caller ID showed it was Nyla—Nyla, with her calming, responsible ways.

Sarah said, "I've got to take this other call."

"I'm on my way over." Dulcet sounded more on her way under, as in drinking herself under a table somewhere.

⸎

"Line 'em up!" Ben said. It was his turn to buy. Humble drained his pint. When Hum said something, he turned his head away and Ben couldn't hear him very well over the music, but he caught the words *Dead girl* and *Skoal* and *Make a bet*. He followed Hum's gaze and saw a cop show rerun on TV with an underweight Asian girl in a bikini dead on a slab, her ribs architectural under her thin satin skin.

The regulars along the bar roared. They slapped the wooden bar top. Humble leaned forward and smiled at the masses. He lifted his glass. Everybody drank.

Cheers, dead girl!

A skinny woman in a nearly sheer shirt—she wore it like a dress, but it was a shirt—bumped Ben's elbow as she leaned on the bar, trying to catch the bartender's attention. She whipped her hair around and flashed a look at him just long enough to say, "Sorry." Her eyes were green. Her teeth were small. She was barely twenty-one, if even that, Ben guessed.

He said, "It's okay."

She stopped, stared, and pulled a strand of hair out of her mouth. "What happened to you?"

He smiled. He couldn't help it. He was happy to be out on the town. Before he could come up with the right clever line, Hum leaned in and yelled through the music, "He slipped in the john."

The woman's face moved into an uncertain smile. "Really?"

Ben let the conversation unfold across him. Humble nodded, said, "Hit the sink," and smacked one hand against the other.

She said, "Oh my God. This is the guy you told me about!"

Humble and the woman both busted up over it. Ben asked, "What?"

The woman said, "You should sue somebody."

Again? Ben let that wash on by. He said, "Maybe I'm already a rich man."

The woman, or girl, said, "I'm sure. The Humster told me all about you."

The Humster?

Hum grinned back like he was used to flirting with underage drinkers, or drinksters: the Humster and the Drinksters.

What did Humble know about Ben's smashed face, anyway? Not the real story. Ben tipped back his glass. The girl-woman ordered her drinks, holding a few bills in one hand and running the fingers of her other hand over the ends of them.

Then Hannah came on the TV over the girl's shoulder—Hannah, the newly appointed senator.

Or state senator, really.

She was a floating face, an angel or devil, ready to whisper in the young woman's ear, to whisper in Ben's ear. She was the mother of all those children in the bar, high above, a concerned talking head.

It was a newsbreak. Hannah spoke with authority about some vague plan; Ben missed the lead-in, and what was she talking about?

Maybe because of the beer, or maybe because of his broken face, to show he was more than a buffoon, Ben elbowed Humble in a way that made both their beers slosh. He said, "I used to date her."

Humble looked again at the busty young chick in the sheer shirt. He smiled. "Her?"

Ben said, "No, her," and pointed at the TV. "In college."

Humble looked up at Hannah, with the blank stare of the unimpressed. Ben tried to shake it off like Humble's opinion didn't matter, but yes, it was her, his old girlfriend, on TV, and she still mattered.

He had her photo torn from the newspaper folded in his wallet.

.‿ ‿.

At home, over the phone, Nyla asked, "Does it hurt more or less than the time the cops showed up and you fell out of that tree and couldn't catch your breath, you hit the ground so hard?"

Sarah said, "You know, I was so wasted back then. That was a long time ago. . . ." It was a landmark in their shared ancient history. They'd been under drinking age but over eighteen—old enough to throw in jail—on a night when a party was busted. A close call.

"But that's what it feels like, isn't it?" Nyla said. "The one I had was quick. Like an afternoon. It was intense, but only lasted for a few hours."

Sarah flipped her magazine closed and reached for her glass of wine, but she didn't sit up all the way and knocked the magazine into the wine instead. The glass spilled; wine rolled across the coffee table, under magazines and junk mail, and across the old maxi-pad. "Ah, crumb!" She grabbed the first thing she could reach—more pads—and started blotting.

Nyla said, "What is it?"

"Nothing. A spill, red wine. Second one today. I'm so wiped out, it makes me clumsy." She stood up, and when she stood she heard and felt, in a mixed sensation, the suck of blood and clots tumbling. Her head tipped back like somebody had put a palm to her forehead. She said, "Oh, jeez!" and reached for a wall.

Nyla said, "What?"

She said, "Just dizzy, for a minute."

Nyla said, "Sit down. Right now, right where you are. Are you okay?"

She said, "The bleeding's a little heavier."

"Hang up and call 911. Call, and I'm coming over. I'll call right back. When I call back, I want to hear that they're on the way." It was a plan.

Humble's voice was loud when he said, in Ben's ear, "Ever think about it, like, what if you were still with her? You'd be in politics."

Ben said, "No way, man." He shook his head. It seemed the thing to say. Why tell Humble about pining?

Hannah, on TV, was dressed in the worst kind of clothes, a self-imposed frump. But even in her politician costume, she was beautiful. She was hot. If he'd married her, by now he'd be the public husband lagging behind his successful, hot politico wife. It'd be good—she's a powerhouse. And it'd be lame—he'd look useless.

His own wife was a crazy hot mix of brilliant and sexy, and she loved him in a way that made him confident. They made each other's lives rich.

"I don't think about that woman at all," he said.

The girl in the sheer shirt across the way, surrounded by drunks, shook out her hair. Overhead Hannah nodded, a crease between her eyebrows, and took a question from somebody offscreen.

When Ben first moved from his small town nowhere to Eugene, for college, the city felt huge. Now he knew Eugene was a relative backwater town. But then, the bars were different from the cowboy taverns at home, and he was old enough to get in, and sometimes he and Hannah would drive to Portland for a show, and mostly he remembered sex with Hannah. She was his first girlfriend. Sex was a trip. It was a hard-won prize, his daily dose of bliss.

He missed it, now. That person he'd been.

But that wasn't about Hannah—it was about lost youth.

Ben wanted his wife, Sarah, with her stretch marks like a tiger's stripes, and their shared squalor. They were at the start of good things. Even if they never had kids, Sarah was enough to make Ben's life worth living.

As long as his cell phone didn't vibrate, he knew she was fine. She was sad, at home, but they'd get through it. She wanted him to have a night out. He put a hand to his thigh, where he didn't feel the usual lump in his pocket. His jacket hung on a hook under the bar. The phone would be in his jacket—for Sarah, at her request. It was away from his sperm. One more drink, then he'd go. At home, he'd clean up. He'd make something like dinner. If not tonight, then other nights. Sarah understood him. He pushed away his ludicrous nostalgia for Hannah and the boners of his youth. He loved Sarah. He really did. Being out in a bar in this guy way, it wasn't his thing. He was ready to go home.

Dulcet got to the house first. She banged on the door, rang the bell, then banged again. When Sarah answered, she leaned against the wall like she needed that wall in order to stand.

Dulcet said, "Oh, darling, you look like hell." She pushed her way past Sarah and tripped over a pair of scattered shoes in the hall. When she saw the rest of the house, she said, "It's a bloody war zone in here!" Her breath was full of red wine. Her teeth were purple.

In vino veritas, Sarah thought, but didn't manage to say. She slid down the wall, to the floor. There was blood on the wall in fingerprints and blood on the floor. Dulcet screamed, stumbled again, and dropped to her knees.

The paramedics pulled up soon enough. They took Sarah's blood pressure. It was low, but it was always low. That ran in her family.

Except now it was really low.

When blood pressure reaches zero, veins collapse. There's nothing to keep the freeways of blood and oxygen moving. Sarah was close to zero and losing pressure, losing blood.

"Hello?" a voice called, over the low roar of the ambulance's generator. It was Nyla, trying to see around the paramedics. Dulcet stepped past Sarah to reach Nyla. Sarah was still on the floor, flat on her back.

"Oh God," Nyla said. Sarah was in a white hall streaked with bloody fingerprints. Georgie, in her old sedan, pulled up to the curb.

Dulcet and Nyla stood under the porch light and watched as Georgie leaned into the car. Georgie's skirt jiggled, thick with the clinging pounds of her pregnancy.

Dulcet looked out. "She didn't, did she?"

"Yes, she did."

Georgie unpacked her newborn baby from the car seat in the back of her Honda. She'd brought her baby to the scene.

Dulcet said, "What is she thinking?"

But Nyla had the picture. "She can't leave the baby at home, if Humble's out with Ben."

Georgie hoisted the basket half of the car seat contraption, full as it was with all eight pounds of baby Bella.

Dulcet pointed one skinny finger and, in a loud, drunken stage whisper, hissed, "Leave the baby in the car."

Georgie froze, midstride. "What?"

"Leave the baby . . ." Dulcet started again. Her elbow was a jagged crook, her finger a weather vane.

Nyla grabbed her arm. "Shush . . ."

Georgie, talking louder now, said, "I can't leave her in the car. That's illegal, for one thing. Like even if I would."

Dulcet lurched into a Frankenstein walk across the front yard, a walk choreographed by a mix of drink and high heels that stuck in the dirt. "What's going on?" Georgie asked.

"Wait," Dulcet slurred, heading over. She shook a finger in the air.

Georgie sat back in the car. She dialed Humble again, in an effort to reach Ben.

·⤳ ⤴·

Humble's phone buzzed in his pocket, and the noise disappeared into the music and drunk talk and laughing. On TV, a girl lay dead and blue against a disco floor. The girl in the sheer shirt slapped Humble's back. Ben couldn't hear what she said over the noise, but saw her laugh and slam half her beer before it ran over her chin and onto the floor. Her friends shouted, "Skoal!"

Humble ordered a round of Jägermeister. He leaned in and said, "Here's how you play." They put their heads together.

The girl in the sheer shirt already knew the dead girl game. Her friends knew it. Ben, in the warm rush of a whiskey shot, went along with it all, drank and laughed and kept a body count on the TV and let himself have this night.

·⤳ ⤴·

Paramedics put Sarah on a stretcher, pale but conscious. Her face was blotchy. One said, "You're going to be fine."

She grabbed Nyla's hand. "Tell Ben. Write him a note, would you?" Sarah's voice was a breathy whisper, almost sexy, entirely fragile.

Nyla said, "Sure, honey. We're going to clean up a little. Then I'll meet you at the hospital." Sarah could see in Nyla's face she was trying to look calm.

They carried her out past where Dulcet stood smoking and leaning against a car door, where Georgie sat in the car, where baby Bella slept in her cozy, overpriced, guaranteed-safe-forever car seat.

·⤳ ⤴·

Ben dropped his keys. He stooped to find them in the dark and the cobwebs of their badly lit porch. He found them and dropped them again, and it took a few tries, between the booze and the pain meds, but he got the key in the lock. He hadn't been really drunk in forever.

It felt good. His face was warm, and the night was cool. He opened the door. Inside he kicked off his shoes. The kitchen light was on, and somebody was moving around. He walked down the hall, glad to be home.

He'd left the bar early, or it seemed early when he paid the tab, but now it was late, after midnight. How did that happen?

He walked into the light of the room, welcomed by the fine rear ends of three beautiful women on their hands and knees. They scrubbed his kitchen floor. Three women, the three graces—beauty, charm, and joy—showed him the loveliest of human anatomy in their rounded, Tae Bo–sculpted, kickboxing-toned asses. Okay, Georgie's wasn't so toned, but it was still all right. His wife was probably upstairs asleep. Ben didn't see the baby at first. When he did see the baby he had to stop and think—a baby?—before remembering: Georgie's. The newborn slept in a car seat carrier.

The dishwasher sang its song. More dishes were washed and stacked neatly to one side of the counter. He was glad that his wife had such good friends—that they had friends, their friends in common. He made that leap now, to think of them as his friends, too. His heart expanded. Actually, he was so full of love, he felt the blood swim to his drunken cock, a half nod to the good fortune of being surrounded by sexy women.

Hannah felt like a weird dream, an old TV show. He was over her. He tried hard not to slur or spit when he asked, so gently, "How is Sarah?"

One after another the women, beautiful, curvy women, stopped scrubbing and lifted their heads. They were cats. Busy house cats, cleaning their pretty fur. They turned toward him. Each face was a closed mouth, narrow eyes, and he saw it, plain as a billboard on the side of the road, the headline on a newspaper: He'd been kicked out of their cat paradise. Each one offered the closed face of a woman who had vowed to never speak to him, to Ben, that bastard, ever again.

Sitcom

*B*en arrived at Emanuel Hospital with his buzz fading. The fluorescent lights were a quiet violence. Sarah sat in a cranked-up bed with a tray attached to a long mechanized arm adjusted to hover over her lap. A stack of short plastic cups rested on the tray. When Ben walked in, Sarah turned toward him and patted the mattress beside her hip in an invitation. "Ready to try again?"

She looked thin in all the wrong places—around her cheeks and under her eyes. Her hair seemed longer, lank and greasy. Her nails were painted but already chipped.

Had she been that pale when he left her at home?

Her blanched skin under hospital lights let every old scar come forward, a visual journal of the times Sarah had fallen down as a kid, when she had chicken pox, a map of her life in bruises and nicks. He looked for the scar that blamed him—he'd let her down.

She poured dark grape juice into a cup full of chipped ice. When she drank, her lips turned a deeper shade of purple. She wore a hospital bracelet, and a Band-Aid covered the spot where an IV had been.

The TV news showed a pregnant monkey. "Oh, Jesus," Sarah

said. "They're still running that story?" There she was on TV, huddled against the garbage cans. She tortured herself by watching. "I'm not that hairless primate, am I?"

She was high on painkillers.

Ben found a wheelchair pushed against one wall. He sat in it and used his heels to roll himself closer. "Sarah, I'm so sorry—"

She flipped the channel. "It's okay." She drank her juice and watched TV. She found some kind of sitcom: an office, people talking. A laugh track.

Sarah said, "They didn't knock me out, but they gave me drugs so I wouldn't remember the *procedure*. That's how they put it. Feels like I was knocked out."

A fleck of purple-stained ice bounced off her lip and hit her blue hospital robe. Ben reached for it. He put his fingers to Sarah's mouth even as the ice disappeared with the heat of his skin. He wanted to help her, feed her, whatever he could do. She pushed his hand away, then held it and squinted at the television.

Sarah said, "The egg sac or whatever, the 'products of conception' they call it—our little messed-up dead baby?—it was hanging out at the edge of my cervix. It didn't want to go. Could've killed me. How was your night with Humble?"

He shrugged. What was the right answer? "He's a little creepy."

Sarah laughed. "He's a sweetheart! What's creepy about Hum?" They'd both seen Humble hold the baby and do a slow dance in the dining room until the tiny girl fell asleep on his shoulder.

Ben started to explain, then couldn't bring himself to say "dead girl shots" to Sarah's pale skin, with the IV tape still gummy on her hand. "The nurse tells me you're ready to go home."

She said, "When this show is over."

The TV laughed at itself.

"Our insurance pays for about ten minutes in this hotel," Ben said.

Sarah shook her plastic cup. "Can I get another drink?" She had a stack of juice cups, one inside the other. It was past two in the morning.

He said, "Your friends think I'm a jerk."

A janitor came in. With his back to Sarah and Ben and his head down, he emptied the garbage then ran a damp mop over the floor. He mopped around where Ben sat in the wheelchair, the only chair in the room. The janitor turned the lights out when he left, as though the room were already empty, leaving them in the dark with the glow of the TV and the monitors and buttons around the bed.

Ben's broken nose throbbed. His head ached under the ebbing of his personal alcohol tide. "We're supposed to be out of here."

"It's almost over." Sarah flicked a damp, juice-stained finger at the TV. The show had twenty minutes left. Kathy Griffin rattled around at Brooke Shields's ankles yelling, "Calm down! Calm down!"

Ben gave in to Kathy Griffin's demands. He felt calm. He wheeled his chair closer and held his wife's hand. He rubbed his thumb over the back of her hand, where thin bones lay under the skin, under the residual gum of IV tape. He said, "I can't watch this without pain pills."

"Meds make it way better." Sarah never took medicine. She didn't believe in it. She never watched TV, either. Now, with this fourth miscarriage, though, she'd changed. She tapped the piece of paper, the prescription, on her tray.

Ben said, "We have pills at home."

She said, "Not enough. Find a twenty-four-hour pharmacy. Let's make it our best friend."

The New Rules

Nyla stood in bare feet on the metal rung of a short ladder and earnestly scraped layered paint off a windowsill in her store. She wore a blue paper mask to keep dust out. Her shirt read YEAR OF THE POLAR BEAR! like it was a celebration instead of a cry for help, a big party instead of the year polar bears as a species could fall between cracks in melting ice caps.

She had enough inventory to call the room a store. She had a countertop and a green ceramic bowl filled with burnished red chestnuts off the street, and a plate of lavender shortbread. The shortbread wasn't for sale. Nyla baked, just to give back to the world. What was more wholesome than simple, organic ingredients turned into sweets?

She chipped at the paint and hummed along to Amy Winehouse on her old CD player—because honestly, she didn't have an iPod, and who needed all those new techno gadgets with their conflict minerals and strip-mining anyway? She chipped until she had maybe one inch of one windowsill cleared, with six more windows to go.

This chipping would take a lifetime.

Her store was just wider than a hallway and ran along the forgotten fringe of an industrial building. Amy Winehouse's voice echoed against the cinder blocks, smooth, smoky, and contemptuous. Nyla stretched an arm for the remote. She turned up the tunes.

Her lower back moved with the crick of the car accident ten years before. Her psychic yogi healer said she held on to that pain, and even at the time she'd countered, "Why shouldn't I hold on to it?" Her husband, her beautiful, sunny-haired kayaker, had died in the car wreck. In cold weather the memory of him beat in Nyla's back like a cracked steering column.

Another car had crossed the line and smashed their Subaru on the driver's side. Arena was five, in back, in a booster seat in the middle. That day, Nyla saw her daughter's chest pour blood. An old metal camping lantern had cut through the girl's Crater Lake shirt. Nyla had actually fallen over—had learned what it meant to be weak in the knees.

When she tried to look at the disaster of her husband's death as a cosmic lesson she knew only that she could pull a little salvage from the wreck. She built a life for her kids. Nyla had the gift of finding her husband in her daughters' gestures and the color of their hair. They grew more like him all the time. If she could hold their lives together after that accident, adapt and move on, humanity could sure as shit band together, wise up, and head off the disaster of climate change. The trick was to stay positive.

Amy Winehouse's voice wound its way through the room like smoke.

The secret of Nyla was that under her layers of cotton and Gore-Tex, under her fleece vests and scarves, her body was muscular, sleek, and flexible despite her car accident. She did everything possible to keep the synovial fluid washing her joints, and her muscles strong. She was in the slim minority demographic of women over forty who could still do the splits, both ways. She was practical in the way she dressed, and a hardworking machine, but under those clothes she was built for pleasure.

Her store pressed up against a boarded-up dry cleaner's. Crack addicts curled in the recessed doorway and cans of OE8 littered the curb, but there was a Starbucks practically next door. Starbucks, with their market research, was an indicator the neighborhood was poised for an upswing.

She stopped chipping long enough to give her throbbing callus a minute off. She hadn't been on vacation since forever, not even to Dubuque, where her cousin lived. But at the same time she'd barely ever held a steady job, so every day was kind of half vacation, right? She got by through teaching yoga classes and substituting in a cardio-kickboxing gym. Her husband's life insurance policy made the house payments and supplied a basic college fund for the kids. Now she'd have her store, LifeCycles.

Paint flakes gathered on the cement below, loaded with lead and chemicals. Nyla had a vacuum with a HEPA filter. She'd soaked the windowsill because wet paint gave off less dust than dry. None of this was healthy, but somebody had to get the work done, and Nyla was invested in that store.

With the singing and the roar of the vacuum and the rush of her own thoughts, she didn't hear the door open behind her. She didn't hear it close.

It was hot, breathing behind the blue paper. She lifted the dust mask and went back to vacuuming. She swung her hips, giving a fling to the vacuum cord. She shook her hair out. There was a tap on her shoulder. Nyla screamed!

She dropped the vacuum handle and her upright Kenmore fell on her foot. A hand jostled her. She couldn't turn fast enough. It was all in slow motion, a Hitchcock scene.

When she did turn, there was Georgie, smiling, holding a green bottle of prosecco. Nyla's heart squeezed under her ribs. Her face flushed. Dulcet loomed behind Georgie, white bobbles of earrings swinging.

Nyla switched the vacuum off. Instantly, the phone rang. Maybe the phone had been ringing for a while? Her hands were still shaking, her heart tight. She said, "First business call! It's official. You're here to witness it."

She turned down the music, reached for the phone, and tried to put a smile in her voice. "Thank you for calling LifeCycles."

Nyla gestured for Georgie and Dulcet to use the coat hooks. Amber candles burned on a side table. There was a couch covered with a blanket. Into the phone, she said, "Pardon me? No, we're not a bike store. No, I understand, sure. That's okay."

When she got off the phone she gave her friends a hug, a real hello. She said, "Welcome to LifeCycles!"

Dulcet pulled out the bottom of Nyla's T-shirt to straighten the image. YEAR OF THE POLAR BEAR. She said, "Nice. That comes just before the Year of No Polar Bear, right?"

Georgie said, "You shouldn't leave the door unlocked."

Nyla said, "It's a store. People have to come in." Then she looked at Georgie and added, "Where's Bella?"

"With Hum. Their first time home alone. We're practicing, with the conference coming up." Georgie lifted a hand to her breast as though adjusting her bra; it was the gesture of a nursing mother. "I should go back."

"You just got here!" Dulcet said.

"It's hard." Georgie almost whispered this, into her own hands.

A sound like a sudden rain cut in and added to the low notes of music playing. It was a splatter on the window, a man peeing. A drunk. It was an old man, or maybe only a man weathered enough to look old. A "hard liver," as people said—but did that mean his liver, or his life?

"Jesus," Dulcet said.

Georgie squinted at the glass.

Nyla waited it out. "Sometimes that happens."

Dulcet opened the door. She said, "Look what you're doing." The man's wrinkled face was red, his eyes so swollen and narrow he seemed practically blind. Dulcet, in her heels, towered over him. She said, "Go on, get out of here. Go!"

The man struggled to zip up as he stumbled in his slow dance away.

"The neighborhood's in transition," Nyla said.

Dulcet asked, "From what to what?"

This neighborhood had been in transition since 1805. It had been a working-class German settlement, an African American community, and home to many a *quinceañera* celebration. Now it was a hipster corridor mingled with drug house holdovers and a lot of hardworking families. It had an edge of racial tension.

It was what Nyla could afford.

The sky was an evening bruise. The stooped man pushed a shopping cart, and the rattle of loose wheels over ragged macadam drowned out Dulcet's question.

Nyla said, "Look at all the great parking!" She flung her hands wide. The street was nearly empty. "You don't get parking like this downtown."

Across the street sat a Ford truck with a camper shell on the back, makeshift curtains, and an orange tow sticker on the window. A back tire had been replaced by a stack of cinderblocks. Another car was stripped: no hood, no doors. Wires hung out of the exposed seat covers.

Ever optimistic, Nyla said, "I'm practically next door to Starbucks."

Her friends looked up and down the block. Nyla pointed. They followed her hand. Far off down the street, up a shallow hill, there it was: the green double-tailed mermaid, a siren.

Dulcet said, "The Safeway kind of Starbucks."

It was indeed on the side of an old Safeway. It wasn't the kind that meant market research. It was the kind that came blindly, one corporate franchise tied to another in parasitic relations.

The phone inside rang again. Nyla went to answer. Sarah, the last of their party, stepped off a passing bus, breathless and expectant, holding a fistful of mums in green paper.

Inside, Nyla said, "Hello?" Then, "No, I'm sorry. We aren't a funeral parlor. Yes, end-of-use planning. It's a little different." She pushed the plate of lavender shortbread toward Georgie, and into the phone said, "End of use? It's about objects. Recognizing planned obsolescence, factoring disposal in." There was a lull while she listened. Her friends crowded into the tiny store. She said, "That's all right. Thank you. Sorry for your loss."

She put the phone back into its cradle and held it there. She leaned on it as though she might keep another call away if only she held it down tightly enough. She said, "It'll take a while to familiarize a clientele."

Sarah said, "The place is gorgeous!" The walls were painted deep ochre and decorated with bundles of dried lavender. Candles burned in small golden glass orbs. One wall was a dusky blue. Sarah ran a hand over it.

"Pipe Dream," Nyla said. "That's the paint color."

"Of course it is," Dulcet added.

Sarah nodded, offered a smile, and handed over the mums. It was the first time they'd all been together since the night of the miscarriage. She'd already made it clear she wasn't sentimental about that loss—she was determined to *not* be sentimental. A baby that dies at eight weeks gestation old is a collection of cells that hasn't come together right. It wasn't a thing meant to live. And that was the end of the baby conversation. She picked up a horse chestnut from a ceramic bowl.

"Lovely, aren't they?" Nyla said.

"Like a testicle." Sarah moved the nut through her fingers as though kneading a petrified ball sac. It was an embryonic plant. Everything was reproductive.

Nyla sold cloth bags made out of undyed hemp canvas, with the words THE NEW RULES OF LIFE screen printed on one side over a silhouette of a genderless human seemingly giving birth to a bush. Sarah picked the bag up. A tag said the bag was meant to be used a thousand times then buried—given back to the earth.

Who would keep count?

Nyla lifted a basket full of notebooks. "A hundred percent sustainable. Recycled paper, vegan glue. There are tiny wildflower seeds in each page, the seeds of honeybee-friendly flowers." She passed the notebooks around. "I'm waiting on a delivery of organic tea in compostable tea bags. No packaging at all, coming by bicycle."

Sarah flipped through the notebook and saw the flecks of seeds embedded. Each page was laced with embryonic plants waiting to be born.

Dulcet cracked open the prosecco. The cork flew, knocking into a bundle of dried lavender and sending leaves flying. Georgie pulled a pomegranate from her paper bag and split it open in her fingers. Juice ran down her hand and over her wrist and dripped onto the cement floor.

There were so many seeds inside that fruit, each one white as a tooth, wrapped in its translucent, garnet coat. The edible part of a pomegranate is an aril. Sarah had studied pomegranates in school. They used them as models. "A pomegranate is like an ovary," she said.

They were the image of fertility both literal and symbolic.

Georgie's fingers were pink with juice, her body round with baby making. Dulcet poured four glasses of prosecco. The booze whispered and hissed, tiny bubbles bursting. Georgie said, "It's decorative. We don't have to—"

"Throw them in," Sarah urged. Who was she to censor fertility signs?

The arils hit the bubbly and laced the light drink with red, like blood in clear water.

Dulcet asked, "What's the theme of this store?"

Nyla had found a rag and rubbed at a spot on the floor where pomegranate juice seeped into the concrete. Now she sat back on her heels. She said, "To go beyond sustainability. Beyond recycling and the common cycle of consumption." She used the side of her arm to brush hair away from her face, and held her rag on her lap, where it bled a damp spot. "Reduce, reuse, repair, and recycle—we say that all the time, teach it to kids, but what's 'reuse,' really? A purse made of fifty plastic bags? That's crafts, not environmentalism."

Sarah's bag was made out of fifty used plastic bags. The bag was cute. It was plastic and crocheted. She felt a little ashamed of it now.

Nyla said, "Before the industrial revolution sustainability was a whole other question. People produced what they needed."

Dulcet looked around the room. "So, the plan is to sell what people need?"

"The plan is to showcase what I value."

Dulcet said, "Honey, you can't make a living anymore selling hippie bags and clover. The seventies are dead."

"It's not about money. It's about taking a stand." She stood and brushed off her paint-marked yoga clothes, ready to pledge allegiance to her own dream. "Money is a construct, a made-up system, a fiction next to the reality of water and air."

And the anthem that played behind Nyla's speech was Amy Winehouse crooning, "No, no, no . . ." It was a CD set to repeat.

"I've got a development grant. I can promote the world I want, here, in this cheap spot. People buy what's for sale and designers pave the way. I'll be a positive link in that consumer chain."

Sarah expected Nyla to break into song, complete with hand gestures.

"Cheers!" Georgie said. She raised her glass. She said it quickly, having found that spot to interject.

Dulcet refilled her own glass. Sarah lifted a glass, too. Nyla was the last to reach. Then the four clinked their glasses, spilled prosecco, and sipped in celebration—only Nyla put her glass down without drinking.

Sarah knocked on the wood of their small tabletop.

Dulcet grabbed her wrist. "Stop knocking."

"It's bad luck to not drink for a toast," Sarah said. She knocked to call on good luck, to offset the bad.

"Why aren't you drinking?" Georgie asked. "I broke my no-booze-while-nursing rule for this."

Outside, a bus broke wind in a cloud of diesel and pulled away from the curb. A short woman with heavy bags in each hand had climbed off the bus and walked away like a slow-moving windup toy, a roll to each side with every step. Wind shook the leaves on a skinny tree. The world was toxic, dark, and cold out Nyla's window.

After a thoughtful pause—a pregnant pause?—with the determination of a mother ripping off a Band-Aid, when a swifter move could mean less pain, Nyla said, "I might be pregnant."

"What?" Sarah squawked. She couldn't help herself. Nyla had two kids already! She was old. Older than Sarah. At least two years older.

Georgie said, "That's fantastic!"

"Ugh. I can't even imagine." Dulcet drank again, without putting her glass down.

"It's either that or menopause," Nyla said. "Missed a period, and that old familiar feeling." She gave a squeeze and a lift to one of her boobs.

Georgie said, "Who's the father?"

Nyla waved a hand, then picked at a spot on her table. "This man."

Dulcet said, "Obviously."

Nyla said, "Speed dating."

Georgie said, "Five minutes?"

"You move fast," Dulcet purred.

Nyla said, "He was nice."

Sarah didn't say anything. Her face had turned splotchy below her eyes. Her ears were red.

Nyla said, "I've been a single mom a long time. I can do it again."

Sarah knew the stats—women became pregnant more often after one-night stands than in long-term monogamy. Right before menopause. It was an evolutionary strategy.

It was a desperate move.

Sarah was desperate! Precisely. So why was she so monogamous? Because she wanted an actual family, that was why. Her ghost babies gathered around her, all of them clawing at her, not one of them alive.

"How do you feel about—" Her voice cracked, but she went on. "Population, and the environment?" She nodded at the store, the slim eco-merchandise. Sarah didn't have one baby yet. Nyla would have three. That was edging on baby hoarding.

Nyla said, "This could be the child who saves us."

Dulcet laughed. "That's a lot of pressure on one kid, darling."

Georgie said, "Have you seen a doctor?"

Nyla shrugged it off. "I'll find a clinic. But I'm pretty versed in pregnancy."

The phone rang. She said, "Probably somebody wanting a bicycle, or a funeral, or a funeral on a bicycle." With a smile in her voice, she answered, "Hello? LifeCycles." Then she said, "Yes, that's me," and she listened.

She turned her back to her friends. She turned the music down until Amy Winehouse was a whisper.

She said, "What do you mean?"

She said, "Arena wouldn't sell drugs. She doesn't do drugs." There was a pause. "I'm sure all parents do say the same thing, but this time it's true."

When she got off the phone, she found her keys. She said, "I have to go. Lock the door on the way out."

Dulcet asked, "What's wrong?"

"I think it's fine, but the police detained Arena. They say she sold kids crystal meth. Where would she even get that?" Nyla grabbed her purse, though it wasn't really a purse. It was one of the hippie bags.

Georgie called, "Want me to go with you?"

Nyla was at the door, then out.

A sprig of dry lavender fell from the wall in a discreet hiss and rattle. The women sat together at the high, small table. Sarah rapped her knuckles against the wood of the stool she sat on, wanting to bring anything like luck her way.

Georgie said, "Crystal meth?"

Dulcet said, "At least Arena has a product."

Georgie said, "That's my future babysitter." She reached for her keys, too, as though to run home and protect her child.

Sarah said, "She's pregnant? Nyla's pregnant? She's almost forty-five." Sarah's face was still blotchy. Her shoulders slumped. She said, "That's just not fair."

Dulcet's phone rang. She checked the number then silenced it. "Mr. Latex." She added, "This guy wants to see me in my rubber skivvies. Private show." She rubbed her thumb and fingers together: money.

Georgie asked, "Are you going to do it?"

Dulcet said, "Are you crazy? For all I know, he's a cop."

At the word *cop*, Georgie scanned the street. It was a nervous tick, since the day they'd showed up at her house. A flash of paranoia made her want to run home and clutch her daughter. Instead, she put a hand on Sarah's wilting back. She asked, "Sarah?"

Sarah waved her away. "I don't want to talk about it."

Dulcet reached for Sarah's hand. She said, "Honey, sometimes the worst things in life are free."

Sarah straightened up only long enough to reach across the table for Nyla's untouched drink. She wasn't pregnant. Maybe she never would be. She poured Nyla's drink into her own glass, and she drank.

Sugar

*N*yla tried hard not to be the kind of mom she never wanted to be. Still, in the car with Arena she couldn't help but say it: "What were you thinking?" Her old car seats sank in the middle, forcing mother and daughter to rest in grooves they'd made over years of driving together.

Arena said, "I don't know what everyone's freaking out about."

"You're expelled, for one thing." Nyla had to work to keep her foot from pressing on the gas pedal and racing home, as though home were some kind of safe place, a place where Arena could be a kid again.

"It's not fair," Arena said, and sounded like every child ever called on the carpet.

One thing Nyla had learned through raising children was that kids' emotions run deep. They resonate against the tight landscape of inexperience, but even from the first day they're about the same struggles as adults, navigating unsteady terrain between love and loneliness.

A truck in the next lane released a dark cloud of diesel, visible where it cut across the arc of a streetlight. The world smelled like breast cancer in the making. To live in a city means living with other people's choices.

Arena said, "Dulcet was kicked out of high school, too. You don't rag on her for it."

"That was twenty years ago." Dulcet had been kicked out for smoking hash on school property. She didn't graduate; she went to summer school instead. Nyla could've been kicked out, too, back then, but on that particular day she was working on a letter to the editor of the *Oregonian* about landfills and the use of Styrofoam in the lunchroom, petitioning for change. Her decision to stay in the library that afternoon involved perhaps an hour, and separated her reputation from her best friend's ever after. She could smoke hash all summer! She could stand outside the party store midafternoon looking for old men to buy them booze, and nothing changed—she'd become the good girl. Now she said, "Besides, that was different."

"Right." Arena looked out the window, then dragged a strand of dark hair across her cheek.

Nyla should've been spending more time with her daughter, not opening a store and reading *Peace One Day*.

This was her fault.

Arena was a good student, with a distinct learning style. She wasn't a fast reader, but was committed to ideas. She'd been reading one book all year—*Red Azalea*—that's how dedicated to ideas Arena was. She read the pages backward and forward and drew illustrations in the white space.

Now there would be a hearing. There'd be a big fine. There'd probably be a social worker sent to the house. There was a yellow slip of paper in Nyla's bag documenting the charges and dates in question. Nyla said, "You're kicked out of Maya Angelou High." Arena's high school, in a lousy neighborhood, was close to bottom rung. The school slogan was "Still I Rise!" a line from an Angelou poem.

Arena said, "I'm not the only one who does it, you know."

Nyla said. "Dulcet only sells prescription drugs to friends. Adults. And only when she's broke."

Arena blinked her eyes. "Dulcet sells drugs? To which friends?"

Nyla realized she'd screwed up. In a fast effort to redirect, she said, "We're talking about you."

Arena said, "I mean at school, now. Other kids sell it. It's really not that big a deal."

Nyla wanted to say all the right things, only the right things, and at the same time she wanted very much to scream. She said, "Listen—just stay away from those people."

Outside the sky was dark. In the winter in Portland the days were short, the sky was so often solid clouds, and what little they saw of the sun set by four o'clock. Now it started to rain, a fine mist that built up on the windows and blurred the lights of oncoming traffic. Nyla's wipers made a muddy smear across the windshield. A scrawny man lurched across the street at a crosswalk. His hair was scraggly, his teeth half gone.

"You see him?" Nyla pointed at the man as he struggled to cross the street. A history of meth showed in his flat lips and missing teeth. He dragged one leg. "He's a cautionary tale."

"Mom!" Arena looked appalled. Her mom had taught her to be kind. They served men like that food at the mission. She said, "You don't know his story."

"I'm old enough to know a few things." Sure, it was wrong to turn a man into a symbol, but this was about saving her daughter. "You need to rethink your actions."

Arena said, "Kids like to have something to buy. Makes 'em feel street-smart."

Nyla sputtered. She could hardly hold back her fury. "Does that man look 'street-smart'? Does he look any kind of smart?" She tried to pace her words. She squinted through the muddy windshield and said, "You think you're doing kids a favor?"

The windshield cleaner only made the smudges worse. Arena said, "Mom, are you still using water for wiper solution?"

"Solution. Ha," Nyla said. "That's a euphemism for poison. It doesn't solve anything. Put enough 'solution' in the groundwater and we'll all have liver cancer."

Arena ran a finger over the glass from the inside. "Can you even see?"

"Ignore the windshield." This was her baby girl! What about all she'd done—the breast-feeding, the co-sleeping, the family camping trips, the day trips to the mountains? "You need to take this seriously."

Arena said, "It's not serious. It's a game, Mom. I've got more at home. A whole box."

Nyla said, "A *box*?"

Arena fiddled with the car's stereo. She picked up something she found on the dash—a seashell or a rock. Nyla's car was cluttered with nature brought inside.

Nyla said, "Meth in a box?" It sounded so corporate. Drugs had come a long way since Nyla was in high school, since Dulcet was expelled. Those days looked innocent, back when the focus was on homegrown pot and magic mushrooms that popped up in local parks.

Arena looked at her mother, and her mouth opened. "Meth? That's what they told you?"

Nyla nodded.

"Crystal meth?" Arena asked again.

Yes. Arena was being expelled from high school for selling crystal meth. Her daughter! Her good, quiet, thoughtful girl. A student had turned over evidence to a school security guard. He'd pointed Arena out and said she sold him the powder. Nyla had to meet with the guard, the principal, and the police. The wipers slapped the windshield, moving lines of mud across and back.

Arena said, "Mom. It was Crystal Light, not crystal meth."

"What do you mean?" Nyla's voice quavered. She drove a little slower, easing her foot off the pedal.

"Crystal Light? A drink mix, like Kool-Aid for grown-ups." Arena quoted a slogan older than she was: "I believe in Crystal Light because I believe in me."

"Where'd you hear that?"

"YouTube."

The car ahead of them showed only red taillights haloed by rain, and Nyla almost ran into it—had to put the brakes on fast. Then the line started moving again.

Nyla took a yoga breath, then said, "You're telling me you sold kids Crystal Light, the drink mix?" She let this new version of the story sink in.

Arena nodded her head the same way she'd been doing her whole life, yes, like a child. Yes to all those questions over the years: Did Santa bring you something nice? Do you want a tuna sandwich? You mean you didn't sell children hard drugs?

Yes, yes, yes. Nodding, nodding.

"The student had powder. Did you tell him what it was?"

Arena said, "Mom, it was in a Crystal Light stick. It was a package."

Nyla was so relieved, she felt half-sick. She asked, "You didn't fold it inside a bindle?"

"A what?"

"You know, a paper wrap? You take a square and fold it in half, and make triangle, then fold the ends in—"

"You sure know a lot about drugs, Mom. But no, no 'bindle' or whatever." Arena picked at the car's threadbare roof liner.

Nyla had to check one more time. "It definitely wasn't crystal meth, then?"

She needed a meditation tape! She was ready to laugh and vomit at the same time. Her body didn't know what to do with the chemical systems of alarm, how to turn it around so quickly—on a dime, as the saying goes. *On a dime bag*, she thought.

Arena said, "No, Mom. They put it in their water. I bought a box of six. They buy it for a dollar a pack. There's fruit punch, lemonade, caffeine flavor—"

Nyla cut in, "Caffeine isn't a flavor, honey."

Arena said, "Whatever. Energy flavor, then. There's one for your skin. Every jock with acne bought it. Are you crying, Mom?"

"I'm not," Nyla said. But she ran a finger under one eye, then the other. She said, "Crystal Light is a corporate product with artificial sweetener, artificial color, artificial flavor, and way too much packaging." Her voice was shaky. Nyla was dizzy with relief, afraid to give in to this new and improved version of events.

Arena said, "Not at all, Mom. They have real sugar in some of them. Studies show women who drink Crystal Light drink twenty percent more water on average."

Nyla said, "You're quoting ads as truth?" This wasn't how she raised her children. She wiped her eyes again.

Arena looked the other way when she said, "I am."

Nyla added, "They drink chemicals."

Arena said, "You *are* crying. Mom?"

Nyla's nose had started to run. She said, "Did you tell Mrs. Cherryholmes it was Crystal Light?"

"I thought she knew."

"Well, Crystal Light's not exactly high crime." Nyla tried to quit being so emotional about it. She couldn't stop her voice from quavering.

"They don't like us selling anything at school. And I sold packets individually, or whatever. Where it says 'Not for individual sale' on the side?"

Her darling child!

Nyla exhaled. She wiped her nose on the back of her hand. She took another deep breath, started to laugh, then choked up again, and felt herself lost in an emotion between elated and crushed, and that's what it meant to have children: happiness tempered with terror, panic laced with love. "We'll clear it up." She gave two more squirts from her water-filled windshield cleaner reservoir and left muddy rivulets down the glass.

Arena nodded.

Outside the car it was dark, raining, and cold, but in the car she felt close to her strange, quiet girl. She missed Celestial, who had always been so ready to tell Nyla everything, who thought out loud and asked questions. But maybe now, with Celeste at Brown, she and Arena would learn to talk. This problem with school could be a catalyst.

Arena asked, "Mom, what do you think happens when we die?"

"You're not going to die. You're just expelled." Nyla was happy.

"We'll all die. What happens then?"

"I have no idea." A strange question. Nyla kept her eyes on the sea of orange and red taillights in the stop-and-go traffic, each light haloed by rain.

Arena said, "I met this cool guy?"

Nyla froze. This was it—the moment of mother-daughter bonding she had hoped for. Nyla had to be careful not to scare her shy daughter away.

"Let me show you a picture." Arena dug in her backpack. Nyla held her breath, ready to see what kind of man or boy Arena took an interest in, ready for any clue to her daughter's internal life. Arena pulled out her worn copy of *Red Azalea*. She leafed through it. There between the pages she found a photo. "Here."

In the dark car it was hard to see what Arena held. Nyla tried to catch a glimpse as they passed under streetlights. "What's that?"

The photo looked like twin taillights in the rain.

"It's him," Arena said, "and me. We share the same energy field."

Nyla looked again. She looked closely. She gave her daughter her full attention, forgot to brake, the taillights brightened, and she saw her daughter's head jerk forward then back as they slammed into the rear of the car ahead of them.

Risk Assessment

Ben couldn't stop to check his makeup; he was late for an under-writers powwow where they'd hash out details on tricky loans. Early that morning, Sarah had worked on his face, using a tube shaped like a bullet casing or a lipstick container, only the makeup inside was pale green. She tapped green dots under his eyes then across the cracked bridge of his nose. "Green covers bruises," she said, leaning so close her breath beat against his lips.

A temp passed Ben in the wide corridor of their office, arms full of folders. She eyeballed him up and down. "Nice look!"

Was that ironic or sincere? He was wearing Dockers and a button-down, along with his smashed nose. Maybe that auburn-haired, ponytail-swinging temp could tell he was hidden under an oil-free coat of beige? The temp was young and thin, and slung her files like she had no investment in any of this.

He didn't have time to talk, not even with a sexy, ironic temp who knew how to sling files. It was his first day back.

He'd sat on the edge of the bathtub at home while Sarah leaned over him; her nightshirt hung low, all cleavage and freckled skin. She'd put her tongue to the corner of her lips and tapped the green makeup with a fingertip. Her eyes scanned Ben's face, looking everywhere except back into his eyes.

The beauty of Sarah was she knew how to take charge.

She patted a cool liquid foundation over the green dots and used her second finger to work the makeup down and out, toward his ears. She found a fat brush in her bag of tricks and swirled it in a plastic dish. "Setting powder," she said, and gave the brush two good raps against the porcelain sink. He could still feel that brush coming at him with its crazy tickle, obnoxious and soft and sexy at the same time.

He'd watched this routine his whole life; now he was an insider, brought in on the makeup ritual.

"Powder makes it so it won't travel," Sarah said. "Longer coverage."

"How long?"

Sarah shrugged. He lost heart, and said, "I don't know about this."

"Think of it as war paint." She dropped the tube of concealer in his blazer pocket.

Wearing the face Sarah made him, he walked with long strides down the open corridor between cubicles and saw his meeting, already started, through a conference room window at the far end of the offices. People were seated around a rectangular table, trapped in the soundproofed capsule of office space.

Ben nodded through the window at his coworkers and offered what he hoped was an enthusiastic, warm yet professional expression. It was hard to look friendly with a smashed face. He felt the warrior paint of his makeup where it lay heavy on his skin. Would it crease?

His boss, Trisha, swiveled and turned a lever. The white blinds tipped. The room was cut off, his smile wasted on the dusty contours of louvered blinds. Had she done that on purpose?

Her timing was precise.

Not one person in the office had welcomed him back yet after his bloody nose vacation. He'd expected to groan at an office card on his desk, or to crowd in the break room for well-wishes and cheap cake. He didn't want the card or the cake, but he wanted the connection a card could stand for. They circulated cards with every birthday, new baby, divorce, promotion, and vasectomy.

But apparently not for a crash in the john.

They acted like it didn't happen.

That'd be fine, except it did happen, and it felt weird to leave so much unsaid. Could he be on the verge of losing his job and everybody knew but him? Or had somebody seen him with his pants down, nose pouring blood, blacked out? He had given them reason to look away, and here they were, still looking away.

What if there were pictures? Oh, God. Totally possible. Everybody had a camera phone. There could even be a camera hidden in the bathroom, some kind of corporate Homeland Security.

He'd Google it. Key words: *bathroom, underwriter, nosebleed, cock.*

He'd run *jacking off* through YouTube. How many videos would that call up? His palms started to sweat at the thought. His neck tightened.

He opened the conference room door. His coworkers were deep in discussion, a file on the table. Most people who worked at that level of the bank's mortgage lending office were women, and the women were all divorced single moms, high school educated, who'd climbed the ladder from claims processor on up. This was their ceiling.

Management was all the same kind of tall, large-knuckled men. There were three managers with corner offices on that floor. Ben was tall, but apparently not tall enough.

He'd drifted into the pink-collar ghetto.

He found a chair, and kept a wary eye to see if anyone noticed his makeover. The underwriters didn't look up from their pages. The only other man in the meeting pushed a credit report, bank statements, and a home appraisal toward Ben, without looking at him.

Trisha was assessing the file. She said, "So we've got low income going on. . . ."

"But trending upward," the man said, and he raised a finger toward the ceiling. "And job stability." That man was very small, with narrow bones and compact ears. He'd never be management.

Ben scanned the credit report. The primary borrower worked in a munitions storage facility in eastern Oregon, not far from where Ben grew up. The borrowers were a couple, a man and a woman. The wife, the secondary signatory on the loan app, was in nuclear waste containment.

He looked closer at the county on the form.

It was the same nuclear waste facility Ben grew up downwind of. There weren't too many of them. He could picture the low, broken grass that lined the highway, the silhouette of industry against his old running ground. That woman had a long commute on empty roads.

She had great job stability. Nuclear waste would be around longer than the ozone.

He touched the edge of his eyebrow, then drew his hand away. If he didn't touch it, the makeup would last longer. He tried not to think about his face.

Every file tells a story. It's an underwriter's assignment to read the story and decide if the financial narrative arcs toward happy or tragic. Each debt is a choice; character shows in accumulated debt.

In one month, four years back, the husband had racked up a major balance with an appliance store. After four years of minimal payments, it was still a high enough debt load to mean a top-of-the-line refrigerator, or a lower-priced full kitchen set: Either way, Ben would bet that spending spree indicated a first marriage.

The man's name had been taken off a previous home loan, but the loan still made its way to the man's credit report. That was a sure sign of divorce.

The two current borrowers shared an auto loan and a maxed-out credit line with Ethan Allen furniture: the sweeping outlay of fresh debt, fast signatures, an exuberant new start.

That'd be a second marriage.

Weddings are only the first step in learning to blow money together in the name of love.

The credit history of each borrower detailed the pursuit of happiness; love and money were mingled. When a dishwasher broke, or a garage door refused to open, when the transmission blew out on what had been a new car, the marriage would feel it.

Divorce was a cumulative response to designed obsolescence, warrantees running out.

He and Sarah lived with a nicked dining room table they found on the side of the road, and when he looked at the dings and scratches of somebody else's life, he knew they'd done okay: They'd made a home for that table. They'd made a home without the false promise of happiness through overspending.

Credit reports were clean, pared down, beautiful in the details; debt illustrated the skeleton of interactions stripped of both romance and couples counseling, stripped of everything except the money trail.

Ben lost himself in the borrowers' history and forgot about his own broken face, the makeup mask. He rubbed a hand along his chin.

Trisha said, "Eighty K in savings. Where'd that come from?" Her hair was thick as a wig, a blond helmet. Her face was well fed. She furrowed her eyebrows, then flipped back and forth through bank statements.

The applicants didn't earn enough to have savings. Not in the past year. Their tax papers didn't show interest earned, meaning they didn't have money in savings the year before.

Another underwriter, a woman in her late thirties, with an actual pink collar sticking out from under a home-knit vest, asked, "Should we go there?"

That was underwriter's shorthand: *go there.* Were they required by regulations to ask about the source of funds?

An older woman, breathing through her mouth, cut in, "I wouldn't go there." With twenty years' experience, this woman always moved like her back hurt. She had a bag of potato chips open on the table and chewed like she meant business; those chips didn't have a chance.

The man said, "I'd go there. If we don't go there and the loan is audited . . ." He looked to Trisha.

The woman in the pink collar looked up and down the table.

Trisha said, "We'll go there if those funds are necessary for closing."

Ben's head hummed, the bruise over his sinus cavity ripe and singing. He put two fingers to the bridge of his nose and closed his eyes. He used his thumb to move the chip of bone that sat on the side of the bridge of his nose, just under the skin. That chip was his tiny friend, with him but not part of him anymore.

The man on the loan was a veteran. He could qualify for a VA loan, a more complicated form, but they'd chosen the simple route.

Ben cut in. "It's a conventional loan. If it's not part of closing, we're not required to go there." He heard himself say it: *go there.* The phrase itself was a hit of poison.

Where was anybody going?

He pressed against his nose, and the pain radiated. It cut against his thoughts, and he liked the way that pain kept him present. The rest agreed, *No, we won't go there. Let's not go there. We don't have to.*

They called off a major voyage.

The potato chip eater shook her bag upside down in celebration, crumbs tumbling into her thick palm. The way the makeup rested, visible, on the pink-collared woman's face was what Ben thought of as a suburban mask. It was smooth, perfect, and a shade too dark. He saw now the line along her chin, where foundation came right to the edge of her pale neck. Why did people do that?

It was the lights. Then it dawned on him, and the moment froze—was his own haze of beige cream too dark in the flicker of fluorescents? It made his stomach knot. He tried to see himself in the aluminum bar of the office chair: There his face was warped.

He wanted to leave—put his hands to his face and flee. He was an actor in potentially fucked-up costume. He tried to focus on the job: Get it done and get the hell out of the meeting.

He flipped past the credit report and on into the appraisal. Where a picture of the house in question should've been, there was a photo of a squat and gleaming corrugated building cut halfway into the hillside, surrounded by land, on the edge of a river. It was a grain silo. He said, "Is this a farm sale?" He squinted at the numbers: It was a slight quarter acre, with a low estimated land value. He looked at the photo again.

"Now you get the situation," the man said. "No comps."

Ben asked, "Of what?" Comps were meant to be comparable home sales to show relative value. There wasn't even a house here.

The man said, "Our borrowers plan to live in a grain silo." He reached over and turned Ben's pages for him until he found one with a few blurry faxes of interior rooms. "That's our home." He tapped a finger to the pictures.

The silo's outer walls were curved. Windows lined the walls, looking out over the hills. The kitchen was modern.

Ben examined what passed for comps: old farmhouses, old kitchens, broken screen doors. He knew those other houses. One was his old best friend's uncle's house, or just like it. He knew the layout: two bedrooms, one bath, no dining room at all.

They were the working-class shacks of his hometown.

He flipped back to the subject property. The silo was sleek. It was a castle, a turret. One picture showed a spacious, simple bedroom with a bed in the middle of the room. An individualist's dream—somebody had personally converted that silo. It was like nothing he'd ever seen.

Trisha looked for the appraiser's signature. "You can't just take a house, make a few adjustments, and say it's equal to a grain silo."

The veteran and his second wife, with their bad health and their Ethan Allen debt, wanted to move into the silo and make the dream their own.

The small man said, "What about a geodesic dome?"

Trisha said, "A dome's not a silo. We've done domes."

The pink-collared underwriter in her genuine pink collar tapped the eraser end of her pencil against the table.

Trisha declared, "No precursor." She pushed the file away.

One glossy photo showed how the sun hit the curve of the silo's corrugated aluminum and sprang into a gleaming star, shining like a fever dream.

The army vet's file told a simple story: The man had done everything a man is asked to do. He finished high school, joined the army, got married, bought appliances, had kids, and got divorced. Like a good soldier he got back in the action and married again. He worked forty hours a week at a job nobody wanted. His wife put in forty at her own toxic industry. All they wanted was to buy a grain silo on the edge of nowhere and call it home.

Ben said, "Three bathrooms?" That was a lot, for a one-bedroom. He pulled the blurry photocopies of photos closer to his face.

The pink-collared single mom looked at Ben. She said, "Want to go there?" She smiled, and tapped her eraser against her white teeth.

Somebody laughed, or coughed, or stifled a laugh. Three bathrooms.

Then they all looked away. Was that on purpose? He got it—he was Ben the bathroom guy. He wanted to say the word again, to check. He dared them. He tried it out. He said, "Full bathrooms, each one."

Nobody looked at him.

He said, "No half baths."

They kept their eyes on their pages. There was one throat clearing. He'd run that through YouTube: *Ben + bathroom*.

Trisha said, "No comps, we can't go there."

Ben wanted to go there, literally—find his way to a rolling hill with no neighbors—a cheap, gleaming grain silo of a home like a fort. Better yet would be a missile silo, insulated and hermetic. Just Sarah and him. It wouldn't matter to him if they never got pregnant. He'd be happy with Sarah.

Trisha said, "Not in this lending climate." She pushed the papers away.

Sorry, borrowers! Sorry to anybody who might want out. No precedent means no money. Banks don't lend on the rebel dream.

Ben started to fold his pages closed. Then he ran a finger under the single glossy photo of the silo house and pulled it from its glue. He slid it into his blazer pocket. He saw the soft smudge of concealer where his mask had rubbed off on his fingers, onto the empty square left where the picture had been.

Energy

Arena couldn't go back to Maya Angelou High—what the kids called My-High—until her mom talked to the principal. Energy is neither created nor destroyed, only transferred. She was expelled, and that was a massive transfer of energy: transferred from school to what?

She wore a T-shirt that said UPTOWN IS NEARTOWN. NEARTOWN IS DOWNTOWN. What the shirt didn't say was the logical conclusion: Uptown was downtown. It was a syllogism, and syllogisms were beautiful. There was a name, PETE'S DINER, and a street address for uptown or downtown in some other city. Arena loved that shirt.

She flipped through her dad's vinyl. The records were old and warped, had that great smell of their old paper covers, and they were hers. Her dad had written his name on them: Pete. One name only.

The Wipers. The Jackals. Those records told her that her life would've had a different sound track if he'd stuck around. Her mom listened to new age flutes with a trickling waterfall in the background that made Arena have to pee.

How was that remotely relaxing?

She looked at Lou Reed's picture on the front of *Transformer* and said, "Hello, Father."

On the back of that album there was another guy dressed as a hooker on the left-hand side of the cover, and then as a cowboy with a major boner on the right side, hot for himself. She put Lou Reed back in the stacks, because all the albums needed a fair chance to be her father's voice for the day.

She closed her eyes, walking her fingers along the frayed paper spines. When she felt the right energy—one thin slip of a record casing calling to her—she slid an album from the stack and pulled it to her lap. Only then did she open her eyes.

Television, *Marquee Moon.*

That was auspicious. Tom Verlaine's vulnerable, venerable croak would be today's voice of her father's wisdom, punked out and bitter.

Okay.

She opened the dusty, smoke-colored cover of an old Sears turntable. She took out the vinyl, held it so gently between four fingers, and blew across it. Someday those black discs would break, and the last bit of her dad would go.

Her room was jammed with clothes in piles, books in stacks, her bed. But the stereo was a temple and lived in a cleared space.

She put the album on the system, dropped the needle, and let Tom Verlaine channel her father.

She sat cross-legged, hugging her knees. Television, the band, was her father's broken heart. Arena drank it in and waited for the sentences that would speak to her.

It was like reading tarot cards, or throwing the I Ching. It was better than a horoscope.

It didn't take long before Tom Verlaine sang, "I understand all destructive urges . . . I see no eviiiiiiil—" The words stood out like a letter written to her. That was her dad!

He understood.

Tom Verlaine wouldn't fault her for being expelled from school or even worse. Her father understood Tom Verlaine. If uptown was neartown, and neartown was downtown, Tom Verlaine was her papa and he understood everything.

Her dad's unconditional love went on until the album ground to the end, the needle's voice turned to a hiss, and the disc kept up a pointless spin. Arena lifted the arm.

To play it again would ruin the magic. Her job was to interpret her father's wisdom, and what she heard was love.

. ⸝ ⸜.

Downstairs, almost noon, her mom was on the couch and on the phone. She was wearing her "sardine apron," an apron she'd bought at a garage sale and used mostly to keep sardine oil off her clothes. Nyla ate a steady diet of sardines for her health. The house smelled like fish and olive oil. There was an empty tin with the lid peeled back on the coffee table.

She hung up the phone as Arena came down the stairs. Her hair was still in yesterday's ponytail. Her mascara had traveled beneath her eyes. Nyla said, "Well, that went exactly nowhere."

Arena knew without asking: Nyla'd been on the phone with Maya Angelou High. Instead she said, "Don't you have to open the store?"

Nyla said, "I have to go down to your school."

There was an awkward silence. Arena didn't want to think about school.

"Maybe afterward, I could take you out for lunch," Nyla said.

Her whole life, Arena had never spent so much time alone with her mom as in the months since Celeste moved out. Before, she'd gotten by with listening. How did anyone ever know what to say?

"Mom?" Her voice sounded uncertain. Nyla cocked her head and waited. Arena asked, "Can I show you something? It's near your store." Arena heard herself say it: *Near.* What did that mean? When did something near quit being near and move into far? What was in between?

The words echoed in her head: It's near the store, we're near the store. Uptown, downtown, neartown.

Her mom made as much sense as anything: Expelled + lunch date = good again. She could feel her mother's brain compute the math. But Nyla didn't understand destructive urges. Her mother was about preserving the planet and every ecosystem on it. Her mother was about trapping energy, preserving her children as babies in photos all over the house. Arena said, "I want to show you the Temple Everlasting of Life on Earth."

A New Heaven, a New Earth

A line of geese decorated the flat of the gray sky overhead. Each one found a place in the line. Nyla offered her silent blessing: *I love you, geese, stringing together your necklace of selves against the sky.* She wanted to blow them kisses. Her eyes teared up with love for the world, and for her place in that world, her daughters, and the baby in her stomach, and then she knew for sure she was pregnant. Who needs a test? Pregnancy was about being in love in a big way. She was glad to have her sunglasses on. Nyla was in love with the beginning of the life story, the human birth moment.

As she drove toward the temple, she cleared her throat and asked, "You sure it's not the Temple *of* Everlasting Life on Earth?"

Arena was sure.

Temple Everlasting.

What was really everlasting was the string of cults that popped up in Portland, each one all bright ideas and tax evasion. When Nyla was Arena's age there'd been the Holy Order of Mans, a mystical branch of Christians with a coffee shop called the Wheel of Fortune. They sold a cheap breakfast all day. In the old days, Nyla had done her high school homework there, where Dulcet could smoke.

The Hare Krishnas were always around town, setting up temples in old houses, offering free vegan curry dinners.

When she was twenty Nyla and a broke date ate gritty lentil soup from a stoneware bowl sitting on the splintered wood floor of the Krishna temple, in a cloud of incense.

The Scientologists brought Chick Corea to play piano outside city hall, in a protest concert.

Nyla didn't even let herself think about the Love Family, or the Church of Jesus Christ at Armageddon, as they called themselves, with their evangelical orgies and "cum-unions." There were grown kids in town now, Nyla's age, born as "Jesus babies," from straight-up religious prostitution.

The Rosicrucians were still around. They had a saying: Every potential convert was a "walking question mark." When they found a seeker, they knew it.

And the Bhagwan Shree Rajneesh, with his followers, had been Portland's biggest cult influx until they crashed and burned over a food scandal—intentionally lacing salmonella in a salad bar. What a disaster. It was still the only case of large-scale bioterrorism in the United States.

Nyla had been in Portland through all of it. She'd danced in the Rajneesh disco and seen their used pink clothes filter through the resale stores then clothe the homeless when the cult shut down.

"There it is!" Arena pointed, and tapped the car window.

The Temple Everlasting was in a tight strip of stores on a run-down street. It was another narrow storefront, like LifeCycles. Nyla could guess the rent. They got out and went to the door. It was locked. A white sandwich board inside leaned against the glass. Arena put her face to the window and cupped her hands. "It's amazing."

A sign taped to the window read FOR I AM FASHIONING A NEW HEAVEN AND A NEW EARTH, AND THE MEMORY OF THE FORMER THINGS WILL NOT ENTER THE MIND OR COME UP IN THE HEART.— GOD, OLD TESTAMENT.

The Church of the Lousy Childhood. That'd attract a crowd.

In a bid to stay neutral, Nyla said, "So, you're interested in religion."

"It's science, Mom." Arena scooted along the window. "See Einstein, toward the back? His light is out."

Nyla put her face to the glass, too.

With a flash of light inside the building, a naked man came through a door further back. His brown hair stuck up in a spiky imitation of Einstein's style. His chest was more of the same. He scratched his balls and brushed his teeth.

Arena slapped the glass, then waved.

The man took the toothbrush from his mouth. He grabbed some kind of cloth to cover himself.

Nyla pulled her face away fast. She stepped back. "I'm pretty sure they're closed."

But Arena knocked again and waved, and soon enough the front door opened. Now the man was in a robe like something from another country, a priest's robe, or a relic from a seventies wedding. It was floor-length white polyester with a rope of gold swirls along the neck and hem. The Church of Goodwill castoffs. He lifted the hem from the dusty floor, keeping his eyes on Arena. "Come in."

Arena went first. Nyla followed, but the man in his dress dropped the door on Nyla like she wasn't there.

The Church of Rude.

He followed at Arena's heels. "You drink coffee?"

Arena said, "Of course."

Cult food? Nyla said, "No, we're fine." She tried to catch Arena's eye.

"I'd love a cup," Arena said.

Pure death. Potentially. Nyla's palms were sweaty. She followed them both past old TVs on white pedestals. In the back of the store, Arena made herself at home at a chrome dining table. Other mismatched chairs were claimed by books, clothes, dishes. The man ducked behind a wall. There was a crash and shuffle, the sound of pans and glass.

Arena said, "Isn't this place cool?"

Cool as the Goodwill bins, that grimy last stop where they sold mixed junk by the pound—Nyla had burned out on that scene a long time ago.

What was up with her daughter? First Crystal Light, and now religion? Welcome to teenage-land.

The man came out from behind his wall with a dusty percolator. The cups he found were ringed with stains. "I've got coffee here somewhere," he said, and dug through a box of jumper cables and aerosols.

Arena said, "This is my mom."

It was as though he noticed Nyla for the first time. He said, "Hey. Welcome."

Nyla said her own name. She reached to shake his hand.

He said, "Mack."

Arena laughed. "Really?"

Mack shrugged. "You expected something more Hindu? It's short for Macheath. The 'rents were *Threepenny Opera* fans."

He found a rusted can of Maxwell House. If he didn't poison them on purpose, he'd do it by accident.

Don't drink the Kool-Aid. Don't trust the salad bar. Don't go to Applebee's. Sometimes you can trust the lentil soup. Sometimes. This is what Nyla had learned from cults.

Mack said, "A name is a pointless point of separation, when on a cellular level, we're all one, right?"

Arena beamed at him.

Mack said, "Your name and my name could be the same, right? The name of all life."

Nyla's jaw tightened. She wanted to physically push him away from Arena. Nyla took a careful look at Mack's chiseled face. She said, "Didn't you used to tend bar?" She'd seen him around.

He was closer to her age than to her daughter's. Jesus Christ.

He said, "I've done all kinds of things."

Nyla said, "I'm sure."

Arena picked out a stained mug, like choosing a flower from a garden.

Nyla was determined: We are not drinking that coffee.

Mack said, "Now I'm doing what matters," and gave her a wide smile, like one of the blessed.

To a lonely teenage girl, what was more seductive, sex or religion?

Arena flipped her hair out of her eyes. She said, "Show Mom your equipment."

Mack gave a nervous blink.

Nyla said, "I don't need to see your equipment."

Arena said, "Can we use the camera?"

"Camera?" Nyla echoed, as her mom instincts kicked into higher gear.

Mack cleared his throat and made his voice deep. "We, here at the Temple Everlasting of Life on Earth, are able to document aspects of energy fields. There's a magnetic field produced by the emotions of the human heart."

He stopped to find a carton of powdered nondairy creamer under a stack of clothes.

Old white powder that could be anything, really.

"The camera is phenomenal. It shows us we're not as alone as we might otherwise feel," Mack said.

Wasn't loneliness every pornographer's justification?

He said, "Let's not set it up now, though."

"What have you taken pictures of?" Nyla braced for the worst.

"Kindred spirits."

He turned his religious beam toward Arena. Lust made visible. Yes, this was another cult out to poison babies. If it wasn't salmonella in the salad bar, it was porn. Nyla said, "She's in high school." Her voice was low and steady.

He said, "Really? Why isn't she there?"

Arena sucked in her breath, a habit she'd had since she was a baby, a flash of anxiety.

"The Temple is about honesty. When we choose to feel our feelings, and share those shared feelings, we come closest to our truest truth."

Feeling feelings and truest truth? Was this guy kidding?

He lifted the percolator. He couldn't move far from the wall; it was still plugged in. Arena got up to go to him. This was a man who wouldn't go out of his way for her.

Nyla said, "We don't need coffee."

"Mom," Arena said.

"Show me the camera." This was a command. Nyla said it with the conviction learned through years of being a mother. There was an implied threat in her voice: or else. Or else what? She'd start counting? Or else they were in trouble? It didn't matter. She wanted to see the setup, if only to tell police.

Mack shuffled in his slippers toward the front of the store to the black cloak that covered the machine. "It's an old machine. Very special. It has to warm up."

He gave it a pat through the cloth.

Arena followed him. She said, "Mom, everything here is substantiated theory." She waved a hand at the pyramids, at Einstein and Tesla. "I love substantiated theory."

"I'm not sure this qualifies." Nyla almost whispered it.

The photography machine clicked and hummed. Mack said, "I don't believe in binaries, like religion versus science. It's about the unifying element: particle theory." He found a bag of tortilla chips on the floor. "Chip?" he asked.

More food.

No sex, no food, no naked pictures; Nyla took the bag and rolled the top closed, then shoved it in her purse. Nobody would be eating those chips.

"It's about energy," Arena said. "You know what this means, right?"

Nyla saw in her daughter the Rosicrucian saying: Arena, with her teenage slouch and her T-shirt that made no sense—uptown is neartown?—she was that walking question mark. She was it.

"No, what does it mean?" Nyla tried to stay calm.

Arena blew stray hair away from her face. The hair settled back across her cheek. Nyla wanted to find a hair clip in her purse, something pink with flowers, something for a kid. She wanted to take Arena home. With one hand she smoothed the hair, and tucked it behind her daughter's tender ear.

Arena brushed Nyla away like she was shooing off a mosquito. But she smiled, through chapped lips. She'd only just gotten her braces off the year before, but was one front tooth drifting?

She said, "It means Dad's still with us. He's not gone. He's energy."

Baby, Cry It Out

*G*eorgie flossed her teeth in the upstairs bathroom and when Bella started crying in the next room over, she paused, a white line of dental tape still laced around her fingers. It was almost midnight. She could see Humble in bed, reflected in the slice of bathroom mirror, framed by the open door. He was watching a cop show on TV.

He said, "Did you fill out the life insurance papers?"

Ah, crumb! Again. She didn't want to think about ever dying, about leaving her daughter, leaving this world. Georgie stopped flossing long enough to say, "I'll get to it in the morning."

"Get to it? What do you do all day?"

The baby monitor was on her side of the bed, where it cranked up the volume of Bella's crying and brought it out in stereo like they had unhappy twins, one in each room, one a little more electronic than the other. Humble didn't let on that he even heard it. He had a beer on his side of the bed. Bella kept up the howl. The heartbeat of the white noise machine, with its steady *thump-thump*, seeped through the monitor, too. Georgie dropped her floss in the wastebasket.

This was the first night they'd moved Bella to her own room.

She was a tiny baby on a raft of cushions on a big, flat mattress in a lovely maple crib.

Georgie walked into the bedroom, ready to sink into bed, but couldn't relax as long as Bella was crying.

With his eyes still on the TV, Humble leaned over and clicked the monitor off. The heartbeat and the baby's cry were muffled but fought their way through the walls.

"Should we check on her?"

Humble said, "She'll get herself to sleep."

Georgie felt the baby's cry crawl through her body in a steady low-voltage electricity that powered a nearly constant tension in her neck. The heartbeat matched her own. "If we let her cry, we're teaching her that we don't listen."

Humble said, "That worked for my parents."

"You think your mom listens to you, even now?" Humble's mom was present only as an absence, a grandmother who made no promises.

Bella coughed, a choking little baby cough. It was a whole drama going on in the next room.

Georgie said, "We're teaching her she can't affect her environment. We're teaching powerlessness."

Humble reached for his beer and took a sip.

"If I bring her in here, we can turn the heartbeat off," she negotiated. The baby would hear Georgie's heartbeat through her chest. They'd sleep that close together.

Humble put his beer bottle down. He said, "I can't sleep with her in the bed."

With that bottle, and his bed, Georgie saw him then as a grown baby. This is how his mother raised him: a crib and a bottle.

He was a tired baby, his eyes ringed with exhaustion.

But to let Bella cry, alone like that, even though she was only one room over, was to Georgie like leaving her on the side of the road, lost in a vast world.

Georgie went to check on her.

Bella was a red-faced bundle of hot tears and clenched fists. She'd kicked her blanket off.

Newborn babies are freaky alien fish slipped from another dimension: big eyes, heavy heads, useless limbs—they swim in a climate laden with gravity; the air doesn't support their efforts so they cry. They need support.

Georgie put Bella on her back, in the middle of a baby blanket. Bella kicked and howled, wrinkled her face, opened her mouth. Georgie put a hand on her daughter's chest and pulled the blanket snug around the tiny body. The first time she'd done this, it'd seemed so very wrong. She caught her daughter's arms and legs, trapped them in the blanket, twisted the cloth and tucked one end in, making a package, a human present. Bella stopped crying. It was instantaneous: The blanket was tight, and her whole body relaxed. She closed her puffy eyes and slept.

The womb is a snug place. A tight swaddle is as close as a newborn gets to going back home.

Georgie picked up the package that was her newborn and carried it in one arm. She went downstairs for a glass of water. She patted Bella's back and sang a song made up of sounds that weren't words, and every sound was all about love. Halfway down the stairs in the dim light she took a step that didn't work out, and she fell. That easily, her foot swished. Down she went two steps at a time. Georgie's knee bent wrong and her body weight cut through the air until she hit the wooden floor in the downstairs hall. The baby was against her shoulder. Georgie hadn't tumbled, she'd gone straight down. Her knee was jammed, and one hip hurt, but Bella was fine.

There was this new clumsiness that came with motherhood: always one hip cocked out, a baby in her arms, her spine still recovering from the baby weight, her C-section scar along the front. All of it conspired to make her lose her footing.

When she looked over her shoulder, the light of their open bedroom door cut through the dark hallway.

"I fell down the stairs," she called out.

There was the sound of TV voices.

"I wrenched my knee."

Still no answer.

Georgie patted Bella's back. "I don't know if I can stand."

"Did you try?" Humble's voice was slow and gravelly.

Georgie pictured his tired eyes. She got up on wobbly legs. She leaned with one hand against the doorway and got to her feet with less grace but the same trepidation as Bambi. Her balance was off with swaddled Bella in one arm. She hadn't broken anything. A place on the side of her hip, maybe technically her ass, her lower ass, felt hot and as though a hand was pushing against her there. "My hip is wrecked," she said. But she could walk. That invisible hand didn't push her over.

"You'll be fine," Humble said.

She called back, "Really? That's all you can do?"

There was an ambulance wail on TV. A voice said, "... hasn't been dead long." Humble's bottle clinked against the nightstand.

Open the studbook

So say you're a female Asian elephant, shy, tall, and pretty. A good part of your evolutionary success is because you have the ability to grow the weight of a refrigerator in your gut, in your womb, as you carry it for nearly two years, then push it headfirst out the birth canal, the pocketbook, the elephant pussy, in a splashing river of blood and tissue.

That's a requirement.

You'll have blood down your legs, a baby on the ground. The amniotic sac should break, and if it doesn't, that's a problem. Make your baby breathe when it won't. Kick it with your feet if you have to, let it slide in the blood one way then another until its eyes open, its mouth moves, air goes in.

If you're that newborn, your job is to walk immediately. It's crucial. Walk away from predators, and keep close at your mom's side even as you blink eyelashes still gummed with afterbirth, dust, and blood.

Sarah stood outside the dry moat and wall of the outdoor enclosure watching three elephant cows and their massive offspring. How could something so big look so charmingly diminutive? Even the largest elephant moved with the dreamy grace of a parade float.

Their ears were freckled and looked as soft and ruffled as the edge of a silk skirt. Their backs were topographical maps. Even the babies had eyes like old men, like sea turtles.

She tapped her pencil against the metal railing. The rail was decorated with chipped paint, like old metal playground equipment. *They should test the paint for lead*, she thought, and she'd care about that more if she were still pregnant.

The cows raised their calves together in a happy co-op. The fathers, two bull elephants, were kept in separate enclosures.

Bulls could turn murderous.

In other countries elephants are work animals. Often enough, bulls kill their masters. Mostly they kill when they're in what's called "musth," a state that comes on like really bad PMS, only in the males. It's a physiological thing, a psychotic shift. It's a problem. There'd be money in developing a Prozac-type drug to keep male elephants emotionally stable, if a company wanted to take that on.

Some trainers starve the bulls to keep them docile, but musth comes anyway.

In Asia, nobody blames a rampaging elephant. Trainers know the odds: Males go mad; it's par for the course. In the United States, stomping a trainer'll get a bull killed. "Put down" is the phrase, as though to kill an animal and a little insult, a put-down, are at all the same. As though bringing an animal to its knees—down, closer to the ground—is the whole of it.

It left a serious dent in breeding programs when zoos became scared of the liability involved in keeping a postadolescent, sexually active bull in the stable. The Oregon Zoo held the international Asian elephant studbook.

Sarah had stood in the same spot weekly for months, watching each baby elephant flop its short trunk and learn to use it. They had to develop those muscles! Supercute.

But after miscarriage number four all this family shit had started to get under her skin. The zoo was a place for endangered animals to fuck in safety. Her job was to watch babies, hoping to see animals make more babies. She was a barren voyeur, a babysitter.

Everywhere she looked, small bodies orbited around larger bodies like Galilean moons.

Sarah was in her own musth.

She'd been robbed. She had been on her way, a baby! And now, nothing.

A studbook recorded who had babies but also highlighted who didn't.

Around her, the zoo was packed with families, mostly women and children. Dads were rare, but not so rare as to be either exotic or endangered. One woman pushed a six-seater stroller. Six kids? Whose idea was that?

Baby hogs.

Hoarders.

Dulcet was right, they were all addicts.

Children climbed on fences and pressed themselves against the animals' enclosures in a visual display, a reenactment, of humans encroaching on an already diminished terrain.

As compulsive and indulgent as alcoholics, some people couldn't have one without going overboard. Even lab rats were kept with set limits on offspring, due to the Animal Care and Use Protocol in research. Too many rats in a cage? That's a mess. They'll eat one another alive. Too many humans in a house?

Sarah wanted one single child. She wasn't greedy.

Down in the Africa exhibit, a sign attributed as a "Masai Elder Blessing" read, "May you be peaceful and prosperous with many cattle and children."

Sarah passed that sign at least once a day, sometimes more. Now she was not peaceful. She didn't have cattle. She didn't have kids.

What was the Masai curse? That's what she got.

Every baby she saw was an anxiogenic substance: Babies made her anxious.

To see them in plague proportions? That had grown into her personal panicogen, no chemicals needed—flat-out panic.

Her timer peeped. Her charge, a six-month-old male elephant, tapped its trunk against a stick, left and right. He was doing well. "Play behavior," Sarah marked on her list.

An elephant cow named Rainy Day paced incessantly. It was a coping mechanism. Years before, Rainy had been traded to another zoo, swapped for a male who came to Oregon on a short-term breeding loan.

She was pregnant when they traded her off. Her baby was born at the new zoo, but neither Rainy nor her calf were accepted as part of the elephant social circle there. The other elephants crowded her and pulled rank. Her infant fell off the edge of their artificial lot into a dry moat, hit his head, and died.

Rainy went nuts. They tranquilized her, but that's when she started pacing, and she never stopped.

Elephant handlers sometimes use what's called an elephant hook. It's a long pole. The end is curved like a scythe only with a round ball at the tip, instead of a blade. The ball is supposed to offer a nudge, like a fist, to an elephant's sensitive temple. After her baby died, when Rainy Day started pacing, when she was high on tranquilizers and frantic with grief, zookeepers at the new zoo tapped Rainy with an elephant hook. But she moved fast, and the ball at the end of the hook knocked her eye out.

That's when they sent her home.

She was a sweet elephant, half-blind, forever walking off that dance to her lost son. Her new baby was the thinnest in the herd; he ran all day at his mother's feet. It was hard to say if she seemed to be running away from her child or trying to lead him somewhere better. Either way, a nervous mother set the pace for his world.

A happy mother makes a happy family!

Rainy's dead calf was in the studbook, alongside the success stories. Sarah's miscarriages? They'd be in a book, too, if anyone were keeping track.

She heard Dale's voice before she saw him. "You've got the easy job," he said. She turned. He'd come out of the elephant enclosure through a back door, down a fake-clay tunnel, a place used by staff and camouflaged from zoo guests by a thicket of bamboo. He wore waist-high rubber waders, and he was soaked. "Jesus, I hate urine collection."

Sarah asked, "They've got you doing that?"

"Short on handlers," he said. The air was already ripe with the green scent of elephant poop, and now the acrid component of that stench was intensified and close; Dale reeked of piss. He said, "I'm glad you're back at work. Sorry you've had a rough time of it." He looked at her as though to say more, but what was there to say?

"It's not your fault. No need to be sorry." Sarah was embarrassed. She didn't want to talk about it. Any fault lay somewhere between Sarah and Ben, in the ways their bodies came together.

Her timer went off. The elephant child ran alongside its mom's frantic stride. "Locomotion," she wrote on her chart. She'd heard about urine collection, though never seen it. Handlers tried to keep it behind the scenes. Sarah's job was out front. "How do you collect urine from an elephant?"

"With a bucket and a prayer." Dale stomped his feet. A newspaper blew past. It stuck on the wooden rails of the elephant info kiosk. Sarah took it from the rails. A headline read SPEEDERS KILL 1,200 MORE PEOPLE THAN DRUNK DRIVERS.

And what about drunk speeders?

She said, "Let's raise the speed limit another ten and clear some room for the rest of us."

Dale offered, "I like a woman with a warm heart. But the crowd'll thin out once the rain starts." He was talking about the zoo. Sarah meant the planet. That population would not thin out with the weather, unless global warming kicked in some really severe times.

He said, "Hey, you want to see a show with me?" He leaned on the metal bar that marked the edge of the elephants' space.

Was he asking her on a date?

That was a new kind of anxiogenic move. She was married.

He ran a hand over his short hair, in the warm light of the fall sun. He said, "It's a science show, at OMSI."

The Oregon Museum of Science and Industry was another anthill of offspring. School buses lined the OMSI parking lot to bring kids in by the herd. The "tactile experience center" was a pet store of babies.

Depressogenic, totally.

Dale said, "This show is about reconstructive surgeries, artificial limbs, skin grafts. You'll love it." He added, more softly, "The thing is, for me, it's kind of a big deal. My ex has work in it."

She'd heard about Dale's ex, a scientist in Chicago. The woman had left Dale overnight and broken his heart. He was still her biggest fan.

He said, "I haven't talked to her in a year." His cheeks flushed, a shifting of color near his jaw, across his pale skin. Sarah's heart melted. He looked to the elephants and said, "Seriously, though, she's a pioneer."

A pioneer? It was hard not to picture Dale's ex in a rugged sack dress, crossing the prairie in a wagon, devoted to science.

"She gets huge grants," he said.

Sarah's field was observation, her focus behavior and interpretation. Lodged in the soft sciences, she hadn't practiced dissection since college. Sarah asked, "What does she reconstruct?"

"Anything you want," Dale answered, with the embarrassed smile of vicarious pride.

Behind him, a woman walked five kids, each one on a furry leash and halter. The woman's hand was full of monkey tails. She was like a balloon vendor, strings in hand—only her fat balloons scrambled over the zoo grass. She was a dog walker of children, readily making herself genetically redundant and proud of it.

Excessive baby making was a quiet war: building up troops, everyone secretly worried about their team. Would the Mexican families take over the small towns? The Catholics or the Mormons? *Go forth and multiply.* Those were fighting words.

Make war through love.

We've seen the family annihilators, though, from the patricide of Oedipus to the parricide of every spoiled suburban kid to turn a gun on his parents. There was no guarantee of team players. Each one of those five babies could be a little ticking bomb.

Sarah ached for one uncertain little future hellion to call her own.

Two men, elephant handlers, burst from the fake-clay tunnel. As they came out of the tunnel, Sarah saw the men themselves as sperm.

Dale whispered, "Watch. They'll want help with sperm collection now."

He leaned over the railing to eyeball a cow's feet. Captive elephant feet always need vet care. Microscopic bacteria could find a way in around cracks and poorly tended nails, and those tiny bacteria could kill an elephant. He said, "She's due for a pedicure."

One handler called over, "We need backup with the old bull."

Dale gave a glance to Sarah. "Duty calls. See you later." He jogged off to the indoor rooms of the big elephant cages, the private porn motel of elephant ejaculation. Elephants at the Oregon Zoo mostly mated the natural way, but as part of the Species Survival Plan, and as the strongest Asian elephant breeders in the world, their zoo shipped frozen sperm around the globe for artificial insemination.

Now, where Sarah stood, kids twirled and crashed around her like so much litter.

A litter of children.

In the spring when gnats hatched out over Oregon's damp grasses, they flew in uneven spirals, ran into things, and reminded Sarah of toddlers, with their little twenty-four-hour lives. Everyone resented gnats every moment they were around. Sarah tried to give them their space. But now these children ran like gnats over the zoo lawn, the same loopy circles.

A pack of hellspawn jumped up and down yelling "Chimpanzees!" or maybe they yelled "Chips and cheese!" Each one was a prized little consumer.

Their mother, that mother gnat slave, frantically opened juice boxes and freed one straw after another from its plastic sleeve. How much garbage did it take to make a juice box? The woman turned, looked right at her, and said, "Sarah! Jesus, it's been, like, what? Ten years?"

The woman morphed from a stranger into an old friend, and from a mom with a surplus swarm of dirty chimp-kids into Sarah's old neighbor, when they were, like, twenty, back when the woman was thinner, and younger, and was an excellent drinker with a big laugh and a bottle of Bushmills in her freezer.

What was her name?

Georgie would remember it. They'd all lived in small rooms in an Old West–style apartment building in deep northwest Portland. Nights they'd walked home together, drunk women stumbling in high heels, watching one another's backs.

The woman asked, "Which kids are yours?"

Sarah could see her own babies out there on the green grass as though they'd grown. Now one was walking, another was still more of a toddler, the third able to walk only if it held on to the stroller, its light curls blowing in the cool breeze.

"None." She looked to the elephants and tapped her pen on her chart. She was there to work.

"You got married, though, right?" the woman asked.

"Yep." That was the last time they'd seen each other, at Sarah's wedding. She held up her hand with the ring on it as though that proved something. "Ten years."

She was married, but no kids. Was that so freaky?

Why did people think zoos were for kids, anyway? Grown-ups could take an interest in animals. It was the real world.

Four kids orbited Sarah's old friend, and Sarah asked, "Are these yours?"

The woman nodded. "Four in three years. Twins, even." She waved a hand at a big-eyed boy, then a girl, who looked nothing alike. "Crazy, isn't it?"

. Sarah nodded back. She really did agree—it was crazy. Flat-out crazy. *This*, she thought, *is why we need speeders*. A population can't just triple, every two people turning into six.

In zoo terms, there was plenty of genetic surplus.

She looked at the flock of smiling faces, little hands, cute mall clothes in mini-sizes, and knew she was horrible for even thinking about thinning the population.

Other people, she imagined—like this made it any better. Send the speeders to take out other people. Somebody had to make room.

She was still horrible.

Was it so wrong to want space and water and resources for her own unborn? Save a little something, please. But she and Ben were turning out to be snow leopards, calm and barren, while everybody else got to be gnats, or even better, happy elephants, breeding and grazing and wandering the fields.

Sarah wanted to be an elephant cow, like her old drinking friend!

Population control: The world needed barren women to balance out the numbers. Sarah pushed that anxiogenic, panicogen, depressogenic, loserogenic thought away fast.

Who assigned her the role of barren?

Mrs. Fertility let her kids trample the zoo lawn. She said, "You heard about that girl who used to live upstairs from us?"

Sarah tried to remember.

The woman said, "She got shin cancer, from all those years as a stripper. You know, cowboy boots, bare legs. They treat the leather with chemicals that give you cancer. That's what I heard."

The baby elephants ran like clumsy ballerinas. Sarah listened to a string of stories about old neighbors. The mom talked about meth and somebody getting shot while she handed her children slices of apple.

Rainy paced the edge of the elephant enclosure. Her baby kept up a steady trot at her feet, and Dale stumbled from the elephant enclosure's back rooms.

Sarah said, "That was fast."

"I'm good at what I do." He dropped the suspenders on his waders and stepped out. His shoes caught on the pant legs. He held on to a small tree for balance and tugged one foot free. He said, "It's called animal husbandry, and sometimes that feels a little too accurate, you know? As in—why am I that elephant's bitch?"

The mom-friend was in the center of her own storm, working her diaper bag, managing a pack of Wet Ones. She helped her kids and littered the ground in a living illustration of perpetual consumption.

Dale let his waders fall in a pile. He pulled off the shirt half of his scrubs. He had another shirt underneath. The two shirts hitched up together, flashing an expanse of a strong back, soft skin, hard muscles. His stomach had only the inevitable folding of skin as he bent, no gut rolls, no spare tire, no muffin tops or love handles.

Sarah started to introduce him, but his face was hidden. The other woman looked, too. She ate one of her own brown apple slices.

Still under his shirt, Dale said, "Next month I'm assisting on an elephant vasectomy in Orlando. That'll be a first. The thing about elephants is, their testicles are inside, up near their kidneys. And they have a trunk-sized penis, if you can visualize that." His shirt slid off, and he straightened up, in his Hanes T.

Again Sarah moved to introduce him, but before she could, he cut her off. He said, "So, are you going to that show with me?" He was sweaty from work and too many clothes.

She saw Dale the way her friend would see him: hot.

His flushed skin caught the sun and cast it back in a glow. He said, "Maybe next week?"

There were perks to not having kids. She didn't have to sort out child care. Ben would be at work. She'd make the most of it, because, why not?

With the audience of a mom who now wiped her oldest boy's snot with the edge of her sleeve, Sarah said, "That'd be great."

Dale said, "We could have drinks."

She said, "Sure."

Arrangements

Nyla went to the school, found the vice principal's office, and explained how Crystal Light wasn't crystal meth and never had been. It was all pretty much a game! Kids' stuff. The vice principal was a dark-haired woman in the middle of filing papers, bent over a cabinet. She straightened up with a groan. She adjusted her wool skirt at the waist and said, "The report was detailed and specific."

"But it's wrong," Nyla insisted. She felt about twelve years old. The vice principal let her in to see Principal Cherryholmes.

Mrs. Cherryholmes was petite and beautiful, maybe even younger than Nyla. She had frosted hair and frosted fingernails and tipped her head sideways as she sat behind her desk and listened.

Nyla said, "When you saw it, did it look more like baking soda or salt? Did it smell like cat urine or more like lemonade?"

A look of disdain flickered across the principal's face, then she was back to her polite composure. She said, "Our security personnel worked with the police. I don't know what it looked like. I certainly didn't smell it."

"It wasn't drugs," Nyla tried, one more time.

Mrs. Cherryholmes took a deep breath. She reached a hand

halfway across her desk—not far enough to touch Nyla, but dip-lomatically far enough to make a gesture of communing. She said, "Understandably, many parents fall into what we call a truthfulness bias. They need to believe their children tell the truth."

"And that's wrong?" Nyla's voice broke. She knew her daughter.

"The police have tests for substances."

"Then they must not have tested it." Nyla felt her nose grow congested and tears well up, but she blinked the tears back and hid it—stoic! She'd be stoic. Nobody could tell. She'd cry later, on her own.

Mrs. Cherryholmes slid a box of tissues closer to Nyla's side of the desk.

Okay. So she could tell. Nyla wasn't stoic!

"If you really feel there's been an error, I encourage you to re-visit this with the police. They have the evidence. They'll sort it out."

Nyla coughed to clear her grief-choked throat. "There's still a chance?"

Mrs. Cherryholmes shook her gleaming hair. She smiled. Her lipstick was frosted, too, in a sheen of confidence. That was probably the actual lipstick color: Administrative Confidence.

Nyla asked, "How come nobody here followed up on it? Nobody noticed or investigated?"

The principal tightened down on her smile of success. She said, "Please. We have twenty-four hundred kids in this school. We have five security guards a day rotating through. Our job is to curtail any culture of drug trafficking or other problematic behavior, and maintain a quality education. When there's a problem, we shut it down. We don't test drugs ourselves. If there's an error, the police will find and fix it."

It sounded so easy. So rational. And so very impersonal.

"Understand this—we can't afford a situation like they're hav-ing in Washington right now."

A sexting scandal going through a southern Washington school district had been all over the news. A photo of one girl's naked body, forwarded through the whole school system, left every child involved charged with distribution of porn. It was a nightmare. Parents had filed lawsuits against the district, citing a hostile learn-ing environment. The lawsuits had started piling up on top of one another.

"Your daughter will be fine," Mrs. Cherryholmes offered. "The support of a concerned parent like you makes all the difference in the world."

The principal stood up, and Nyla stood with her. They nodded their heads in unison. It'd all be all right. And in that way, the principal silently convinced Nyla to leave. She walked her out of the office and down the hall to the school's front door.

"Good luck with it. Let us know," Mrs. Cherryholmes said. "You're doing everything right."

Nyla was happy for the talk. It felt like they were friends. It almost made her want to volunteer in the school again, though she'd given that up years before when she got in trouble for letting kids play with matches in the name of an art project, working with burnished driftwood and melted paraffin.

Back then, one of the girls had long, curly hair. They were supposed to tie their hair back! But anyway, Nyla had put the fire out fast, using her own wool jacket even, and the girl had only a few singed bits, and she looked good with her new short hair the next day. She did! It could've been worse, and it wasn't, because Nyla knew what to do in a crisis, and that was something they needed around schools.

Nyla didn't want to remember that scene too much but knew if she'd been there when Arena was accused—even if it was someone else's daughter who had been caught selling a mysterious powder—she would've seen the project through and had the substance in question tested. Definitely.

The truth was, Nyla hadn't given up volunteering back when Arena was in grade school—she'd been banned. Maybe they'd forgotten. For now, though, she wouldn't volunteer anyway because she had her own project, and that project was her daughter.

⟋ ⟍

At home, Nyla called the nonemergency police number. She went through the hoops, pushing one button to indicate her precinct, then another to tell the computer it wasn't a stolen vehicle problem. No, it wasn't domestic violence, which would mean pushing two. It wasn't assault, corporate crime, a traffic incident, or a food poisoning grievance. They had a whole menu of options.

It wasn't a mass cult suicide. She thought of the Temple Everlasting, that creepy dive, and hoped to never push button six.

When the option came up, she chose "evidence room"—"press eight"—and then listened to Muzak for a tooth-grindingly long time, but toughed it out. She listened to that shitty excuse for hold music because this, the phone call, was about Arena.

The Muzak cut. A man said, "Case number and date of complaint."

It caught Nyla off guard. She fumbled. "What?" She'd expected something more like a conversation.

He said it again. "Case number. Upper right hand. Sixteen digits, two letters."

She dug through her purse for the folded yellow paper they'd given her the day it all started. She read her case number off the slip. This was the path to the solution. She'd do it their way. Eye on the prize.

There was the light click and tap of a keyboard on the other end.

She asked, "Can we revisit evidence without bringing in lawyers?"

The man on the phone coughed. Then, in his tired voice, he said, "We show no evidence on hold associated with that report, ma'am."

She said, "None?"

He said, "Sorry. Nothing listed. Maybe it's still in processing."

The legal system and the school system both had their own paperwork, their own rules. Nyla made phone calls, memorizing the pattern of buttons to push to move through electronic instructions. She had a constant sound track of Muzak in her head. Out of all her calls, nobody could come up with "evidence," and at the same time, the school wouldn't agree to let Arena off the hook.

It was like she'd fallen, her feet moving in two different directions, all of it tangled. The paperwork was in process, Arena's name was on it, and there was a gap between the humans who worked at the school, the paper pushers in the district's legal offices, and the law, which was inhuman, disembodied, and looming.

Somebody, somewhere along the way, had made a human error. Somebody operated based on an assumption. Maybe it took more than one person, but nobody was willing to step up and fix the error, which could, at least theoretically, involve laying blame.

Another day, another call, a man from the local district attorney's office said, "The report says she was selling a controlled substance, ma'am."

Nyla said, "I know it does, but she wasn't."

She heard the crunch of food on the other end of the line, as though the man was eating chips. He took a deep breath. He said, "You'd want to get yourself a lawyer."

His words sunk to her stomach like rancid fat.

She'd worked with court-appointed lawyers after the wreck that killed her husband. Lawyers like that? They're budgeted for a limited amount of standard paperwork. You can't even talk to a lawyer without accruing a bill. To ask a lawyer to read a single sentence of e-mail could cost more than a hundred dollars. To send three lawyers the same short note was a fortune.

She wouldn't contact a lawyer if she could help it.

The DA's office man said, "I'd recommend you let your daughter go through the process. It's a small thing. It'll be like water running its course. She might even learn from it. You can have it expunged from the record later."

Nyla asked, "Does expunging take a lawyer?"

"It does." The man's voice was forgiving, but his facts stayed the same. After a pause, he said, "I've seen people spend more time and money fighting the law than it takes to just participate in it."

Posterior for All Posterity

On a porn shoot, you'd call it the "C-light" and use it to cast a cunt or a cock into the brightest glow. The C-light directs a viewer's eye, leads the way like the yellow brick road right to the money-maker. Dulcet had one hand on the black casing of what would be her C-light. She gave the piece a twist and a tap, and aimed the beam. She said, "Stand on the X."

Georgie, with Bella in her arms, shifted uncertainly to an X made out of duct tape on the floor.

Dulcet's photography studio was a rented room on the first floor of a warehouse building in southeast Portland. There was a black cloth backdrop rolled down and ready. The windows were covered with poster board and silver duct tape. Bitchy Bitch slept curled up in a well-worn overstuffed armchair.

Dulcet said, "Taking photos is about creating a relationship between the subject and the photographer. And we already have that. This'll be fabulous. Ready to strip?"

Georgie adjusted one of the nursing pads lodged in her cotton bra, cradled Bella, and looked around. "It's cold in here."

It wasn't that cold, though, really.

The walls were lined with pictures, a few framed and more un-framed, and then even more on the floor, leaning against the wall. There was one of a naked woman on a beach, her body echoing the planes of sand and driftwood. Another showed a curvy, nude blonde alone in her retro kitchen with a Wedgewood stove.

Georgie let her eyes rest on it and felt a pang of stove envy.

Even more, she had a hit of envy for the way all these women could stand naked and made-up and act casual.

Some of the photos were theatrical: There was a bare naked black-haired, ivory-skinned princess sprawled on a polished bar top, a cherry floating in an amber Manhattan, the tumbler tucked be-tween her thighs; in another, the light hit a woman's ass, close up, and the woman turned her head to look back at the camera and laugh, playing off an exaggerated angle between her narrow face, lower down, and her broad fanny, which loomed large.

Dulcet hauled out a space heater. The heater hummed its own song.

Georgie held her baby's wobbly head close, glad for the cotton sling that kept her daughter's gaze veiled. A newborn's eyes aren't strong, but a baby is wired to learn fast, and it didn't seem right to let a two-week-old girl baby look far into Dulcet's panopticon of female sex.

In one photo, a satin-skinned woman, dressed only in high heels, talked on an old-school phone with a long curly cord. She seemed to have gotten terribly tangled, fallen over in her tipsy shoes, then pulled a pillow under her stomach just enough to lift her rear and give a glimpse of an inner-thigh tattoo.

Georgie moved closer, inching away from the X on the floor. She said, "What's the story here?" She looked for the narrative line, the rhetorical angle. She read a picture the way she'd read a book.

"Story? That was a blast. That's the PE teacher."

Georgie looked at Dulcet. "The one who got you kicked out of the schools?"

Dulcet laughed in a way that meant yes, of course, and no at the same time. "I got myself kicked out the schools."

"The famous PE teacher." Georgie smelled Bella's head, her soft hair, the scent trapped and condensed inside the fabric of the dark, cradling sling.

Posing nude was esteem building. That's what people said, anyway. *The immergence of the gaze invests itself in the legitimation of the gendered body.* The photo shoot was Dulcet's postpartum gift to Georgie: a mother and child portrait, which sounded like a great plan back when Georgie pictured herself reclaiming her pre-pregnancy body, back when she still bothered to wash her hair.

She wanted pictures of Bella, so new and delicate. But photos of her own naked ass? That she could put off forever.

"All systems go," Dulcet sang.

Georgie hesitated. How did other women do this? This was not self-esteem building. Not at all.

Dulcet said, "Stand on the mark. We'll take a few test shots."

Georgie kept her clothes on and held Bella in the sling in front. She walked over the sheet on the floor, stepped onto the X, and claimed her fate.

Dulcet snapped away, then squinted at the image on the back of her digital Nikon, checking light and composition. She took another. Georgie smiled into the lens and winced under the flash.

"I vote you get naked. At least get the baby out of that hammock. You'll look totally hot."

Georgie said, "Do we have to go for 'hot'? Maybe something more Madonna-ish."

Dulcet lowered her camera. "Madonna? That's what you want?"

"Madonna-like." Georgie nodded and lifted her baby from the sling. Bella was in a sweet pink terry onesie, with even her little feet covered.

Dulcet asked, "Like mid-eighties Madonna, when she was cute and round?"

Georgie gave her daughter a pat, as though to say "All good," and the eco-unfriendly disposable diaper crinkled beneath her hand. She said, "I mean, like early AD Madonna, the timeless one. Mother and child?"

Georgie wore a pink, nearly skin-color dress that she imagined as a drape, a Grecian wrap, or maybe even the plain cloth garb favored by Élisabeth Vigée-Lebrun, the French painter at the center of her dissertation. Vigée-Lebrun was famous for making everyone look beautiful, even though she dared dress her subjects in muslin during the era of lace, the rococo days, in the Palace of Versailles.

In the photos around the room, Dulcet had made everyone look gorgeous. Still, Georgie wanted that muslin.

Dulcet put her camera on a cabinet. She came forward and lifted Georgie's hair, and Georgie shivered. "If you want classical, definitely strip." She unzipped the zipper on the back of Georgie's dress. "Naked is as timeless and sacred as it gets."

The synthetic material gave no protest. The dress slithered down Georgie's shoulders. She still had the baby sling on, like a beauty queen's sash, and the dress caught on it, not yet fallen.

Around the room all those naked women laughed and leered. They paraded their confidence—Esteem! Built from posing naked!—smiled at Georgie, and dared her to smile back. She cowered. Bitchy Bitch lifted her head.

What kind of role model was Georgie if she couldn't pose naked—couldn't stand proud in her meat suit, as the saying goes?

Dulcet lifted the sling to take it away. Georgie let her and maneuvered Bella through the sling, though she held on to her dress with one hand. She asked, "Do you ever take photos of naked men?" Her voice came out a little thin and desperate, vying for a distraction.

Dulcet put the baby sling on her filing cabinet. She glanced at the lights and kicked the step stool to another corner to adjust another one. "Not often. With men, the whole focus is on the cock, you know? Erect, curved, relaxed. That's it. With women, you can find more complex planes, invert conventions, find a cultural charge."

Georgie hid behind her dress and her baby, uneasy with that cultural charge. Her nursing bra was heavy cotton, decorated with snaps where function trumped form. Worse than the bra, she still wore granny panties hoisted over her C-section scar.

Dulcet disappeared behind a tall rolling bookcase that served as a room divider, then came back out with an old cotton battery-operated jiggling baby chair on a metal frame. "Voilà!" She plunked it down. When she turned a switch it played a slow and garbled song. "Let's start with a few of just you, until the room warms up."

Georgie walked over to the bouncy chair. "What do you have this around for?" She put Bella down. The girl didn't fuss. Without her baby in her arms, she felt naked already. Dulcet was stripping Georgie of props.

"I photograph some moms," Dulcet said, and picked up her camera again. "You don't have this much rock-solid sexual energy and not make a few babies. Now, you ready?"

"I'm fat."

Dulcet snapped a picture. She said, "You're gorgeous."

Bitchy Bitch jumped off the chair and settled in closer, blinking big eyes. What's more powerful, the male gaze, or a blinking bitch's calm stare?

Dulcet let the camera hang around her neck and ducked behind her wall-shelf again. "I've got a little something to put you at ease."

Georgie could hear her dig through a box. A little *something*. What did that mean? Georgie called over, "I'm still not drinking. And I'm staying away from pills. All of them."

Dulcet came back around the corner tossing a silk scarf. It caught on the air, hung, then fell without going much distance. Georgie bent and picked it up, still holding her dress in place. As she bent she felt her bottom grow larger—expanding! Impossibly large. Her knees pressed together, she felt like a hippo. This body! She didn't love it.

There, she admitted it to herself: She didn't love her body. Was that such a crime?

She reached one hand down in front and pulled the damp nursing pads out of her bra. Her nipples were sweaty and cramped. She tossed the pads out of the way, off the backdrop. She reached back and unhooked her bra, under her dress. She'd known Dulcet twenty years, since before she became Dulcet Marvel, back when she was Tina Stanton and got her first job as a waitress at a French restaurant. They'd gone camping together. They'd been naked at hot springs. It was different with a camera. She'd have to trust Dulcet's eye.

It really was about trust.

Georgie stared at the robust ta-tas and damp love lips of the women on the walls. "So are these all about developing relationships? Photographer and subject?"

Dulcet took a breath. She thought about the question. "Sometimes, secretly, I think maybe really it's only about my relationship to me."

Georgie let the scarf unfold. It was a wide scarf, and long, though sheer. She let her dress drop. The cold air was a chill.

Dulcet said, "A naked woman's body is a commodity, as natural and common as homegrown pot. Strip everything away, like a stripper, and you've got this radical object. Take a picture of a woman's back, it's art. Show the vertebrae and ribs, it's architecture. If you take the same picture from the front, straight on, it's confrontational. Spread her legs, and the photo's illegal to show in public, most places.

"And I am one. That's the part I can't get my head around. I am that object."

Georgie reached a hand down and slid her fuchsia granny panties to her knees. She stepped out of them.

Dulcet said, "I've found two galleries to show my stuff. Both times, the show closed early."

Georgie said, "And they sold out, right?"

Dulcet said, "Yes, that, too." She snapped a photo of Georgie naked and veiled.

Georgie tried to relax. She tossed her head back. She twirled the scarf experimentally.

Dulcet said, "These'll be a gift for Humble. Imagine he's here—that he's the one you're posing for."

Ha! Georgie hardly thought Humble would care. He was a simmering pot on the stove, the way he skulked around the house these days.

Dulcet said, "He's one of the good ones." Then she lowered her camera. She looked over the top of it. "What is that?"

"What?" Georgie looked behind her. Then she looked at her own front, at her soft stomach and pale thighs. Her scar was a red grin along the top of her pubic bone. She'd only just started to relax. Now the anxiety meter shot up again.

Dulcet said, "Above your ass, next to your tattoo?"

Jesus. Embarrassing! What was it? Georgie twisted to one side. She brushed her fingers over her skin and ran a hand down between her own legs.

Dulcet walked over to touch one finger lightly on the back of Georgie's hip. "It's huge."

Georgie twisted around the other way until she could see a bruise the size of a softball, purple and yellow and faded at the edges like a storm cloud.

Dulcet traced a line up Georgie's back. "And you've skinned

your spine. In another kind of shoot, we could use it as a prop, it's that dramatic."

There was nothing between naked Georgie and the world. "I fell down the stairs."

Dulcet let out a long whistle.

She found an oversized tackle box. She opened one drawer, then closed it again and opened another. She took out a tube of makeup, a container of powder, and a few triangular sponges. She dabbed pale green concealer on her fingertips. "I'll Photoshop it out, but it'll be easier if we lighten it now."

Georgie let Dulcet paint concealer on the round backside of her hip and dot cool makeup along her vertebrae. Dulcet asked, "Does that hurt?"

"No." Georgie closed her eyes. She felt nerves radiate a hot pain under Dulcet's fingers, and then again as Dulcet swiped her skin with a sponge.

Dulcet said, "Has Humble seen it?"

Georgie kept her eyes closed, without answering. The fingers on her back could be anyone's fingers, taking care.

Why go into it?

When Georgie opened her eyes, baby Bella, in her pink onesie, was a sweet rosebud there on the floor, in her bouncy chair. She was pink and fresh, still figuring out how to lift her own head, a newborn baby girl. Bella smiled her small, toothless smile, glad to be part of the world, happy to be alive. She was beautiful. Georgie's heart ached. Her skin warmed under the glow of the C-light as it poured light like an artificial sun kissing her bruised back.

Sentencing

Arena had been raised to walk abandoned dogs at the pound—beautiful dogs they couldn't take home. She'd planted trees every Arbor Day, though the trees mostly died the same season. She, her mom, and her sister had a tradition of forcing their way into Thanksgiving meals at Sisters of the Road, a shelter where Nyla thought it was edifying for a kid to serve a holiday dinner to black-toothed drunks.

Community service didn't faze her—but what was up with the idea of unearned punishment? Sure, she sold Crystal Light on school grounds, and she sold those individual packages marked NOT TO BE SOLD INDIVIDUALLY. So what? Lesson learned.

But no. Here was community service coming at her again. Her assignment: litter. Also, meetings where she'd meet other losers.

Each meeting cost $75. If she was one minute late, they wouldn't let her in. If she missed a meeting, she'd have to pay anyway and then pay again at the makeup session. It was rigged.

Her mom was totally lame about it. She'd said, "Take notes. Keep a journal. Later, it'll all seem like a great story."

They were still trying to fight the accusations, but the truth was, Nyla could not afford a lawyer. Instead, she gave Arena a bound book made out of recycled paper, with a recycled cover, and a recycled card where she'd written, "Keep an Attitude of Gratitude. Life is an adventure! I love you always."

An Attitude of Platitudes.

Nyla would quote a teacher she'd had: "Interesting stories happen to people who can tell them." Arena was supposed to collect interesting stories.

Arena wrote "My Prison Journal" on the cover in silver Sharpie.

On Nyla's bumper, another sticker declared NONVIOLENT, NOT SILENT. Arena had never noticed how ineffectual her mother's political opinions were until now. Her mama had no power.

Nyla gave Arena a ride to the work crew pickup station. As she saw her off, onto a county bus, she waved and said, "See you at dinner! Remember, it's all material, right? Tell me how it goes."

The bus was short and yellow, like a school bus but without the name of any school or district on the side. Inside it smelled like sweat and loserdom. It smelled like old backpacks, lost lunches, and guys who needed to shower. It was all guys, and her.

On the short bus there was no way-back, no far-back, no place different from the front, no place to use her hiding skills. She sat in the second seat and put her forehead against the dirty glass of the window.

In *Red Azalea*, Anchee Min, assigned the role of peasant under Chairman Mao, was taken away in a truck, starting from someplace called "People's Square" in China.

Was this any different? Arena was assigned the role of criminal.

Anchee Min wrote, "My family stood in front of me, as if taking a dull picture. It was a picture of sadness, a picture of never the same."

Arena replayed her mom's words: "See you at dinner. Tell me how it goes!" Her mom seemed almost happy, like this was a scholarship to science camp or some extended writing exercise.

The bus took them to a barren hellhole strip outside of Tigard, a suburb. They got out and walked along a culvert on the side of the highway. A coordinator handed out orange reflective vests, plastic garbage bags, and gloves. He said, "Stay three feet apart minimum. No talking, no breaks."

The bus took off. The man in charge got busy with his iPhone, moved away, and lit a cigarette.

Picking up garbage was as easy as picking blueberries in season: McDonald's wrappers, Big Gulp cups, cigarettes, diapers, soda cans, a pair of pants, three pairs of underwear—two ladies' and one pair of boxers.

Arena had never touched what she still thought of clinically as a "penis," and had no ready list of familiar pet names, stories about banana shapes and commas. She heard those stories, but she was a loner and a listener and school was one big reality TV show where up until getting expelled she'd been cast as an extra.

Now, she held a blue and twisted rubber condom in her gloved hands, then put it in her bag.

How many other hands had slid into the work gloves Arena wore? It was cold out, but the gloves were rubber and her hands started to sweat. The reflective vest smelled like old cigarettes. She was in the costume of somebody else.

Arena could write that in her new journal: "Punished for crimes I never committed, made to wear the costume of a criminal."

The guy picking up trash beside her inched closer, breaking the three-feet-apart rule.

He said, "Hey. You new?"

She heard him, over the rush of traffic. She didn't answer, though.

He said, "I've been here three months." He kicked his foot through the grass. "I'm an expert." He walked right past bottles, cans, and chip bags.

She picked up a brown paper grocery bag and put it in her plastic garbage bag. If her mom saw this, she'd get on the city about recycling the trash. She'd do more about that environmental injustice than she was doing to get Arena off the chain gang.

The guy said, "You find good stuff. Last week I found this awesome bong, no shit."

Arena looked at him then. He was tall and thin, with skin like coffee ice cream.

"It was, like . . ." He held his hands apart, his plastic bag swinging in one, tongs in the other. He whispered, "Had to smuggle it out in my pants. Looked like I had a woody so big I couldn't bend my leg, but none of these homophobes wanted to pat me down."

Arena had to laugh. She said, "You did not."

He nodded. "I did. I'm AKA."

She said, "That's not a name."

He said, "It's mine. You can call me AK, like the assault rifle." He made a gesture as though to gun invisible people down.

He was pretty and girlish and handsome all at once. He seemed kind of gay, but also like he was flirting.

She said, "I'm Arena."

He said, "Beautiful name."

"If you like sports." She practiced looking him in the eyes. His eyes were so dark they were all one shade, almost black. His hair was shaggy, a short haircut that'd grown out, and his cheekbones were high and narrow.

He asked, "What'd you do to get here?"

"Sold Crystal Light to kids."

That cracked him up. He said, "Jesus! She's dangerous." He turned to the guy behind him, a red-haired slacker with tired eyes. The wind and rush off passing semis stole their voices.

Arena's hair blew in the freeway corridor's draft. She asked, "You?"

He said, "Knocking over old ladies."

The red-haired guy said, "Knocking up. And wasn't that your mom?"

They were clustered together now.

AKA gave his friend a fake jab, a swing to his jaw that only pushed through air. His teeth were white, his fingers long. He was so tall and thin, it made him seem fragile as an insect, like his arm could come off under his heavy coat. He said, "I robbed 'em blind, and cashed in. It's a cakewalk."

He giggled in a way that was no kind of threat.

Arena said, "Right."

He said, "Serious."

Their leader marched through the tall grass, wheezing when he reached them. He made a gesture with his hands, like swimming frog-style, pushing the air, telling them to move apart.

Arena nodded, and moved away. She let the roar of traffic fill the lull in voices, and disentangled another mangled condom from the scrub grass, then another pair of underwear. Who would lose their underwear on a freeway? How did that happen?

Low-Hanging Fruit

$\mathcal{D}$ulcet called Sarah and left a jumbled message: "God, I think I dropped my underwear somewhere along the freeway!" Her recorded voice launched into a story, even as Sarah deleted it. She didn't have time! Now was the time to be ruthless, to play hardball—or blue balls, or whatever it took.

Why wouldn't Ben get his sperm checked? It'd been on their to-do list for months. Late one night, in bed, she'd asked him if he was scared to find out. She said, "It's something we can address."

He said, "I haven't had time."

But time was what they were losing, along with fertility. She was the one with the ticking clock, eggs, and ovaries.

He was afraid of doctors—afraid to learn the limits of his own body.

She'd be the most loving, nurturing, proud mother on the planet even if she had to kill somebody to get there.

Reproduction is not passive. Ben didn't get it. Adaptation occurs under stress. Four miscarriages had taught her a few lessons. Everybody knows about the black widow and the mantis, insects that eat their mates. On a relative scale, Ben would be fine with whatever happened.

Outside town, fall chinook were making their way back to rivers to spawn and die. *Spawn and die, spawn and die!* Their stomachs would disintegrate while the fish were alive, starving the host bodies, making room for eggs or sperm.

Sarah was old!

She'd spawn if it killed her.

She drove her Subaru down Martin Luther King, Jr., Boulevard. On the radio, a man with a clipped British accent reported that toxic levels of vitamin A in an energy drink had killed nine people. A computer error had moved a decimal point one space over and each individual serving was accidentally filled with enough vitamin A to blow out a liver.

Nine people?

Did nine people matter on a planet crawling with seven billion poorly evolved primates who called themselves human?

We could lose a billion and still stock the grade schools and temp agencies, keep Starbucks hopping. We could lose over three billion, almost half, and only be back to a 1970s population. Who ever missed the current crowd, the masses, before they were born? These days people stood in lines around the block for brunch, for movies, for a free dinner in a church or an overpriced meal downtown. More and more, there was always the threat of some population vigilante with a gun out to cull the herd, a psycho unleashed under the pressure of crowds.

With half as many people, though, humans had still been, apparently, expendable enough for World War II and Vietnam. Procreation and destruction walk hand in hand. With fewer than two billion people, it seems we afforded and weathered the losses of World War I, sixteen million people. The way to stop war would be to stop having babies, stop raising foot soldiers.

Sarah was only one of the masses. She knew it. Her child would be one more.

Reproduction is about survival of the species, but to an individual animal it's about the nuclear family, the survival of biological offspring. The rest of the population is competition.

She'd be a loving mama.

The other humans, the ones who burned through fossil fuels, jammed the express lane at the grocery store, faked their way through the carpool lanes, and pissed in the communal well? They could screw themselves.

She snapped the radio off. When she found a prescription bottle on her car's console, she drove with her arms on the wheel and worked with both hands to open a childproof cap. It was her most recent post-miscarriage anxiety prescription.

Sarah had, by now, completely given in to pills. Doctors wrote out prescriptions like love notes, trying to turn her into Dulcet—to make her not care. The pills helped! In a warbling, temporary way. They helped her to focus her concerns. And with the help of those pills, she resolved to *spawn or die, spawn or die, spawn or die.* She sang the words to herself.

She was relaxed and desperate at the same time.

She chipped the side off a tablet of Klonopin with her teeth, ignored the dosing instructions, and instead nibbled pills all day long, a little now, a little later. The smallest flake of a pill on her tongue, and the world mattered less. Time mattered less. She'd started to see the benefit: a military dose of Klonopin with red wine, dished out like a free lunch, would end the troubles in the Gaza Strip, no joke.

Why didn't somebody prescribe mood pills for whole countries?

Her car was speckled with pink, pale yellow, and white pill crumbs, Klonopin, diazepam, Vicodin.

Martin Luther King, Jr., Boulevard was lined with junkies and hipsters.

Sarah couldn't stand their passivity.

She couldn't stand that she had to get older, and there was no way to stop it.

A shaggy-haired waif on the side of the road held up a battered and grease-stained cardboard sign: PREGNANT. NO JOB.

Bragging! Totally.

The street corners were littered with the ever-present stacks of free stuff, and today most of it was baby gear: cribs, strollers, changing tables, and car seat carriers. These stacks of junk arranged themselves into nurseries, baby-friendly spaces artfully waiting at each curb. Each one said, "Our child is off to Harvard! Have our garbage!"

At a stoplight, Sarah idled next to a free pile. A mobile jutting out of a box turned in the wind and played a soft, discordant song.

That song, that noise! It was the Empty Nest song. The free piles mocked her.

This was the deep life pain of snow leopards at the zoo. Those two animals would have a better chance at avoiding extinction if they were asexually reproductive, making autonomous biological choices. Instead they were locked in a cage, one with eggs, the other holding the sperm, at a standoff in their collaborations.

And this is what bothered her about Ben: his foot-dragging.

If she were a lesbian lizard of the desert, a whiptail, there'd be no problem: The whole tribe is female, all potentially reproductive. The lizards put on a fake sort of sex show, a physical routine sans sperm. Only the lizards who do the sex dance lay any eggs at all.

Sarah could totally fake sex—straight, queer, three-way, you name it—if it was the dance that brought about a baby.

They had ten weeks until the doctor said they could try again. Her last egg might drop in that span. Then what? She'd be old. It'd be over. They'd donate their baby books to the library's fund-raising book sale. Ben would pat her on the back and look at her in his apologetic way and they'd go to the Ringside for a steak dinner. They'd have mixed drinks and talk about saving for a trip to Hawaii or Thailand.

They'd be old people.

She was a problem solver. She could see the problem of mortality coming from way down the road. To do nothing was a maladaptive survival strategy. Even a lowly burr in a field knows how to scatter seed.

Soon enough it'd be summer, and somewhere the summer aphids, those tiny green specks, would reproduce without the need for all this partnering, finagling, relationship building. Summer aphids, like Christ, are born from virgin mothers. The first mother in a lineage is a fundatrix, a foundress.

Sarah should be the fundatrix of her own line.

She drove past day laborers waiting for work on the side of the road. Men waited for yard work, building sites, anything unskilled. They visibly waited out their lives in hope of work. She and the men had that in common: forced passivity.

So many men. So little work.

So many swimming sperm under faded denim.

She slowed her car, ignoring the traffic on her bumper. She looked at the men, because they were men—looked at their shoulders and faces and thick, dark hair. Some were tall, others weren't. Some had awful teeth. Most looked strong.

Every one of them was a walking sperm bank.

Who defined the limits of "day labor"?

They could help her; she'd help them. She had money. It was cheap labor, no paperwork. It was only the cost of copulation, that human risk.

Survival of the species is about creative adaptation.

Where did thriving sperm cluster? The day laborers were rugged men with hard lives, troubles that showed in their skin and teeth. But there, in with the broken and worn, was one man with a Burt Reynolds mustache. He wasn't handsome, but he had confidence. Then she spotted a dark James Dean. His hair held a shine like the water of the river, that churning, toxic ribbon of the Willamette that cut the city in half only a block away.

Behind the day laborers a building had been imploded. There was an empty lot full of rubble wrapped in cyclone fencing. Sarah had driven that street for years, but couldn't remember what building stood there.

That'd be her own life story: here for a while, then gone, and who'd remember Sarah? But to see these men selling their bodies, their skills, on the side of the road, gave her a new sense of possibility. One man held a guitar. He handed it to another guy when a car slowed. She pulled to the curb, still a ways back. She watched him lean in to talk through the passenger-side window of a stranger's car.

She could do that: pull over, talk to them. They'd come to her.

She circled the block, hoping for a red light, a chance to scan the crew without swerving. She drove slowly, ignoring the honking horns—those mechanical howls of domesticated primates—and passing the line of waiting men a third time. Then the man with the guitar stretched. His guitar leaned against his leg like a devoted pet. He looked good, solid and relaxed.

Relaxed was a trick that didn't exist in her family gene pool so far.

Sarah was high. Those nibbles on pills added up. Who kept

track? She was high and desperate. The man with the guitar leaned against the chain-link fence, his shoulders big and rounded.

She pulled over to the side of the road and powered down her passenger-side window. The pills whispered, "It's okay." More than okay, it was brilliant. It was survival. *"Hola!"* She waved a hand.

How awkward: Spanish or English? Her Spanish was lame. She put a smile on her face and pointed, picking out her man. It was that easy.

He left his guitar on the curb and walked to her car window.

"Quiere trabajar?" Sarah opted for the formal verb. She admired any language that offered a built-in distance.

He nodded. *"Sí, sí.* Yes. You have work?"

Oh yes, she had work.

"How many men you want?" he asked. His eyes were deep brown, with long lashes. They weren't Ben's eyes, not at all. She pressed on.

"Solo uno," she said. *"Solo usted."* It wasn't clear if Spanish was even his language.

He gestured with a hand toward the open city. "I have tools." Somewhere, out there.

He had the tool she needed. "No worries. Let's go. *Vámonos."* He got in the car. He sat, then lifted himself from the car seat and ran a hand underneath himself, coming up with a Klonopin vial.

"Sorry." She took the vial from him. Their fingers brushed. His hands were rough, his fingers short and thick.

She watched the road. What came next? The man was big in her car. His shoulders blocked the side window as he twisted to look at her. It was like bringing a Christmas tree home! He was bigger than he looked on the lot. Traffic urged her forward, in a stream of busy people driving with conviction.

The man rested his hands uneasily on the wide expanse of his thighs. He could strangle her. What had she done?

His thighs pressed tight against his clothes from inside, ropy with muscle. Sarah felt her cell phone in her coat pocket. That phone, with a loaded speed dial, was an umbilical cord to everyone she cared about.

What now—take him home? This was adaptation through experimentation. She saw a car wash on the side of the road and pulled in, buying time to gather her medicated thoughts.

TOUCHLESS, the sign said. A touchless car wash.

She pulled up to the booth and handed the car wash attendant a prepaid card. He punched the card and handed it back, keeping his cap low as he leaned back into his booth and disappeared.

The man looked out the window, as though a parking lot full of self-serve auto vacs was scenic. The sky was the mottled gray threat of an Oregon winter rain.

If Ben were in the car, he'd say, "Why wash the car when it's getting ready to rain?"

Sarah would answer, "Why eat, when you'll be hungry later?" It always rained in Portland in the winter.

Ben pretty much was there in the car with them, the way she heard this conversation in her head. The man she'd picked up looked at the sky, and Sarah could tell he'd agree with Ben.

She shoved her punch card in the ashtray, alongside Klonopin crumbs. One whole pill lay there round and white, as promising as an uncut cake. Sarah asked, "What's your name?"

"Frank." There was the flash of a gold tooth halfway back. His feet were in worn Adidas. The white leather was like raku, it was so covered in cracks. If things worked out, she'd buy him shoes.

Frank?

It was possible she'd picked up the only Germanic day laborer in town.

She followed yellow arrows on the ground, around a semicircle, toward the maw of the wash.

She steered the car onto the short track. A teenage employee came through a narrow doorway, waving a hand for her to move forward. She pulled in slowly.

"Pull up, pull up, pull up," his hand beckoned. When he flashed the flat of his open palm, she took her foot off the brake and put the car in neutral. She moved as though it were all according to this kid's plan—fated on the lines of his creased palm—not hers.

Jets of water started as a trickle then grew stronger. The jets themselves lifted as though by the force of the water, and turned toward the car on mechanical arms. The car lurched. Sarah kept her hands on the steering wheel, even as she leaned against the door and turned to appraise Frank.

Inside the car grew dark. Frank, cast into the dusk inside the wash, tapped his fingers against his thigh. The sound of his breath disappeared, subsumed into the louder voice of machinery, mechanical arms, and water pressure.

This was a fine first date, the short version of a drive-in movie, just long enough to smell each other in the compressed space of the car. It was an exercise in intimacy.

It was a trespass, against Ben.

Sarah asked, "You have family around here?"

Water beat against the roof and the sides of the car like a storm. The car was a private cabin on a rainy night, a weekend getaway. It was Noah's ark in a car wash flood and they were two in a pair. There was a pressure in the dark; even the air felt limited and tense.

Hot foam covered the car windows.

"Yes, family." He pointed in a circle around his head. Family around. His breath was the warm smell of a jar of pennies.

Family didn't mean a wife. Not necessarily. They were in the heart of the wash. In the dark, in the gears, with the windows covered, and equipment up close, all sounds blocked by the hum of machinery, the world was gone.

"Kids?"

"No, no kids." He smiled as he said it. She almost believed him. "You?"

If her car were to slide off the track they'd be jammed in the machinery, trapped at the mercy of slow-witted teenagers. She'd marry her day laborer—a marriage of convenience, married by gears, crushed together.

Then he opened her glove box and looked inside. He shuffled through her papers. What the hell was he doing? This was too forward. There was nothing in there except Burgerville napkins, tampons, and car records. She reached to close it.

His hand was in the way.

He gave her a smile, showing his gold teeth. Who had she invited into her car?

This risk was the new cost of copulation in her survival strategy. The Klonopin made her head thick and had started to give her a headache. Either that or the Vicodin was wearing off. She ran her hand over the console between the seats until she found a pink crumb to slide between her teeth.

He closed the glove box, in his own time. She refused to flinch.

A car wash compresses time and space; it takes forever and then is over in minutes. The dark inside the car lifted. The windshield cleared. The black gaping mouths of wide hoses nodded up and down like snake heads, blasting the hiss of hot air over the car. Six hands reached for them; three attendants, palms draped in soft cloths. A girl with a long ponytail pressed herself against the side of the car. A boy patted the fender.

The world was bright and painted with rainbows in the prisms of chemically tinted water, a spray of polish illuminating the windshield. The track ended; the car dropped to the pavement. Sarah shifted into gear.

She was still the driver, and the driver is in charge. She pulled into traffic and moved down Martin Luther King, Jr., Boulevard. The day laborers would be there again the next day and the day after that.

This didn't have to be the end of anything.

For now, she reached the patch of sidewalk where they clustered, pulled over, gave Frank twenty dollars, unlocked the doors, and let him go.

Energy Fields

After work crew Arena took AKA to the Temple Everlasting. His long grasshopper legs barely fit behind the seat in front of them on the city bus, and he sprawled into the aisle. Arena asked, "Do your parents wait for you to come home, or whatever?"

"Parents?" He blinked, like she'd woken up a sleeping corner of his brain.

At the temple, Arena pushed open the front door and called hello to cluttered rooms. The battered TV was midsentence, in its guppy routine: ". . . able to live upstream from the threat of violence . . ."

AKA said, "Upstream from violence?" He slapped a hand on the Sony. When he turned the old-style knob to switch channels, the guppy track screwed up, making a crash of static.

AKA was violence; the guppies were fried.

Arena said, "Don't touch it. We don't know how that works."

"It's a TV. I grew up with one." He flipped the channels, then turned the whole thing around to mess with switches on the back.

She looked for a remote, and while she did, Mack emerged from a back room. He said, "Arena! What're you doing here?"

"Meet my friend."

"Dude, I busted your set."

Arena offered a nervous giggle. "It's not broken. Can we use the camera? Let's see AK's energy field." Arena pushed AKA forward and held his arm like they'd come in for prom photos.

Mack only nodded a tight nod, like he had checked something off a bitter list.

AKA said, "Nah, I don't know if I'm into that." He seemed more gangly than ever in the cluttered store. "Maybe I'm, like, a vampire, right? What's vampire energy?"

Arena assured him, "Your energy is great."

Mack unplugged the guppy TV, hoisted it off the stand, and carried it to his back room. "Arena, I'm not a photo booth at the county fair. This is science. You don't play with testing energy fields. Besides, the Kirlian machine's broken."

Mack came back out with a broom and swept the floor like he was beating it into submission. He swept where they stood and then again where they moved to. He swept until AKA moved away from Arena, and then he swept AKA's feet.

AKA asked, "What's that smell?"

Arena sniffed. The place smelled like leaking pipes and molding floorboards.

Mack said, "Weird. It just started when you got here." He dabbed at the floor with his broom, pushing dirt into the air and in a pile.

Arena said, "That dust in the air? That's matter transferred, like energy."

Mack kept up his work. "You're a doubter."

Arena said, "No! I mean it. I see it everywhere now."

"Right." He swept closer to AKA's feet and AKA stepped back, again and again, until he'd backed them all the way to the door.

AKA opened the door and went outside, and Arena followed. She waved a good-bye that Mack ignored. Like, when did his job get so busy? But it was beautiful out, they were free of the musty temple, there was a Cajun bistro down the block with an oil drum–style barbecue out front making a smoky cloud across the sidewalk, and the city smelled like grilled shrimp.

AKA said, "Wow. Talk about a negative energy field. That dude is gone."

They passed a corner bar where hipsters played pool inside.

The door was open. They heard the crack of balls and smelled beer. There was a 1914 church, then a second hipster bar, then a gangster church with a PT Cruiser complete with flames outside. It was that kind of neighborhood: young drunks and people looking to be saved. She asked, "What do you do? When you're not picking up trash."

He said, "I'm in a band."

Of course! Who wasn't? Phone poles were wrapped in rusted staples and band flyers, a show every night.

"Eco-emo. Angry songs about the trashed environment."

Arena said, "Really? My mom'd love it."

"She should come to a show," he said. "Maybe you'd come with her. We've got this one tune, 'Whose the Nero Now?' I totally wrote it. It'll make you cry. Feel. Break up with your boyfriend."

She said, "I don't have a boyfriend."

"Wow. That was easy," he said.

"Ha." Arena ducked into a junk store and AKA followed. It was all random resale: buttons and Barbie dolls and picture frames sold as art supplies. A woman with a thick waist, a heavy sweater, and a head of hair like tumbleweed sat on the floor sorting through a bucket of rocks. In a dusty back corner, a bolt of white mesh fabric rested against the wall, caught what little light there was, and glowed in its plastic white aura like a synthetic ghost. To Arena's eyes it was white as heaven, even with a waffle-shoe footprint on one spot, keeping it tied to the earth. It was perfect. "How much for that?"

The woman put her hands beside her on the floor, pushed off, heaved herself into an upright position, then lumbered over to the mesh.

She dug in her apron pocket until she found a stack of Post-it Notes and a ballpoint pen. She wrote "$5.00" on one page and stuck it to the mesh. "Sound good?"

Arena hoisted the bolt of fabric to her shoulder.

When the woman moved behind the cash register, she checked the price on her own Post-it as if she hadn't just written the note. Arena dug in her backpack, found a five, and handed it over.

They walked down Martin Luther King, Jr., Boulevard. Arena balanced the bolt of netting on her shoulder. A stray strip trailed her like a veil. "I've been looking for exactly this."

This mesh was Arena's mosquito net made visible. It was An-chee Min's mosquito net, from *Red Azalea*. Arena said, "AKA, if I tell you what it is, will you help me with it?"

Arena wanted a partner. She didn't know how to ask.

He said, "Tell me."

"It'll be an installation. *Synthetic Heaven*, I call it." She couldn't look at him. Then she did look his way, looked him straight and steady in his dark eyes, though it made her own eyes water. It was a muscle-building exercise, to hold his gaze. It was an exercise in personal energy. She collected her words in her head before saying them out loud. Finally, fast and soft, she said, "All you have to do is be naked."

Georgie's Big Break

*T*he day of Lit Expedition, Georgie woke up before Humble and the baby—woke up like a kid on Christmas, ready for her first day back at the work she was born to do.

By the time Humble got up, when Bella started to cry, Georgie was already out of the shower and drinking coffee. So many days lately her head had been cloudy. From morning until noon could pass in a blurry haze, one diaper change after another. Nursing hormones make a woman's brain less engaged in aspirations. Georgie had read that. And she was prone to barometric migraines. Under a constantly cloudy Oregon winter sky, she could feel the atmospheric pressure shift inside her head. Today her head was clear, with a chance of thinking. Beautiful.

"Big plans?" Hum asked. He scratched his stomach and reached for the coffeepot. He'd forgotten.

That was okay.

Georgie didn't need Humble's validation; her plans were important to her. It was a certain kind of peevish wife's role to begrudge him his own forgetfulness, and she thought of Mrs. Joe Gargery, that belittling drudge, that cautionary tale of an unwilling wife and surrogate mother in the gendered society of *Great Expectations. I may truly say I've never had this apron of mine off since born you were.*

"Lit Expedition," Georgie said, calmly. She had Bella in one arm and was patting the girl's back. "Arena's coming to babysit." She touched her iPod in its docking station. It was already cued to her sound track, and blasted Brahms's Academic Festival Overture through the house.

"Jesus, that's loud." Humble was puffy-eyed. He moved like an older man, totally hungover.

"It's good for Bella and good for us."

Then she remembered: Nurse Ratched, in *Cuckoo's Nest*, blasted music through the psych ward. Agh! But this wasn't a ward. It was her house. Humble wasn't a patient. He could go out if he wanted to.

Anyway, maybe it was time somebody rewrote that book from Nurse Ratched's point of view.

Upstairs, with the overture still playing, she put Bella in a rocking swing, then squeezed into her best pre-pregnancy skirt. She let her shirt hang out to camouflage the snug waist. It was a gorgeous and generous indigo blue, spun hemp and silk. A lucky, luxury shirt.

Today would be Bella's first experience with an actual sitter.

It would be Georgie's day out on her own.

The rocking swing ticked like a metronome, counting down the seconds.

The thought of leaving her baby in anybody else's care made Georgie half-sick. Really, it did. But she'd see it through. People did this all the time.

The doorbell rang. Humble was in the bathroom, his morning office, and Georgie gave Bella a second look—the girl was buckled in, half-asleep, safe—then ran to get the door. Arena was on time, thank God. She was wearing a tiny T-shirt that said I ❤ OLD PEO-PLE. Her jeans were striped jeggings. The girl was tall and thin and made being human in a human body look easy; everything fit and hung and tucked and moved in all the right places.

Georgie felt suddenly short and fat and a little oily. A minute ago, in the mirror, she'd looked fine. Now, she was definitely not sleek. She smiled, invited Arena in, and led her back upstairs. "You've changed a diaper before?"

Arena said, "Not really."

Not really? What did that mean? The girl was still in trouble for selling crystal meth, but Nyla swore up and down that was all a mistake, that it was Crystal Light. Expelled over Crystal Light?

Highly unlikely.

"But you've given a baby a bottle? I pumped fresh milk. She'll be hungry when she wakes up."

Arena shook her head. Her hair slid down over one eye. "Couldn't be too hard."

Downstairs, the front door opened then closed. Humble had left for the day.

Georgie stared at Arena. She'd changed Arena's diapers. She'd helped give this grown girl a bottle. How was that even possible? Arena ran a hand through her loose hair, but instead of moving it out of her face, she drew it to her lips and slid that forelock between her teeth. She was like a tall five-year-old.

An abandoning mother isn't a mother. Leave your kid behind and words like this will forever sing in that child-animal's mind. Leave, and you don't get it back, you don't get to erase the mistake, it doesn't go away. Georgie sang the words back to her own absent mother. To leave for a conference when Bella was so small? That'd be a tiny bit of what Georgie experienced when her mother left for Malaysia.

She couldn't do it. "You know what? Come with me." Georgie bent and started packing a diaper bag. "Come to the conference, hold Bella, keep her calm, stay close. I'll do what I'm there for." She'd introduce speakers and network.

"Really?" Arena slouched even more, a fragile flower wilting.

But it would be good.

If the baby needed to nurse, Georgie would be there. If Arena bought or sold drugs, Georgie would be there, too. Right?

She tucked extra disposable diapers in her diaper bag. Yes, disposable diapers! She used them. Each diaper took five hundred years to degrade in a landfill, longer than Oregon had been a state, longer than the United States had existed so far. The grandchildren of her grandchildren's grandchildren would live with that waste, but so what? Today she needed the godsend of high-tech diapering.

Arena slunk along the wall, down a hallway to the dining room. She followed Georgie. "So, what exactly are you doing at this thing?" Her teeth were white and charming in their awkward alignment. Her lips were doll lips.

"Introducing a speaker. It's part of a conference." She'd been assigned at least one, and maybe only one as far as she could tell.

"Somebody famous?" Arena picked up a postcard on the table and turned it over as though there was a chance it would be addressed to her.

"Might be," Georgie said. "They're all pretty big in my world, anyway." She packed picture books, a pacifier, extra blankets, a rattle, and a soft toy—anything to calm a screaming baby in a tight moment. Mostly, at six weeks, the answer was always nursing. Boobs, boobs, boobs.

The point of the day was to let Georgie feel like a person with a brain, not a milk dispenser. That's all she wanted. She put a bottle of frozen breast milk in a side pocket of her diaper bag. Arena leaned on the arm of the couch and stared at the TV like the TV was on, but it was off. Arena said, slowly and quietly, "I like to read, too."

·シ ▽ ✦·

The conference was in the Convention Center. The parking lot was so big they had to take a shuttle from their car to the entrance. They actually may have parked closer to Georgie's house than to the place—they were that far away across a broad expanse of parking lots. The three of them sat crowded in two of the shuttle's sideways-facing seats. The folded stroller jutted into the aisle. Georgie held Bella in her lap. The diaper bag was as big as another rear end, like a person crouched on the floor, a Seeing Eye dog.

Georgie smoothed the dark, silky swirl of her daughter's hair, looked down, and saw a mark at the edge of her own lucky shirt. It was a milk stain, or a water mark. It was almost invisible but no, there it was. Had that been on the shirt when she put it on?

Then she saw another one, higher up. And a little splatter. Breast milk or toothpaste? Either way, the flickering shuttle bus lights, with their hint of green, brought the stains out like subliminal patterns.

In the Convention Center, Georgie put Bella in the stroller then broke into a power walk to keep her from screaming. Movement usually did the trick. Arena loped along at her side. They found the volunteer coordinator in the lobby at a lone freestanding booth. The woman handed Georgie an envelope and a name badge. Inside the envelope was a form letter:

THANK YOU FOR VOLUNTEERING. . . . YOUR GUEST TODAY WILL BE MR/MRS/MS. CLIFFORD. PLEASE MEET MR/MRS/MS. CLIFFORD IN THE GREEN ROOM AT LEAST ONE HOUR BEFORE THE ASSIGNED TIME OF THE EVENT

There was a map, a schedule, and a coupon for a cup of Starbucks.

Mr. Clifford? Georgie's heart picked up. James Clifford was brilliant. He was a well-known anthropological theorist. But then again, there'd also been a woman named Anita Clifford doing widely recognized work, briefly. Maybe it was her.

Arena twisted back and forth, her legs wrapped around each other like a little noodle ballet, her fingers laced. She asked, "Get somebody cool?"

Bella yawned and blinked.

"I think so." Georgie scanned the schedule until she found the name, Clifford, highlighted. She had less than an hour. She was already late. She hoisted the diaper bag back on her shoulder and gripped the stroller's handles. "He's an interesting man. You'll meet him."

But where was the Green Room? She turned again to the volunteer coordinator. "Excuse me—"

The woman was busy with somebody else.

Bella hated the stroller. She gave a mewling, fussy cry, trying it out.

Georgie waited her turn. Everywhere she looked, she saw people who looked like somebody she might know. She thought she saw

Al Gore, but it was instead a man who looked like Al Gore. Then another one, who looked like Al Gore crossed with Alec Baldwin.

They waited too long—Bella's cry climbed, louder, then burst into full song. They were already late. Bella screamed and then threw up. Her tiny hands were covered in baby spit and shaking.

Arena wandered off and fed coins into a Coke machine ten steps away. Georgie picked Bella up. She found a wipe in a bag to clean those darling starfish hands, even as the hands grabbed Georgie's clothes, her best effort at dressing up. "There there, sweets. You're okay," she whispered.

Finally, the volunteer coordinator was free. She started packing, ready to leave the booth. Georgie cut in, "Excuse me?" She bounced Bella. "Where is the Green Room?"

The woman hitched up her Dockers. She took a short breath and clicked the cap off a Sharpie. She marked a big X on a map over one tiny room, a square, and handed the map to Georgie.

"How will I recognize my guest?"

The woman took the form letter from Georgie's hand. She read it, then handed it back. "You'll see 'em," she said. Job done, she waddled off.

As soon as Georgie pushed open the Green Room door, she saw him. Right next to a tray of salami and Havarti. Clifford. She saw the red hair on his back, his giant head as it swung her way. His big cartoon character eyes and ever-present smile. Georgie said, "Clifford?"

The dog bobbed its massive head.

There was no mistaking the situation, and no way out.

Arena, behind her, giggled. Georgie shook the dog's stuffed paw. Then Georgie turned and introduced Arena, because what else could she do? She was ready for full retreat—time to go home. It was time to hit the couch, cuddle with her baby, forget about work, career, networking. Forget about the world. It was time to drink the glass of wine she'd been denying herself since even before she got pregnant and take those pain pills the hospital had sent her home with. They had forty-five minutes to kill with a big red stuffed animal. Her job was to introduce a person in a dog suit.

Another volunteer handed her the assigned script.

"Okay," Georgie said. She tried to smile. "Let's go find your stage."

Bella screamed when she was back in the stroller. Georgie offered her blankets, pillows, and a rattle that attached to the stroller bar with a martian-esque bobbly head, but the baby kept crying. Georgie broke out in a sweat, then gave in and carried Bella, letting the blankets and toys ride. Arena pushed the stroller through the crowded wide conference halls like some kind of middle school science lesson on birth control.

Right away they passed a group of three faculty from Georgie's school. Georgie nodded, smiled, kept walking. She saw a former student who looked glad to catch her eye. She nodded back, adjusted the baby in her arms, and didn't break her clip.

Who wants to mingle when your date's a guy in a dog suit?

Then she saw Brian Watson. Maybe Brian Watson saw her first. Whatever. She saw her ex. The married professor, her professor, the man who never left his wife for her after all. That'd been so many years ago. It should've been forgotten. It was forgotten. They'd grown up. They grew out of it. She'd met Humble and fallen in love! Still, she lurched, stumbled against the carpet, tried to turn away.

His rock-star curls were silver—they'd been half-gray before—and still fabulous. He was a Fulbright fellow, an award winner. His skin had a perma-tan, weathered like a cowboy.

Georgie scratched the side of her face and held up the conference paperwork, a map of the booths and stages, to hide behind it.

"Georgie!" he called. His social skills had always been better than hers. Particularly if you count fucking around as a social skill.

She said, "Brian!" and hoped it sounded spontaneous.

He said, "Look at you, you haven't changed at all."

She knew it was a lie—her hair was thinner, her ass was bigger, she had toothpaste on her shirt. She hadn't changed her clothes at all, was more like it. In this moment, Georgie wanted Humble by her side. She wanted her sexy man, her life.

Brian Watson said, "You brought your family," and waved a hand.

"Family?" If only. Georgie kept a smile on her face. She followed the wave. There was her crew: Arena, tall and thin and rumpled, who made the world into her own little Calvin Klein ad. Clifford stood with his hands on his hips. The stroller was full of blankets, rattles, a stray pacifier, and the martian-esque bobbly toy. There was something demented about pushing a stroller with no baby in it. Georgie tried not to slouch and not to stick her hip out under the weight of tiny Bella and the massive diaper bag. As a group, they were a family right out of the toy box, a hodgepodge of creatures pulled from different boxed sets. She forced what she tried to present as an easy smile, and said, "Sure. That one's my husband," and pointed at the big red dog. "And that's our latest addition," the empty stroller. It seemed funny, like a kid's game, until she said it out loud.

Brian Watson, the smartest infidel in academia, the most gracious of liars, leaned forward so easily, so readily. He glanced at Arena's boobs. He read her shirt. He said, "I heart old people. Fabulous!" He offered a hand to the dog suit. He said, "Nice to meet you. You've got a gorgeous family."

How did he manage to come off as sincere?

His sincerity made Georgie feel like the cad, like she'd set him up, told him a lie.

Clifford's smile never faltered. It couldn't—it was sewn in. Clifford shook Brian Watson's hand and nodded his big fuzzy head. It was like the dog was half-deaf in that outfit. Who was in there? Knock-knock. Georgie wanted to rap the dog on his head.

She said, "Really, only the baby is mine."

Brian Watson tipped his chin up, like he was working out a philosophical angle, sinking into brainiac musings.

Georgie said, "The dog, Clifford, is a social signifier employed in this context to convey that interstitial terrain between childhood and adulthood, the locus between television, the great equalizer, and the individuality inherent in fantasy, as seen through the eyes—yes, plastic eyes—of an almost human form intended to elicit a sympathetic response while gratifying basic urges through purporting to know what we can never know, the mind of animals and the mind of the other . . ."

Georgie was looking for the end of her own sentence, while Brian Watson watched her like an infomercial. Maybe he was thinking about a new paper on hostility and comedy, one disguising the other. Maybe he thought Georgie was a jerk. Either way he held a relaxed, pleasant look on his philosopher's face. He took one step away. He didn't laugh. He said, "Did you ever finish that book you were working on? What was it, Vigée-Lebrun?"

She flushed. How could he possibly remember that, and—Oh, God!—had she really been working on it for that long? She said, "I've started another book." The hypochondriac's guide, her book about baby ailments. He, an academic and an award winner, wouldn't count that as professional work.

He said, "Really? What's it about?"

"Health," Georgie said. "And psychology."

"Psychological health?" He dragged the words out in an awkward combination of syllables, making the whole thing sound preposterous.

Georgie nodded. "It'll be a significant contribution to women's studies—"

"Women's studies?" he said, nodding as though he understood, but raising his eyebrows at the same time, as though she were talking about unicorns and fairies.

She said, "It's a nonfiction work offering advice based on a particular study...." That study was her, Georgie's life, her own experience.

But Brian Watson had already quit listening. A tall, thin woman half his age ran her arm through his, and he shook his silver hair. He said, "Take care, okay? Don't be a stranger, kid." He tapped her with a rolled-up program.

The dog turned its big head Georgie's way. She saw a second set of eyes behind sheer black screens, hidden in the dark fabric of the animal's mouth. Those eyes—did they look at her with pity? Georgie couldn't tell if it was a man or a woman inside. An androgynous judge. It was somebody who refused to talk. Did this outfit, this Halloween joke, this toddler celebrity, really need an introduction?

Georgie walked. Arena, with the empty stroller, fell in line. Clifford, too.

What kind of parade has my life become? Georgie thought.

She avoided everyone she could until she saw the department chair, her adviser. Part of her tenure committee. "Hello, Dan," she said.

"So, I see you found your guest," Dan said. He rocked up on his toes.

"Can you believe it?" Georgie whispered. She turned away from the animal, afraid it could read lips. "Out of all the visiting stars, the professors, the writers, I end up with a stuffed dog."

The department chair closed his mouth into a thin smile. He gave a slow blink, and said, "I was sure you'd be thrilled."

"Wait, you knew about this?"

He said, "I set it up. You're perfect."

Georgie felt her face grow hot. Her fingers were trembling. She needed to sit. Why was she suddenly "perfect" to introduce a cartoon character?

This didn't look good for tenure.

She wanted to put the baby down, to walk away, to pull herself together. Her arms were weak and strong at the same time—it was like there was no weight to them, no blood, but like she could swing, could hit something and pack a punch. She wanted to run, to jog, to get off the planet.

"Because I'm a mom?" she said.

"Sure, and it's fun, right?" Dan clicked his fingers down low, a habit he had.

Not "fun" in any way that he might take it on himself—his serious, academic, male self. He saw her now as a mother, existing in the world of children's books, not literature.

He saw her as a child.

She wanted to throttle him.

She called to Arena and handed over the baby. Bella screamed immediately, in that psychically attuned way that infants can give voice to the parent's inner life; Georgie wanted to scream, too. She reached for the stroller. She turned around to grab her diaper bag, too fast, and bumped into a group of men coming up on one side. One man's shoe hit the side of her wedge heel and knocked her leg out from under her.

She was kicked down.

As she fell, she saw it was a pack of frat boys, strong men in slacks and T-shirts. They had square heads and bodybuilder arms. They had Bluetooth headsets. It was frat boys knocking down intellect, knocking down the academy, the faculty—or just her. A person.

The crowd against one. Georgie. She landed on her side, padded by her weight. Oof!

She wanted to cry.

But there was one guy in the middle of the crowd, a man with a lighter build. He was different from the others. He had a nicer suit. He leaned toward her. He had long hair. He tucked a wayward strand of his hair behind his ear as he leaned in. His eyes were wide and brown. They were kind. His mouth opened as though to say something. He licked his lips. Reached a hand. It was Johnny Depp. The frat boys—they were bodyguards, or handlers. They were security.

Brahms's Academic Festival Overture boomed in the auditorium of her mind.

Georgie reached back. Her fingers were inches from his, from Johnny Depp's hand. Then she felt herself lifted. Two fuzzy red paws took her by the armpits and helped her up. They pulled her away from Johnny. The brown-eyed man—was that Johnny Depp?—disappeared so quickly. Manly bodies closed in like doors and cut him off from the masses.

Clifford's paws beat against Georgie's lucky shirt, her tight skirt, to dust her off. She couldn't see around the dog's stuffed and swinging cranium. Where was Mr. Depp? Where was her angel? Johnny!

Clifford picked up the diaper bag in one thick paw and slid it onto his arm. He managed to collect the scattered onesies in his hairy paws and shove back into the bag. Instead of handing the diaper bag over, the big red dog hoisted it to his own shoulder. The bag looked at home there. He bent for a fallen rattle and rested it on the shelf of the stroller. Baby Bella still screamed in Arena's arms. Arena was a good kid, but her top skill as a sitter seemed to be acting deaf. She was a shy girl, with no leadership skills.

Clifford reached for Bella. Arena handed her over like a bag of laundry. Bella quit crying. She snuggled in. The dog bowed his massive head over her tiny one and swayed back and forth in a clumsy big-footed waltz. Bella closed her eyes, wrapped in the plush folds of red poly-fibers.

She knew who was inside that costume: a mom. Somebody unemployed. Maybe someone with a graduate degree, out to network.

Maybe it was a writer-mom with a book in process, an agent in New York, a dream big as all Manhattan. It was somebody who knew how to sling a diaper bag, push a stroller, and not miss a beat. A person who could take care of a kid without being sidetracked even by Johnny Depp in the flesh. Inside that big dope of a dog, inside that dancing red costume, was at least one part of the woman, the caretaker, Georgie tried to pretend to be. *This*, she thought, *this dog, is how we dress a mom.* Her own head felt like a puppet's then, big and fuzzy, blinking under fluorescent lights, hiding another brain deep inside.

Needs

The school halls were quiet when Nyla signed in at the front desk. Students were in class or out on the fields for PE. She took a butterscotch in a translucent wrapper from a crystal bowl on the counter, and was given a laminated visitor's pass. The principal's office was down the hall. She made her way over squeaky linoleum floors so clean she could see up her own skirt.

Despite a queasy feeling, she wanted to dance, to slide on the polished floors, raise her arms, and chant, "We got it, we got it, we got it."

That morning during their daily phone negotiations, Mrs. Cherryholmes had said there was a way, perhaps, to get Arena back in classes sooner than the initial terms of her expulsion. Yes! Victory! Her hopes were high. Nyla had come down to iron out the details.

The butterscotch settled her stomach and obscured the bitter saliva of pregnancy mouth. The vice principal had the outer office, in front of the principal's rooms. She was on the phone making a soothing cluck and murmur. Still behind her desk, she nodded hello and waved a hand toward a second door, the door to the principal's quarters.

Mrs. Cherryholmes's door was open.

Nyla spit the butterscotch into her palm. She tapped on the narrow rectangle of paper-covered glass that marked the door, then went in. Mrs. Cherryholmes stood, tall and composed. She reached out a hand. Nyla flipped the butterscotch from her right to her left. When they shook, that trace of sugar clung and her hand stuck to the principal's.

She tugged her ponytail into place and sat down.

The principal smiled, all good news. She said, "We have room in a program for your daughter. We're willing to reconsider the terms of her expulsion, in light of this opportunity. It's a transitional class specifically for students who benefit most with an additional level of support."

Transitional sounded good—Arena would be transitioning back in.

The principal said, "We'll need you to sign a few forms." She opened a drawer. The paperwork came out. "This is an award-winning educational model designed to maximize a student's abilities while recognizing the many levels of needs we address in the school system."

Nyla tried to read the papers. Each page was marked with a red X, directions where to sign. The teacher would be Barry Gibb. Ha! Barry Gibb? She imagined the Bee Gees playing softly. Then she saw the words "documented disability." She saw words like *medication* and *therapist* and *delayed learning.* There it was: *special needs.*

She said, "This is special ed?"

Mrs. Cherryholmes took her time. She spoke carefully. "It's not what you'd consider special education back when we were in school. This is supplemental education, a holistic program designed to integrate learning styles with behavioral challenges and social dynamics."

Nyla said, "Arena is not a slow learner."

"It encompasses all levels of challenge. We have space and funding. It's an opportunity." Mrs. Cherryholmes looked happy with the plan.

"Funding?" Nyla sensed a state quota to fill. "She's a perfectly good student."

Mrs. Cherryholmes said, "She's an expelled student. I know we don't want to see our own children as falling behind, but Arena is a student at risk who may have difficulty reentering. Besides, in this program?" Mrs. Cherryholmes paused briefly to let Nyla catch up with her words. "We have fully funded federal art programs five days a week, along with math, science, and twenty-three minutes of physical education daily."

Nyla asked, "You don't have that in regular schedules?"

Mrs. Cherryholmes laced her fingers together. She shook her head slowly, and let a frosted lipsticked smile spread. "In this program, all funding is federally protected. They can't take it away."

She said it as though, as an educator, she was letting Arena in on a special bargain.

When Nyla hesitated, her pen hovering over the page, Mrs. Cherryholmes added, "Behavioral problems *are* learning problems. You're both welcome to meet with our guidance counselor if you'd like to discuss it."

Nyla touched the tip of the pen to the signature line.

This classroom, designed for special needs, would be a starting place. It didn't sound awful. At least Arena would be inside the same school as her peers and on track to graduate. She'd only be in a different room. She'd have a specialized teacher. It was better than picking up trash on the side of the road, or staying home, or wandering down to the Temple Everlasting.

Nyla signed the forms, one page after another.

It was dark out by the time Arena swung open their big entryway door. Nyla was in the kitchen and heard Arena drop her backpack then kick off her shoes.

Let the girl settle in, she thought. It was hard not to rush her in the hall and blurt out the news. It'd been hard to wait patiently all day.

Arena padded down the hallway in her socks. She said, "You're baking?" The house was full of chocolate-infused air. Two layers of cake rested, each on its own cooling rack. Nyla baked when she was stressed and when she was thrilled, and now she contained both emotions at once, practically vibrating with new hope. "We're celebrating. You're back in school. I worked it out."

Arena walked up to the kitchen counter, found a cake crumb, and ate it. She said, "Really?"

"Yep. And guess what? Your new teacher is Barry Gibb. How's that for a laugh?" Nyla was tickled to have it sorted out.

Arena shook her hair out of her eyes or maybe back into her eyes. She looked at her mother. "Barry Gibb?"

Nyla said, "Well, probably not *the* Barry Gibb . . ."

Arena knew exactly who this teacher was. He held a place in her school. She said, "No way, Mom. I am not going to special ed. I'm not. I'm not in that class."

Nyla tried. She said, "It's not exactly special ed. . . ."

But it was. "It is, exactly. So, what, now they think I'm retarded?"

It'd sounded so much better when Mrs. Cherryholmes said it. "I don't think they use that term anymore. And it's a good program—"

"Sure, a great program, for kids who need it."

"Kids who need extra support—"

"Mom, I sold drink mix. That doesn't mean I'm a lame student."

Nyla heard her own voice sound false and broken when she said, "It's where the funding is. They have room for you." Portland's schools all struggled for funding. She said, "It's mostly art classes. You love art."

Arena said, "I'm not going."

"You are going. It's already decided."

"I'll drop out."

"You are not going to drop out of high school." Nyla kept her voice low and steady. "They can arrest you for that. You're still underage. It's only for a few hours of the day."

Arena's voice broke when she answered, "It's eight hours of the day. And they can arrest me for anything. They already did. It was totally unfair. But when they say 'do restitution,' or whatever, I'm out there doing it. They put me to work, I go along with it, and now *I* have the problem?"

"You can't just hang out at the Temple Everlasting. It's morbid." She put a hand to her stomach, as though to reach for the unborn child, to hold that one close.

Arena turned and walked back down the hall the way she'd

come in. Nyla followed. Arena slid her feet back in her shoes and reached for her coat where it lay on the couch.

"Where you going?"

Arena said, "Wherever. I'll meet up with a friend from the work crew."

She had friends? "Who?"

Arena's tennis shoe was stuck on her foot like a clog. She bent and untied it, straightened it out. "You don't know him."

Still Nyla wanted information. She said, "What's his name?"

"AKA." Arena slid her cell phone in the front pocket of her jeans.

Nyla said, "His real name."

"What do you mean?"

Nyla stepped in Arena's way, between her daughter and the front door. She said, "AKA? That's not a name. You didn't know Mack's name, down at the Temple Everlasting. And that guy's not normal."

"You want me to know their names?" Arena asked. It came out like a challenge.

Nyla said, "I want you to make thoughtful decisions." She tried to lower the tone of the conversation, to bring sweetness into it. She dropped her voice and put her hands on Arena's bony shoulders. She said, "This isn't the life I want for you." She wanted her daughter to have a life of meaning, with a good education and *all* good things, like love. Most of all, love. Without the girl's dad around, she wanted to be Arena's first source of support, both mother and father, to be everything.

Arena said, "Guess what, Mom? You don't get to pick a life for me. I do." She pushed her way past.

Nyla let her go, because really that was exactly the kind of life she valued and offered: one where the girl got to make her own choices. Arena went out the door, down the front steps.

She called out to her fleeing daughter, "Don't stay out too late."

Arena was already far down the block.

Nyla yelled, "Darling, you're still on parole! And you've got school in the morning."

Proof

Arena slid her phone out of her pocket. She only had two names in her contacts: her mom, and AKA. She didn't call her mom now. When AKA answered, his voice was raspy, lower than she'd noticed in person. She asked, "Where are you?"

"Home. You're welcome to join me."

She'd never been to his place before. He gave her the address. It was across the river, downtown, a short ride on the city bus.

She found him waiting for her at the bus stop. She smiled at him and he smiled back, and she loved how he didn't always need to talk. He took her hand, and they walked together to an old brick building with a mini-mart and a Chinese restaurant with a bar downstairs. He pushed buttons to unlock the apartment door. Inside, he led her down a hallway lined with a narrow strip of stained rug. The building smelled like grease, kung pao, and mildew.

She'd never met anyone who actually lived in these old-style downtown apartments. She'd thought the buildings were where alcoholics went to drink and die, and hipsters filmed music videos.

The elevator was rickety with a metal accordion door and yellowed buttons with big numbers on them that looked like they could've been made from ivory, or at least fake ivory. It felt like another town, another time.

Arena loved it.

They got out on the third floor. The hallway air was thick with the smell of bacon and cats. AKA had a key to a room at the end of the hall. He pushed the door open. The apartment started out as narrow as a coat closet, and she walked behind him until it opened up into a wider space. There was a man sacked out on a couch, and somebody else in what must've been the kitchen off to the side, banging pans. The central room split into halls that led in all directions, like burrows. He pulled her toward one hall, then to a room at the end of it. He closed the door behind them.

The room was big and empty, with a tall row of windows. It was dark outside and the dark turned the windows into mirrors; still, the windows made the claustrophobic web of hallways and the people in the common room not matter so much. AKA had a mattress on the floor. He and Arena dropped down onto it, side by side. There were three pillows, each one thin and flat. He let her have two. He rested on one folded in half, and he rubbed the back of her hand. She said, "Are those your parents, out there?"

He laughed. "Those two? No way." After a minute, he said, "I answered an ad. I can't actually figure out how many people live here. I haven't even seen all the rooms."

"You're moved out?" He'd be the first person she met who had moved out of his parents' place without going to college.

He said, "Something like that."

Outside a siren sang from far away. AKA wiggled his feet in his high-tops where they rested on top of his blankets. The blankets were thin, like they'd been stolen from a hospital.

Arena looked around the big, empty space of his room. "You know, we could work on my project here. With the mesh?"

He put a hand on her hip. "You mean the one where I'm naked? Bring it on."

They were so close on the bed.

"I'm not ready for that yet," she said.

He said, "We'll take it slow." His breath moved over her skin. He tugged at her T-shirt.

She said, "I mean, I don't have a camera."

"Camera?" His dark eyes opened wider. "We didn't talk about a camera. What's the project, porn?" But already he'd relaxed again, like he didn't object all that much. He traced his finger along the stitching on her jeans.

He had a guitar on a stand in one corner. A few shirts hung in a doorless closet. The chipped floorboards were as textured as the best kind of painting. There was one rickety desk on long, thin legs near a window.

Arena's cell phone rang in her coat pocket. She let it go. When it rang again, she said, "That'd be my mom."

AKA rubbed his hand along her thigh.

"She's freaked out about the Temple Everlasting of Life on Earth."

AKA said, "Maybe I am, too." His hand crept up to Arena's waist, then along her ribs.

She asked, "You think Mack's trying to brainwash me into a death cult?"

AKA said, "That's his job."

Arena pushed away the distraction of AKA's hand.

He said, "Why do you go there?" Now he sounded exactly like her mom—her mom in a guy suit. The conversation was going off course. Arena needed an ally.

"He's read a lot," she said. "I go to talk about heaven, death. The big mysteries."

"You can talk about heaven right here." He pulled her closer.

"Seriously. I mean, what's the point of life, if we're just going to die?"

"You're not the first person to wonder." He inched toward her, and he kissed her. He ran a hand under her shirt.

Arena put her hand over his. She stopped him.

She didn't know if she wanted that hand under her shirt. There was the scar, near her shoulder. That scar had been there as long as she could remember. It was hers, and it was private.

It was the scar from the car wreck. Her dad, his death, his life, drawn in stitches that had melted into her skin. Sometimes she listened to his records and touched the scar and could almost remember back when she had a dad.

She said, "Mack's not trying to convert anyone."

AKA sat up and started unlacing a high-top. His shoelaces made a slapping sound as he pulled each one through the eyelets. He said, "He's afraid of death."

"He's not afraid to think about it." Arena kicked her worn shoes off easily, one toe against the heel of the other.

AKA tossed one of his shoes toward his closet. He said, "He's afraid to die alone so he made up a religion." He unlaced his second shoe.

Arena said, "He didn't make it up. It's from the Egyptians, and scientists. It's a collage of super-respected ideas."

AKA said, "What I know is, people who're afraid to die alone? They're the scariest crew, fueled with apocalyptic fantasies."

"I don't think he's an apocalypse guy," Arena said.

Her phone rang again. They lay side by side and listened to the short bar of dance music. Arena said, "I can't wait to move out."

AKA said, "If you've got a free place to live, and decent meals, I wouldn't ditch it too soon."

Arena said, "My mom has all these ideas. . . ."

"Like keeping you safe?" he asked.

"Like keeping me trapped," she whispered. The phone gave up; the ringing stopped.

He said, "You know, I actually own a house and an acre and a half of woods." As he said it, he wrapped one broad, long-fingered hand around her thin wrist. The gesture fell somewhere between hand-holding and handcuffs.

"You're joking." Sometimes he said things like that. She looked into his eyes, practiced, but this time it didn't feel like practicing. It felt natural. He was the first person whose eyes didn't make her gaze skitter.

He said, "It's in Boring. A farmhouse, with land. In the winter and spring, there's a pond in back." Oregon land was dotted with vernal ponds—shallow seasonal ponds that soaked into the ground and dried up in the summer sun.

Boring was a town outside of Portland. The name was a local joke.

She said, "Right. A country estate. And why would you live here?"

He shook his shaggy hair and peeled himself away from her.

She felt the draft against her feet where his feet had been. He stood up and shuffled through a clutch of papers. He crossed the room and looked in one warped drawer of his old spindly desk. He closed that one and opened another drawer. He flipped through his stacks until he found a photo, and he handed it to Arena.

"Proof."

It was a picture the size of the photo from the Kirlian photography machine. But this one was a picture not of orange energy, but of a pale green house with a gravel driveway and a tire swing hanging from a crooked apple tree. A dog stood in the sun. A tanned shirtless kid ran barefoot across the lawn. There was a mailbox up close, near where the photographer must've been standing.

"I'll take you there."

Arena looked at the house, a one-story box.

He put a finger to the photo, as she held it. Arena had never seen AKA smoke, but she could smell smoke on him, and his fingers were stained from nicotine. His nails were bitten low.

The kid in the picture wore torn shorts. His face was as wide and open as the face on his soft-eared dog. The two of them looked happy. The house was big-eyed and welcoming, like it didn't know a gutter had fallen off. The boy was the same. AKA pointed a nicotine-stained finger at the kid in the picture. He said, "That, right there. That boy is me."

Scent of a Party

*H*umble walked in the side door of their house, and there was Georgie with Bella in one arm, her other hand in a bowl making meatloaf: raw hamburger mixed with raw egg clung to her wrist. Jesus, Humble thought. It was a bowl of salmonella, E. coli, parasites—could she get their baby any closer to death?

Thump-thump.

The white noise machine was on.

Bella was still awake, her round eyes two little walnuts. The house was warm and smelled overripe with tomato sauce, a bowl of apples, and noodles boiling on the stove. Humble was drunk and trying not to be, mostly glad to see Georgie and his baby girl but also guilty—he said he'd be home earlier; did it matter that he wasn't? He was always guilty. Home was where the guilt lived. He smiled and said, "Hey."

The single word came out slurry, longer than it needed to be: "He-e-e-ey."

Thump-thump.

Georgie, her pale skin splotched, looked tired, like she had too much face and not enough features; and with that sound track the house was absolutely creepy. "Welcome home," she said.

Was that sarcasm? He couldn't tell. He'd turned away just then and dropped his keys on the table.

He said, "Did you get to those life insurance papers?"

She hadn't. The papers were still on the table, now ringed with a beer stain. The heartbeat machine kept up its rhythm. "What if you died today?" the life insurance papers asked, through the stain.

Any minute now, he thought. Any minute and she'd ask where he'd been, how many drinks he had. Who counted drinks?

She'd say, "So you're drinking alone again?"

He drank alone, except for all the other people in the bar, and the bartenders, and everybody who'd learned the dead girl game and called him "Dead Man" because that was his nickname these days and he didn't mind. He drank alone except for Justine, this twentysomething with big tits who showed up with her skater boy-friend and a rotating cast of girls, and this guy named Max, who said he just got fired from Taco Del Mar. Humble was like their dad, if they drank with their dad.

"Why's the machine on if she's awake?"

"I was just about to put her down," Georgie said. She mixed bread crumbs into the meatloaf.

He waited for her to say something as he put his coat on the back of a dining room chair. He used the toes of one foot to coerce the heel of his shoe off the other foot, and as he did he tipped and started to stumble. He put two hands on the back of the chair and acted like that was what he meant to do: He meant to hold on to the chair, do a little dance, and work his shoes off. His socks were wet with sweat and rainwater that had seeped in on his way home. He kept his eyes on his shoes as he took them off but felt Georgie and Bella waiting.

"Every time I change her diaper, it's clean." Georgie said.

"What's that?" Humble said. He'd been prepared for a different grievance. This was a relief. He said, "Then don't change 'em. Sounds like you're makin' work."

Georgie stepped into the living room and picked a dirty diaper off the coffee table. Like she'd saved it. She said, "Look at this." She held the diaper in the air and bobbed it up and down. It was like a fat pelican. "There's two pounds of pee."

Her wrist was covered in raw hamburger.

"Throw that out, Jesus." Humble ducked around the diaper. Did he want that in his face? Did she really expect him to look at it?

She said, "They're all like that. She's not dehydrated, but she hasn't pooped in days."

"Days? I doubt it." Hum walked into the kitchen. He opened the fridge. Georgie and the baby and the diaper full of pee followed.

Georgie said, "I can't remember her last poop."

So Georgie counted drinks and counted shitty diapers. Humble said, "The house smells like baby shit. Somebody's cranking it out."

"That's the diaper pail." It was designed to keep odor in, and it didn't. Usually it was up in Bella's room. Now it sat by the front door. Georgie said, "I washed it and put baking soda in. But really, seriously, she hasn't pooped for days."

Thump-thump, thump-thump . . .

She held Bella close to her body, a heavy, wrapped bundle. Humble couldn't see his own kid's face. It was like they were merged, his wife and his baby.

Humble wasn't ready to worry. He said, "Sounds like the perfect kid. Maybe she's more evolved." He found a bottle of Fat Tire amber ale in the crisper in the bottom of the fridge. Then he needed an opener. Why the hell couldn't microbrews use screw tops?

He riffled through a drawer. They had, like, three openers—where did they all go? There was a latte frother, an olive spoon. He ran an impatient hand through the clutter, and a paring knife flipped out to the side. It swished between them. The knife fell blade first and stuck in their wooden floor.

"Humble!" Georgie's voice was shrill. He couldn't let that knife of a voice in. He let it go by like the wind. She said, "Somebody could've been hurt by that. You could've put Bella's eye out, blinded your own daughter."

That heartbeat in the background was driving him nuts. It made everything into a drama.

"Nobody's blind." He found an opener and opened his beer. It gave a satisfying crack and hiss.

Georgie picked up the knife. She said, "How much have you had to drink?"

There it was. Humble finished his swallow. He said, "You're so predictable." He wiped his mouth with the back of his hand.

Georgie looked shaky. She said, "Oh, nice. You're wasted, and that's predictable. I'm sick of it."

Hum said, "You threatening me?"

"What're you talking about?" Georgie bounced the baby. She stepped back and forth, her bare feet on the kitchen floor.

"Put down the knife. I don't talk to anybody holding a knife." He took another drink of his beer.

"Oh, Jesus Christ." Georgie tossed the knife in the drawer. "You're crazy."

"Name-calling," Humble said, and turned to walk away.

Georgie followed. She said, "I don't want to be the only one worrying here. You don't get up when she wakes up. You don't care if she has a rash. She hasn't pooped in days. You think it's a big joke."

Her voice didn't stop.

Humble turned around then. He said, "You're tedious, you know that? You're tedious." He yelled it. It felt good to yell. Yes, maybe the neighbors could hear, their houses were close, but so what?

Georgie, her voice lower now, almost a whisper, said, "Don't raise your voice around the baby."

He yelled, "I don't want to come home and talk baby shit!"

Georgie hissed, "This is not about what you want. I'm sick of being alone in this parenting thing."

In the kitchen, a timer went off. The noodles were done. Still, they boiled on, and the heartbeat played in the background, and the timer sang its song. Georgie said, "You're never even here."

Humble watched her mouth move up and down. Her chin shook. Her chin never used to shake like that. She was talking but all he saw was that mouth moving and Bella screamed in her arms and he couldn't hear over the screaming. It was two women, yelling. It was the story of his life: his mother, his sister, always this noise. His wife loved his jokes. This wasn't her anymore.

"Who are you these days?" he said.

She said, "I'm not your mom. I'm not here to police you and keep you in line, and drag you in from the bars, like some big drunk baby—"

He reached a hand out and grabbed Georgie's neck and slammed her into a wall and then she shut up and it was only Bella screaming. Georgie, her eyes wide with shock, wrapped both arms tight around the baby, and held her close. Georgie's neck was soft under Humble's hand. There was a smell like a party now, like a moment from high school Humble could almost remember. It smelled good.

It was the smell of being unencumbered, out all night. It was the smell of freedom.

It was beer—his beer had spilled. The bottle was in his other hand, and the baby and Georgie were soaked. Georgie's face was red. Her mascara bled into the creases under her eyes the way it did when she got sweaty in the heat of summer, and when they had sex, except now it was like she couldn't see him, her eyes weren't focused, and he let go.

She put a hand to her throat. She curled around Bella.

Humble turned away. He put his shoes on. Georgie said, "Humble?" She wasn't crying but her voice cracked in a way that meant she was ready to. She said his name like it was a question. Then she hissed, "Get out."

He was already going.

He had both shoes on now. He took his keys and went out the door. She followed him to the doorway. It was all he could do: leave. He could've killed her. He knew it. He knew it, and his heart pounded inside and his hands shook and he felt like somebody else, far away, not the man in the body that moved with him, and he walked. There was a rhythm to the lurch. His steps beat out a word: un-en-cum-bered. All he'd done was push her away. By the throat, yes, but shit, he needed her to stop talking. The further he got from the house, the more he could believe he'd just overreacted, that was all. He wasn't a complete bastard. Unencumbered. She wasn't hurt.

Jesus.

He wanted to scream. He was a bad husband, and bad father, and he knew it, and the voices in his head sang a different song, and he kept walking. His phone rang in his pocket. He pulled it out, saw his wife's name, and put it back. What would they do, yell? He couldn't do it, couldn't talk. The phone was so small between his fingers. What did it say, that he had such a prissy little phone?

He hunted for a bar that would feel like home.

.ﾞ ﾟ.

Georgie held the baby and breathed baby smells. The meatloaf was raw in its bowl on the counter. The noodles, undrained, grew fat. Bella was sound asleep, but Georgie was afraid to put her down. She stayed on the couch and picked up a ballpoint pen. What came next—kick him out? Fix things?

It's hard to build a family when you didn't have one to begin with. It's harder to know when to let your new family, the one you made, go.

She called Humble. This was a nightmare. Maybe, she thought, if they talked, they could fix it. But her head throbbed where she hit the wall, Bella was half-awake now, in her arms, and Humble didn't answer.

On the rhetorical triangle, that tattoo on her arm, she wrote "Mom," in a scrawled hand caused by reaching over the sleeping baby girl. That was one point of the triangle, one corner of the making of meaning. At another juncture, she wrote "Baby." And who held up that third side?

Relapse

AKA tagged along beside Arena like a stray dog, but no worries. He had his clothes on again now. They'd started "the project." He did what he could to keep his hands off her.

He walked with her on the street, both of them dressed, and remembered being naked in front of her—the feeling was still with him—and though maybe it looked like he walked beside her, he knew he was really a step behind, following her lead.

Overhead, there was one heavy cloud in the sky, a floating mountain, Mount Hood's weightless cousin. It was a place they could live. AKA entertained the dream. He said, "What do you see?" and gestured at the cloud.

Arena squinted to the sky. He waited. If she said a floating mountain, their dreams would be in sync, like two iPods with the same playlist.

"In the cloud?" she asked.

He nodded yes, hungry for communion.

She said, "Drops of water and frozen crystals, suspended in the atmosphere."

Gawd. Not the answer. Her words made him want to lace his

fingers through her hair, pull her head back, and kiss her until she agreed to see what he saw. He wanted to demand.

She said, "Isn't that amazing enough?"

She didn't wear makeup. Her mouth was red, always a little open. Her skin was pale. She was weird in the way she could go forever without talking, and then when she did talk, it was only to him, not to anybody else that he'd seen, and that was cool. It was like he could be her translator.

He had a monopoly, and she let that happen.

As they walked, their feet kicked out in front together, each step. She said, "What happened to your shoes?"

The rubber toes of his Chuck Taylors had been turned to blackened cheese. He said, "Radiator." He'd been trying to dry the rain soak out and left the shoes a little too close. "Shoulda seen the smoke, Jesus."

Arena said, "You should get a new pair."

Like he had money. That was the difference between her and him.

They walked side by side in silence, past a brick wall with an ad for a bar on the side: FINE CHAMPAGNE AND CRAFT BEER! A little rattle-can art had altered the message to read FINE CHAMPAGNE AND CRAP BEER! Which was probably about right, too.

AKA nodded at the wall and jostled Arena's shoulder. "I did that," he said.

"Really?"

"You don't believe me?" He was proud of his work, his voice. It was supposed to stay secret, that was part of the tagger's code, but he'd told her and right away he felt exposed: He wanted to share. He hated even trying.

They reached a bus stop. She started to say something. Her red mouth opened. She looked away. Her tongue touched the corner of her lips. His eyes were on her mouth. She said, "I'm going to leave you here."

Here? AKA felt her words like a shove.

Leave him?

That was a gut punch.

He could push back, there in the middle of nowhere, a dead zone between industrial and new built. It was a city block with a short row of stores—some of them boarded up, others with businesses—across from an abandoned warehouse. He tried to smile and felt his mouth twitch. He said, "Where're you going?"

In one cube of a store, a man changed an overhead lightbulb. In another, a woman rearranged her furniture. The woman pushed and shoved, directing a love seat across the floor.

Arena said, "I'm going to catch a bus."

He said, "I'll wait with you."

She said, "That's okay. No need."

Behind Arena, in the store, the woman moving furniture stopped pushing the love seat. She put her hands on her hips, then wiped stray hair away from her face. It was dark out and light in her store, making her as good as on TV, under those bright lights. Hers was another yuppie dive.

Arena hung on the bus stop pole. She was so thin. She and the pole were twins.

"What're you going to do with the footage?" AKA asked. He felt weird about letting her take a movie of him naked. That's what she had asked for: him, naked, in his apartment. She asked him to dance, just a little, and slow. She filmed him letting his jeans fall to the floor. Now that would go out in the world? She could do anything with it. She could show it as art or post it on the Internet. And she was leaving him.

She said, "Trust me. You'll like it."

She made him nervous. He knew he'd like it. He liked everything that had to do with her. "Trust isn't my strongest thing," he said. "I didn't sign a release form, right?" He tried to sound cool, like he knew things.

She said, "We have an oral agreement."

God. It made his cock hard, to hear her say it: oral. Her red mouth. She held the video camera, in its case, at her shoulder, her arm bent at the elbow. It wasn't her camera; it was borrowed from school, in her new classes.

She was back in school. That made him nervous, too. She was moving forward. He never graduated and never would. She had a mom who cared.

Of course they had an agreement. Oral, written, written on the body even: She could have what she wanted. Arena won. Arena would always win.

He said, "Next time, maybe I won't be the only one naked." He lifted her hair and came in for a kiss. She shrugged him off, and she smiled, but she looked over her shoulder like somebody might be watching, and he had that feeling of pushing things—he wanted to push, to tear her shirt off, make something happen—and he held back. He kept himself in check. This kind of situation was why he didn't drink and had cut out the weed. Not just because they made him do it, in juvenile detention. He had to work hard to keep his impulses in check.

His counselors at the Donald E. Long Juvenile Detention Home told him that. He wanted to be a better person. But he wasn't. Not inside.

A TriMet bus came down the road, wheezing and belching diesel. Arena stepped away from the stop. When the bus came near, she waved it on, shaking her head. "I thought you were waiting for the bus?" AKA knew he had trust issues. But still.

"I'll catch the next one," Arena said. "Go on. I'll be fine."

Behind Arena, the woman in her store was alone, with her little black dress and her ponytail, puzzling something out. She was maybe the most vulnerable woman in town, her head full of the wrong problems. Maybe she had an SUV and a husband, a house in the hills. She probably had a tiny little phone that she thought could save her life. Women did that, even men did it—clung to their phones.

It said LIFECYCLES on a bare white sign that hung in the window. LifeCycles? What did that even mean? Part of a life cycle is death.

He said, "You're going home?" He had to double-check, couldn't help it.

"I have my own life." She followed his gaze, to the store, to the woman inside. "What're you looking at?"

That woman was everything AKA never wanted to be: Tame. Working. Building her own little trap. A store! Oh, so nice. Consumerism nobody needed for sale in a part of town nobody came to. More than that, she was a woman and looked like the kind of mother he never had. A woman who might bake. Who might wash her kids' clothes, not pile 'em out in the dirt and say they'd get to the laundry soon. Not break a window when she was high, or date a guy who barely knew how to run a meth lab but was always willing to wing it. AKA was outside, looking in.

Arena looked at the store, too.

He nodded. Okay. If Arena wanted him to, he'd go. He'd put on the right show.

He'd go, he'd go, he'd go. He had to tell himself, like the trained dog he was, the half-trained feral dog. He made his feet cooperate and turned as though to leave. Then his feet turned back; he was facing her again. "See you at work screw." He hoped she'd laugh.

She only nodded.

He said, "Don't forget." They had a plan to meet up after.

There was no bus coming. Arena said, "See you then." Her eyes glittered in the fading light, and AKA wanted her to love him more. She had to love him—he loved her! He wanted to cram her in his pocket. She stood there, on her own.

He remembered a class he'd had, part of probation: He was responsible for his own actions, she was responsible for hers. He'd bring her around. Money would help. Money always helped.

If he had cash, he could lure Arena to him.

The need for dollars was an old ache, like a best friend just out of prison calling his name. The urge for pocket money grew like a lie, like a fever, and he felt his childhood illness of deep need coming on.

Breeding Ground

At the mandrill cage, the zoo's Community Outreach department had laced a pole with pink and blue crepe paper and set up an awning. Volunteers sliced and served a sheet cake with a square footage the size of a studio apartment. They offered coloring pages for the kids, little packs of crayons, and a contest: Guess how big around Mama Mandrill is?

It was a citywide baby shower!

Really it was a desperate plea to get people to visit the zoo in these colder months.

Helium balloons bobbed like cartoon heads. A face painter drew mandrill stripes on the willing, kids and adults, blue lines down their cheeks. All those testosterone-indicating alpha mandrill stripes could pose a threat to the zoo's mandrill patriarch if there was any realism to it. A fine mist in the air made the face paint streak and blur into bruises. It looked like a zombie party, or an orgy of domestic abuse. Sarah stood in the thick of that scene and worked on her animal observations through a hot glaze of blinked-away tears.

Baby Lucy came to the bars, behind the glass, and wrapped her fingers around them. She looked out into the crowd, with big eyes. A family of six looked right past her, saying, "Where's the baby?"

She'd grown, and it was like they couldn't see her. The public wanted their babies tiny. This was biology, for Christ's sake—the mandrill grew at mandrill speed. To tear up over it was even dumber than crying over a song on the radio, or a Dove soap ad. Dale skidded to a stop on his Nishiki, and Sarah wiped her eyes.

He said, "This is not good."

She felt accused. "What?"

"Spotting. Blood, discharge on her hindquarters." He nodded toward the mandrills.

Sarah felt it in her body like it was her own. She'd been jealous of that monkey, she really had. Now she merged with her, was there alongside her in the pregnancy. Her job was so removed from the bodies of animals—she wasn't allowed to enter the cages. There was a constant and reasonable fear of anthroponosis, reverse zoonosis, human-to-animal disease, like she—and anyone else not trained in handling animals—carried the plague.

But Dale handled their genitals, palpated their stomachs, and studied their gums. The mandrill was spotting?

He shook his head. "We're taking her off exhibit."

Already a handler had opened a door to the enclosure and was luring the mandrill in question out with food. The crowd was a swarm, with their face paint and slabs of sheet cake.

"How will they guess the mother's girth?"

"Nobody here can tell which one is pregnant. We'll point to another one." His voice was nearly a whisper.

The city was compiling baby names on a computerized screen, right then, even as she and Dale spoke. Each child had a celebratory paper mandrill mask. Some put them on right over the face paint. Two mandrills in one, two man-apes over a human face.

He said, "Could be placenta previa. That worries me. Or an infection, or early labor. We'll try to get an ultrasound. We'll definitely be able to save the mother. I mean, we'll try to save them both." He was sweaty and distracted. "They should get these people out of here. It's too much."

Sarah's heart melted. They were in complete agreement: too many humans. "Is she in pain?"

"She's showing anxiety signs." He folded his arms. The cold, damp air made Dale's skin blotch in a way that only made him more clearly alive. He turned to Sarah, as though to see if she, too, were showing anxiety signs. "I'll do what I can."

He was there to help.

Then he changed the subject. He said, "Listen, you still want to catch the show today?"

This was the day they'd planned to go to OMSI, that other sea of children across town, to see his ex's work.

It seemed completely wrong to leave the mother mandrill now. "Don't you need to be here? We can cancel."

"I'll stick around for the next hour or so, monitor things, see if we can get the ultrasound set up. I hate to anesthetize her if it's not necessary. Mostly, chances are, we'll have to wait and see what happens."

Behind him a woman with a troop of kids picked out crayons, while they all kept one hand on a rope to stay together, a chain gang family.

That's how many of them there were! They were slaves to one another.

Sarah wiped her nose on the back of her coat collar. How could Dale not notice she'd been tearing up? She wasn't crying over the mandrill. She was crying over her own dead babies. A volunteer passed by with her hands in plastic gloves held up like a surgeon going in for surgery. She said, "Can I score you a slice of cake?" and gave a wink.

That cake screamed A BABY IS COMING! in giant cursive on the top, and was laden with plastic storks and monkeys in a scientifically confusing array.

Dale said, "Let's take a break from this place."

Sarah's timer went off. She checked "Motoring" for Lucy.

"We'll take my car," Dale said. "Meet you in an hour."

It was a date.

After her shift she practically ran away from the pink and blue baby balloons to join the relatively sparse crowd of winter visitors on the zoo's twisting back walks.

Dale was at the gate. He said, "Two hours till they close."

Sarah was taller than Dale. She swung her legs as they walked to his car, and thought, *Motoring*, one in a pair of awkward animals.

Dale opened the passenger-side door of his car and held it. She folded herself in fast, afraid he'd shut it too soon and accidentally catch a foot or ankle. She said, "I don't want to see OMSI's baby exhibit, though."

"We won't, then." He closed the door gently.

At the museum, Dale paid for them both. They sunk into a mass of couples, in the maze of halls. The crowd was full of acne-faced teenagers, families shuffling in packs, and overweight and underweight men and women holding hands. Everyone looked uniformly unhealthy under the green of fluorescent lights.

A lek is the place where male animals gather to fight and preen, to establish a hierarchy and attract mates. It's a team sport, all competition and cooperation: The alpha male might score the best breeding rights, but the group brought females around, increasing the reproductive odds for the species as a whole.

In a species on its way to extinction, without enough males to form a lek, females don't even know where to look.

It's like a town without a good bar.

If OMSI were a lek, Sarah wouldn't know who to root for. A prairie chicken would look for a male with bright air sacs and a loud cry. An elephant cow would seek out the bull with the largest proboscis. A certain fish would amass sand, building what researchers called a sand castle contest, no joke.

They passed the doorway to the babies exhibit. Those dreaded, haunting little babies. A red and white sign on the wall said ATTEN-TION! VIEWER DISCRETION ADVISED!

The sign was like something you'd see on a biohazard bin or a nuclear waste site. In smaller letters it read THE HUMAN EMBRYOS AND FETUSES IN THIS EXHIBIT ARE REAL.

Real human babies.

And some of those babies? They were older than Sarah.

It was a permanent exhibit of dead babies through all stages of development, preserved and on display. She'd seen it as a kid, then later as an adult, waxy little babies with knobby backbones and wrinkled skin. More than one sucked its miniature thumb in the clear glass display case of its cold womb. The babies who had lived past the first four months of gestation were coated in fine hair, lanugo, their little woolly down. Sarah wanted to pet them.

Dale said, "I thought we agreed to skip the babies?"

"We will," she said.

It was a lie. She couldn't walk past. She was drawn into their rotunda, a round, dark room where the babies lined the walls, each one mounted against black velvet and glowing with a hidden light. The first were weekly embryos. Sarah found the tiny curl of a child at week eight, smaller than a bay shrimp, with its big head and tadpole body.

She leaned her forehead against the glass. It was already marked with the handprints of children.

Mine, she thought. That was her baby: eight weeks.

There was a woman on her knees changing a baby's diaper. Really. In the back of the dimly lit display room. OMSI had bathrooms and changing tables. What was that woman thinking? Sarah saw the live baby's fat, healthy thighs.

"I hate babies," she said. Another lie.

"Babies are assholes." Dale's voice was gentle. He'd make a good father. His hand wrapped around her arm. His body heat quieted her skin. She let him lead her out.

The first part of the reconstructive surgery exhibit was cosmetic—rhinoplasty, dental work, and tattoo removal. Then it moved from elective surgeries to the more serious—tragedy and recovery. Sarah and Dale stood in front of a series of light boards, like giant slides lit from behind, documenting the trauma of a woman who'd been in a car wreck at seventeen. According to a sign on the wall, the car had blown up and the fire burned 80 percent of the woman's flesh. She'd spent the next ten years in clinics. The woman's skin had been regenerated and grafted to create a puffy, red, and inflamed covering. Her lips were tattooed on. Hair was grafted in the place of eyebrows and tattooed underneath. After ten years of medical technology, the woman still looked nothing like the girl she'd been.

A row of microscopes made the steps of regenerating skin visible, each one offering a view of a more advanced stage of growth. When it was Sarah's turn to lean over and watch cells divide, at first she saw only her own eyelashes flickering back.

"Adjust the distance," Dale said, and helped move the lenses until she could focus on the thin, penciled-in-looking lines of transparent cells. She felt his hand on her elbow, his breath a soft motion in the air alongside her cheek.

They watched a movie of an endoscopic ACL replacement: A freckled leg rested on the edge of a metal table. A hand in a rubber glove punctured what the voice-over called "portals" into the skin—bleeding holes, really. The same hand wrestled a cannula under the kneecap, through the skin. The cannula held a camera that brought viewers inside the body to see the torn ACL where it floated, barely attached to the femur.

Dale said, "Like hardware. The body is just parts, put together."

"And sometimes falling apart," Sarah said.

The next light board showed a blown-up photo of a giant pale, hairless ear. The ear was perfect, sculptural and smooth.

"This may look like a human ear," a recorded man's voice said when Sarah touched a flat red button, "but what you are looking at is an artificially cultivated growth of human cells structured to re-create the curving form of ear tissue."

The next image showed the ear was attached to the back of a live rat.

Tissue engineering.

Dale said, "That's it! This is her work!"

His ex helped engineer a human ear grown on a rat?

The ear didn't look real, so much as it made all the other ears in the room look waxy and fake, even against living heads.

Five more photos illustrated how the ear had been grown through cloning human skin cells and farming them on the back of the rat.

"Initial cells are harvested from human foreskin," the recorded voice said. Dale loved it. The rat looked hungry and frightened and oblivious to the ear. Its eyes gleamed under the photographer's lights, and its dark, handlike paws were tense.

The picture was horrifying, the whole idea wrong. Sarah paused. People gathered behind her. She said, "Why do this?"

Dale answered, "Someone loses an ear, they want another one. But the bigger point is, tissue engineering is the basis of stem cell research, heart surgery options, brain reconstruction."

Sarah couldn't leave the rat. She stayed, fascinated by the shine in its eyes, the tension in its body. Every inch of the animal addressed the camera. The ear grew like a fungus from its back. The more Sarah looked at the growth, the less it looked like an ear. It was smooth, pale, and unmarked. It was nobody's ear, just a crazy work of art molded from human foreskin.

After the rat, the rest of the show appeared desperate, a collective effort toward recovery and anticipated loss: emu-to-human cornea transplants. Tendon replacements harvested from a bird called a rhea, reconstructed in a human.

It was all animals serving human needs.

Someone, somewhere, would be grateful for that ear, and for the rat that carried the ear, the foreskin, the grafting.

Dale reached for Sarah's hand. He touched her smallest finger. Sarah let her fingers slide, one between each of his, to feel the bones of his knuckles, the muscle and skeleton underneath. It was an experiment. She folded a second hand over the top of his, to find the thick rope of vein that ran along the back.

It was evening as they left OMSI. In the zoo the cats, nocturnal, would skulk along the edge of their confines. Good-bye rabbits! Sarah would soon be home with Ben, making dinner. The mandrill was in her holding area, with a few mandrill friends to keep her calm, and Dale would visit her. He would take care of his pregnant animal.

Sarah shortened her stride to match his. Their hands pressed together like there was a wound between them, something they needed to keep direct pressure on.

He reached his other hand to unlock the car door and brushed against her. Then he brought his lips in. His breath touched her first. His lips were on hers. She kissed him, too. It was awkward. It was skin. Grafting on each other: She felt that ear grow on the back of the rat—a mismatch, and a solution. She was the ear on the rat now.

Punch It Out

*B*ecause she lacked the cultural reach to demand reforestation of the world's mangrove trees, Nyla put paper in one bag and bottles in another. She couldn't stop oil from seeping along the floor of the Gulf of Mexico. She couldn't save baby oysters in Oregon's own Willapa Bay from death by acidification of the waters, but she could dig her fingernails into the magenta paper wrapped around a bottle of natural cherry soda and peel it back like so much sunburned skin.

She worked the way she'd weed a garden, dig a pit toilet, rock climb. She'd done all of it, always as a multitasker: Now while she sorted and peeled, her body built a whole new person, a baby.

A baby who she'd send to OMSI science camp and every other science camp—everything she herself never got—until maybe that child would have what it took to save the planet.

It was late. Her store was closed. Arena had stayed after school to work on art. Barry Gibb encouraged her, and the class had a show coming up.

Nobody expected Nyla to make dinner. Nobody needed Nyla at all.

The cure for despair? To do good work. The store was her art installation, her perfect world, her new pet. She hummed an aimless tune, her back to the door, then heard the doorbell's fairy chime. When she turned around there was a man in the store, gawky and stooped. He pulled his stocking cap off.

"I'm sorry, we're closed." She ran a hand down her ponytail. Outside it was dark.

He shuffled from one foot to the other, and tugged off his gray fingerless gloves. He said, "I'll turn the sign around for you."

She kept a careful eye on him. He turned the sign in the window from OPEN to CLOSED, and she waited for him to go but he didn't. He said, "You don't have to sort that stuff, you know. It's all one bin now, at the curb, right?"

He looked about twenty, maybe older or younger, who could tell. He had black hair that needed cutting, and it danced in lines of static from his hat. He could've been part Chinese, or Mexican, or Native American. Maybe one parent from India?

His shoes were screwed up, burned and melted rubber-toed tennis shoes. Maybe he lived in a hobo camp kept warm by a fire in a hidden lot somewhere. Nyla had the urge to find him a pair of shoes.

"Have a good night." She pulled the paper label off a can in her hands, and dropped the can into one bag and the label into another. He was right, you didn't have to sort anymore, but she did it anyway—this was how she was raised, old-school enviro—and hoped her extra effort helped the recycling program. She walked forward, a move meant to urge the man out the door the way the principal always led her from the school office.

He said, "Except for bottles. Glass. That's still separate." He took a step into the store and balled his knit gloves in one palm. His thin mouth curved into a half smile.

"We open at ten, tomorrow." The canvas bag Nyla called a purse, with her phone and keys inside, was at the end of the couch closer to the door. She meant to leave soon. She wasn't used to anybody actually coming into the store.

"What do you sell?" He looked around.

She hadn't sold anything, ever.

A knife rested on the glass top of a bistro table in the middle of the room. It was a long butcher knife. Nyla used it for slicing cheese and sometimes for breaking up thick squares of bulk dark chocolate.

She'd brought it for celebrations, in anticipation of hosting events at the store, people in their good clothes, talks about the environment. Parties. Maybe a rain forest fund-raiser? It was her old kitchen knife, a wedding present, bigger and sharper than it needed to be to do the party cheese slicing. She saw the man notice the knife. Then he looked at her.

She said, "You need to go."

"You're inside and I'm outside," he said, but he said it quietly. Nyla wasn't sure she'd heard right.

She asked, "What's that?"

He said, "You got a bathroom I could use?"

She shook her head no.

He said, "Where's the money?"

She said, "There's no money here." She tried to keep her voice steady. Really, there was no money. The last of her money had gone to fabric for her undyed hemp curtains.

He smiled wider, almost laughed. He said, "Everybody's got money," like he knew something Nyla didn't. "The only difference is how much."

The mini-fridge hummed. The computer emitted a steady hiss. When the man moved in the direction of the knife, Nyla moved, too, and she moved faster than he did. She had to. She shot out her right hand, from the shoulder, and hit him in the jaw. His head jerked back. She swung with the left, in a crosscut.

She had surprise on her side; the look on his face was mostly shock. He came forward, angry now.

As she swung, Nyla's muscle memory knew the steps: She heard the electronic Middle Eastern mash-up of her kickboxing DVD sound track and saw in her mind's eye that Barbie doll coach, a beautiful blonde, all white teeth, long hair, and a boob job, in a pink and black workout outfit. That angel of fitness, Barbie, smiled and said, "Remember—arms up, protect your face!"

The man reached out to grab her. Nyla's arms were already up. She ducked, knocked his hand away, then pulled back, danced in a boxer's shuffle, and offered a fast uppercut to his soft jaw that made his teeth click together.

She'd done this thousands of times—five days a week, an hour a day for more than ten years, in Tae Bo, kickboxing, weight training, and cardio.

Angel Barbie in Nyla's mind prompted, "Remember to breathe!"

Nyla's foot hit the man's ribs in a roundhouse, from the right then the left. Her shoe, a soft leather clog, flew off on the way. It smacked the wall.

Barbie said, "Good work! This is your cardio. Keep your focus, ladies!"

The man grabbed his side. His face contorted, and he came at Nyla in a rage. He was a man she'd been waiting for, the man her father locked the house against at night, the man she wasn't supposed to speak to on the city bus, the guy who offered her a ride once, the dangers. He was here. She brought out a front kick as he lunged— "Heel first! Straighten that leg!"—and used his momentum against him, doubling the impact. He bent in half, hands to the groin.

"Okay, up the tempo! Do it again!" Barbie smiled, her glossy hair flipping side to side.

Nyla dealt another roundhouse from the right automatically because it was the routine and she was deep into it and she was terrified. The man fell toward the floor. *Thwack!* Her foot found the side of his head on the way down. She panicked. She couldn't let him get up, he'd kill her. If he wasn't going to kill her before, he definitely would now. *Don't move, don't move*, she prayed. What came next was up to him. His decisions would fuel her own.

Barbie said, "We're halfway through, keep moving! You can do it! Eight more."

Eight more? Nyla bounced in her boxer's shuffle and watched, ready.

The man didn't get up. He moved one hand slightly, that was all.

Barbie said, "Don't poop out on me now! Finish strong."

There was blood on the floor and on the side of the man's face— what had she done? Nyla didn't want to hurt him! She only meant to protect herself. She bent down and asked, "What's bleeding?"

He said something garbled, something like "Fuck you," or "Kill you," or "Would you—"

Nyla said, "What's that?"

His eyes, when he opened them, were furious. He grabbed for her ponytail, catching her hair in his blood-marked fingers. Nyla swung a cocked elbow hard into the man's bloody nose. She ripped her own head backward, leaving hair in his hands as she stood up fast and stepped away. He grabbed for her foot. Her second shoe slid off. She gave a ballet leap over the crumpled man, snagged the knife, and reached for the strap of her canvas tote where it rested on the couch. She made it out the door and pulled the door closed, but couldn't stop to lock it. She'd have to find her keys—too slow! She kept going, then slid the rusted, reticulated metal gate across the outside entryway. The padlock was easy to find: It rested heavy in the bottom of her bag. She forced the padlock through an old metal loop, clicked it, and locked the gate. Inside the store, the man started to get up. Nyla's heart kicked into higher gear. He got up, his head swaying, and then went down again.

Her phone was in her bag. She called 911.

"March it out!" smiling Barbie said. "Punch the sky! Great for the abs."

Over her own pounding heart, Nyla told the operator, "I've been attacked." She said, "I have a store, on Williams. Somebody may be hurt."

The operator asked, "Are you hurt?"

Nyla couldn't catch her breath. She said, "No." Her hands were numb, and she couldn't breathe, but she was okay.

The man in her store howled. From inside, he threw a vase against the front window, and the window shattered in a web of fractures. Nyla hid in the shadows alongside the building but kept an eye on her storefront. Her heartbeat didn't know the fight was over. Adrenaline made her move.

Her fingers tightened around the knife handle.

When the police cruiser turned the corner, what officers might've seen first was a barefoot woman doing a victory dance on a dark patch of sidewalk. At Barbie's command, Nyla marched it off. She punched the sky and lifted her knees and took deep breaths. The butcher knife in her fist glinted when it caught the streetlight, each time she raised her arm. Blood-darkened spots marked the blade, Nyla's skin, and her clothes. If she stopped moving, she'd cry. When she tried to stop, her legs shook; her chest was ready to explode.

An ambulance siren called to them from far down the street. A fire truck was on the way, too. They always sent a fire truck, like every emergency involved some kind of fire.

The man was trapped behind the locked gate, just out of the store, but not free to leave. He let out a yodel, yelled to be *let free.*

Amber police lights circled and played over the metal gate. Nyla walked in her cooldown, trying to shake this techno-pop dance version of terror. The police pulled over to the curb.

One officer got out of the cruiser. He said, "Drop the weapon."

Nyla, still on the verge of tears, yelled, "Don't shoot! He's not armed!" She bounced up and down.

The officer flinched. He said, "Drop the weapon." His gun was pointed at Nyla.

She slowed in her jog.

"Weapon?"

"Drop the knife." A second officer got out of the car. He put a hand to his holster.

"Ah, the knife!" Her fingers were numb, far away, and curled around the black knife handle. It was a weapon! She didn't think of it as a weapon, not when it was in her own hands. It was cutlery. It was a wedding present.

"Now," the cop said. She was in his sights!

She let the knife fall to the ground.

The attacker yelled, "She tried to kill me!"

The wedding present butcher knife hit the sidewalk with a thud and rattle. She said, "No. I called help. I called help for you."

Breeding Loan

*H*umanity was trampling itself in search of reported action!

On the other side of a plate glass window, in an enclosure, the mandrill patriarch lumbered through the artificial landscape to approach a female from behind. He reached a hand, spread the soft pads of her relatively compact butt, touched her, then smelled his fingers. When he licked his fingers, somebody outside, down below, beyond the window, barked, "Dude!"

Sarah was at tree canopy level; her room looked down over the top of the enclosure, a secret perch. The female must've smelled like a hot monkey in estrus; the male stood on his hind legs and mounted her leisurely.

Sarah felt the male's push and thrust as though in the cavities of her own body. We could be asexual populations, single-celled drifters, built to reproduce without fusing gametes. But we're not. The mandrill touched his mate with a gentle, determined hand. Sarah held her breath.

Guffaws broke out beyond the glass, out of her line of sight.

The female shook off the male's long-fingered grip and scampered across fake rock, hesitating near a clump of hanging foliage.

The male rocked back on his striped ornament. He ran his thumb over the folds of his pink member, picked something off the head, and flicked whatever he'd found into the shrubs.

Male mandrills drip a secretion. They rub their sternal gland drippings on mates and on trees, too, until their chests are bloody and riddled with splinters. Their world is one ripe advertisement of virility. Sarah stood above the habitat where the air was thick with musk, breathed in man-ape, kicked a foot through straw scattered on the floor—debris left from bales stored there—and willed her last good egg to stay viable.

She could feel the heat of her own body fluids gathering.

Her timer beeped. She peered through the grate. Baby Lucy picked at a tire on a rope, and trailed a finger through the straw. "Foraging," Sarah wrote. *Ignoring the adults getting it on.*

A horde of teenagers shrieked the mixed yodel of excited pack animals. The patriarch followed his mate. She waited. He checked her scent again, pulled apart the folds of her vagina, and touched his tongue inside.

It was science!

It was a peep show. The mandrill put his hands on her hips. This time, she stayed still.

"Dude, you taping this?" somebody yelled below. There was a cackle. The humans were loud; the mandrills were silent and purposeful. The patriarch bent his knees and pushed his erect baby maker into his mate. She stayed on all fours. Humans hooted, their voices an ever-expanding choir.

Sarah's cinder block cell, bleaker than the cheapest of hotels, was pungent with animal sex. She was paid to watch, and now it was like watching porn. The male pushed his hips back and forth, in and out.

Sarah leaned against the bars of the narrow window. Where was Ben? Her mate, her only mate, her legal love.

The door to the outside stairs opened. A cold breeze cut through. "Hey," Dale called out. "I checked on our expectant mother. The baby still has a heartbeat. There's signs of placenta previa, though—"

Sarah turned to him.

He said, "I want to apologize, for the other day, by the car. I was out of line."

She put her clipboard on a folding chair, met Dale halfway as he walked over, and lifted his T-shirt over his head. He said, "Hey. What're you doing?"

She tugged. He gave in, raising his arms. She had him trapped inside his own shirt; his head was hidden, his armpits said a big hello, his torso was that model of anatomy, pale and lightly marked with the curl of hair. He tugged an arm out of the shirt. Sarah sank into his skin. He smelled like Dial soap, clean and chemical, a man fighting off his own dripping secretions. She breathed his scent in until she found the real smell, human sweat trapped in the hair under his arms, the smell of an animal, new genetic material.

Sexual selection.

She unbuttoned his jeans, following the happy trail of curled hair down his belly. He said, "I don't know—" His voice was gentle. His pants dropped to the floor. He stepped out of them. His cock tented his briefs. Sarah kissed him openmouthed, felt the warmth of his breath.

This was imperative.

She'd be doing Ben a favor. Not a biological favor so much, but a sociological assist. He'd be a father. She'd be a mom. Pressure off.

She'd be faithful to him ever after.

It wasn't about love. It was about maximizing reproductive chances. They'd retain the marriage paradigm. She curled down to the straw-covered cement floor, in air heavy with mandrill secretions. Dale followed her down. He didn't say anything, but let his body follow her lead. She took her clothes off in the cold. They could hear the hoots and hollers down below, the audience gathered for the mandrill porn show. Sarah pushed her clothes away, felt her skin rest against the near-frozen concrete, and against Dale's heat. Those clothes had been a costume, hopeful and civilized, hiding and holding back her animal urge.

Wise Up

Arena spanked a lump of red clay with her fist until it grew warm and soft under her knuckles.

"Paper!" the teacher, Barry Gibb, barked across the room, and shook out the tendrils of his honey-toned mullet. He wanted her to lay newspaper between the damp clay and the nicked tabletop—a table laced with cutout hearts and the etched curses of kids who'd already graduated or maybe just wandered away. There was a stack of *Oregonians* in the middle of the table. Arena took the Metro section and spread the sheets out.

She picked up her clay and the words *ekiM sevol aniT* were raised in the back of it, lifted off the table's carved face along with half a broken heart. She poked a finger through the words.

Other kids were busy, their heads bowed over the fat strokes of tempera paintings or the crazy hatch marks of detailed ink cartoons. One guy seemed normal except for a crying problem; he charted whale migrations on big sheets of white paper tacked to the wall. His drawings were beautiful.

Who wouldn't cry over that?

There were smart students in the special room, and others who lagged. There were kids struggling with autism and Asperger's and extreme hyperactivity. One tapped his pencil all day, the same rhythm, *tap, tap, tap-tap-tap*. There were kids with problems Arena didn't understand, who managed well enough and then suddenly broke, and didn't manage at all, like their little internal computers had been hit with a virus.

In that room they ate snacks, like in kindergarten. Granola bars and cut oranges! Snacks left them smelling like children.

She dropped her clay hard against the paper, and pushed her thumb into it.

"Hey, dealer!" A voice broke through the room. It came from a guy who leaned in the doorway. The pencil tapping stopped. All the kids looked, like maybe they were all secretly dealers.

They were all *dealing*—they were coping. Arena knew he meant her: drug dealer.

He said, "Seen your mom on the news."

The pencil tapping started again.

Barry Gibb waved a hand and said, "Keep moving."

The guy at the door flashed a peace sign, pointed at Arena, and said, "Righteous!"

Was that a good thing, or bad? She gave him a thumbs-up. It seemed expected. He disappeared.

She couldn't read by herself in the cone zone anymore without smokers saying how awesome it was, her mom kicking butt like that. They'd say, "Awesome," their heads bobbing.

She tried to pass it off as cool points.

The thing was, now her mom moved like she'd been the one beaten up—limped like she hurt her leg or her back but wouldn't admit it. She mumbled broken sentences like, "God, I hope not," or "Geez," or sometimes "Holy mackerel"; she'd murmur to the toaster or the shower curtain or their potted plants.

She'd quit doing her workout DVDs. Instead she spent her afternoons fussing with a bread dough recipe, a baking project, the "mother starter," she called it. Nyla said baking was wholesome. It was science. It was love. Arena saw it as food. They had plenty of food.

AKA was the face on the other side of the conversations in her head. She stored her thoughts to tell him later. He'd skipped work crew. She'd asked their group leader where AKA was, but he'd only muttered, "Confidential," and put a pair of gloves in her hand, then gestured for her to get going on litter patrol.

Maybe it actually was confidential or maybe that word was code, meaning their crew leader didn't know squat.

She pummeled her clay, pulled off a piece, and rolled a clay snake. Her hands turned rusty brown. Making art kept students busy and gave the teacher and his assistant time to focus on kids who needed more help.

They didn't focus on Arena. What help did she need?

She'd called AKA's phone and gotten his voice mail, his own voice saying, "Sorry. Not here! Ha! Leave a message or whatever. I'll call you back."

"What about our trip to the country?" she said, into his machine. They'd made a plan the last time they talked to see his house in Boring. Maybe it was about meeting his parents. The way he talked about it, it was like the trip mattered to him. Besides, he'd end up back in the Donald E. Long Home if he didn't finish work screw.

Mostly, Arena needed him. He was her only friend.

She'd gone back to the Temple Everlasting once, since bringing AKA there, but Mack treated her like a customer, like she needed a reason to be there, like she'd come looking for something.

Like he had anything to offer?

She coiled her clay snake into a low bowl. The class was working toward an art show. Her project was the installation. She had a roll of gauze. She had Anchee Min's mosquito net. She had an ache like she was meant to be somebody else and was trapped in this body, this place, this school.

The thought of putting her art up in the school gym for people to see made her queasy and have to pee, but it was better than picking up used condoms on the side of the highway. Dulcet showed her work. Arena aimed to be brave, like Dulcet.

She noticed a grainy photo in the Metro section of the *Oregonian*, the paper under her clay. It was a close-up of her mom's face looking older and anxious. Her mom's hair was wispy. She needed to put whatever people put in their hair to make it lie flat, product, something her mom would call toxic chemicals.

This was different from the earlier stories she'd seen about her mom and the attempted robbery.

There was a picture of AKA. There he was! Arena's heart picked up. Her only friend! It looked like him, but more sulky. Wait—was that him? She started to doubt it. She'd already seen him a few times in strangers on the street—the slouch of his back, his shaggy hair— the way it happens when you're looking for somebody, the way it happened when she thought about her dad. She'd see men on the street who could've been her dad, if he were alive.

She looked closer. This was her mother's attacker, the man who'd left her mom limping like an old lady. The guy who wouldn't leave the store. Alvin Kelvin Aldrich.

Aldrich, an emancipated minor, is on probation for property theft and menacing . . .

Arena couldn't breathe. The air was thick with the dust of tempera paint and dry clay. She folded up the paper. Her stomach was a knot. In the back of the room, Barry Gibb helped a student into a smock.

She took the paper and slipped out into the empty hall.

Her mom had beaten up AKA. Her mom beat up her boyfriend, the only eyes she could look back into and not squint and skitter.

An alarm went off, blaring loud, like a fire drill, only this time it wasn't a drill. It beat against the inside of her skull. She couldn't hear anything else. It was in her head, in her brain, in her heart.

She couldn't breathe until she got out the front door. In the school parking lot, she took out her phone and called, clay dusting the phone's tiny buttons.

There was his voice—"Not here! Ha!"—and it was all a big joke except he really wasn't there and he could even be dead because that voice had been his message for as long as she'd known him and now for all she knew he was nothing but energy in the cosmos and his voice was sound trapped in time and all of physics couldn't explain why her heart hurt and her gut hurt and outside she wanted to see the city bus round the hill.

She wanted that bus like it was her breath.

She crushed the newspaper in her hand, then smoothed it out. She looked at AKA's face, glowering and worried, and he was lost, and she was empty and he was hers, and her mother had done this, and no way was it AKA's fault, and Arena was in love.

Animal Behavior

The partnering side of mating is a bodyguard arrangement, about sticking around to protect new babies and the mother while she's vulnerable. Was that still so relevant, in the modern world? Sarah, on the couch, was a snow leopard on a rock ledge, patient and edgy. She wore an invitingly short T-shirt dress with a pair of high-heeled mules and called it good.

She ran a hand over Shadow's knobby back, and watched the clock. She had strong coffee ready to make those spermy sperm race. Go, little soldiers! All she needed was Ben.

A footstep landed on the front porch. Sarah got up and Shadow got up fast, too, underfoot. Together they scrambled for the door. Sarah lost a shoe, and then she wasn't a snow leopard at all but a stray and starved dog—not the plan! She stopped and tugged at her dress. She told Shadow to sit. She slid her foot back into her shoe and did her best to walk calmly.

She heard Ben make his way to the door. She poured the coffee. He'd have his hands full, his big satchel, and his crumpled, oft-reused paper lunch bag.

She flung the door open and threw out an eager thigh: *Hello, Sugar!*

A rusted wheelbarrow sat in the front yard, tipped to one side like a drunk trying to remember the way home. A man came from across the street carrying a shovel and hoe. He had dark curls and big shoulders. Ah! She'd forgotten: her latest date with lawn care, a day laborer.

Shadow made his way to the door slowly and started to bark an aging dog's bark, deep and weak and slow.

Bags of mulch were stacked against the side of the house. They'd booked ahead—this guy was in demand. His teeth were white; his arms were strong. He was, he said himself, the day she met him in a parking lot, "good and fast and clean."

He was kind of a young Orson Welles, if Orson Welles had worked out. He was beautiful genetic material.

"Coffee?" she offered, and held out the cup.

"Hey! Looks good!" Ben's voice was sudden and booming as he came up the walk from the other way.

Oof! He'd seen her, offering coffee.

Sarah turned fast. Her hands shook, the coffee spilled, and the cup fell to the front steps and smashed. "You're home."

His medium beige foundation was broken by a five o'clock shadow. That was why men didn't wear makeup: Their facial hair ruined it. The shadow was manly! He was half in drag. His nose looked better, really, or maybe she'd just grown used to it.

He bent and picked up a piece of the cup.

Sarah took his hand. "I'll get that later."

The day laborer started laying mulch, getting their flower beds ready for winter. Privately Ben had already asked Sarah more than once why they were hiring laborers for work they could do them-selves. It was charity, she said. Giving men work.

She pulled Ben into the hallway, shut the door, and closed young Orson Welles and the rest of the world out.

Ben said, "Well, got through my stack of loans. I was working on a VA loan at the end of the day that looked like it'd never come together, but I think we've—"

She put her arms around him and kissed him. She didn't care about loans. She unbuttoned his work shirt. He dropped his bag on the hallway floor.

He said, "Your doctor said wait two months."

Sarah said, "We can't wait."

He said, "We might lose another one."

Her body felt ready. Who could say when her last good egg would move from her ovaries to her fallopian tubes? "Anything can happen. I'll take my chances." She moved behind him and pushed him toward the stairs, upstairs to their bedroom.

Ben let her take his shirt off. He had on a ribbed tank, sweaty with the day's work. He smelled like a man. A little like powder and makeup, too, but mostly a man. He smelled familiar. He smelled like hers.

The curtains were pulled. Outside, it'd grown dark, and the inside room was a cave against the winter. Sarah kissed his face. She could tell he was nervous. She said, "It's fine."

He said, "You're sure you want to do this?"

"It's what I live for." When she pushed him onto the bed it was a loving shove and he was compliant.

"Our lives are good," he whispered.

"We'll make a good life for a child."

"I worry about you—"

She said, "Shhh. It's not about me." She put a finger to her lips, then her lips on his, and she stopped him from talking.

He pulled away. He said, "Ow, Jeesuz!"

She'd hit his nose with her own.

He winced. "I'm okay."

Sarah tugged at Ben's boxers. She pulled her dress over her own head and kicked out of her underwear.

Mother Bread

A child's heart, that first functional embryonic organ, built in the mother's own body, is no secret to a mother. Nyla's unborn baby would show itself soon, through evolving morning sickness and later kicking. All she had to do was pay attention. For now, though, any embryonic struggle was overshadowed by the nuisance of a throbbing pain in Nyla's side.

She'd pulled a muscle, probably when she executed the roundhouse.

Maybe when she broke the kid's ribs.

God, she hated to think about all that! She could still feel the way her foot had made contact, the bone cracking. She had a bruise on her instep. What was a bruised foot and an aching side compared to broken ribs? She could've punctured that boy's lungs. They were lucky he was alive.

She beat up a child! Sheesh. Yes, he was a grown kid, almost eighteen, menacing and with a record, but still.

It was worse to her mind that he was brown skinned, maybe Native American, or African American, part Latino or from India, or all of those ancestries. He was a disenfranchised, disadvantaged youth. She'd made his future a little more screwed. From what she'd read in the papers, he didn't seem to be a gang member. He wasn't a murderer.

Her store was poised on the edge of a neighborhood forever in transition. She was only blocks from Unthank Park. The name of that park always sounded so ungrateful, but really it was named for Doctor DeNorval Unthank, one of Portland's early African American doctors and a civil rights activist, maybe by necessity. He'd been chased out of Westmoreland, a white neighborhood, by hardcore racism. Now Nyla had become the very last thing she ever wanted to be.

She was gentrification. Even on her slim budget.

She was whitey! A scared white lady.

Dulcet treated the whole thing like an unexpected victory, a reason to slap a high five, pour another vodka 'tini—shaken, stirred, dirty, dry, laced with barbiturates. Georgie looked baffled, but that was sleep deprivation. Sarah only chirped, "Your training paid off!" Like Nyla had been doing yoga and kickboxing all these years to kick teenage butt.

She was ready to forgive that almost-grown boy for entering LifeCycles. He was misguided. He didn't need money. He needed love! If he should perhaps want a foster mom, a friend, a big sister, a mentor, she'd be there for him.

What kind of mentor could she be, though? Jeez. The shame of liberal guilt climbed through her bones: a foster mom, really. Because why? Because she was white and old. Those were her credentials. That was nothing.

And she'd raised a couple of kids, true. She had experience there.

But she lived on her husband's life insurance policy and had a narrow storefront like a toy store in a crummy part of town.

Nyla reached up to a high shelf for a bag of organic flour. As she reached, the muscle in her side gave a twinge that made her sweat. She breathed through the pain, visualizing letting it go like leaves drifting down a river.

This was her health care plan: visualizations.

She was seven weeks pregnant. The baby was still too small to feel except in nausea. Somewhere in the world was a man with a deep voice and black hair on the backs of his hands, who had left his DNA for the child that he would have with Nyla.

She could e-mail him. But she could never muster the level of naive optimism she'd had before the car wreck, the optimism that it took to build, again, a two-parent family.

On the same high shelf she found a metal tin with sugar inside. She slid the tin onto the counter next to the flour, then got out a quart of milk. She pressed one hand near her hip bone, over the ache. She was expanding her Amish friendship bread dough starter to give to friends. Baking was Nyla's way of giving back. This round, it was a formal request to the world for forgiveness for her failings.

Norman Cousins, the writer, said, "Life is an adventure in forgiveness." Nyla exercised her own forgiveness muscles daily, with the same rigor she brought to Pilates. She forgave the shortsighted, greedy politicians and the local land developers who filled in wetlands, killed off ecosystems, and flattened her childhood sledding hill to build a strip mall nobody needed then sprayed the place with neurotoxins in the name of pest control.

They'd killed the last beaver in Beaverton, a suburb of Portland.

This boy had only pulled her hair. It could've been worse. She limped across the kitchen, held her side, and found a wooden spoon in a crock of utensils.

Nyla had covered her fridge with inspirational notes, mostly in her own hand. One read, "A dirty coffee cup isn't *clean*, but it's never very dirty either." That was hers. Another read, "The further off from England, the nearer is to France," from the "Lobster Quadrille" by Lewis Carroll.

Nyla felt herself in the sea, and swam toward that further shore, seeking a way out. She lifted the ceramic bowl. The Amish friendship bread starter was a life form doing its job: yeast rising. She tended that starter like a child, every day.

She tended it the way she cared for Arena.

Who were the parents of her attacker, her victim? What kind of parents didn't know when their child was heading toward trouble? That would be a mother who didn't know her own child's heart. Arena was safely in school.

Actually Arena was downtown, in the street, standing in the way of a barreling TriMet bus. She yelled at AKA's apartment building, calling his name. The bus driver hit the horn without slowing down.

Arena gave the bus a glare as though her fury could stop it. TriMet barreled forward. She dove for the curb at the last possible minute, tripped on the sidewalk, rolled in the passing crowd, and flipped the bus off.

A raspy and low voice said, "Get yourself run over, that way."

She turned toward the voice. It was a man in a long army coat and a floppy, oiled-leather hat. He had a paper grocery bag under one arm and a short cigar between his teeth. It was the hippie she'd seen in AKA's place, the guy who wasn't AKA's father.

She stood up fast and brushed herself off. "We met, remember?"

He looked her up and down, took the cigar out of his mouth, and raised his eyebrows. "I'd like to remember." His voice pawed her like a hand.

"I was with AKA."

The hippie put his wet cigar back between his lips. His teeth were dark and crooked. He worked a key into the lock and muscled the door open. "He owes us rent." The cigar danced against the man's lip. The gray sky had started to spit, and the man's bag was dotted with rain. "He needs to pick up his crap."

"Did he move out?" Arena was cold. She was shaking. Her heart was a pigeon, her lungs were all city bus exhaust.

"Disappeared," the hippie said.

She'd already been down to the Juvenile Justice Center and asked about AKA. The suits behind their counters wouldn't tell her anything. Confidential. At the hospital, she had to have a secret PIN number to show she was legally granted access to his information, to know if he was even there. It was all confidential. She had no clues. She'd scanned the phone poles for flyers, looking for a sign of AKA's band. Maybe he'd play somewhere and she could show up.

She followed the hippie's hunched shoulders into the shadows of the apartment's stairwell. He let her. They went down skinny and unlit halls. He said, "Take anything of his you want. The rest is headed for a Dumpster."

When she reached AKA's room, she knocked, then pushed the door open. The windows were already open. A nylon curtain blew in the wind. Rain kicked up the tar smell of the roof outside. Blankets lay in a tangle on the mattress on the floor. There were clothes on the floor, too, like AKA had just stepped out of them.

She read the clothes the way she'd read a book. This place was her mosquito net, the source of her longing. She dropped down on the bed.

The hippie knocked around in the next room over. Footsteps came down the hall. She held her breath. The steps went on by.

Beside the bed there was an ashtray full of cigarette butts, a half-full plastic liter of warm Coke, and a photograph. It was the picture of AKA and his country house. There, for a moment stuck in time, he was a long-haired, shirtless, happy kid with a dog and a tire swing. Arena turned the photo over. Somebody had written a date and an address on the back in the curling, careful letters of a woman's hand. Below the date, it said, "The Boring House."

Of course: AKA would go home. He was in trouble. He was hurt. Arena's own new-age, environmental, nonviolent mom had pounded him! He'd want the safety of his parents.

Her mom was nuts with saving the rain forest, conserving toilet paper—Canadian old-growth forests!—and barely driving the car. But his mom might be the kind to buy Cap'n Crunch and watch TV with him.

She slid the picture into her pocket and left the room.

The hippie loitered in the living room, now stripped down to his post-working-day or whatever tighty-whities and a Hanes T-shirt. His hat was off. His long gray and black hair had the ring of hat head. Without the hat, he didn't look so much like a hippie, more like just an old man who needed a haircut. He said, "You party?" He took a toke on a joint so small it was almost invisible between his thick fingers.

Party?

He held the tiny joint out.

She sucked in her stomach to slide past him. He exhaled and said, "Stay, Princess!" He followed her into the narrow hallway. He reached out. His fingers wrapped around her wrist and he pulled her toward him, smashing his face against hers. It wasn't a kiss so much as their teeth hitting together. She pushed against his body and yanked her arm away. He threw the roach on the floor, then pushed her head down. She fought back. His underwear was tented as he pushed into her, and showed a damp spot. His hand pushed against her head, urging her down, toward that damp spot on his briefs. She brought her knee up and he twisted her wrist. It was all in seconds. He was strong, but wasted and unsteady. She screamed. The hippie was bigger than she was, but he lost his footing when she ducked sideways fast, and she shoved until he hit the ground.

She ran. He fumbled to get up behind her.

.ᴗ ᴗ.

La la la . . . ! Nyla hummed and stirred her Amish bread. Life was good, getting better all the time, if she could only shake the guilt and the ache in her side and the limp of her sore foot.

She'd called the courts and said she wouldn't press charges—the attack was a misunderstanding, water under the bridge, right?—but the boy had a record. He was on probation. His future was in the hands of the state.

She added a cup of flour, a cup of milk, and a cup of sugar, everything in equal proportions. The starter was the "mother bread," meant to be divided.

Nyla was the mother bread's mother.

Every ten days forever that starter would be ready to split, like cells dividing, turning into twins, triplets, quadruplets.

Bread without end, amen.

Every ten days she'd have a new gift to give away. It was a chain letter in dough form. They'd all make bread together, tending that baby. She'd give a starter to the parents of that boy when she found them.

Her answer to the world's despair was bread.

She lifted a cup of dough out of the starter. Two more times, and she had three gifts. Nyla had three lumps of bread dough individually packaged in plastic bags, each one round and white.

She headed for Sarah's.

This was the day to spread her love.

.ᴗ ᴗ.

Dulcet claimed it as a day to spread her legs and her latex. A day to get the bills paid. The banks had shut down one of her lines of credit, though she had made her payments on time and met their incredibly high interest rate. It was the new lending climate. Her other cards were maxed. The schools hadn't brought her in to do the body show since the "incident," as she thought of it, in the closet.

She had options: sell off photography equipment, give up the cheap lease on her studio, or pull out the latex suit.

Mr. Latex was her answer, her angel. He would be her stopgap.

He seemed genuine in his urges. Maybe he was a dedicated cop sustaining an undercover ruse, or a patient and conniving murderer. More likely he was a man pushing sixty who saw death skulking on the horizon and wanted his needs gratified in this lifetime. She slid out a clothing bag from under the bed. Like a vampire, the latex suit didn't do well stored in the light of day. She unzipped the case and lifted her organs out. There was the lung vest, the respiratory system, and the underlayer of ovaries, uterus, and kidneys. The pieces were well oiled with a silicone that gave them a shine. Inside, it was dry and clean and powdered. She laid it on the bed.

The one part that was missing from this woman's body, she thought for the first time, might be a developing fetus in the uterus. She hadn't considered making a pregnant anatomy when she ordered the suit. She always thought of it as anti-baby.

She put her hand inside, behind the uterus, and wondered how a baby doll might work, upside down, against her own skin, under the latex.

She could take a Sharpie and draw in a simple, tiny embryo. Then she'd be in Nyla's body, that fertile, fecund maker of babies.

Nyla was on the verge of an empty nest, and suddenly—Inexplicably! Wham!—pregnant. *Ding-ding-ding!* What were the odds of that? Dulcet was pretty sure Nyla had engineered the situation on purpose.

Clearly, Nyla had lost all sense of herself except as a mother.

Dulcet pulled off her dress, kicked off her underwear, then sat stark naked beside the suit and began to rub a water-based lube across her stomach. She worked lube over her bony hips and along the arch of her ass.

The goal was for the suit to happily glide on, not tear or overstretch. Latex clothes are big bucks. This one was tailor-made, and it was her income; she babied that precious fetish wear.

Nyla, uneasy about leaving the house since she had started showing up on the local news, scrambled to her car. She locked the
doors and revved the engine, always grateful when the car started.
She'd been recognized more than once by neighbors, as *that woman
from TV who beat up some punk.* Her neighborhood business associa-
tion invited her to teach a class in self-defense for small business
owners.

The newspaper found reasons to get extra mileage out of her
photo: ECONOMY WORSENS, VIOLENT CRIME ON THE RISE. And there
would be her picture, the poster victim of rising violent crime. They
were saving money by rerunning the image.

She didn't feel like a victim. She'd put up a serious fight. It was
possible that, out of the two of them, she was the only one fighting.
That kid could not keep his hands up, to protect his face, to save his
life.

Alvin Kelvin Aldrich was the prisoner who set the record for
crowding in the juvenile jails. His sweet, sad face showed up under
headlines such as SYSTEM OVERBURDENED.

She hurried up Sarah's front steps. Her breathing was shallow.
She was kind of a wreck. She cradled what she'd come to think of as
her Bundle of Love, the starter dough, knocked on the door, and kept
her coat collar pulled up high.

The city was a sprawling jail under cement-gray skies. Nyla had
donated what extra money she could come up with to the Oregon
Humane Society that month. She gave money to save ringed seals.
She bought a magazine subscription from a kid who came to her
door even though she didn't believe the magazines would ever be
delivered.

It was her ongoing effort to atone.

When the door opened, it wasn't Sarah or even Ben. It was a
big, silent, brawny, weathered man. Thieves? Nyla's fist tightened,
with an urge toward self-preservation. But she couldn't start another fight, not ever, not in that town. She tried to think peaceful
thoughts. "Is Sarah here?"

The man rotated his thick neck to gaze back into the house.
Nyla took two steps away. She felt hands wrap around her shoulders,
and when she moved she stepped on somebody's foot, gave a yip, and
flung her Bundle of Love.

"Hey, darlin'." Sarah's voice, behind her, was the burble of a river. "I was in the backyard. What'd you bring us?" Sarah picked up the Ziploc bag of white starter dough from where it'd tumbled under an azalea bush and gave it a gentle squeeze. "Salt dough clay?"

Nyla said, "Friendship bread. You can use it to make other starters, too, and expand the circle of friends." Her voice was nervous and thin.

Inside, the house had the smell of men at work: cut planks, fresh dirt, and sweat. Ben came downstairs with damp hair like he'd just stepped out of a shower. He walked in a cloud of berry shampoo—not the smell of work at all. Sarah took the starter to the kitchen, leaving her alone with Ben. Nyla still hadn't forgiven him for abandoning Sarah during the miscarriage.

Now she asked, "What do you have going on?"

"We're adding a deck!" Then more quietly, confidentially, Ben said, "She's been fragile, since the last miscarriage. Home improvements keep her spirits up."

There were the sounds of a handsaw being drawn back and forth against wood. Sarah came back from the kitchen, and Ben put a hand on her shoulder. She wrapped her arms around him. They seemed so happy together, completely partnered. They even looked alike. Nyla missed the days when she'd had a husband. She missed it more than anyone could imagine.

Sarah and Ben's lives were perfect and easy.

All Nyla did, all she'd ever done, was work. She felt it now, watching the hired men. She'd rehabbed her own houses. She knew how to use a Sawzall, for God's sake, that mark of an ambitious, self-sufficient homeowner.

The pain in her side spoke up in its way. Ugh. Nyla put a hand to it.

Seeing Sarah and Ben so happy together, surrounded by all that industry, improving their lives, made her miserable, even as she was happy for them, and she couldn't hold on to both emotions at once. They seemed so suddenly Ken and Barbie, both of them lanky but an average Oregon height, where women ran tall, the two of them like a pair of grande Americanos in that Starbucks daily measurement system, or a Subaru's compact Outback, all those ways of saying middle ground, evenly matched in their long limbs.

She couldn't stay there. It was easy to excuse herself—she was incidental to their happiness. She got out.

She wanted to see Dulcet.

Dulcet, her dear debauched friend, that lone wolf, would be an antidote to the overwhelming hit of Sarah and Ben's domestic bliss.

⸎

Arena marched at the edge of the road and heard her feet crunch gravel along with a symphony of crickets, tall grass rustling, and the hum of electrical wires. The road was empty and the dark was crowded with noise. There were no lights. The stars were clear but small and far away between cloud cover. Starlight? That was a joke. The stars didn't light up anything but themselves.

She'd taken the last bus out.

She used her iPhone to find directions to the address of the house on the back of AKA's photo. She tried to use the same phone to light her way, but that dim light only made her feel more visible against the dark.

She could use the phone to actually make a call. To talk to her mom, to tell her about the hippie. Arena's wrist was red and swollen.

But this was her mom's fault. She never wanted to talk to her mom again.

She wanted to see AKA, cry into his shoulder, smell him up close. The thought of his caramel skin kept her going forward. She thought about her own virginity thing. This was the time: She'd find AKA and tear his clothes off. She'd give herself over—pull his body so close even their molecules could mingle.

Her thigh muscles tightened against the cold night. She came to a mailbox and used her phone to light the numbers of the address on the side of it. She was closer.

Her legs were machines. Her breath was shallow. She could smell AKA's mix of cigarettes, sweat, and soap, and tried to imagine his room in the house he grew up in: clean sheets, a doting mother, a woodstove. Houses in the country all had woodstoves, right?

After forever—miles?—she found the address in black numbers on gold squares stuck to a mailbox. She slid the photo from her coat pocket; it was hard to see the details in the dark. She held the photo close to the light of her phone.

This was the house.

The mailbox, covered in rust, crumbled when she prodded it

with a finger. A car approached from far away. Its lights ran across Arena, illuminating her on the side of the road. She ducked behind bushes that grew in the culvert. The culvert was full of rain, though, and it soaked through the fabric of her Toms.

Could AKA be in the car?

The car slowed, as though looking out into the dark. What if an ax murderer drove down that empty road and saw her stumbling along?

She froze, like a deer.

The car sped up again, kept going, and left the night darker than before. If it had been a murderer, Arena would be dead. That'd show her mom faster than anorexia, which was the way most girls at Maya Angelou called out for attention. It'd be faster than alcohol poisoning even, and more decisive than teen pregnancy.

Her mom would love a teen pregnancy! She was nuts about babies.

Arena walked on trembling legs down the pitch-black driveway, where it was covered with the tangle of branches, leaning trees, and vines. Leaves had fallen, thick on the ground.

The house, when she reached it, looked diseased, with black patches against pale paint. There was a car in the driveway. Something moved. Arena froze.

She saw the movement again. It was so slight—like somebody who didn't want to be seen, the shoulder of a crouched man. No, it was a tire swing on a thin and frayed rope. The screen door was half off its hinges.

"Hello?"

A window was broken. Something had happened here. A fight? The house looked beaten up. "AK?" she called. She stepped onto the porch, reached past the broken screen door, lifted a knocker, and let it fall against the wood.

She jumped at the sound, even as she made it.

When she stopped knocking, there was only the song of the invisible bugs in the grass, frogs, crickets, or the electric hum. The windshield of the car was dark with the rot of fallen leaves. Arena put her hand around the brass doorknob and turned. It gave in. The smell of the house came out to meet her.

She broke a law; she stepped inside.

An open magazine sprawled on the couch. A pan of water waited for a dog, or for the roof to stop leaking, or both. Arena stepped over matted socks and a dirty carpet. A few more steps and she saw the kitchen. The fridge was pulled away from the wall. And there he was—AKA.

He was in a photo under a Disneyland magnet. He was a boy, then older.

A house is a box for a family. She opened bedroom doors. There was a room with a sliding closet door, and the closet was open, crowded with plastic hangers and women's clothes.

Two more doors and then she found a room with a short book-case, a mess of T-shirts, and blue and yellow wallpaper. A boy's room. The bed was narrow and cheap and broken.

This had to be his.

There was a watch on the floor. Arena picked it up. It was the kind with a clock face, not digital, and it had a rotating sun and moon, to show day and night. In an old movie a watch would be a clue—she'd seen that before, in *Chinatown*. Here the only thing it meant was a dead battery.

But something violent had happened; the house was ashamed. The family was gone. Einstein was wrong. Energy was both created and destroyed in that place—she could feel it—and the history of a family was trapped in decay.

Nobody marked off the crime scene because the crime didn't happen all at once. A house was a horrible thing.

She was in that closed-off part of AKA's brain, the home that would haunt him in dreams. There was no bus back to the city until morning. The night was pitch-black, and the light switches did nothing. Arena picked her way over the cluttered floor, stepping around the shimmer of puddles. She went deeper into the smell, to the kitchen. She took AKA's school portrait photos off the refrigerator. She took the picture of him happy in the backyard. She held the photos in her palm and pressed them into a tight stack, each one cut to the same size. She collected the photos the way people bury the dead, because maybe if she got his pictures out of that house, it'd help his spirit.

Her arm hurt from fighting off the hippie. She was so far from Portland, in an awful corner of a forgotten world. There was no way home.

Nyla sang as she limped the halls of Dulcet's apartment building. She sang anything—parts of songs, words, "Good day sunshine," "Think I can make it now"—with one hand to her hip, bearing her second Bundle of Love. The long, yellow hall reeked with cat urine. She passed one apartment door, then another, swimming her way to France, to that metaphoric further shore, a place of forgiveness.

She'd lived in only one apartment in her life. As soon as she was married, they'd bought their old house and torn it down to the studs. They were young. And when her husband died, she kept working on that house, forever. She actually envied Dulcet's cheap digs: Why was she, Nyla, devoted to the temple of her home? She was a servant to her house, a place for her babies.

She knocked on Dulcet's door.

"Christ!" somebody barked.

Did it come from Dulcet's room, or down the hall?

Nyla knocked again then put her ear to the door.

A man came in through a back door marked EMERGENCY EXIT. He stopped farther down the hall, looked at Nyla, and said, "Didn't I see you on TV?"

There was a crash inside the apartment. Was Dulcet okay?

The man down the hall pointed a fat finger. He said, "D'oh! Better get in my apartment! You could be dangerous." He raised his hands and crouched, in a sloppy kung fu posture. "Ha!"

He was a human enactment of the throbbing ache in Nyla's side. Her palms broke out in a pain sweat.

She found a pen in her handbag. She leaned into the wall and wrote on the card she'd brought along, "Love is all there really is, and I love you. Love, your friend, Nyla." Then she drew hearts, which was a way of saying love, without saying it. Could she get any more love on that card? At the bottom she put an asterisk, and a PS, and a little note: "See you at Arena's art show!" and one more heart, and hugs and kisses.

The man down the hall said, "You use a half nelson on that scum sucker?" He fell into a coughing fit that sounded like he needed an inhaler fast.

Nyla took her phone out to call Dulcet, and as she dialed, another call came in.

Arena.

There was another crash inside Dulcet's place. Something was wrong. Nyla could call her daughter back.

⁓

Mr. Latex scurried to put his Dockers on even as Dulcet tugged them away. She hissed, "Shhh—we're okay."

She wore her superhero anatomy suit, complete with thigh-high boots and a length of unspooled rubber intestine meant to serve as a whip.

The knocking didn't stop. Mr. Latex said, "Cops?" He threw a crocheted afghan over the Volcano, where it stood like a major erection.

She said, "Why would it be cops?"

He said, "You're in this with me." He was high and paranoid, on the verge of flipping out. It turned out part of his game, what he wanted, was a booty bump from a latex doll. Yes, Dulcet was his doll, in her plasticized body, and he had asked for an anal administration of meth. At the time she'd said, "You're insane, sir. That shit can kill a person."

It'd destroy a life.

"Once," he said. "I want to try it once. I've never done it."

By the beauty of his good teeth and ordinary, unscathed skin, she believed him. She said, "The future might deviate from the past, you know. I don't want to start something—"

He was a strange bird clawing at the ragged edge of his existence, wanting to find a genuine sensation in life before it was over. Dulcet could relate. She wasn't there yet, but she could glimpse his pain on a distant horizon. He was an adult. He had his drugs. He'd done the legwork, if you could call it that.

There was the knock on the door again.

Mr. Latex Lover was so jumpy! Dulcet wasn't on steady ground herself. Yes, they were high, and who was that at her door?

But the money. "We can finish," she said.

She'd had him half-convinced to stay, even after the third knock, until a man's voice outside the door cut in: ". . . use a half nelson on that scum sucker . . ."

Latex ducked, like they could see him. Dulcet froze. They watched the door.

She whispered, "You still owe me for the hours." Her phone started to ring. She silenced it.

"You owe me for the pot," he said and pulled a T-shirt over his head.

"You said you had pills." The latex squeaked as she moved. She poured herself a whiskey.

He couldn't leave yet. She said, "They're still out there."

He nodded, his teeth clacking together like a party skeleton, Day of the Dead, thinly cloaked in a temporary human casing.

Arena spoke into the phone. "Mom!"

How was there no answer? She'd run away, and what, her mom didn't care? The house around her was a family destroyed. It was awful. There could have been a chalk line around an invisible body in every room of the darkness. She couldn't get her words together, didn't know where to start. She said, "Did you even know who he was?" Her hands were shaking and she hung up.

Division and Subtraction

Sarah and Ben lay across their bed in a mix of postcoital tristesse and elation. She had a pillow under her ass to help the sperm swim deep and fast. Her stomach was sweaty. Her thighs were still wet with Ben's spew. The only sound now in the room was their breath and the dog on the floor lapping loudly.

That dog! Sarah burst out laughing. She was happy, sated, and maybe even on the way to pregnant.

Ben lifted a hand and touched her hip bone, lifted as it was by the pillow underneath. He turned toward her. It was a beautiful moment, not yet dark in their room, the two of them, except the dog, Shadow, and his ceaseless lapping.

Then the lapping did cease. Shadow gagged instead, and vomited on the floor.

Ben said, "Oh, dog," and again they laughed. They'd put up with that dog for years. Dogs are beautiful and disgusting, worthy of love and tolerance.

"Total buzz kill!" Sarah reached to turn on the lamp.

Ben got up, still naked. He said, "There's blood in it. A lot, actually."

When Sarah looked, there was blood pooled in Shadow's vomit, and the dog was drooling. He wasn't usually the kind of dog to drool, but now it hung from his lips in a stream of bubbling white spit.

"Hey, baby," Sarah called.

Shadow walked like he didn't know where his own legs were. He walked like some kind of clown, like he was stuck in glue. Sarah's heart broke at that walk. "He's messed up," she said, and wanted to cry. He'd been fine just a little while earlier. He was old, but fine.

They dressed and drove to the twenty-four-hour emergency vet, the overpriced lifesaving dog ER. When they got there and started to explain, the woman behind the counter looked at Shadow. She picked up the phone and said, "Let's get urgent triage to the front desk."

Urgent.

That didn't sound good.

It wasn't long before the three of them were in one of the medical rooms. Ben and Sarah sat in chairs, Shadow lay at their feet. He looked better now, really. He'd stopped drooling. But he still couldn't walk.

The vet was young and earnest and everything they needed from a specialist. He wrote notes. He said, "We'll need to run a blood panel and take X-rays. When an animal presents in this condition, it's hard to rule out poisoning. It could be an inner-ear problem, though that usually leads to nystagmus, a movement in the eyes. We're not seeing that."

They spoke at length about tests and costs—about the value of a complete blood panel versus a less extensive version.

"He presents as though he's had some kind of neurological event," the veterinarian said. "We'll run him through a few tests. You can wait out front, or leave a phone number with the receptionist if you're comfortable with that."

Ben and Sarah were still in the front lobby, drinking water from the cooler in paper cups, when a technician called them back in.

It was sooner than they had expected.

This time, they weren't shown to an exam room, but to a professionally arranged parlor, a living room of sorts, a tidy space like a good hotel. They sat together on a couch.

A technician brought Shadow in, and the old dog staggered toward Ben and Sarah. Shadow had a catheter in his bony front leg, held on with bright pink tape. "Oh my God," Sarah said.

Ben was already crying, his big manly face folded up in creases under his lips, under his jaw, everything tense and sad and reddened. He wiped a hand at his eyes. Sarah leaned into him.

The vet said, "I don't think we need to run the tests we discussed earlier. Our first X-rays give us a pretty good indication of what's going on." He put the X-rays up on a light board, reminding Sarah of the light boards at the OMSI science exhibit.

A white clouded patch was a mass on Shadow's lungs. The dog had extensive cancer. "When we're dealing with lung cancer, and the animal presents with neurological trouble, it's generally a sign that it has progressed to the brain." The vet said, "I'm sorry. We need to talk about options."

Sarah ran a hand over her old dog's silky ear. Ben took one of Sarah's hands.

They went through a list with the vet: Chemotherapy? Shadow would likely not survive. They could take him home, see how he'd do. He might live a little longer. The vet said, "It all depends on what you're willing to handle. His world is probably spinning right now. He may have had a seizure already. It's likely he'll have more."

The dog slipped, as one foot went out from under him, and Sarah screamed; she'd been holding her dog together with her will, trying to will him back to health.

He walked lifting his feet too high, moving them in random directions.

That fast, the time had come. Shadow had seemed fine in the morning, and in the afternoon, too, but now they'd put him down. His life was over.

He was the dog of Sarah's youth. He was the dog of their early marriage. This was a lifetime. She said, "Why didn't I notice?" She was a goddamn animal behaviorist, an ethologist. She was supposed to be paying attention.

She ran her hand over Shadow's head, and he looked into her eyes, and he was love. Her baby. "We have to do this fast," she said. She couldn't stand it.

The vet left and came back with a kit. He knelt at their side. Shadow got up on Sarah's lap. The three of them were together on the couch. The vet said, "The first shot feels good. It's propofol, made famous by Michael Jackson. I've tried it myself. He'll be calm."

And he slid a needle into the catheter. Shadow blinked, settled, closed his eyes. With the second shot, Sarah felt her dog's heart stop beating under her hand. Still she couldn't quit running her fingers through his short fur, and she couldn't stop touching his ears long after he had left the world behind.

Family

Arena's phone message was cryptic and unsettling. When Nyla called back, she wouldn't answer, and she hadn't come home. Nyla tried not to watch the clock. She left a simple, cheerful message of love and being present: "Dinner's ready! I love you! Love, love, love!" She couldn't say it enough. Then she sat down to dinner alone.

Trust was crucial.

She picked through a plate of quinoa with feta and herbs and knocked the bones out of a slim bit of sustainably harvested Alaskan salmon.

After she'd faked her way through the meal long enough, for an audience of nobody, she got up, put the rest of the salad in a glass bowl, and snapped on an environmentally friendly reusable lid. She put the salad and Arena's dinner in the fridge.

The wait for Arena to come home was killing her. She couldn't do it. She reached for the car keys. She left a note on the table: "Call when you're in, dear!" She slipped on her shoes and went to her store to stay busy.

There Nyla chipped and chipped and chipped at her perfect world. With each swing of her putty knife she was improving her circumstances in all ways, building her self-sustaining economic future while making her mark of environmental awareness.

But when she looked at her clock and it was past eleven and she still hadn't heard from Arena, her self-restraint cracked. What the hell was going on? Her daughter never stayed out this late. Nyla slapped down the putty knife.

She called Arena again, and there was still no answer. She dialed 911, then hung up.

Was this an emergency?

That call would contribute to the city's problem of an overburdened 911 system. She tried the nonemergency police, where she reached a recording. She followed the instructions, well accustomed to their automated system by now, punched in the right numbers, and left a message.

As soon as she hung up, she regretted the call—Arena was still on parole. Had she just turned her own daughter in?

Arena wasn't out of control, only out of the house.

Now Nyla waited for two things—Arena to come home, or the police to call back, whichever came first.

She couldn't pretend to do any more work that night. She lifted her worn canvas bag and locked up the store. The street was dark. Nyla pulled her coat closed against the cold. When a lone man passed, she kept a careful distance. The shadowy stranger materialized into a Kurt Cobain look-alike. Portland was flooded with them these days, now more than ever, as though Cobain's death had spawned his likeness, born the moment he died, and now they were all teenagers, his energy transferred—

She knew where Arena was.

The Temple Everlasting was a short walk. Nyla was barely in her own body, and she ran. The blocks flew by. She ignored the pull in her groin muscle and the ache in her side. That damn human body with its demands. Her body served her children, that was its best use. With each gallop, her bag slapped her hip like an eager jockey.

She gulped air.

When she got there, she pounded on the glass of the Temple's front door. Then she saw the notice: a green tag stuck firmly against the front window.

Eviction due to safety concerns.

The building had been vacated, and the owners had forty-five days to remove property for repairs. Eviction? She ran her hand over the tag as though over a lover's portrait and immediately felt almost a nostalgia for Mack and his little world, because if Arena wasn't there, where was she?

It was dark inside and looked half-ransacked, but it had looked like that before. The cool glass was soothing to Nyla's worried forehead, and even though it was covered in street grime, she pressed her skin against it and closed her eyes, as though welcoming her own mother's soothing hand. When she opened her eyes, she saw a sliver of light that radiated from under another door in the far back.

Was he there? Mack and Arena could be there, behind that door getting it on, drinking booze or church tea. Maybe laughing at her. Sure he'd been evicted, but maybe he hadn't gone.

She slapped on the window again.

When Nyla was that age she and Dulcet had hung out with old men who bought booze, and Greek bar owners, and a drug dealer named D'Loi. One time, at Pittock Mansion, a historic house with a sprawling lawn outside of town, they'd been up there drinking in the dark, overlooking the city with an old rocker who had coke, and Dulcet went to pee in the bushes and the rocker attacked Nyla, rolling her on the grass. Maybe it was meant as a seduction.

She'd been Arena's age.

It all seemed like a good time back then. Really. Even when it was awful.

She smacked her palm against the glass, rattled the door handle, kicked at the wood along the bottom, and yelled, "Open this door!"

After a wait long enough to hide a dead body, long enough for Nyla to almost give up, Mack shuffled out from the back of his place. He was there! He was in a robe, with his hair sticking up, and had a big cardboard box under one arm.

A box? That was creepy. It was only a box but it seemed so wrong.

He came to the door and slid open a lock. Then he turned a key, another lock. He took off a chain. Nyla could see it all through the glass. Three locks, and still anybody could break that glass if they really wanted in. His robe was stained, and his socks had holes. He said, "Not evicted, right? Because there is no true eviction."

His breath smelled like curdled milk. He put the box out on the sidewalk. "We just circulate, like a box of Portland's finest castoffs. I'll find new digs."

Nyla pushed Mack out of the way and went inside.

He said, "Arena's not here."

She marched to the far back and peered through the open door. There was a couch and a fat old TV set with a cop show on. She called, "Arena?"

"How long's she been gone?"

Nyla felt a fist in her gut. She clutched her phone—that severed, invisible cord that linked to her baby.

Mack was sleepy eyed. He poured a glass of water from a speckled Brita pitcher, handed the water to Nyla, and said, "If I see her, I'll tell her to go home. I've got my own kid out there, too, you know."

Nyla had no idea.

"He lives with his mom."

The walk back to her store was a march of anxiety. She held a hand to her side and limped forward. She scanned the crowd in a bar, through the front window. What if Arena was there?

She saw the back of a man and recognized the fit of his jeans. It was Humble, at the end of the bar, his back to the glass of the storefront window.

Was that really him? Was she so versed in the shape of her friend's husband's ass? He turned. It *was* Humble, poised, about to drink. He saw her, gave a nod, and raised his glass.

She wiped her eyes with her palm. She checked her phone, where there were no calls, no texts from Arena or the police. She was afraid to go home and worry alone. Instead she doubled back, found the door to the bar, and went in.

She hadn't been in a bar in forever. The dive bars of her youth had all been converted to yoga studios, as though the buildings in the city had grown up alongside her, their interests evolving together.

This one was hot inside, ready for hot yoga.

She pushed her way through the clusters of drinkers. Humble looked at Nyla like she was coming to check for his hall pass. That ache clawed her side.

She sidled up to the counter in a slim space near the servers' station, near the cut limes and lemons and tiny onions. She wedged herself in next to Humble, still running her fingers over the buttons of her old cell phone.

Her heart was pounding, the bar was loud; she put her mouth next to Humble's ear. "Order me whatever you're having."

He gestured at the bartender, the slightest movement of one finger, like a king.

Then she thought twice: *the baby.*

She pulled him close again. "Change that. I'll have a soda."

He said, "You're sure?" His voice found its way through the noise more easily than hers, as though the whiskey on his breath brought it over.

She didn't want a soda. Would one whiskey hurt her baby? Her hands were shaking. Her heart was a knot. "No. Never mind. What you're having," she said.

Humble had no idea yet what was up ahead, what it means to love a baby who grows into an adult. Nyla said, "You're at the easy part."

He turned toward her, raised an eyebrow, and raised his glass.

She said, "Don't ever let your daughter out of your sight."

He heard her words as a joke, smiled in response, and swirled his drink. "She's out of my sight right now."

"That's where it starts," Nyla said, ready to cry.

The bar erupted in a cheer. Her words were drowned out. Cups raised! What happened? Everyone drank. A short girl gave Humble a hug from behind, and he raised his glass. Nyla looked for the game on TV, but saw instead a woman in a strapless dress with her graceful neck slit, and a serious man in a good suit giving her the once-over. He played with his keys in his pocket. The dead girl looked like Arena, gangly in the elbows, a glossy ponytail. That was it. It was too much! In the middle of the cheers, the drinks, and the drunks, Nyla found her phone and dialed 911.

Concealer

*T*he next morning, at the end of his ten-thirty break, under a pale lemon sun and the haze of city air, Ben left Nordstrom with a silver shopping bag the size of a slim lunch box. The bag twirled from his fingers in the breeze of the traffic's wake. He shifted to his serious visage—his office job face—and put a fast stop to that twirl. He folded the bottom of the bag, rolled it up, and tried to shove the thing in his blazer pocket. It was almost small enough to fit; his pocket was nearly big enough. He was still manhandling his way through the impossibility of that volumetric problem as he crossed the street to Pioneer Square, "the city's living room."

Every brick in the square had the name of a donor pressed into it, somebody who'd paid for that privilege and so funded building the space.

A flock of gutter punks had settled on the orange bricks, their dingy asses covering the names of Portland's philanthropists. They leaned against a slice of wall—a wall that served as nothing except a place for street kids to lean. One of them wore a leather hat, a dog collar, and army fatigues. Others were in torn jeans and flapping coats, their hair half-dyed, half-fried, with a pit bull on a rope. Ben

stepped into the square, and as soon as he let go of it, the silver bag fell out of his pocket onto the bricks.

The bag spit out its decorative tissue and unleashed a plastic disc like a hockey puck that spun slowly in widening circles.

It was high-grade, talc-free, mineralized loose powder, and that didn't come cheap; Ben ran after it. It was a gift to himself, an effort to even out the blotchy skin of crying all night about the loss of their dog.

It was an effort to even imagine talking to anyone about that particular sadness, and to pretend he was fine.

He tried to step on the compact as it rolled, but he missed. He chased after it. People moved aside, raised their eyebrows, and held their satchels and purses and bags. He swung his foot again, in a dance, and strangers danced, too—they danced away, that is; he felt their eyes on him and hated to be the center of a minor scene, but this time the powder lost and—*smack*—he knocked it to the ground.

The gutter punk with a dog on a rope threw a burning cigarette into the crowd. The punk didn't deserve a dog; the dog deserved better. The cigarette skidded and stopped near Ben's feet, near his hockey puck. The gutter punks didn't crack a smile; that cigarette smoldered their contempt.

Ben tugged at his collar. He was clean and crisp and on his way to work. What was so wrong with that?

His face had healed, sure, but it didn't look right to him anymore without the war paint. He'd grown used to seeing himself with diminished pores and highlighter along his brow bone. It was a good look. Why didn't all men do it? Makeup—hadn't those gutter punks heard of *A Clockwork Orange*? All murderous boys loved makeup.

Ben had been cool once. Hot enough to get laid, anyway. He asserted this to himself and silently debated with the punks like they mattered.

Maybe he wasn't fooling anyone these days about his coolness quotient, but he liked himself better behind the Lancôme mask.

The MAX train cut him off at the corner as he started across the street.

The doors slid open, people poured out, and in that crowd he saw Arena. She was tall and pale, and she stepped onto the bricks of the square and squinted into the sun. He was right in front of her, a few feet off, camouflaged by the masses. Why should a kid have such dark circles under her eyes?

He remembered the day she was born.

Now she looked tragic and gorgeous, and Ben had known women like that a few times in his life. Yes, he'd been cool enough to get laid by those very women.

Arena looked lost. Was she lost? He called her name. The train shut its doors behind her, then moved off. Arena's hair blew into her eyes. She shook it away, saw Ben, stepped closer, and gave a timid nod.

He said, "No school today?" He heard his own words and it sounded like he was talking to a child. Ugh. He meant it as a good thing—a day off! Portland Public Schools had all kinds of in-service days, enough that it made the newspapers, because they couldn't afford to keep the lights on, apparently. But the way Arena's lips tugged down he could tell he'd said something stupid, definitely square, or straight, or whatever they called it now.

Was she expelled again? He couldn't keep up with her drama. He shoved the Nordstrom bag back in his jacket pocket, where it didn't fit and wouldn't stay.

Arena said, "You're wearing makeup."

"What're you talking about?" Ben's chuckle sounded fake even to himself—mostly to himself. He was a weak liar. How could she see that expensive foundation?

There was one male makeup guy in Nordstrom. He worked behind the MAC counter, an Asian man who liked to run hot pink under his eyebrows and line his eyes in deep black. He looked ready to star in *Cats*. His was the sort of thespian outsider flair that gave men in makeup a bad name.

So Ben had gone to the Lancôme counter instead. He didn't opt for eyeliner. His makeup was all about concealer.

When Arena did look at him, her eyes were big and brown, and conveyed sincerity and maybe grief; she'd known Ben her whole life. He said, "Okay, a little. To cover my broken nose."

Arena's lips were chapped. She said, "It doesn't look broken anymore."

"Then it's working!" He forced a laugh again, like this was all easy for him.

She let her gaze drift down the street. Maybe she had somewhere she was supposed to be. Like, high school? When she touched her face, her fingernails were dirty.

If she had somewhere to be, she didn't seem to want to go there. What was wrong? Ben was no good at deducing, couldn't tell if it was something big or small, serious or growing pains. Sarah would have it all figured out already.

Once, when Arena was maybe five years old, for some reason Ben had been left in charge of her. He had to watch her, this little kid, for a couple of hours. Thing was, he'd let her cut paper with scissors that were too big and sharp for a child. What did he know back then? She'd sliced her finger and bled all over the paper he'd given her, and she screamed. He remembered his panic when he didn't know what to do. But he'd washed her hand and found a Band-Aid, and she loved that Band-Aid even though it was only a plain one the color of nobody's real skin, the color of cheap makeup. She quit crying, and her resilience made him suddenly feel like an expert in child care. Then they'd walked to the store and he bought her a Klondike bar, and they sat on a dirty bench in the sun.

She needed a Klondike bar now. She needed a meal and a little under-eye brightener. He said, "They do makeup at Nordstrom. It's free."

She smirked and shrugged his suggestion away. Then it was like watching a silent movie, the way her face shifted, falling from smug to broken. Her mouth opened, ready to say something, but there were no words.

He fumbled for something to say, to find their equilibrium. Did she need help? He said, "Your art show's tonight."

She looked at him like she was drowning. She said, "Screw it." After a shaky moment she spit out, "I'm not going."

Nyla had been talking about the show all week. She'd sent out e-mails, sometimes at three or four in the morning. He said, "Your mom posted it as her Facebook status." Maybe they'd laugh at this together, a shared perspective, a healthy distance.

"God." Arena only twisted her hair. She held her own arm, hugged herself, and said, "I hate that school. I'm in the wrong classes. I don't want to hang my work in the show. It's fucking stupid."

The way she said "fucking" was like the word didn't come naturally. She was testing the waters.

Ben needed to say exactly the right thing. This was what it

meant to be an adult; it was his job. He'd never been a parent—wasn't even a coach. Arena bit her lip, and her chapped lips started to bleed.

Ben said, "Listen," and she turned toward him. She really did it—she listened. He'd set himself up now, as though he had advice.

Where was that Klondike bar? The Band-Aid. The comfort of a public bench.

He hated his job the way she hated school. Why go back? He was a punk rock runaway hidden in his own button-downs and Dockers. He tried again, and paced his words. He said, "Sometimes, we have to do things we don't want to do."

She looked at him incredulously. "You're giving me the 'Suck it up' speech?" She took a breath so deep it raised her teenage chest. She started to leave.

He said, "No. Listen."

He couldn't believe it when she turned back—she gave him another chance. Why? She waited.

She made him feel like an adult.

Who was he? He was a fat kid who'd grown taller and thinned out, and now he was a man with a job and two ounces of overpriced cosmetics in his suit jacket pocket.

He said, "I understand. . . ." He aimed to be honest. He wasn't sure what in him was even a little honest or clear anymore. He said, "I get it. I understand your destructive urges."

Arena quit her nervous flickering and looked at him then. Her eyes narrowed. He'd said either the right thing or the wrong thing, and he was working on his next line when she asked, "What did you say?"

He said, "I mean, sometimes we all—"

She said, "No. Say it exactly. Say what you said." She moved in closer. Her cracked lips were open, like she breathed through her mouth, like a kid with a stuffy nose, a child who had been crying, in need of Vicks VapoRub. He took his small, crumpled shopping bag back out of his pocket and found the tissue paper inside it. He used the white tissue to dab Arena's bleeding lip.

She pulled her head away from his hands and said, "Say it."

He tried to remember exactly. "I understand your . . . destructive . . . urges."

Arena scowled, but then it wasn't a scowl, it was tears, and her mouth folded and she looked sick, and her face flushed red.

She wrapped her hand around the bloody tissue paper in his hand and threw herself against him, crying into his shoulder. Her hair was a tangled smell of incense and skin. Another cargo load of people poured off the next MAX and stared as they parted around him and Arena, and Arena sobbed.

He touched the ends of her tangled brown hair. He said, "You're okay."

She tried to talk. She said, "My dad. *Marquee Moon*—" She coughed on her own snot and tears.

Had Ben inadvertently quoted lyrics? It rang a distant bell, Tom Verlaine. Maybe he'd heard that song. Maybe every sentence possible had become lyrics by now. He said, "Shhh . . ."

She said, "It seems so perfect—" and she choked again and couldn't talk and Ben petted her hair and wondered if he'd sweat off his makeup. It was all too much, too intense, it was like he'd found a lost pet and couldn't let it go and he didn't mean to bring this animal home but he was in deep and didn't know what else to do. Arena stayed wrapped around him. If she cared about what anybody thought, she didn't let on. She didn't wear makeup. She didn't hide. Ben hid. Always. These days he wrote an ongoing script for the gutter punks' judgments, for strangers, talking back to a world that talked around him, about him, about how he looked, and mostly about what his life meant or failed to mean.

A coworker came down the street. Ben turned his face into Arena's shoulder to hide. She wouldn't let go. He reached for his cell phone. He'd call in sick—say it was an emergency, because it was, and he was in way over his head.

Live! Nude! Men!

Say you're a fish in the Labridae family. You're a pretty thing, bright and darting out near a coral reef, living to entertain snorkelers. In that family, maybe specifically you're a wrasse. That's a fine name for a creature, a word that comes from the Welsh, based on a word that means an old woman or a hag.

Sarah felt herself a wrasse as she rode in the car alongside Ben.

She'd lost everything. Her dog was dead. Her babies had never been born. Now they were a ghost family frolicking together in her broken heart.

But Labridae are clever fish, adaptive and tricky, and she hadn't given up. Here's their best trick: They all stay female in their harem as long as there's a male in charge. If you lose the male? A female changes sex. It's biological transsexualism.

Somebody has to step up.

Ben's makeup was badly blended near his earlobe. Sarah reached out and smoothed the line away. She looked into his eyes, while he watched the road, and she said, "That under-eye concealer is really fantastic." He had a gossamer shimmer where he'd once had umber circles of exhaustion.

"Thank you. You're not supposed to notice it." He cleared his throat, as though quietly clearing himself of something that might have been shyness or shame.

Arena sat in the backseat, her hands folded in her lap. They were on the way to her art show. They'd called Nyla and had a very long talk. The plan was to mediate a careful reconciliation. Arena had already threatened to run away again. Apparently she'd slept one night in an abandoned house, outside of Portland, some meth lab gone wrong by the sound of it. Ben had persuaded Arena to follow through with the show, when the others failed. Now the show would be a neutral spot, like a public child drop-off point arranged for some feuding and divorced families.

They passed a cluster of lingering day laborers, male *Homo sapiens* complete with their particular gametes. *Homo sapiens*, Latin for "wise man." The old woman that was Sarah gazed at the parade of wise men.

Some people are obsessed with garage sales. Others browse real estate, or "Brake for angels!" Sarah shopped day laborers. She couldn't help it. A rangy man with long ringlets of deep brown hair flashed a scar on his cheek like he'd been in a knife fight, and caught her eye: knockout genetic material, there in the strength of his arms, the saunter of his walk. She touched Ben's shoulder. "Pull over. Here. Stop!"

Ben popped on the brakes. A car behind them honked. He saw the line of men on the side of the road, furrowed his glowing, concealer-laden brow, and put his foot on the gas again. "No. Not now."

Sarah kept a wistful eye on the day laborers as they drove on past.

He put a hand on her knee. "Sarah, it's getting compulsive."

In his glance, she felt the boundaries of their marriage eroding, or expanding. What she wanted was a family in her house to claim as their own.

And Sarah was a wrasse, an old hag in the making. She was her own example of biological transsexualism, and a convert from faithful to desperate, from passive to an effort at taking control. She'd build a family even if she had to do it alone.

Nyla locked her store's gate under a clear sky and a full moon. The city smelled like one big natural gas leak.

She wanted her daughter, and wanted Portland to smell like good Pacific Northwest air even when it was full of enough benzene to bring on leukemia, when the papers called it a "toxic soup," and an unchecked factory in the heart of town spewed microscopic aluminum particulates.

After a third try, her car started. She pined for her girl in a way that hurt more than her pulled muscle. It was like she'd had an organ removed, an open hole in her body.

Halfway to the show, she stopped to buy flowers.

Dulcet eased into her latex suit. She and Mr. Latex had negotiated a second round. There was money involved, and promises. She actually liked him. He wasn't awful.

She'd finished touching up the studio portraits of Georgie and Bella. In the photos, the bodies, mother and child, looked physical, architectural, and seductive. Georgie's hair was a chaos of greasy strands, and it worked. Her body was confident in ways Georgie used to be.

When she saw those pictures, Georgie would love herself.

Dulcet slid the stack of photos between two pieces of cardboard and wrapped silver elastic cord around them as a makeshift portfolio. She'd go to the art show, give Georgie her prints, then meet Mr. Latex afterward. Her suit was on, her body snug and hot inside that perpetual warm hug.

The show was in the gymnasium. Sarah, Ben, and Arena arrived early to set up. Arena had a bolt of netting stashed in her school locker. She had two digital projectors checked out from AV.

A maintenance man was there and had hung the pulleys.

Arena's piece was called *Behind the Mosquito Net: Synthetic Heaven.* If anyone asked, she would've said it was about humanity.

Nobody asked, though.

She would have said it was sex and death. It was about saving her father—keeping him alive, though he was already dead. He'd slipped through her net, his energy scattered. If a person had the right net, speaking metaphorically, you could let the body rot but keep the energy together in human form. Why not? Mack and Einstein convinced her of that. The trick was how to harvest and contain that energy.

Arena imagined a net that could hold life together.

"Put the projector on the floor," she told the AV guy, and waved a pale arm. He sat the tiny electronic projector on the red ring of the basketball court.

She bent to adjust the machine, extending its tiny forelegs until it pointed up. Families filtered in. The boy with the whale migration project set up along one corner of the gym. A girl came in with her mom and dad and a pack of Mint Milano cookies. She'd drawn cartoons about family dinner in Sharpie marker inside jar lids.

Georgie arrived, hugging baby Bella in a swath of blankets, and found her way across the gym. The maintenance man hoisted lengths of cosmic fishnet. Arena was watching it go up, like a captain overseeing her boat's rigging, a dirty seafarer with tangled hair and cuts on her hands, but gorgeous, stern lipped, and steady.

"Where's Hum?" Sarah asked.

"Not coming," Georgie said. She hadn't seen him in days. It took steady effort to not answer his phone calls. Now she'd worked to push her hair into place, to look like she ever slept at all.

Sarah asked, "Are you okay?"

Georgie started to nod yes, then her lip trembled. She pressed her mouth against her daughter's soft hair.

A woman, a stranger, tapped Ben on the shoulder. She gave him a hug. "So good to see you, Benjamin!" Her voice was cultivated in an acting-school kind of way.

He flushed even through the cool, smooth tone of his foundation. He said, "What're you doing here?"

Sarah wasn't used to Ben having friends who weren't her friends.

The woman tapped a fine fingernail to a badge pinned on her suit jacket: judge.

"Sarah, remember I told you about Hannah? My friend from college." Ben seemed nervous. He'd left out the world *girl*. His girlfriend from college, now in politics, Hannah smiled the gracious, munificent smile of the newly elected.

Ben shuffled like a boy. He tried to hold back a smile and it came out broken and warped.

Sarah wasn't threatened. Ben could have his elation. She was drifty and detached behind the veil of her prescriptions, where she forged her own plans: If Ben didn't step up, didn't get his sperm checked, Dale was her backup. If Dale backed out, there were day laborers. Right?

She and Ben had their house together. They were married! A team. They were animals in captivity and they'd caged themselves and she hated the trapped quality of it all—she'd drop dead before Ben took action. They'd have no kids, no grandkids—and that anger cruised through her veins, and she held it in check with Klonopin.

Muscovy ducks might stay faithful to their partners for a whole breeding season—which is to say, not very damn long. A season? Humans get so locked into their little contracts. Why can't the partnership of marriage be split off from that sperm-collecting urge of the fertile female? Sarah could crack open the door on their cage. She could take the pressure off Ben.

She shook hands with Hannah.

Hannah wore a wedding ring, too.

Parents and grandparents came to see the show. Ben and Hannah stepped to the edges of the crowd.

A shrill scream pierced the room, the happy sound of kids playing, as melodic as a murder scene, and Ben couldn't hear what Hannah said. That screech was awful! He wasn't even sure he liked kids. He and Sarah, they had good furniture. Kids ruined furniture. They slept late on the weekends, and little kids didn't let that happen. A baby would grow into a teenager, and who wanted a teenager in the house?

Hannah spoke steadily about her new role as senator. "State senator," she clarified, tapping a gentle hand to his arm.

Ben eyed her eyeliner. She wore a streak of white shadow, a highlight carefully drawn under the arch of her eyebrow, there to brighten her face at the brow bone. The plum shadow in the folds of her eyelid was designed to enliven the hazel of her eyes.

He knew her tricks.

He never realized how much makeup some women wore until he started experimenting with it himself. Sarah went to work in the nude, makeup-wise. Now that he wore the mask, he could see the mask on everybody else.

His ex-lover was more hidden than he was. That girl was gone. He said, "You have lipstick on your teeth."

Hannah's unnaturally white state senator smile faltered then, and she scrubbed her front tooth with a finger. He saw the old Hannah for a fleeting second: a hard worker, an enthusiast.

And she was gone, turned into a politician again as she shook a stranger's hand. She transformed her beautiful, unbridled self into a tame, packaged production.

Dulcet tripped in, in high heels and a long leather coat. She swung her purse and stumbled, but didn't fall, and made her way to her crew, with the cardboard portfolio tucked under her arm.

"This is it?" She looked at the nets.

Arena lifted the remote and turned the projector on. A nearly naked man appeared dancing on the scrim made by a piece of mesh. The fabric was just dense enough to hold the image. The man wore snug white cotton briefs. He looked hopeful and vulnerable, naked and bruised.

Arena turned on the second projector and there he was again. "Reproduction," she said.

On the first screen the man bent, pulled off his underwear, and danced. His cock hung free. As soon as the spectators all saw it, he bent and picked up his underwear again and put it back on. He was bold, then shy. He moved with intention, then something like regret. His regrets set in just as his twin on the other screen peeled his underwear off and did the same dance. They were in front of a mattress on the floor.

One undressed as the other dressed, in a loop.

Dulcet moved behind the scrim.

"You're in the room with him," Georgie said. Dulcet did a shimmy with the man on the screen, waved her portfolio, flashed her latex suit—her beyond-naked body—and gave her boobs a good shake. Then she laughed, wrapped herself back in her coat, and said, "You're with him, too. All of you."

Everybody on the other side of the screen was in the room with the naked man. He faced the crowd from both sides; it was the same image. Ben looked through the screens and saw Sarah in the man's bedroom, and felt the fleeting heat of possessiveness; he was ready to take his wife home. Dulcet saw Georgie and the baby with the naked man, a diorama of family. Sarah saw everyone, the gymnasium full of people, with the naked man front and center stage. She was used to watching animal hordes in cages. The gym was an exercise in overpopulation.

Nyla pushed her way through the gym doors, limped across the basketball court into the masses, and scanned for her daughter, cradling a wad of pink lilies wrapped in neon-green tissue. Her hip screamed. She pushed against that pain with one palm. Her vision was narrow, her mind focused.

The gym buzzed with families cooing over children's art. "Look what our babies have done!" Every child was a genius.

Nyla was queasy, in a cold sweat with her pain, as she scanned that sea of humanity. Dulcet emerged out of the crowd, in front of Nyla. She leaned in. "More speed dating?"

Nyla looked confused. What was she getting at?

"Looks like you've pulled something," Dulcet yelled, over the noise. This was almost as loud as the bar the night before. The sweet-bitter skunk of Dulcet's pot breath was startlingly close.

Dulcet laughed. When did she get so many teeth? She said, "You're limping like you've had major action." Dulcet's coat flashed open as she moved ever closer. Underneath, she was all organs: lungs, kidneys, and ovaries as visible as if her skin had been peeled off.

Georgie moved in, with her baby, and asked, "Yoga strain?"

Nyla had only one person in mind. She stepped around them, said, "Darling!" and held out her arms to her daughter. Arena recoiled. Nyla came at her with the flowers. Arena didn't take them, but instead ducked behind a screen, behind her rippled fabric. Then Nyla saw the dancing man, too. Before then, her eyes had been solely on her girl.

"Look familiar?"

The naked man stepped out of his underwear. He flashed an

awkward glance. Nyla recognized him and gasped. She dropped the lilies. "Him!"

"Yes. Him." Arena spit the words. She broke them off, crumpled them like paper, made them sound recycled and weathered. She hadn't spoken to her mom since she saw the photo in the news. She hadn't even been home.

Nyla felt like she was losing her mind. Was that really *him*? She wasn't sure. She'd never seen her attacker naked. "Who is he?"

"He's a good guy, Mom." The girl's voice choked. "I love him."

The man disappeared from one screen, then the second screen. "We can't show this here." Mrs. Cherryholmes, with her frosted hair and frosted makeup, had turned the projectors off.

She'd expelled the image on the screen from the school. They were big on expulsion here.

"Can't show art at an art show?" Dulcet giggled with a stoner's glee, always up for an altercation.

Nyla picked up her fallen lilies. Arena had the remote in her hand and, in quiet defiance, turned one projector back on. AKA came back, dancing and naked. The principal bent and clicked it off. Arena turned on the other. There he was again.

Nyla whispered, "Alvin Kelvin Aldrich." She stepped forward and back, then forward again, in constant nervous motion. Sarah recognized the movement. Where had she seen that dance before?

"So you admit you know him," Arena said.

Mrs. Cherryholmes said, "This is inappropriate." AKA disappeared.

"It's a celebration of the human form," Dulcet barked, accustomed to the argument in light of her own work. Now she felt lifted into the place of a role model. Despite all the missed birthdays and weak social skills, maybe Dulcet had an influence on the girl after all! Maybe this was her legacy, not a child but an artist. "Turn it on, Arena, honey."

Arena did. There he was again.

The principal took the remote away. "It's sexually explicit content."

Arena turned to her mom. Nyla offered, "It's . . . not?" Then again, with more conviction, "It's not explicitly sexual." The whole time, Nyla never quit walking. It was like she couldn't turn off part of her workout routine.

Georgie bounced her baby and murmured, "Well, it is kind of explicit. . . ."

"What's wrong with explicit?" Dulcet's voice was loud and clear even under the high ceiling of the gym, against the wail of children.

Arena sucked in her breath, that anxious response. She twisted her hair, still the girl-child she'd always been. She said, "Stand up for me, Mom!"

Nyla held no sway in this school or any school; she had nothing but struggles. She pressed a hand to the ache in her side, stepping from one foot to the other. She said, "This is about freedom of expression."

In Portland, even the full-nude strip joints were deemed an exercise in free speech.

Mrs. Cherryholmes held on to the remote. "That doesn't pertain to a public high school, when minors are present."

Then Sarah recognized Nyla's dance: It was the pacing of the one-eyed elephant at the zoo who had lost her baby. It was the nervous dance of a mother in pain.

Sarah could hardly stand to watch. She laced an arm over Nyla's shoulders, but Nyla shook her off, waved at the screens, and said, "This is work my daughter did in school. Here."

"Direct action!" Dulcet said. She bent to turn one screen back on, in her stumbling way, and her makeshift cardboard portfolio slipped from her arms, scattering an arc of black-and-white photos.

At a glance the pictures held the inviting curves of ripe fruit in sun and shadow. Upside down, sideways, and on top of each other, one materialized as a landscape of low hills. A white crescent was a shell, or an ear, until it became an arm wrapped alongside two legs, hands laced together under a knee. Ben was the first to come forward, crouch, and start picking the photos up, always eager to make himself useful.

And if one looked at the photos a moment longer, the curves settled into the planes of Georgie's face and the fullness of her breasts and the dark circles of her nipples, and there was the baby, and it was a mother and an infant, and what was that sheer scarf of a drape? The black-and-white shadows and lights reached across the gray scale.

There was the triangle tattoo. *Any questions?*

Georgie, her arms full of her child, couldn't pick up the photos fast enough.

A woman in a sweat suit bent to retrieve a print that had slid far across the gym floor. Dulcet called out, "Hey, you're still here?"

"So far." The woman held a photo in front of Georgie, to compare the image. "This must be Georgie."

"She saw the shots in my studio." Dulcet was crouched down, too, now, in her high heels. She caught herself before falling sideways. "Remember my friend, the gym teacher?"

Georgie countered, "I saw yours."

"This is not supportive. None of it," Arena said, loudly—loud enough for any child services representative who might unexpectedly be in the area, as though she were talking to the world, not only her mother and her mother's friends.

Nyla half-whispered, "Dulcet, it isn't your show."

"I'm not trying to take over," Dulcet said, surprised.

"Well, you're not trying to smooth things over, either," Nyla added.

Barry Gibb moved through the crowd, shaking his mullet and meeting parents. This was the teacher who'd encouraged Arena, who'd let her do this work in his class. He looked like somebody's way-too-old prom date, in jeans and a sport coat.

Sophomore year, Dulcet had crashed somebody else's senior prom with a guy exactly like that.

The principal unplugged a projector and started winding up the cord. She said, "I'm going to ask you to leave now."

"Ask them, you mean?" Nyla was ready to cut her friends loose, if that's what it took to support her daughter.

"All of you." The principal stood firm, mini-projector in hand.

Arena said, "Good riddance." She walked out first.

"You can't keep throwing us out!" Nyla said. "We just got her back in." The AV guy brought a cart around. The principal slid the projector onto the cart. Arena had already walked off. Nyla called her name and tried to run, but only managed to limp after her daughter.

They found Arena on a post in a gravel stretch across from the school, under a SLOW CHILDREN sign. Dulcet teetered in high heels as she crossed the gravel lot, pushing a palm to the childproof lid of an amber vial, reaching for ever-present pain meds.

Georgie, striding along with Bella in her arms, in her Keds, said, "Why do stoner chicks ever wear high heels? Seems harder than it has to be."

Dulcet gave a grin and put a pill on her tongue. "I don't feel a thing."

"Anybody want to go out for ice cream?" Nyla held a hand to her hip. Her top lip was beaded with sweat. Her eyes were ringed with dark circles, and her hair was all flyaways. She chirped, "My treat."

Sarah looked like she hadn't heard. Georgie was busy with the baby.

Dulcet offered, "Vicodin? My treat." Her latex suit gave a happy squeak against her leather coat.

Nyla winced at Dulcet, then looked to her daughter. "No, really. Dessert, honey?"

Arena kicked the gravel. Dulcet held Georgie's photos jammed under one arm, out of their cardboard binder now. Arena reached over and slid one from the stack. They looked at Georgie's naked body.

"Humble's gonna whimper," Dulcet said.

Humble.

If only he'd whimper, Georgie thought. *If he'd weep. If he'd make amends. If only.* Bella fussed, and Georgie pulled down the neckline of her dress to let the baby nurse. She and Bella were good at stealth nursing, it turned out. Until her daughter was born, Georgie didn't know she had such a talent.

Nyla said, "Where is Hum, anyway?" She reached one pale hand for a pole to steady herself.

Sarah said, "Are you okay?"

Nyla said, "He said he'd be here."

Georgie flinched, like she'd been hit, and said, "You talked to Humble?"

"We had drinks, last night."

That was why Nyla looked so trashed: drinks. Too many drinks.

Humble was out drinking with Nyla? He wasn't laid up with remorse or getting into rehab. He was hitting the bars.

He was supposed to whimper, weep, and wail.

Georgie said, "Drinks? Aren't you pregnant?"

Dulcet cut in, tipsy and loud, "Nyla, honey, we'll do your maternity photos when you're ready."

"Maternity?" Arena turned to her mom. "Oh, God. Mom, no way."

Nyla said, "I was going to tell you—I didn't have a chance. There was the crystal meth thing—"

"Crystal Light," Arena cut in.

"The timing didn't seem right, then you took off—"

"So it's my fault?"

Nyla said, "I'm only eight weeks along. It's still the first trimester."

"When were you planning to tell me, Mom?"

"Further along. Not all pregnancies work out. Look at Sarah." And they all did—they all looked at Sarah, who seemed to visibly shrink under their gaze.

Sarah said, quietly, "Leave me out of this, Nyla."

"I'm sorry," Nyla said. "I'm trying to explain—"

"You're all guppies," Arena said. She handed Georgie's picture off to the air, to the first hand that'd take it. "I'm going to throw up."

Animal Nature

"*D*rinks?" Dulcet purred with the contented voice of the medicated.

Nyla had gone to chip paint or arrange dried flowers or place orders for carbon-neutral products that had yet to be invented.

Arena swore she'd vomit if she had to ride with her pregnant mother. She rode with Ben instead, who said he'd take her home. Sarah, Georgie, and Dulcet stood outside the high school.

Sarah said, "I thought you had somewhere to be."

"I've got a gap." Dulcet wrapped her coat tighter. She had an hour before her date with Mr. Latex. She'd expected to stay at the art show longer. Latex wanted her to arrive dressed. That was part of the deal. Bitchy Bitch danced at her feet, wildly happy about being let out of Dulcet's old Fairlane, the dog always in motion. Dulcet only said, "God, Nyla is a wreck."

"She needs sleep," Georgie said. Georgie herself looked exhausted.

Dulcet said, "She's a walking corpse."

"Too much yoga," Georgie said, then looked around cautiously. Yes, she was postpartum fat and hadn't touched Nyla's Blast the Flab cardio DVD offer. She hadn't lifted one finger, done one roundhouse, or even lowered into a single downward dog in a weak warm-up. Who was she to talk?

Georgie said, "If she makes another fat comment, I'll scream."

Dulcet murmured, "She doesn't hear herself. Nyla doesn't mean any harm. But she's the whore with the store. I don't judge her, but I could offer her a sex ed class." She found a pre-rolled joint in a baggie in her jacket pocket, and a pack of matches. "Medicinal," she said, justifying her habit out of habit as she lit up.

Georgie said, "And, Sarah, that comment of hers was out of line."

Sarah waved away the sympathy. "No, she's right. I'm a living reality check on pregnancies. They don't all last. Let me be your goddamn cautionary tale!" Sarah half-yelled it.

Dulcet cut in, "Where's a brewpub? They let babies in." She fanned smoke away from her face.

Georgie made a note for her hypochondriac's guide to motherhood: Don't worry about not being able to party after you have a baby. There are brewpubs and backyards for drinking with kids.

That was for the alcoholic's guide to parenting, which she could totally write, too.

So they'd drink and use plastic stir sticks and wad up napkins and forget about the rain forest and the petroleum industry and all the other global destruction, without Nyla there to remind them.

Dear Nyla. They loved her. They did. But this was a welcome break.

Mrs. Cherryholmes came out of the school and crossed the gravel to where they stood, smokers in the smokers' corner, stoners in the cone zone, Slow Children of all ages. Dulcet palmed the joint. The principal held out a canvas bag.

"This came with one of you?" She practically held her nose.

It was Nyla's bag. THE NEW RULES, it said. Dulcet held out a hand, and the principal handed the sad, sagging bag over.

They piled in Georgie's car because the baby seat was secured there and Georgie wasn't high. She tucked Bella in. "Who wants to ride in back with the baby?"

Ride with the baby? Sarah twisted her hands, then knocked on her own head for luck. It was body language for a conflicted *no thanks.*

Dulcet wedged her long, thin self in beside the baby seat. The seat sat in the middle of the backseat, turned around backward, with the baby left to gaze out the rear window. Somehow that infant carrier dominated the whole backseat, with its hard plastic contours. Dulcet snapped her fingers. Bitchy Bitch jumped in the car.

Sarah reached back to pet the dog. They'd all been sorry to hear about Shadow.

Bella was warm, quiet, and sleeping. They sailed down Portland's winter weeknight streets. For once, it wasn't raining. It wasn't even cold. Georgie said, "Nyla gave me that mother bread starter. I'm fat—like I need bread? Endless bread that keeps doubling itself. She's the enabler." They cut onto Burnside and drove toward Sandy. The car smelled like dog breath and baby spit. The dog was a white ball of wild fluff barking at the windows. Georgie said, "Endless carbs that keep on multiplying. Amish friendship bread that needs tending every day." Sarah rolled down her window.

Dulcet asked, "What bread?"

"It's like having another baby," Georgie said. "I put it in the freezer."

"You'll kill the yeast," Sarah said. Wind through the open window battered her words.

Dulcet said, "Oh, shit. I might have stepped on mine. There was something in the hallway outside my apartment."

"I killed it?" Georgie asked.

"I killed mine, too." Sarah spit her gum out the window even though she knew better. A wad of gum on the ground could choke a bird who mistook it for food. But Sarah was being reckless, and regretted it immediately. The dog whipped her head around, as though to snap at the gum, as though the gum were food.

They were in six lanes of traffic, where Sandy Boulevard crossed Burnside Street, when Bitchy Bitch, Dulcet's big-eyed baby, bent, lunged, and gave a leap. She went after Sarah's gum and turned herself into a white flag flying against the rush of oncoming cars in the dark night.

Dulcet screamed. Georgie slammed on the brakes and her tires squealed. The car fishtailed and slid into oncoming traffic. Bella woke up and started to cry.

In the back corner of her store, by the small sink, Nyla peeled off her dress and changed into yoga wear.

She vowed to be patient with Arena.

She sat at her desk and booted up the computer to check her bank account. The machine was slow. Then it read FATAL ERROR, and shut itself down.

Dead.

This was Humble's area of expertise. When she called and got his answering service, she left a message. "It says fatal error."

Maybe he'd come.

She wrote out small checks. Writing checks to environmental groups always helped lift her spirits, and sometimes it was all she could do.

She wrote a check to the Rainforest Alliance and one to the League of Conservation Voters. She doubled her contribution to the NAACP and to a group out to save coral reefs, then more to Save the Children. She gave money to stop the slaughter of the friendly, smiling, innocent pink river dolphin of the Amazon.

What can you do with a humanity that kills a smiling pink dolphin?

She wrote checks for a foster child in Sri Lanka, and another for earthquake victims in Haiti. She slid them into envelopes. Should a person have to pay to keep the world intact?

Ben, awkward behind his forced optimism and the mask of makeup, sat on a tall stool at a gelato shop where he tried to celebrate with Arena, because he was willing to go out and he thought somebody should throw her a party. It was the grown-up version of that Klondike bar he'd bought her once upon a time.

Sarah threw herself into the street after Dulcet, who had run into traffic after Bitchy. Dulcet's coat flapped open, her latex organs exposed. She yelled, "Get back here, Bitchy Bitch!" She waved her hands. A second car slammed on its breaks, then drove around all of them.

Sarah said, "Dulcet, get out of the road! Dulcet!"

"Bitchy!"

"Dulcet!"

"Bitchy!"

It was a duet of women raised on the duets of Peaches and Herb.

Dulcet wobbled on her high heels, fell, and hit her knee, turning her leg into a streak of skin and blood, and still got up and kept going, back into traffic, yelling, "Bitchy!" The dog danced in traffic, another car squealed its brakes, and the air filled with the smell of burned rubber.

Nyla was dizzy. Was that from sitting for too long? There was nothing yoga couldn't cure, along with water and clean air. Her hip was a knot and her stomach was sad.

She put a DVD in.

But when she tried to do her first sun salutations and almost fell over, she called Dulcet. Nobody answered, and then she called Sarah. She left a message, and called Georgie.

In a bar across town, Humble tormented himself with a Diet Coke. He didn't have enough friends. Not real friends. Bars were good, because you didn't need an invitation. You couldn't be stood up.

His phone rang, and it was Nyla. He silenced the ring tone to let it go on by.

When he checked the message, it was only Nyla asking for computer help. No surprise there—her PC was recycled junk, old materials patched together. It wouldn't take a small business loan to get a new computer. He laid down a five and pushed himself off the stool. He had something to prove. He wasn't the shit they all believed him to be.

He wasn't the shit he'd come to know he really was.

He wouldn't even charge.

Georgie waited on the curb with Bella in her arms. She yelled, "Please don't get killed!"

It was all she could do.

Another car swerved around Dulcet and the dog, the driver laying on the horn like a screaming voice, and all Georgie could do was hold her baby tightly and curse. A mother's job is to keep her child safe. She sang baby songs and said a silent prayer and wanted that damn frantic dog out of the road. "Bitchy!" she called to the animal, then put a hand to her child's ears, knowing her voice was so loud, close to those precious, fragile ears.

Another horn screamed, and Dulcet twisted her ankle, and a bus heaved its way toward them.

The store was closed but the door was unlocked. Humble knocked, as if going into a house, then opened the door anyway because it was supposed to be a business. "Computer service!" He called it out with a false formality, a joke in his voice. "Here to fix your system, ma'am."

A paper mobile of polar bears drifted in a slow circle. From somewhere in the same direction a woman answered him. She crooned, in sweet, honeyed tones, "You're only as young as your spine is flexible. And remember, your mind is connected to your spine. It's all one. Flexibility is a mental journey as well as the care of your backbone."

Quiet music played.

"Nyla?" Humble called out.

"For our next move, we'll lie on the floor."

Humble walked past the bistro table, around a rolling bookcase made to serve as a room divider. He saw a laptop hooked up to an extension cord. The laptop sat on an office chair, and the chair was in front of the desk, where the desktop computer rested. The whole setup was a mess of cables.

Then he saw Nyla on the floor on her yoga mat, on her stomach, tucked between boxes of paperwork. Facedown, she did the sponge, or the rock, or whatever they called the resting pose down at the 24 Hour Fitness class he and Georgie tried together once.

The woman on the DVD said, "Feel your blood coursing through your veins, fueling your system."

Nyla's arms were blanched. Her mat was wet.

He said, "Sorry—did I interrupt?"

Nyla's hair was plastered to her damp cheek. Her mouth was open, and her lips were almost as white as her skin.

The DVD fitness guru said, "Your body loves you, because you love your body."

Skoal.

Dead?

Humble dropped to his knees. He lifted her hand, and her skin was as cold as the cement floor. Closer like that, he saw her lips were ringed with a thin line of blue. Then he felt her pull her hand back. Did she? It was a small movement. He couldn't tell—maybe it was gravity or rigor mortis, or what did he know? He'd never held a dead woman's hand before. Panic swirled in his thick brain.

Then the hand moved again. Nyla's lips opened. He saw the dry skin cling as she moved her mouth.

"Feel the blood run through your veins. Synovial fluid will wash your joints. This is what your body was meant to do. This is how we come alive."

Humble said, "You're going to be okay." He brushed her hair back. He'd never seen skin so white it was gray, the color of aging teeth. Her eyelids flickered.

Humble wrapped Nyla's arm around his neck. He said, "We'll get you to a hospital." As soon as he started to move her, he knew he was doing the wrong thing—you don't move an injured person. Where was her injury? Was she sick? He tried to put her back down. He said, "I'll get help."

He reached for her hand, to unlink her arm from his neck. She wouldn't let go. She was strong. He pushed her arm away, and she held on. She whispered, "Don't . . . go . . ."

His face was pulled close to hers. He said, "Wait here." She didn't look ready to go anywhere.

Then Nyla wasn't breathing. Or maybe she was. He couldn't get her arm off his neck. He half-stood and she lifted off the ground. She was as thin as a ballerina, but even now she was strong. He had to use some strength to get her to let go. It was so physical, to fight against her grip. It was awful.

The yoga woman said, "It's your job to make life glow through your system, make it glisten. Yoga is about using your body to care for your body."

He fumbled in his shirt pocket for a phone and called 911 as fast as his thick fingers could tap the screen of his tiny phone.

Dulcet wrestled the dog out of the street, with a hand through its collar. She fell to the curb, long and pale and bony, a skeleton with organs on the side of the road in the dark.

Sarah helped her back to the car.

Georgie's phone rang, and it was Humble. She silenced that call, and when she did, she saw she'd missed a previous call, from Nyla.

Dulcet was winded and windblown by the time she climbed in the car. Right away she dug through her purse, looking for her pipe. Pot was her version of a bronchial inhaler. It was her nerve medicine, her teddy bear, her comfort. Her breath was ragged. She said, "Whew! We're all alive!" She wheezed like an asthmatic, with a little death rattle hiding in every breath.

Dead Girl Solitaire Reprise

Skoal. Bottoms up.

Once Nyla was pronounced dead, Humble couldn't force himself to stay at the hospital. His feet wouldn't let him. He walked. Ben arrived first, with Arena. Arena had come sliding into the waiting room, practically running, her boots soft against the linoleum. Her face was round and flushed. Her hair laced in and out of a ponytail fastener in a mix of tangles. "Where's Mom?"

Behind her, the TV news cut to an image of a hairy baby. The mandrill had been born at the zoo. The sound was off but the closed captioning was on, and HAPPY BIRTHDAY TO YOU scrolled across the bottom of the monitor.

The mandrill baby closed its eyes.

Humble tried to talk, to answer her, and he couldn't. His voice was so thick it caught in his chest, and he said what he could then he left. He said, "She's gone."

He'd called everyone. He'd left messages. He told them to come to Emanuel Hospital, and that Nyla had died. He could hardly get the words out—didn't want to have to say it again. He said it over and over again into machines. Nobody answered his calls except finally his last call, Ben, and Ben wasn't who he wanted; he wanted to reach his wife.

He left Ben with Arena's wail.

Humble walked out of the hospital grounds, then down Williams Street, in northeast Portland. It wasn't far before he came to a bar, a nondescript place he'd been to before, or not, or maybe it'd changed hands; it didn't matter—it was a counter and a wall of liquor and a guy who'd pour a beer or a scotch or both.

He followed his instincts, took steps, reached out, and pushed the door open, but he could hardly feel his body. He tried to conjure up a drive toward bourbon, but what he felt was Nyla, pale and cold and sweaty in her yoga clothes on her mat down with the dust, by her space heater and her filing projects.

Her body was still wrapped around him like it was his own; she was his date, his wife, his personal ghost. He couldn't untwist her gray arm from his neck. It stayed crooked there like a sinker, hellbent on pulling him down. He felt Nyla's raspy breath against his cheek, the white of her lips so close, a bone-thin woman in his arms.

What had happened to her?

She was death, hanging on. Humble was tied to a skeleton that whispered. He could smell it like some kind of hippie perfume, the earthy mildew of patchouli and musk. He sat on a fake-red-leather-covered stool at the bar. The place was full of TVs, and every TV showed a dead woman.

A drunk whom Humble didn't even remember knowing yelled, "Hey, Dead Man!" and sloshed a mug of beer in a solo "Cheers!"

Humble muttered, "Fuck you."

The dead woman around his neck leaned on him. She breathed her last breath on his skin, then she did it again.

The drunk guy said, "Dude, you playing?" He tipped his head. The TV flashed a dead hottie in a white baby-doll dress, her high heels falling off, thighs full of life.

The drunk said, "Come on, Dead Man! Make it my round."

Humble reached for the remote, where it rested by the cash register. The bartender raised his eyebrows, but the bartender was small, thin, and young, and Humble wasn't any of those things; he was in charge.

He changed channels: cop shows, hospitals—ugh. There was

HBO, and even real estate was all about dead girls: a dead girl in a house for sale. He clicked through *Cops* and cooking shows where lovely women cut meat, red and bloody, on slabs of granite like a morgue. Vomit roiled in his gut like a storm coming in.

Then he hit VBTV, Vampire-Based TV, and it was all pale girls dead and undead all the time, and he had his own ghost clinging to his neck and that was the last thing he wanted. It was creepy.

He was ready to give up, turn the TV off, and slice his own wrist because what was the point? Live until you die.

He kept the channels moving.

Then he came to a public broadcasting station. An old man sat behind a desk talking with an even older woman. And Humble stayed with it.

The old man's face was collapsed under a river of wrinkles. His hair was mostly gone, and what was left was gray. He seemed to be interviewing the woman, who reached for her necklace with one liver-spotted hand there in high-definition TV.

It didn't matter what they said. It was soothing to see a man and woman who had lived a long time. They'd lived through what, World War II? The Korean War? The Nixon years and two recessions and the days of DDT, but they looked all right. They were on TV!

There was a comfort in this evidence: It was possible to survive long enough to die of age. It looked like such luxury, to have lived. They'd dodged cancer, bullets, and nuclear war, radiation and disease, diabetes and poverty. He remembered a shirt Arena wore: I ♥ OLD PEOPLE. And he did, too! He hearted old people, or at least he aspired to be one.

Nyla would never be that old person her daughter loved.

The drunk guy farther down the bar said, "What is this talking heads bullshit? What are we, geezers?"

Humble sipped a Manhattan, his shoulders hunched against Nyla's ghost hug, and kept the remote in his own thick hand like it had ties to a destiny he might control.

Hell if that loser would take Hum's old people away.

The drunk punk in his skinny girl-jeans made one more squawk, and Humble thought, *I could kill him.*

He could.

He could make a second scrawny arm hold his neck and beg. No doubt. If the kid didn't like old people? He could rob that hipster of his own old age. Humble put his money on the counter and finished his drink.

He walked back to the hospital. With booze in his bloodstream his legs swung easily. He walked like a machine. As he got close to the hospital, he saw his wife inside the lobby. She was there with Dulcet, Sarah, and Ben. He saw their shapes through the dark glass. The window ran from the ground to the ceiling, in one efficient pane of smoke-tinted glass. He saw his friends as though they were on TV.

He stopped outside. They moved like they might leave, might go to the sliding doors, but then they stayed pulled together, a tight orbit. Arena was a crumpled body sloped in a chair. Georgie bent to put an arm around her. His wife's mascara was all over her face. She kept wiping her eyes with a tissue, then putting the tissue back in her pocket and pulling it out again. They took turns hugging each other, and Arena. Humble felt the bar calling his name. He wanted out of there. The last thing he wanted was to cry, with a pack of criers.

A TV in the waiting room showed the news. Who in an ER waiting room could care about outside news?

Humble went on in. In the lobby, he heard it, like adding a sound track: They were all crying and trying not to, blowing their noses and then crying again. Even Ben was in tears, and he looked like he had somebody else's makeup all over his face.

Everyone was crying except the baby—that baby who always cried. Now Bella watched the world like crying was normal, like anything was normal.

Georgie reached down and took Bella out of the car seat. She lifted the baby to her shoulder, and she cried, and then she saw Humble. Her eyes widened.

He moved closer, took the baby from her. She let him take her. He held Bella in one arm and with the other rubbed Georgie's back. Their baby was warm, and he laid her across his chest. That baby's breath spoke to his heartbeat. Nyla's ghost lifted her dead arm from his neck to make way for Bella's soft head. The smell of her body was replaced by the scent of the baby and Georgie's shampoo. Humble's family warded off Nyla's dead weight. For a moment he could forget, in that circle of safety—a child, a wife, a future—and Hum didn't want even one foot outside that circle. Maybe for the first time, he was committed to his own marriage. He wanted in. He wanted that new family to stop time; he'd be the father of a newborn with a full life ahead of them all, forever.

Nyla had died before the ambulance reached the hospital. The IV didn't fill her bloodstream in time, her blood didn't regenerate fast enough. Her veins collapsed. Internal bleeding, they'd say later.

She wasn't alone when she died, and not only with Humble. She was with that baby lodged in her fallopian tube. Ectopic pregnancy.

Dulcet held Nyla's dirty canvas bag and cried big burbling tears. Her broad shoulders shook, her face was red. She said, "We were all having such a good time."

"Were we?" Sarah asked. Her words came out muffled and garbled. None of them could talk. Crying was their language now.

Habitat

Nyla had been dead for three days when Ben came home from work with a plan. He slid his fingers over the slick surface of the photo in his jacket pocket.

Sarah was at the dining table looking over papers. She spent her days now watching the newest little mandrill.

"Are the beasts still mating?" he asked.

"Some more than others." She stretched her arms over her head. A flash of pale belly showed. "Rats, cats, and coyotes."

She couldn't make herself say dog. She still had to stop herself from opening the back door at night to let in her dog, her Shadow, though the dog was dead.

"Cats and coyotes?"

"Not together," she said.

He put his lunch sack down between the pages of her work and pulled out a battered banana. They'd been saving their money since before they got married, saving for a baby's future and their own. Now that money might go to fertility treatments, if you asked Sarah.

There was a shuffling of feet. A woman came down the hall. It was Nyla, in their house. Her hair was wet. Nyla's ghost had just stepped out of a shower. She looked sad, but young and pretty, about the age Nyla had been when Ben first met her, right before Celeste was born.

She came through the front room and paused. She opened her mouth—Nyla had a message for them. She said, "I think you're out of conditioner." She nodded and moved up the stairs.

Ben whispered, "Jesus."

Sarah said, "I know."

It was Celestial, home from school for the funeral and to manage her mother's things.

Sarah turned to the extra chair beside her at the table, and pulled papers from Nyla's undyed canvas sack.

She'd kept it. Arena had said she should.

Arena's shoes lay in the hall, one right side up, the other upside down. She'd been sleeping in their spare room. Nobody wanted to sleep in Nyla's big empty house. Now Celeste would stay here, too.

In a crowded city on a crowded planet overrun with seven billion people multiplying fast, they missed Nyla.

One person.

Sarah felt the loss of Nyla's baby, too, a person she'd never met.

Everybody mattered. Every last one.

Ben went to the table and laid down the photo. He said, "Let's buy it and move. We could cut back on work. All we need is each other."

It was a proposal as good as marriage all over again. Sarah picked up the glossy photo. "It's a giant penis."

It was the silo house.

He looked over her shoulder. "I hadn't noticed that." The house was virile in the way it jutted up from the flat land around it.

Sarah held it to her own lap, a cock, then turned it sideways and pressed it against Ben's crotch. He said, "We could sell our place and offer them cash."

"It's so far away," Sarah said. "I can't move away from Dulcet and Georgie. Not now."

She couldn't. Ben knew it. She said, "We can't leave Arena."

"We could take her with us," Ben said. "For what, another year? Maybe six months, by the time we move in." Then she'd go off to college.

Legally she'd be on her own, emancipated, and financially independent. They were her unofficial guardians.

Weren't they all unofficial guardians of one another?

But theirs was the house she had chosen to come to. They had ghost girls to care for now.

Ben took a drink from a glass of water on the table and swallowed. He said, "People like to visit a house in the country."

"One bedroom." Sarah read the stats.

"One big bedroom," he said. Mostly, it was isolated, and it was near where Ben grew up. It would be like going back home. "We could have camping parties, in the summer. Set up tents. There's nobody for miles."

He ran a hand over her hair. "You know, we might never have a baby."

She smiled, a nervous smile, with a tick on one side. "Round five." She held up a hand, all fingers shown. After she said it, she was beaming, like the sun coming through the clouds, the first time she'd smiled since Nyla died. She tapped the eraser of her pencil against her paperwork. She swiveled in her chair. Ben sensed he was looking at two people at once. He actually was looking at two people: There was a baby between them. It was a risk. He said, "I can't go through that again."

Sarah stood up. She said, "It'll be okay."

He burbled then. Ben cried, and tried not to, and this, he thought, was what the makeup covered: his broken heart. He slid the silo house photo away from them on the table. "Our lives are good."

"They are." She hugged him close.

Ben sunk his fingers into Sarah's shoulders hard, in a back rub that was more about holding on to his wife. She peeled his fingers off. He said, "Nyla was killed by a baby."

A deadly little unborn baby that'd taken up residence in her fallopian tube, death by overpopulation of one; there was no room for a growing embryo there.

It was that misguided collection of cells with its will to live, two people who had come together to create one.

She said, "We have health insurance. We have doctors, primary care physicians, I take vitamins—"

Ben whispered to Sarah, "I can't lose you." He felt her blood warming her skin through its network of veins, arteries, and capillaries.

Vitamins? There was no certainty.

She said, "Shhh . . . ," and rubbed her body against his. She said, "A baby! It'll be different for us."

acknowledgments

I am deeply grateful for the support of so many amazing people. In particular: my writing crew, Lidia Yuknavitch, Suzy Vitello, Chuck Palahniuk, Andy Mingo, Mary Wysong-Haeri, Erin Leonard, Chelsea Cain, Diana Page Jordan, James Bernard Frost, and Cheryl Strayed; Mitch Finnegan, Christine Fletcher, Alicia Zambelli, and Ann Duncan, for their knowledge of animals and animal care; Mickey Lindsay, Cynthia Chimienti, Bellen Drake, Nirel, Lise Pacioretty, Djamilah Troncelliti, Sonya Schmick Carnes, Marne Lucas, and Joanna Berton Martinez, for their inspiration, support, and kindred spirits; Seth Fishman, Alexis Washam, Christine Kopprasch, for their wisdom; PNCA and the Sally Lawrence Award; and always, Barbara Drake, Albert Drake, and Kassten Alonso.

about the author

MONICA DRAKE is the author of *Clown Girl*, winner of an Eric Hoffer Award and an IPPY (Independent Publisher Book Award). Her essays and short stories have appeared in a variety of journals, and she is a regular contributor to the *Oregonian*, the *Portland Mercury*, and the *Stranger* (Seattle). Monica has an MFA from the University of Arizona and is currently on the faculty at the Pacific Northwest College of Art.

about the type

The text of this book was set in Bell, a Transitional typeface created for Mono-type in 1931 and originally cut by Richard Austin in 1788 for John Bell's type foundry. When Bell's foundry closed down, the font migrated for decades under different names: "English Copperplate" at the American Riverside Press in 1792, then "Brimmer," and later "Mountjoye," until font designer Stanley Morrison restored the name again in 1931. Unique to Bell is its break from tradition for numerals: They are two thirds the height of the font's capitals and sit evenly on the line.